PRAISE FOR
LABYRINTH LOST

A Bustle Best Book
An NPR Top YA Book
A *Paste* magazine Best Book
A School Library Journal Popular Pick
A Barnes & Noble Teen Best Queer-YA-Fantasy Selection
A Tor.com Best YA SFF Selection
A New York Public Library Best Book for Teens
A Chicago Public Library Best of the Best Book
A Los Angeles Public Library Best Teen Book
Winner of the 2017 International Latino Book Award
for Best Young Adult Fiction

"A richly Latin American, giddily exciting novel."

—*New York Times*

"The best new series of the year."

—*Paste* magazine

★ "This work is a magical journey from start to finish…"

—*School Library Journal*, Starred Review

"Zoraida Córdova's stunning storytelling and wondrous world-building make this one to remember, and bonus: there's a multicultural, bisexual love triangle to give you the swoons."

—Bustle

"A magical story of love, family, and finding yourself. Enchanting from start to finish."

—Amy Tintera, author of *Ruined*

"Córdova's prose enchants. *Labyrinth Lost* is pure magic."

—Melissa Grey, author of *The Girl at Midnight*

"Magical and empowering, *Labyrinth Lost* is an incredible heroine's journey filled with mythos come to life but, at its heart, honors the importance of love and family."

—Cindy Pon, author of *Serpentine* and *Silver Phoenix*

"A thrilling, imaginative journey through a bittersweet bruja wonderland. I can't wait for the next Brooklyn Brujas adventure."

—Jessica Spotswood, author of *Wild Swans* and the Cahill Witch Chronicles

"An inspired tale of family, magic, and one powerful girl's quest to save them both."

—Gretchen McNeil, author of *Ten* and the Don't Get Mad series

"Córdova's world will leave you breathless, and her magic will ignite an envy so green you'll wish you were born a bruja. An unputdownable book."

—Dhonielle Clayton, *New York Times* bestselling author of *The Belles* and *Tiny Pretty Things*

"The series features strong, independent young women struggling to find their place in the world... I cannot recommend Zoraida Córdova highly enough."

—TOR.com, Alex Brown

ALSO BY ZORAIDA CÓRDOVA

The Way to Rio Luna
Star Wars: Galaxy's Edge: A Crash of Fate

The Brooklyn Brujas Series
Labyrinth Lost
Bruja Born
Wayward Witch

The Vicious Deep Trilogy
The Vicious Deep
The Savage Blue
The Vast and Brutal Sea

The Hollow Crown Duology
Incendiary

WAYWARD WITCH

ZORAIDA CÓRDOVA

sourcebooks
fire

Published by Sourcebooks Fire, an imprint of Sourcebooks
P.O. Box 4410, Naperville, Illinois 60567-4410
(630) 961-3900
sourcebooks.com

Library of Congress Cataloging-in-Publication Data

Names: Córdova, Zoraida, author.
Title: Wayward witch / Zoraida Córdova.
Description: Naperville, Illinois : Sourcebooks Fire, [2020] | Series:
   Brooklyn Brujas ; 3 | Audience: Ages 14-18. | Audience: Grades 10-12. |
   Identifiers: LCCN 2019059979 | (hardcover) | (trade paperback)
Subjects: CYAC: Magic--Fiction. | Witches--Fiction. |
   Supernatural--Fiction. | Families--Fiction. | Hispanic
   Americans--Fiction. | Bisexuality--Fiction.
Classification: LCC PZ7.C8153573 Wc 2020 | DDC [Fic]--dc23
LC record available at https://lccn.loc.gov/2019059979

Printed and bound in the United States of America.
SB 10 9 8 7 6 5 4 3 2 1

YA
CÓRDOVA

For immigrants.
We get the job done!

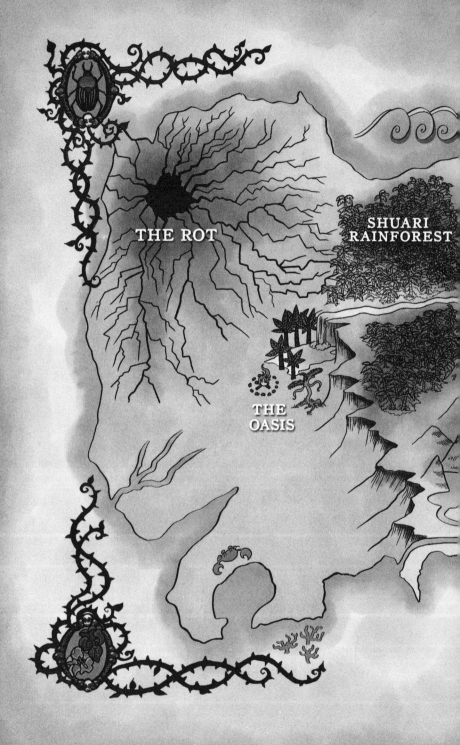

THE ROT

SHUARI
RAINFOREST

THE
OASIS

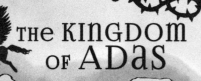

THE KINGDOM OF ADAS

SELVA YARUNI

CASTILLO DE SAL

SOLOMÍA RIVER

GIRASOL GROVE

TANAMÁ RIVER

LAGUNITAS SERPENTINAS

OLAPURA

PUNTO DEL FIN

PART I

THE DEATHDAY

1

Claribelle was lost in the forest.

She stepped between two ceiba trees

under the light of the full moon.

A door opened and she walked through it.

—CLARIBELLE AND THE KINGDOM
OF ADAS: TALES TALL AND TRUE,
GLORIANA PALACIOS

I'm supposed to be the good one. The bruja who studies dusty tomes and respects her magical lineage. The sister who doesn't trap her family in another dimension or raise an army of heart-chomping zombies. The daughter who doesn't talk back, flosses twice a day, cleans her altar without being told to, takes out the trash, and recites rezos to the gods before going to bed at midnight. If I were the good one, I wouldn't be hiding today of all days.

It is, after all, my Deathday and my birthday combined, and like the average fifteen-year-old bruja, I'm spending the party in a hallway pantry, sitting on a crate of Goya beans, with my dress pockets full of chocolate candy bars. A low-hanging light bulb casts a white glow over the open storybook on my lap.

"Have you seen Rose?" My mother asks someone from the other side of the door.

I don't know who she's talking to, but they make a noncommittal sound. Ma shouts my name, and I freeze mid-page-turn. After the ceremony, I said I'd go change into party clothes and be right back, and I had every intention of doing so. Mostly. But I started imagining all those people—friends, family, and strangers—wanting to talk to me. To look at me. To wonder why, after fifteen years of being an ordinary bruja I am suddenly so *interesting*. That's the word people keep using, at least. Since I don't have an answer, I decided to put myself in time-out.

When my mom gives up and the hammering tap of heels dissolves into echoes, I breathe a little easier. I flip to my bookmark and sigh. I'll read one more chapter and then go. I know. I *know* I can't stay in here forever.

If you ask me, and no one ever does, it's too soon to celebrate my freakish new abilities. I mean, one minute, I was a seer, speaking to ghosts and the world beyond the Veil of the living. Now I'm something completely different that no one in my family, our network of brujas, or supernatural allies have ever heard of. There isn't even a name for it since I've forbidden everyone from calling me a "magical hacker." It's a miracle our lives haven't been threatened for a whole six months, so I haven't had to put my power to the test. Honestly, I'm not so sure my family even wants me to try.

Lula told me to enjoy the moments we get to be normal and danger free, but there's no "normal" when you're a bruja. Unlike the rest of the Mortiz family, I can't pretend like the last year and half hasn't been filled with monsters and blood and guts and secret societies and more resurrections than I am personally comfortable with. We've just accepted Dad's magical memory loss from the years he was gone. Alex is all One with the Force after she accidentally banished us to Los Lagos. Lula unleashed dead hordes across the city, but no worries, she's back to her old self again. Ma finally has her family whole and together.

I'm the only one who seems to notice that there *is* something wrong around here, but every time I work up the nerve to speak, I convince myself that it's all in my head. Things are peaceful. Things are fine.

Aren't they?

Sandals slap against the tiled hallway floor. I recognize the cadence of her walk instantly. I hold in a sneeze brought on by pantry dust as my eldest sister starts yelling for me.

"Rose Elizabeta Mortiz, get your bedazzled butt out here and dance!" Lula manages to walk right past my hiding spot.

I sneeze, and a handful of pink and white petals fall between the pages of my book. The flowers in my ceremonial crown are already wilting. So much for fresh carnations. I've tried to undo the braid Lula and Alex artfully twisted around my head with gold twine, but they used so much hairspray and so many bobby pins that I only managed to yank a few strands out by the root. I blow on the petals. They scatter on the blush-pink tulle skirt of my dress, stuffed around my feet.

The door opens, letting in the bright kitchen light and the rhythmic tap of drums from the living room.

Lula purses her lips. There's a flash of relief in her gray eyes before she shouts, "Found her!"

Alex pokes her head around Lula's body. Her brown hair is in a braided ballerina bun, decorated with a glittering crescent moon. "I *told* you she wouldn't have been in the garage. That's where all the old folks are playing cards."

"I have to say, I'm disappointed in your hide-and-seek skills." I turn the page of my book and clear my throat, hoping they'll take the hint and go away. "Good thing neither of you are going into search and rescue for a living."

"Um, *rude*," Lula says, dusting her bare shoulder, but the pantry dust only mixes with her body glitter. When she leans into the light, the four claw marks that scar my sister's face are iridescent as pearl. Over the summer, she started accentuating them with colorful eye shadow because she says people stare anyway, so she might as well get creative. "There are too many rooms in this house. I keep confusing the guest bathroom for the guest closet, which is not a fun surprise when there are a hundred people in the house and *no one* locks the door."

"And yet"—I slam my book shut—"you managed to find me in the only place I've been able to find some peace and quiet since the ceremony finished."

My sisters ignore me and shove their way in, party dresses and all. I groan in protest when one of them steps on my foot and another one jams an elbow in my ribs as they squeeze on either side of me and close the door.

"Come on, Rosie!" Lula says. "You're missing out. Tía Panchita says she's dancing with a ghost but really she's had six cups of Tío Julio's coquito."

If I were still connected to the Veil I could debunk her theory. Instead, I ask, "Are you sure *you* haven't had six cups of Tío Julio's coquito? Or is a certain *thirsty* hunter here?"

She elbows me, and in an attempt to move away, I slam into Alex, who bumps into the supplies stacked on the shelves that surround us. The jars wobble precariously, and a dozen of them tip forward. I shield my face from the impact, but Alex thrusts her hands up, conjuring a gust of wind. The chilly air funnels around us, and the force of her magic sets every jar of spices and bird bones back into place. When our arms brush against each other, I jump at the electric charge of her lingering power.

Alex dusts her palms, and even in the dim light, her smug grin is unmistakable. It's a welcome change to the days when she rejected anything that had to do with being a bruja. But now she's just showing off.

"Okay," Alex says, "Why are you reading a book you've already read a thousand times instead of enjoying your Deathday after-party?"

As if on cue, a chorus of laughter filters from the living room, followed by the scaling notes of a saxophone. I don't know why my parents insisted on hiring a real live salsa band to perform when the only salsa I like is the chunky and spicy kind I can scoop up with tortilla chips.

"Excuse you," I say, frowning, "but if I remember correctly *you* didn't even want to have a Deathday, and we all know how that turned out."

"Rosie…" Alex says, the smugness completely gone. "You know I'm sorry."

Lula's brows shoot up, her gray eyes darting between Alex and me.

Frustration knots in my throat. I know Alex regrets what she did. Despite being the only encantrix in her generation, she is still a cautionary tale brujas tell their children at night. How was she supposed to know her canto would backfire? How could she have known that her family was so intrinsically tied to her magic that removing it would have been like trying to carve out an organ with a butter knife? When Alex tried to cast her powers away, she changed everything. Sometimes I want to blame her. If not for Alex, Lula would have never tried to resurrect the dead. We wouldn't have had to fight for our lives and watch our home burn down and had to move to Nowhere, Queens. I would still be a seer. Then again, if not for Alex, we wouldn't have Nova in our lives or Dad back.

In my heart, I know that if we were the kind of family that verbalized our feelings, things might be different. But we bottle our fears and sadness and sometimes even our joy. I know I'm no different.

"I get it, you're sorry. Look," I say. I wish I was better at trying to untangle my emotions because I don't want to hurt my sister, either. "All I'm asking for is an hour by myself. Conjuring dozens of ancestral spirits doesn't exactly make me want to get on the dance floor and mambo."

"What about perreo?" Lula muses, followed by Alex flicking the bare skin of Lula's arm.

"I'd rather not see a bunch of old brujas dirty dancing," Alex mutters. She nudges my shoulder playfully like we're in on this

8

together. "I could tell you stories about Agosto that aren't in this book."

"In the living room," Lula offers brightly.

And Alex adds, "While we eat cake."

"I don't *want* your stories of Los Lagos," I say, perhaps a little more roughly than I meant to. I will always be a teeny tiny bit jealous that Alex got to meet Agosto the Faun King in real life. Then I remember that while she was running around Los Lagos, I was inside a ball of energy waiting to get served up for dinner to an old hag. I tell myself that Alex came through. She saved us. We saved her too. "It's just—I want my own, that's all."

Lula wraps her arm around my shoulder. She isn't using her healing magic on me—not exactly. She has a different kind of power that usually calms me just by being near. The times I was holed up in bed because the spirits whispering in my ear were too loud, Lula was at my side, singing and brushing my hair to distract me. On the day I found out I had to switch schools because we moved here, she bought me a tray of cupcakes and didn't even have one for herself. I can think of a thousand more ways Lula is my rock. But I don't want that today.

"Rosie, come on," she says. "I know being the center of attention isn't the most fun—"

Alex scrunches up her face and holds out her hand like she's ready to catch the lie in Lula's words. "But you *love* being the center of attention so…"

"This is true," Lula admits, tapping a red nail against her chin. "We're still talking about a once-in-a-lifetime rite of passage. Like sinmago parties. You had fun at Claudia Toloza's quinceañera."

9

"And you danced all night at Rishi's sweet sixteen," Alex chimes.

I grumble. "That's different."

"If I could do my Deathday over—" Alex starts to say, and that's when everything I feel tips over.

"First of all, I don't need your philosophizing on the mistakes you made and what you'd do over again," I tell her. "I'm *not* you."

Lula and Alex stare at each other and share a look only older sisters can, like I'm acting petulant and unreasonable. But they don't see things the way I do. The frustration of it all makes me want to scratch at the itch beneath my skin, the one that started ever since my new magic appeared, but when I did that last night, I just clawed my arms raw.

"Rose—" Lula starts.

"No, I need you guys to listen to me. Please," I beg.

My sisters nod and remain quiet for a whole minute. Call the *Guinness Book of World Records*.

I take a breath and say, "Ever since I was little, all I wanted was to be like you guys. I never noticed that we weren't like other families because you never made me feel strange. We are who we are. But lately, it's like you're all trying to make us something we're not."

"What do you mean?" Alex asks, her voice deep with worry.

"I mean me. You don't know what it's like to be me right now. You don't see what I see."

They're quiet again. They scratch their scalps and shift in their glittering party dresses and sigh like they're trying to understand but there is something missing.

Lula brushes my stray baby hairs. "We can do more research into your power, Rosie. I can ask the Alliance to try new sources—"

I let go of a long grunt. "*No.* I mean, it's weird having this new magic and I'd like to find out more about it, but it's not just that."

"Then what?" Alex asks, her brown eyes cast in long shadows from above. "Talk to us."

How am I supposed to know what to say? I know the ingredients that will conjure luck and I can brew a potion to talk to the dead, but no one ever taught me how to speak a truth that is uncomfortable.

I take a deep breath, trying to figure out how to explain what I'm feeling. My sisters are pretending everything is square, just like our parents. It's like we got to the end of the storybook and everyone has their happily-ever-afters. Our dad is back after having vanished without a trace for over seven years. Alex claimed her magic. Lula put the dead back to rest.

But am I the only one who notices the way Dad stares into space like he's forgotten where he is? I've woken in the middle of the night to Lula screaming her dead ex-boyfriend's name. Alex wanders around the house at three in the morning, checking all the locks, making sure our warding wreaths and salt bricks are in place like she's waiting for something to attack. Then there's Nova, our adopted brother, and the magic that marks him and is literally burning through him, using him up like a candlewick. I think of Ma's tense, rigid body, like she's holding her breath because she's afraid this happiness won't last. We are all incomplete and not talking about it. I don't know how to make them see that the Mortiz family hasn't reached the end of their story yet.

Or maybe, just maybe, it's me.

I'm the one who can't move on. My normal is the paranormal, the supernatural. Some people thrive in chaos, and maybe I feel at home when things are wrong.

I look at my sisters, my beautiful and messy sisters, who made mistakes. They are the bad brujas who have raised the dead and traveled realms. They've figured out a way to continue to live and laugh and love. They're all right. Aren't they?

Maybe I'm the one that's wrong. Maybe I'm just so used to everything being on the verge of disaster that I haven't acclimated to harmony. Maybe this is it.

So, I decide to let it go, because I'm the good one, and I don't want to stir up any trouble. I just want to get them off my back. A dull pain pulses in the pit of my stomach and spreads throughout my body. More rose petals fall when I shake my head.

"I think I'm just having a hard time with the move and being at a new school. I got detention for arguing with the social studies teacher and practically failed my science test."

"You got a B," Lula says.

"My first! I had straight A's," I groan. I don't mention that I can't study because I have headaches, and I can't sleep because I miss the whispers of spirits.

They both rub my back like they're washing a car, waxing on and off.

"I started this," Alex says. "I can fix it."

"*I'm* the reason our old house burned down and we had to move," Lula says, managing to sound indignant and apologetic.

Carnation petals rain on my shoulders and hair. "No. It didn't start with you two. It started with Dad."

12

Lula gnaws on her bottom lip and Alex sighs. I bet if I closed my eyes and listened, really listened, I'd hear their heartbeats, just as frantic as mine. But Alex is the one who wants to squash my doubt because she needs to be in control of our family's happiness.

"But he's back now. Everything is fine. We're safe," Lula says.

That right there is why I can't talk to them. They've dealt with so much, and I feel wrong prying into this tentative peace. But I can't shake the feeling that we're all lying to ourselves. To each other.

I palm the top of my book. I can get it together for tonight. I can. I relent because they need me. "*Fine*. I'll go party with New York's finest magical creatures."

"And select fine sinmagos." Alex winks and Lula claps her hands in victory.

"But if I ever spawn, I'm not putting them through this," I grumble. "I don't even know half the people out there."

"You know how it is, Rosie," Lula says. "First you invite one tía, and then the other one is like, I hear so-and-so got an invitation, *pero like*, where's mine? And then the list goes from close friends and family to family six times removed, and even the bodega werewolf that flirts with Ma ends up getting an invite."

"Don't even talk, Lula," Alex says, wagging a finger in front of her face. "You're just like Ma. You'll make friends with the person who bumped into you on the subway. You literally befriended Death."

Lula gives us her cheek and turns her gray eyes to a row of canned tuna. "I'm a little too *busy* lately with important Thorne Hill Alliance business to make friends. It isn't my fault you two get your introvertedness from Dad."

"That's not a word," I say.

"And," Alex adds, "Dad didn't used to be introverted."

"I don't remember," I say. Sometimes I think I remember my father's face while he read me a book or his voice singing while he seasoned a pork shoulder for dinner. But I can't help wondering if those things really happened or if I made them up because I didn't want to be the only one of my sisters who didn't have memories of him.

"Give it an hour," Lula says, tucking a loose black curl behind her ear. "You don't have to hug anyone or kiss anyone on the cheek or be fake polite if you're not comfortable. Just be yourself. Our beautiful, smart Rose."

"And if anyone bothers you…" Alex wiggles her fingers in the air and tiny sparks of electricity thread around them. "Just say the magic word."

"What's the magic word?" I ask.

Lula scrunches up her face, then says, "*Pamplemousse!*"

"I don't know what that means."

Alex rolls her eyes so far I can only see the whites for a second. "It means grapefruit. The *hunter* is teaching her French, so she thinks she's fancy. Also, if he decides to take you on vacation again, he'd better invite all of us or Ma is going to curse his—"

"We were on a *mission*, Alejandra, not vacation!" Lula flips her curls in Alex's face and sucks her teeth. "And I like the sound of the word is all. Anyway, if you can't get out of a conversation just shout *pamplemousse*, and we'll come and save you. Promise."

"Promise," Alex echoes.

"I said I was going," I say, exasperated with them.

14

"Wait, aren't you changing into your after-party dress? I spent weeks combing through thrift stores for both of these," Lula says, because of course that's what she'd be worried about.

"She knows," Alex mutters. "We all know your sinmago power is finding a bargain."

It's customary to have a wardrobe change after the ritual summoning, since there's usually blood spatter from the animal sacrifice. I look at the brownish Texas-shaped stain on the pink fabric of my dress. If I asked a creature to give its life for the security of my power, then I'm going to wear my actions right on my sleeve. Or my skirt.

It's just one night, I tell myself. *You can do this for just one night. For your mom because she spent so much time and effort on this party.* I would do anything for her. Once when my mom made herself sick after healing an older bruja and pulling a ten-hour receptionist shift on the same day, I asked her why she stretched herself so thin and didn't ask for help in return. She said, "Our community needs me. Besides, I have you three. That's all the help I need." After everything my mom has been through, after all she's given of herself, she needs me there. Suddenly, I feel terrible for hiding.

"Let's go," I say. "But I'm not dancing."

We sit in silence for a moment longer, arms linked like a chain, listening to the joyous cacophony outside.

Then, Lula reaches for my wilting flower crown. "Can I fix your hair though?"

"Oh my gods, Lula, leave her be!" Alex lightly slaps the back of Lula's head, and Lula returns it.

"I'm just *saying*. These flowers were supposed to last a whole day, and there's a certain shape-shifter Rose has a crush on who's here tonight." Lula smirks.

"Nope. He's probably a hundred." Alex frowns. "I disapprove."

I try to get out of the pantry just to get away from this conversation and to hide how hot my cheeks are. My sisters follow, bursting into a fit of giggles at my expense. We spill out of the pantry and into the kitchen, three brujas ready to own the night.

2

Her fire inside can never be extinguished.

—Song of La Furia, Goddess of All
the World's Rage, Book of Deos

Our new house in Queens Village is twice as big as the one that burned down in Brooklyn over the summer. This house was a gift from the hunters, the Knights of Lavant. A little "you saved the city and only lost your worldly possessions" thank-you. The ceiling doesn't have the same cracks that my dad kept forgetting to fix. The smoke of palo santo isn't seeped into the carpets. We don't even have carpets now, just artfully arranged rugs over ceramic tiles where our guests can twirl in graceful dance moves.

Instead of an ancient wooden table, our kitchen comes with a marble bar top currently crowded with trays of pernil and rice and beans and Mom's famous lasagna. Instead of an old basement with rickety steps and bloodstained cement ground, our new house has a laundry room and more cabinets than we have things to fill them with, but all our little cousins have clustered down there to see if they can raise their own ghosts.

This house is like wearing an expensive dress that's just a size too big. Maybe we'll learn to fit into it eventually.

At least the kitchen still has Ma's collection of good-luck chickens. Metal chicken ornaments arranged on the kitchen door. Rooster magnets and table toppers. Chickens made of blown glass and porcelain decorate the terrariums along the windowsills. Baby chick salt and pepper shakers my mom found at a garage sale for a quarter. I wonder how many more we'll need before the luck starts kicking in.

"Alex!" Mom's disembodied voice shouts from the hall. "Where are those empanadas? Have you seen your sister?"

I know she means me, so I shout, "I'm here!"

Alex swears, and she rushes to the oven, which she most definitely forgot about. The braided pastries are charred at the edges but still look edible. Hunger slams into my stomach, and I realize I never had a proper dinner. Alex transfers the empanadas to a serving platter and balances it on her palm, using her magic to gently dissolve the smoke as she rushes for the living room.

I snatch one from the top and bite down on deliciously oily ground beef and carrots wrapped in a crispy flour shell. I don't even care that I'm burning my taste buds off.

"Isn't everyone tired?" I ask between bites, crumbs spilling on the bodice of my pink dress. "It's almost midnight."

"I'd give it until sunrise," Lula says, with a mischievous smile.

Her creamy brown skin and scarlet dress make her look like someone out of a Renaissance painting. Even the gold headband she made with wire and white roses from our garden is a crown fit for a fairy queen. She glances at the kitchen entrance to make sure the coast is clear, snatches an open bottle of champagne from an ice bin, and pours the remaining liquid in two plastic champagne flutes.

Lula winks at me. "Here."

When Lula was my age, she was sneaking Mom's vodka and taking it with her to slumber parties, then she'd refill the bottles with water. Ma either never noticed or just didn't mention it. I've only tried sips of wine during equinox celebrations and never understood why adults like fermented fruit juice, but I take the drink my sister offers.

"Happy birthday, Rosie," Lula says. She taps her glass to mine, watching for my reaction.

We drink, and I wrinkle my nose at the bitter bubbles exploding on my tongue. "Gross."

"Come, let's celebrate," she laughs and pulls me into a strangling one-armed hug as we make our way down the hall.

A gaggle of little kids race past us, chasing two stray black cats. Tía Azucena is at their heels, shouting something about rabies and how they're letting out the heat.

"It's a good thing black cats aren't bad luck for us," I say.

"I'm making a list of the upsides to Queens." Lula absentmindedly sways to the music. "Bigger yard and neighborhood cats are high up there."

"What about the downside?"

We stop at the open living room arch and share a look of understanding. I know exactly what she's going to say before she says it.

"It's not Brooklyn." She leans against the threshold and scans the revelers moving across the dance floor. "But we've made it home."

I take another sip of my champagne, and this time it's less gross but still too bitter for something that looks like it should be sweet and sparkly.

All of a sudden, everyone notices me. Mayi and Emma are flushed from dancing. Alex is bombarded by hands grabbing empanadas off her tray. Strangers, friends and family blur together as they all raise glasses and arms, shouting, "Viva la bruja!"

There's a brief moment when people come to shake my hand, congratulate me, or just say hello. I smile and I'm grateful, but it's too much.

"Pamplemousse," I hiss, and Lula dutifully stands beside me, hurrying our guests along until my fifteen minutes of celebrity is over, and the party returns to full swing.

My mom's High Circle of Brooklyn keeps to one corner, tight-lipped and rigid, while brujas and brujos dance right alongside hunters and werewolves and solitary fairies. I don't think we would have been able to do this in our other home, so this goes in the upside column.

"Are you sure there isn't something else you want to talk about?" Lula asks, reaching down to massage the leg that has bothered her since the accident. Some things can't be fixed with magic, and she will always have a small limp. "I don't need my powers to sense your anxiety."

"Nope." I scratch my palm against my dress and shake my head, making wilting petals fall to the ground.

"Good, because this is my song and we're going to dance." She grabs my hand and yanks me forward, but a young guy blocks our path.

"Happy birthday, Rose," he says in that deep voice of his. Then his entire attention shifts to my sister. I see the moment he becomes breathless. "Lula."

"Rhett." She looks at him in that way of hers that makes boys forget themselves.

I bite down on a smile at the sight of the nervous hunter. He shoves one hand in his pocket and unbuttons his bloodred blazer with the other. His brown hair is pulled back into an elegant topknot. On principle, can a topknot be fancy? Rhett helped us last summer with our undead problem. I know Lula liked him, but she wasn't ready to date. Now that she is, they're playing this insufferably cute and awkward game. Rhett stares at Lula like she's a miracle, and after having to impale her boyfriend with the Spear of Death, she deserves someone patient and kind. And living.

Rhett extends his open hand. "Dance with me?"

"You can dance to this?" she asks skeptically.

"My gran taught me a bit," he says, biting his bottom lip.

Lula threads her arm around mine. Somehow, I can feel the nervous flutter of her heart, and the indecision twisting her actions. I know that if I asked my sister to stay and keep me company, she'd forget about doing what makes her happy. She shakes her head but rests her hand in his waiting one. "Maybe later."

Rhett folds himself into a little bow and kisses her knuckles. "I'll be here."

We watch him grab a glass of wine and fold into a group of other hunters.

"If you're just going to stare longingly at each other from across the room," I tell her, "why don't you just dance?"

Lula presses the hand Rhett kissed right over her heart. Her dress covers the black mark left there from the recoil of magic she used over the summer. I wonder if she's remembering those awful few days. I wonder if she'd tell me.

Instead, she flashes a smile and brushes my baby hairs away like she's done my whole life. "Brujas before bros, Rosie."

I roll my eyes. "If you don't want to dance, that's fine. But you've been thirsting after each other for months. Don't use me as an excuse."

"You're not an excuse!" Lula says. "And I'm not *thirsting*. Plus, if I leave, you'll just go hide in the pantry again."

"I won't! I'll dance with Mayi or Adrian."

She bites her bottom lip, and I see the indecision and excitement that makes her radiant. "You sure?"

"Positive." I give her a push and take her half-empty glass. "It's my Deathday slash birthday, *and* my wish is that you have a good time too."

Then she's gone, and I make a beeline for the kitchen to dump out the champagne. As promised, I don't go back into the pantry, but I never said anything about my room. I am shoving an empanada in my pocket when I hear a familiar voice.

"So, you have your Deathday and you start sneaking drinks already?"

I whirl around to find Nova at the kitchen door, leaning casually against the door frame, arms crossed over his chest.

"How are you so stealthy?" I ask.

22

He shrugs and flashes a rueful smirk. "I'm good at not being seen."

Nova's in dark jeans and a blue long-sleeve sweater that brings out the strange shade of his eyes. Ink tendrils of his Sacred Heart tattoo peek from the V-neck trim. His light-brown skin has a paleness to it that doesn't feel normal, but it could also be that he's spent the last couple of months working the night shift at a bar in Coney Island, so he hardly sees the sun.

"It's my party," I say. "I don't have to sneak anything. Plus champagne is gross."

"Good. Keep it that way." He runs a hand along his freshly buzzed fade. I try to not look at his fingers because it makes him feel self-conscious. The black burn marks of his magic have spread to the middle finger joints. He begins to say something, but it comes out as a frustrated sigh. Then, I notice the duffel bag at his feet.

"What's that?"

"I have to go."

Go? Go where. A frantic rush of adrenaline makes my head spin. I realize that I'm not the only one who vanished at the beginning of the party. So did he.

"What's wrong, Nova? Where'd you go after the summoning?"

"I don't really like Deathdays."

"But you do like parties," I say, trying to find something to cheer him up. When he gives me another strained smile, I ask, "Where are you going?"

He takes my hands in his. "You look beautiful, Rosie. Maybe I should stay in case someone tries to get fresh and I have to put on my big-brother hat."

"You didn't answer my question." I hold my finger up to his face. "And I won't take part in your patriarchal nonsense."

He barks a laugh, deep from his belly. "I'm going to miss pretending I understand some of the things you say. Makes me look smarter."

I lightly punch his shoulder. Nova's not my biological brother, but I've learned that there's more to family than blood and duty.

"Why are you leaving now?" There's a hitch in my voice, and I try to breathe through it. "Why today?"

"I don't like messy goodbyes. Plus, now everyone is distracted with the less-bloody parts of the ceremony."

"Is it your magic?" I hold his hand again. Maybe he doesn't like messy goodbyes, but I can't just watch him leave. "We can try to bind your power again. We can find something. You don't have to go."

He looks down, shielding his blue-green eyes from me. Only after he moved in, I noticed how different they were, the blues and greens constantly shifting like light on Caribbean waters.

"No, Rosie. Your parents already did everything they could for me. Nothing they can do is stopping these burns from spreading." He splays his fingers to show the damage. Nova's marks aren't magic. They're the absence of magic. His power burning through him. It's what happens when a brujo's body can't handle their gift. That is why we have Deathdays—to balance our power so we won't singe up like a wick. Family, living and dead, give you that balance in the form of a blessing. We tried to give Nova the Deathday he never had, but the spirits of his ancestors didn't answer the call.

24

I wish my new magic would let me draw the burn marks out, the way I have done to other powers. But I can't.

"I can feel this curse eating right through me. But I think I might have found something."

My eyes go wide. "What?"

"It's a hunch, but I have to go to the DR first."

"You don't have a passport. And you can't exactly take a *bus* to the Dominican Republic."

A playful smile breaks his somber features. "You know by now I have my ways. I'm sorry I couldn't be more help with your pops's memory."

I shrug and ignore the gnawing feeling I already hid from my sisters. "It's not your fault. You're the one who brought him back."

Suddenly, I'm overwhelmed by the things that are unresolved. Nova with his cursed magic and my dad with his lost memory and me with my inexplicable power. I wish I could freeze everything at a moment when I felt hopeful. But if I'm honest with myself, I don't know if that time existed.

"Alex isn't going to let you get away with this," I tell him. I feel like I'm grasping for him, but he wants to be let go. Isn't that why he's leaving in the middle of the night when no one will notice? Except me. "She'll chase you to the ends of the earth. We all will."

"Alex wouldn't miss class if the gods themselves gave her a hall pass." He takes out a little leather pouch. "I made these for you. Just something to show my thanks."

I pull on the drawstring and shake the contents onto my palm. Three braided leather bracelets, each with a silver pendant at the center—a crescent moon, a sun, and a star. "They're so beautiful. Thank you."

Nova clears his throat and blinks until his eyes stop glistening. "The moon is for Alex and the star for Lula."

I slip the sun bracelet around my wrist. There's magic in it. I can feel it deep down. A part of Nova that he's leaving behind. I set the other two back in the pouch and try to act stronger than I feel.

"Don't go, Nova. We can help you." Can we? A few months ago, it felt like we could barely help ourselves.

"This is something I have to do with my blood. It always comes down to blood, doesn't it, Rosie?"

I touch the stain on the front of my dress and nod. I remember what my dad used to say. *The Deos ask for too much.* "I wish it could be different for us."

He brushes a petal stuck to my wet cheek. "I used to think I could find a cure. I did terrible things for it. But it's bone deep. Blood cursed. At least now I know that it isn't me. I inherited it. I have to find a way to end it."

"I'll see you, Rosie." Nova picks up his bag and shoulders it. "Don't do anything I *would* do, and—"

"I know, I know, be good."

He frowns and shakes his head. "That's actually not what I was going to say at all."

"What then?"

"You've got this power, and it will get difficult. No one can understand what you're going through. You might not even know half the time. The only thing you can do is remember yourself." Nova flashes one last smile, and then he's gone into the winter night.

Remember yourself.

I know exactly who I am. At least, I think I do. An idea takes shape as I stand in the empty kitchen. Perhaps, if Nova can take a leap and chase something unknown with a fraction of hope that he can heal his burn marks, I can do the same for my family. This power might be new and different, but I'm still me. I'm still Rose Elizabeta Mortiz Vargas. I can figure out how to fix everything that's broken along the way and make us better, stronger.

A clock strikes somewhere in the house. I gather the skirt of my dress and march back into the hall. It is my party, after all, and what better time to begin working magic than at midnight, after I have been blessed by my family spirits and all the gods?

3

Shine your light on secrets past.

Unravel shadows. Let truth outlast.

—TRUTH CANTO,
BOOK OF CANTOS

Our family altar is in the wide foyer, nestled into the wall by pearls and blue mosaic tiles. The three-foot statue of La Mama, Mother of all the Deos, is especially decadent today. Every part of her, from the golden sun crowning her forehead, to her black skin, to the folds of her gown, was polished for today. Upon entering the house, every guest laid a token around her bare feet—glittering crystals, pennies, baby teeth, cherry-flavored Jolly Ranchers, parrot feathers, wishes scrawled on paper folded so tight the secrets within could never spill out. Tapered candles and flowers overflow onto the floor in a waterfall of wax and petals.

I strike a match and light a new candle to ask for help from our family's patron goddess. Pure, raw magic lingers here hours after my Deathday ritual. When I breathe deeply, I can almost taste it, sugary sweet. Our family's Book of Cantos is locked upstairs. But I don't need it. I know our sacred text, detailing generations of insight and magic, almost by heart. When I close my eyes, I can see the words written in homemade ink by one of my ancestors. A canto to reveal the truth. I wonder what secrets she revealed with it. I wonder if she imagined that decades later, I'd use it on my most blessed day. I am sure that this is what needs to be done to break this cycle of uncertainty and sorrow.

Tucking the slender candle in the open space between La Mama's waiting hands, I pull on the magic around me and concentrate. My power answers with a buzz that smothers my skin. Sifting through the bright souls gathered in our house, I find the people I want to focus on—my parents, my sisters, myself.

I whisper, "Divina Madre, shine your light on secrets past. Unravel shadows. Let truth outlast."

A light breeze tickles the back of my neck. When I open a single eye, my candle does nothing but flicker. Revelers drift past me without so much as a comment. I suppose the good thing about having a party in a house of magic is that no one bats an eye when you're casting cantos. Aside from a distant ringing in my ears, the party goes on.

I mean, what was I expecting? The doors to shake and the electricity to sputter? A little thunder and lightning would be nice. My mother always warned that magic requires patience and that means waiting. So I'll wait. I am totally good with waiting.

On my way back to the living room, I avoid a throng of little kids trying to catch a sparrow that flew inside the house, turn, and nearly bump into a young couple walking out of the guest closet. I feel my face flash hot at the sight of their swollen lips and messed-up hair. They wish me a happy Deathday, and I'm so awkward I make a left for the side entrance, but blocking the door is Marty McKay, a shape-shifter from the Thorne Hill Alliance. He's talking so animatedly with my dad that they don't notice me. I spin on my heels and shuffle back down the hall and return to the dance floor.

Okay, maybe I was wrong to hide for so long. I did *help* with the flower arrangements and choosing the color theme—gold for La Mama, pink for healing, black for protection and for the dead. Fairy lights strung across the high ceiling wink, and snow flurries drift across the ceiling thanks to a glamour canto Mayi cast. It's a perfectly beautiful after-party. So why do I feel this way?

I park myself next to the gift table, waiting for my canto to manifest, and watch my guests salsa and spin to the slap of drums and strum of guitars.

Alex and Rishi are dancing, or whatever passes for dancing when you don't know the steps. Rishi looks like a mermaid in her sequin skirt and matching tube top, which practically doubles as a disco ball when compared to Alex's simple black dress. My sister told me once that Rishi was her light, and I didn't really understand what that meant until I saw them together. Mostly because I'm fifteen and I've never been in love with anyone, but also because I don't think I'd ever want someone to be so much to me that I'd be in the dark without them. It's terrifying.

Like Lula for instance. She and Rhett are leaning against the wall where the shadows are long and romantic. He's handsome in that my-nose-has-been-broken-so-many-times-it-gives-me-character kind of way. His casual red-and-black suit is tapered to his lean muscles, and I'd give him a B-minus at being a hunter, at best, but is he funny? He's patiently waited for her to be ready, but what has he learned about Lula in the months they've spent together? Does he write her love notes? Does he know that when she's sick, the only thing she wants to eat is chicken broth and peppermint tea full of honey candies? Lula has always loved too hard, too quickly. But when she loves, it is forever. (Or until you become a member of the undead and she has to kill you, like with her last boyfriend, but that's an exception.) I can already see how much Lula cares for Rhett in the sparkle of her cloud-gray eyes and how she makes any excuse to touch his hands, shoulder, hair.

Dad blocks my view as he shimmies right past me, in a better mood than the last few months. The sight of him dancing is a pleasant surprise to everyone, and they whistle as he makes his way to my mother. She's holding court on a long couch with other brujas, and they bat their lashes and throw flirty hand gestures at my parents.

So in love. So strong. So together.

Ma is in her favorite ocean-blue dress dotted with tiny mirrors and beads. Dad spins her under his arm, and they settle into the flow of the song. I don't think I have any memories of them together from before. In pictures, he was tall and muscular, with a mess of black curls and a wry grin. He's still tall but slenderer, like when a tree loses all its foliage and suddenly you can see how frail it is. Only his mustache and eyebrows are still ink-black, despite the rest of his hair having gone gray.

He whispers something to my mother, and it feels like I'm invading a private moment by watching.

I pick up the first present in front of me to busy my hands. I shake the small box to my ear, and if I'm not mistaken, it's the rattle of tiny bones. I'll open these tomorrow, while I finish my birthday cake for breakfast. Right now, I'm frustrated that I might have been wrong.

To anyone looking in, my sisters and my parents appear perfectly happy. Panic coils in the pit of my stomach. Maybe my truth canto to La Mama won't reveal anything. Maybe I haven't stopped waiting for the next crisis and have been holding my breath for the last six months.

But then, from where I stand, I notice the fissures in the glass. When Rhett moves to brush a stray curl from Lula's face and she flinches, is she remembering how Maks tried to kill her? Is Alex glancing at the windows because she's also afraid the bruja of our nightmares is going to somehow reappear, seeking vengeance? When my mother's smile falls, just for a second, is she worried that my dad will vanish again into the realm of Adas?

"Talk to me," I whisper, gnawing off the pink nail polish of my manicure.

Their momentary fears lapse, and my family returns to dancing and smiling, and I'm left with a deep ache in the bones of my hands that wasn't there before. I shake out my hand. It must be the recoil that comes with using magic.

The song slows, the singer's deep voice dripping with regret and longing. The band doles out a rhythm that entrances everyone on the dance floor, sweeping them into the melancholy of the romantic tune. The weight of it hits me in the gut because suddenly I know why this feeling of impending doom lingers. It *is* the fissures in the glass. If our happiness is fragile enough to shatter at any moment, are we even happy at all?

When the sweet scent of magic begins to turn sour, I feel someone tap my shoulder.

"Hey, Rose, right?" I look up to find a young brujo, handsome in that way moms and aunties go wild over, with his ironed trousers and checkered button-down tucked into his waistband. His blond hair is brushed to the side, and before he speaks again, he licks peachy lips that probably always say *please* and *thank you.* "I'm William, Azucena's grandson. I stole twenty dollars from her purse while she was in the bathroom."

I could catch a fistful of flies as my mouth hangs open. "Uhh, okay. Nice to meet you."

He blinks rapidly, horrified at what he just said, then scurries away.

"Oh no," I exhale. I glance around the dance floor. Are the lights dimmer than before? Alex dances nearby with Rishi, and I whisper-hiss, "*Pamplemousse!*"

I try to grab my sister, but Mayi blocks my path. She covers her wide grin with one hand. Her onyx eyes are glazed over, but a triumphant giggle escapes. "I made out with Junior in Lula's room just now."

"Oh *no.*" I slap my hands on my head, and a new shower of wilted petals fall from my crown. The pads of my fingertips heat up, pinpricks jab beneath my skin. I examine at my hands to see where the foreign sensation is coming from, but there is nothing there.

Mayi leaves, spinning away in a ruffle of chiffon. Before I can

33

make a run for it, an older woman waddles over to the refreshment table and ladles herself a glass of sangria. She puckers her lips and slides brown eyes at me as if we're in on a secret. "Tasty but the pernil was a little dry. Don't tell your Mami."

I whirl away from her. Okay, okay, okay.

So, my truth canto is working, just not in the way I want it to. I can fix this. I cut through the throngs of dancers, secrets lobbed my way—*Alex Mortiz ruined my life. I've been in love with Lula since the first grade. I think my brother-in-law is my son's real father.* I walk so fast I can't match the faces to the whispered confessions.

"Rose?" Alex asks, gripping me by my wrist. "What's going on?"

"Nothing, I have it under control."

"Good. I'm worried we messed you up too much." She starts, but the minute she speaks those words, her eyes flutter. She smiles and then returns to Rishi.

Is that what they all think? That I'm messed up? I don't have time to linger on Alex's worry about me. My nerves kick up my heartbeat. I follow the flow of the party, where bodies crowd into the hallway on their way to get fresh air on the porches and open windows. I pick up my tulle skirts and run back to the front of the house, back to the three-foot statue of La Mama.

The candle I lit before is already halfway melted into a puddle of wax, but the flame is not extinguished. *When the Deos answer your call, they snuff out the lights.* That's what we've been taught since day one. Cantos and spellwork have to run their course, but I have to stop this before someone says something they'll regret, like telling my mother about her food. And that's the best-case scenario.

34

"Please, La Mama, I beg your forgiveness. Stop this. I don't want to know any more."

I snuff out the candle myself and wait, my heartbeat in my ears like a bass drum. Slowly, even the strange ache in my hands recedes. The air no longer smells like sugar turned sour, and the salsa band is literal music to my ears.

"Thank the Deos," I sigh, relieved. I curse myself because I know better. Or I thought I did.

"There you are, Rose!" Valeria's saccharine voice calls over the song.

I pretend I don't hear her and head for the stairs to hide in my room, but she shouts it a couple more times. I stop at the base of the steps and paint a strained smile on my face before turning to her.

"Oh, hey, Señora Valeria, I didn't see you there," I say.

My old mentor's cocked eyebrow tells me she knows I'm lying. Her plum lipstick runs into the lines around her mouth, proud brown eyes settle on me like a magnifying glass over a curious specimen. This is the woman who delivered me into this world, taught me everything about being a seer when I still thought that was my only gift. Then, she stopped talking to us after Lula's accident. You'd think we're the only family to raise the dead. At least we put them *back*.

"I just wanted to tell you what a beautiful ceremony that was," she says, pressing her hand over her heart. Fear digs cold finger nails into my back because I don't think the canto is quite over. I brace for whatever she's going to say. "But if you were still my student you wouldn't have chosen such a simple offering for such a *fascinating* power."

The "simple offering" she referred to was a mouse.

In the old days, brujas waited for a sacrificial animal to come to them. That was when people lived closer to forests and mountains and didn't shower every day from fear of dying from a cold. My reason for wanting a smaller party was to honor what Deathdays are supposed to be about: the bond between a bruja and her power. These days, Deathdays are all about dresses and guest list politics. My mom says it's because there are so few brujas left, and I get that. But unlike my sisters, who went to the pet store to choose their birds, and unlike some of the brujos who convinced their parents to import exotic gerbils, I went to the park across the highway.

Alley Pond Park had a decent stretch of trees and a muddy basin of brackish water that looked like a Queens mob might have dumped bodies in it fifty years ago. I sat on a blanket inside a ring of white quartz crystals and prayed to El Terroz, Lord of the Earth and its Treasures. Then I waited. It was almost thirty degrees, but my sisters brought me a travel mug of hot chocolate and kept reminding me that there was a pet store on Hillside Avenue.

I'm possibly more stubborn than the pair of them. It got dark, and to be honest, I was scared. Queens Village is too quiet, suburban in a way Brooklyn just isn't. I could sense Alex and Lula nearby though. Their magic brushed against my cold cheeks, and I realized that they were insulating the air around me all while giving me space to do what I needed to do. In that moment, I thanked the Deos for my sisters.

Then, the pale gray mouse ran across my lap and I took it home.

So, when Valeria makes light of my sent-by-the-gods sacrifice, my anger simmers. I breathe deep and take her sideways compliment, because if my mom catches me making a face, she'll say it's going to get stuck that way and to also respect my elders.

"Thanks again for coming." Another cluster of petals falls over my face from my crown.

"I'm very proud of you, Rose." She pinches my cheek hard. "Let's make sure you keep being a good girl. We don't want a repeat of your sisters' mistakes, may the Deos bless them, of course. I keep wondering if things would have been different if your father had been around."

The comment makes me reel back and bump into two women standing behind me. I vaguely recognize them as members of the High Circle of Queens. With their little party plates in hand topped with my mom's fried shrimp puffs and chimichurri sauce, they're a welcome sight.

"Rose! I'm Anaís and this is Juliette," says the bruja wearing a pink silk headwrap. She gives a curt nod in Valeria's direction. Her accent is thick, from somewhere in South America I can't place. "We're honored to welcome you to our wonderful borough. I hope you and your sisters will consider joining our humble High Circle of Queens."

"Yes!" the younger bruja with brown skin and bleached-blond curls yelps. "Oh my Deos. It's so nice to get fresh blood."

Anaís smirks. "And I couldn't help but overhear, but in *Queens*, we show our loyalty. All are welcome, no matter what mistakes you might make."

Valeria turns to me. My former mentor who held my hands and guided me through the Veil of spirits and taught me how to use my power to avoid being possessed by the dead. Except the whole time, I was hacking her power and using it as my own. She used to look at me as if I had potential. Now, her gaze is disapproving, like I've personally set out to insult her. "Is that what you think, Rose?"

I don't think it. I *know* it.

But this conversation has my skin sweating like a Coney Island hot dog on the Fourth of July. From where I stand, I have a direct line of sight to Lula in the crowded living room. I concentrate, like if I put all my power into it, I'll conjure words into her mind.

"*Pamplemousse.*" I hiss it once. I don't care if the brujas from all five boroughs think I'm nuts.

"Is she all right?" Anaís asks Juliette.

"You know I *thought* I smelled the workings of a canto a few moments ago," Juliette says.

"*Pamplemousse!*" I finally shout, but it's no use. Alex and Lula are both too busy dancing and flirting to notice that I *need* them.

The three women start to argue, their words changing to a rapid-fire Spanish that I can't keep track of, and soon enough, they're so busy arguing about *me* that they forget that I'm standing here.

At last! It's my moment to escape.

I tiptoe away, which is decidedly difficult to do while wearing a tulle skirt better suited for a fairy-tale princess. I'm forced to stop when something tugs on my gown and there's a loud *riiiiiiip.*

I look down to find that Marty McKay, shape-shifter and one of the leaders of the supernatural organization the Thorne Hill Alliance, has stepped on my dress.

"Oh my gods, I am so sorry," he shouts, then slaps one hand over his mouth. He's wearing a T-shirt that reads *Taking Back Thor's Day* with a black blazer over it. The sincere apology in his wide brown eyes make me forget to be mad though. "You can't take me anywhere, I swear." He shoves a half-eaten empanada into his mouth and gets down on his knees to survey the damage.

"It's fine!" I grab the tulle skirts and finish ripping off the piece he stepped on. Heat crawls up my neck in a way I've never felt before. "I mean, between that and the bloodstain, it's not like I can wear this to prom, though prom isn't for another three and a half years, and I probably won't go anyway because I'll—"

"Rose?"

"Yes?"

"I'm still sorry."

I let myself breathe in McKay's chill presence. He dusts crumbs off his hands, then lifts his cap to muss up brown waves. Every time I've seen him, he's worn that same black Yankees cap. I wonder if he washes it. I think he'd look cuter without his hat on because you can see the oval shape of his kind face and it doesn't obstruct the dark brown of his eyes or his long lashes. When he smiles at me, my abdomen tightens with a strange anticipation, and I have to look down at my feet so he doesn't see me blushing.

McKay's eyes flick to the stairwell I was aiming for and the brujas still arguing. "What's wrong? Did I interrupt your great escape?"

"You wouldn't understand."

His lips quirk at the corners and a dimple appears. "You're right, I wouldn't. But I can take your mind off whatever is bothering you."

"How?" My heart hiccups. I hear Alex in my head: *He's probably a hundred.* Stupid Lula and Alex ruining my life.

"You can laugh at me while I try to dance. Come on, birthday girl."

39

It's not that I don't like dancing. When I'm alone in my room, I definitely have dance parties for one. It's the people-watching-me part that I want to avoid. But now, I let McKay lead me through the crowd because it's better than staying in the middle of a bruja turf war. The tension around my shoulder unwinds a bit because other than too much information from some people, my canto didn't do much damage.

The salsa band is taking a break, and Lula's iPod is plugged into the speaker, blasting reggaetón that has most of the old folks scattered, except Tía Panchita and her ghost.

"This is my *song*!" Lula shouts.

And I go, "Every song is your song!"

McKay makes his best attempt at break dancing, and a crowd forms around us. I move to the downbeats and quick rhymes and wish Nova were here. Alex and Lula take turns spinning each other around, skirts billowing around their strong legs. I can't help think about how I'm going to have to give them the bracelets Nova made. Tell them that he left us.

But that's a problem for later tonight.

For now, I let myself enjoy this moment. Dancing bodies moving in the hall, the kitchen, and probably the backyard. Our house is full of literal magic and music. Juliette from the High Circle of Queens conjures soft sparks of light across the ceiling, and Rishi's dark eyes widen with glee. She kisses Alex's cheek, and they fall into each other like missing pieces finally finding their match. Tía María Azul cuts in front of Lula to dance with Rhett and she moves over to me, bumping her hips with McKay. Then the song abruptly ends and is followed by a slow ballad.

My face is hot enough to melt the snow outside as couples return to each other, and McKay twirls me around in place. He rests one hand on my waist and takes the other like we're about to waltz, his hands cold even through the fabric of my dress.

"See? This is better than hiding in the pantry."

I laugh and petals rain. "How did you know?"

"I was in the kitchen shoving empanadas in my face and heard you all. Sorry. Is Queens really that bad? I do suppose *Brooklyn Brujas* has a better ring to it than *Queens Brujas*."

"Queens is fine. Though sometimes it's so quiet I feel like I'm being watched."

"We can put more warding on the house."

I shake my head. "We have plenty of protection charms. The house is fine. I can't really explain it."

He scrunches up one side of his face. "With new powers comes great confusion?"

McKay had been there the day I discovered my magic was different. He called me a "magical hacker" because I latched on to his power. I could practically see everything in his makeup down to a cellular level, shifting molecules and tissue and bone. Then I used his power as mine, something I had been doing to Valeria without realizing it for over fourteen years.

He gives my hand a gentle squeeze.

I don't want to tell him about my family business, so I settle for my own. "More like with new powers comes lots of rubberneckers. I feel like everyone is watching and holding their breath for me to screw up."

He laughs, a deep beautiful sound. I start to laugh back when

41

I realize Lula, Alex, and Rishi are all staring at me, making kissy faces in my direction. I glower before turning back to McKay. He's not handsome in the way Lula's hunter is. Or the way Nova is, with his sharp features. But there's something about McKay that makes me like staring at him. Maybe it's because he always exudes happiness, and I wonder: *How can someone sustain that all the time?*

Two couples bump into us, forcing us to stand closer together. I take a deep breath because I don't think I've ever been this close to a guy who was not related to me, and I *hate* that all of my family is watching.

"There's always a new Chosen One around the corner," he says playfully. "You'll be old hat soon enough."

"That's fine with me. I just—I wish everything felt more settled."

"Settled how?"

"I don't know anything about my power. The limits, what it can do. It's like my story is already finished, but I don't feel like it ever started. Maybe if I knew my full potential, I could use my power to make everything right."

"Like you tried to do tonight?"

I scoff. "Lurk much?"

"I had several strangers give me too much personal information, including mental pictures that are now branded in my skull, and it's not because of my charm."

My tongue feels like the time I tripped on my own shoelaces on the first day of junior high. "I undid it. It didn't work right anyway."

The laughter leaves his eyes when he says, "Be careful, Rose."

"What do you mean?"

McKay leans in and whispers, "I can't pretend to know why you're forcing the truth out of people. That's on you. But the rest? I've seen friends grapple with great power. They lose themselves to the expectations of that gift. Let people hold their breath. Let them watch and have their expectations. You will understand your power in time."

"I don't think you know anything about brujas. I can't just worry about me. Everything I do affects my family and my people. It sucks to feel all that pressure, but until I have a handle on things. I need them."

"You are wise, young wizard." He winks.

"Young bruja." I correct him and feel a flutter within my rib cage. My hand is sweating in his, which is embarrassing, but he doesn't let go.

"So that's what's troubling you?" he asks, genuine curiosity in his features. "Not being able to help? The Alliance can always step in. That's why it was created."

I sigh. More petals fall. "Do you ever feel like things are terrible, but everyone is pretending like it's fine?"

"I live with a vampire who is in constant denial about his immortality, so yes, I think I do know how that feels."

When we turn, my parents come back into my line of sight. Only, my dad's walking away from my mom and her body is tense. She dabs at her eyes and hurries off into the hall. Is she crying? Or is she trying to cool off after dancing? A cold sensation takes hold of my gut because I know she's upset and trying her best to hide it.

"It might seem patronizing," McKay says, "but revel in the

moments of peace because they don't last long. You've got this new house and a new school. Your father is home. I mean, I can't blame the man for being so happy after spending all that time eating nothing but fairy food and working in the king's salt mines. Did you know that the fairies in the Kingdom of Adas eat flowers covered in sugar? I wouldn't make it a day. I have to be fed every ninety minutes or—"

Something snaps in my head. "What did you say?"

McKay frowns, holds my hand a little gentler. We stop swaying. "A fairy kingdom would be the end of me?"

"Salt mines?" There's a roaring in my ears. A sick, hot sensation swells in my chest, threatening to leap to my throat and choke me.

"Yeah, your dad mentioned it."

"No." That can't be right. I pull away.

"Rose, did I say something wrong?" Marty's eyes dart around the room, but no one is paying attention to us. Alex and Rishi are gone, and Lula's dancing like she's gliding on air. They don't see. For all their talk about coming to my rescue, my sisters are in their own worlds.

I think about the fissures in the glass. They're spreading. When my dad reappeared, he barely remembered us. Months went by and he said he had no memory of the seven years he was missing. We tried healing cantos, memory charms, séances to wake the spirits. Over this summer, Nova went in search of an item that could be the missing ingredient. He found an acorn from the Kingdom of Adas, the land where my dad had been trapped. We cast a canto that revealed a flash of an image from Dad's time there. But it was a dead end. My father said he still couldn't remember how he ended up there or how he got out, and we let it go. We accepted that the time lost will always be blank spaces in his mind and our lives.

It isn't *possible* that my father would tell McKay something so small—throwaway memories of food and salt mines—when he's been home for a year and has said over and over again that he has not a single memory of his time in Adas. Not a *single* memory.

"I'm sorry if I said something stupid," McKay says. But he sounds far away. "It's my fatal flaw."

"It's fine," I say. But it isn't fine. Maybe nothing will be fine again. I asked for the truth, and I intend to have it. Shaking, I leave the dance floor to find my father—find him and force him to tell me why he lied.

4

The Bastard King of Adas longed for a queen.

He found her in the orchid grove.

—CLARIBELLE AND THE KINGDOM OF ADAS:
TALES TALL AND TRUE, GLORIANA PALACIOS

D ad?" I shout throughout the house.

Dad and *father* are words that I'm still not used to saying. In school, I'd always make an excuse for why he wasn't around. Every time, my lie was different. I didn't know how to explain, and I always felt the judgment in their eyes: *There's that Rose Mortiz with her two sisters and her single mother, abandoned.* At home, we never even talked about him. I watched Alex withdraw while Lula and Ma cast searching cantos and prayers, and burned candles until they gave up and the wax was melted so deep in the wood it would never come out.

I go to the kitchen, but there's no one in there. I run downstairs to the basement, but there are only the little ones playing with Lula's old spirit board. A pinching sensation in my rib cage erupts, and I don't know if it's shortness of breath or my magic, but I pant when I race back upstairs. I realize Lula is right. This house has too many doors. All the bedrooms are empty, and so is the infirmary and the in-progress library I've been working on every weekend. Suddenly, my dress feels too tight, and pinpricks of magic needle beneath my skin.

That's when I spot him. From the hallway window on the second floor, I can see him standing on the front lawn. Staring at the sky. He's always just staring at nothing when we're right here.

I race downstairs, ignoring whoever is calling after me. An aunt, a cousin, a neighbor. I wish I could make everyone leave.

I slam the door behind me, activating the porch lights. I hear something fall but I can't bother with it.

My father turns around at the sound, surprise in his pale gray eyes. "Rosie."

I march down the front steps, glancing back only once at the silhouettes that dance across the windows like will-o'-the-wisps. The heat from the house clings to me through the early December chill. The sky is pitch-black, but twinkling Christmas decorations make up for the streetlamp that has gone out.

"What are you doing out here?" I raise my voice, my hands fists at my side.

"I'm not used to crowds."

It would be easier, better, to let the past be the past. But his calm words send a blind rage through me I didn't even realize was there. "I don't like crowds either, but I have to be there. That's why we had this stupid party, right? Because Ma wants to feel like every-thing is back to normal."

"Rosie, why are you upset?"

47

"You said— You told us you didn't remember your time in that place." Tears threaten my senses and I stop. Start again. My breath condenses. "You said you didn't remember!"

"I don't." His voice is so small and mine is so big and I know I shouldn't yell at him, but it's hard to stay calm when he's lying to my face.

"You're still lying!"

"You did something, didn't you?" He looks down at his feet, the shadows long and overpowering. I don't answer. "I wondered why I said those things…"

"All this time, we were trying to fix your memory. We should have worked on your lies instead."

"I'm—" He starts.

"Don't say you're trying because you're not. You told McKay that you worked in salt mines. You told him you ate flowers. And with us—nothing. You gave us nothing."

My father shakes his head. Droplets fall on the tops of his shoes, and when he looks at me, he's crying.

"I wish I could explain." He reaches for the crown of flowers in my hair, and I slap his hand away. My skin sizzles with the clash of our magic.

"There's nothing wrong with your memory, is there?"

He remains silent. There's sorrow in his voice, in his eyes. I've had the same sorrow in my heart since the day he vanished. I think of Nova saying he inherited his blood curse. Maybe we all get a fatal flaw from our parents. I inherited this silence. No more.

"Tell me the truth," I say, even though I know the answer.

"No, there isn't." His breath is shaky. "I remember everything.

Rosie, listen to me." He grabs my sleeve to stop me from walking away.

I snatch his wrist, and the magic within me unravels. It wraps around his and draws on the living power he holds—the power of storms. My heart races, and I know it shouldn't be possible, but I can see my own molecules shifting, drawing his magic into me. Then he wrenches free and the connection is broken. There's a rush of wind encircling us, the gathering of clouds that weren't there moments ago. Beneath all of that, I rewind his words. *I remember everything.*

I can't stay here.

I can't go back inside my house and pretend everything is all right.

As I run away, he shouts my name.

"I don't want to hear anything you say!"

I run faster than I ever have before. Thunder rumbles overhead as the cluster of storm clouds follows me. Lightning strikes in the park across the street, and the December air fills my lungs with every breath. My father's power is to conjure storms, and for a borrowed moment, it is now mine. I can't control it, only try to run. Beads of moisture cling to my skin, the shake of thunder in my bones—my blood calls to it.

His footsteps are right behind mine, as he gives chase. I don't wait for the light to change. I dart across the parkway, cars honking as they swerve around me. My muscle memory leads me along a paved road that cuts into Alley Pond's tall, bare trees. Silvery light from the full moon illuminates the dirt path into the darker parts of the park. My party shoes sink into the cold mud, slowing me down. My chest hurts from running in the cold.

"Rose!" he shouts. "It's not safe. Please come back. Please let me explain."

"No!" I glance over my shoulder. His gray eyes are sparks of conjured electricity. "A year. You've had over a year to tell us, but you *chose to lie*."

Here, the trees are skeletal, black, and covered in mounds of frosted leaves, snow, and litter. Dad holds his hands up, trying his best to not scare me. If he knew me at all, he'd know I am not scared.

I am furious.

And when he takes another step, that anger shakes loose along with the magic I've stolen. The sky breaks open, hail pelting down as a lightning bolt whips between us. My muscles seize just as the force of our power explodes, sending us flying in opposite directions.

I don't move, listening to the blood rush in my ears, the heaviness of my breath. My body begins to break through a layer of freezing mud and sink into the shallow pond. Cold spreads across my skin, and the ache of recoil makes my leg muscles seize and cramp up. I flip over, mud and who knows what else weigh me down like cement.

"Are you okay?" my father calls out, crawling through the freezing muck to get to me in the crystalline moonlight.

"What was that?" I grunt. Everything hurts when I stand.

For a few steps, there's only the sound of the two of us wading out of the shallow murk. Then, there's something louder nearby. The crunch of feet. The snap of branches. A deep, guttural snarl.

We're not alone.

"Dad?"

"Don't move," he whispers.

I listen to my own heartbeat, my father's heavy breathing, and the percussion of hail. Something followed us into these woods. My adrenaline spikes. My eyes don't quite adjust to the dark.

"Is it gone?" I ask after a stretch of silence.

But whoever, or whatever, is hiding in the trees wants to be heard. The crunch of feet is everywhere at once, pounding and shattering the winter night with a thrilled howl.

My dad grabs my arm and squeezes. "I'm going to clear a path for you. Run home, do you understand?"

"I can't leave you."

"You will." Dad claps his hands, rubs them together. A yellow ball crackles at the center of his palms. Lightning bolts as thin as copper wire draw a clear path through the trees. "Run!"

That's when I see it. A black shape—a horned creature. It disappears into the park shadows. Then I see another, and another.

"Get out of here!" my dad shouts. His fingers shake as the lightning threads flicker like bulbs ready to blow out.

I grab his sleeve to pull him with me, but my fingers close around air.

The horned creature knocks my father to the ground, where they tumble. I scream at the sound of fists beating against skin, and the crunch of bone. My feet are ensnared in roots and leaves, and I stumble once again. With numb fingers, I search for something—a rock, a branch—and close around the neck of a glass bottle.

I jump to my feet and crack the bottle over the creature's head.

"I told you to run!" my father shouts.

51

His hold on the creature slips, and my dad falls into the ice-cold pond, thrashing to get out.

The creature whirls to face me. The threads of light fizzle, but not before I've caught sight of its furred face. Skin green as July leaves. Sharp gold teeth bared to bite.

"I've not forgotten the scent of your magic, Florecita," the creature says, its rotten breath filling my nose.

I clench the bottle neck and raise the jagged glass to attack. "I'm not your *little flower*."

The horned creature is faster than I am, seizing my wrist into a vise grip.

"I've found them both, Your Highness," the beast says.

Your Highness?

"Indeed, you have," a smoky voice cuts through the night. "Here is the king's reward, as promised."

The horned creature's eyes widen as he grunts and staggers a few paces back. The silver point of a blade juts out from his belly, surprise frozen on its green face even as the body falls at my feet. I scuttle back because even though one of these creatures is dead, I am far from safe.

The killer is a figure, cloaked in shadow, that towers over me. I can make out only the barest glint of light on a bloody sword and a second body among the leaves, identical to the one who attacked me. Dread numbs my senses because I can't see or hear my father anywhere.

"Into the portal," the hooded figure orders.

"I'm not going anywhere with you," I say, voice shuddering from fear and cold. I grab a fistful of dirt and aim for the killer's eyes. All that does is anger it for a brief moment. Breathless, I try to run. Alex will know what to do. I have to get home. But a gloved hand closes around my hair and yanks me back. I kick and claw and scream. With a hard shove, I'm falling into the muddy pond. I flail and sink faster. The word it used rings through my head. *Portal.*

I thrash, but there is nothing to hold on to. A chill racks my body when the frozen ground loosens and the muddy water drags me down into the earth.

"My family will come for me." It is a silly, stupid thing. I know it the moment I say it. The creature laughs at my threat.

As I take one gulp of air, ice water and dirt close over my face, and the cutting voice speaks.

"No one will come for you in the Kingdom of Adas."

PART II

THE
SIPHON

5

Claribelle took the prince's hand.
She loathed to leave her family behind,
but her heart was already given.
She had to follow it.

—CLARIBELLE AND THE KINGDOM OF ADAS:
TALES TALL AND TRUE, GLORIANA PALACIOS

When I was a little girl, I liked to play in the mud. If it rained, I found solace in dirt and water beneath my bare feet, under my fingernails. If we were at the beach, I planted myself in the wet strip where waves dissolved. I was not quite a mermaid, or even a reverse mermaid, just a sea beast with hands. And in some ways, I wonder if, back then, a part of me knew I had a power that was still evolving, like some creature that emerged from the belly of the ocean and learned to walk on land.

As I try to hold my breath in this earthen pit, I flail my limbs, eyes shut against the weight of mud. It seeps into my nostrils, the tight line between my lips as they quiver. It's in my pores, my ears. I'm going to choke on it.

An average healthy person can hold their breath for two minutes, maybe. But having spent most of my life being possessed by spirits who don't let you breathe, I've learned to do it for longer and without complete and total panic. Still, my heart is a steady foot drum in my chest, begging, begging, begging for me to open my mouth and gasp for air.

Suddenly, my feet are wet, my calves sliding through a layer of earth and into cold water. I wriggle and push my body until I'm through the other side. I use the muddy ground to hurl myself up and hope that it is, in fact, up. I kick and kick, my arms outstretched in front of me until my fingers touch a vacant space I hope is air because I open my mouth and take hungry, ragged breaths.

I cough until my windpipe is clear. My throat and nasal passages burn. I let myself go under once to rinse mud out of my eyes. The water is a murky green, covered in patches of algae that grow in clumps around browning lily pads. I swim in a circle to stay afloat. There's only one part where the bank looks stable enough to climb out. I swim toward it, each kick warming up my tight muscles.

A figure emerges between the trees ahead, and despite everything I felt not an hour ago, I'm so happy to see my father that I swim faster. He's here. I'm not alone.

"I've got you," he says, grabbing a fallen branch and extending it out to me.

I hold on and let him tug me onto sturdy ground. I shake as I climb into his arms.

"Are you hurt?" he asks between pants. There's a long cut on his cheekbone and bruises shaped like fingers around his neck. Pond scum clings to his mustache and droplets of water fall from his graying curls.

I take an inventory of my body. I'm not bleeding. My scalp hurts where the hooded figure yanked my hair. There's a bruise around my wrist. All things that can heal. We have bigger concerns.

"No. I don't think so." My teeth chatter uncontrollably, so I hold him until I stop shaking and my breathing calms a bit. We're safe. Well, as safe as two people can be after getting sucked through a swampy portal.

"How did you get here?"

"Another pond a few yards that way." He points in the direction he came from. "I tried to fight, but one ada killed the other and shoved me into the portal."

A small brackish lagoon lays in front of us surrounded by tall trees that grow like snakes undulating toward a sky so sharply cerulean it hurts to look at. Black moss clings to stones nested in the ground, and though I can't see any creatures, I can hear the chitter of birds and croak of frogs nearby.

"What is this place?" I ask, wringing the greenish water from my tulle skirt. My throat and nasal passages burn when I breathe in the humid air.

He picks crud from his ruined shirt. "This is Lagunitas Serpentinas."

"There are snakes in there?" I'm not afraid of snakes, but I don't exactly want to cuddle them either.

Dad gives me a wan smile. "The lagoons are named after the shape of the trees. But something's wrong—the water used to be clear as glass."

He remembers, I think.

I ran and we were attacked and now we're here. I push down the anger I feel. Right now, we have to survive. To get home.

59

"Maybe the portal did something to it?" I say. My throat tightens and my lungs ache at the thought of being back in the murky dark we wriggled out of. "Maybe the Alley Pond mud came with us."

Dad shakes his head slowly and points. "Look at the grass along the bank."

It's all yellow. I move the grass stalks back and find red worms as fat as my thumbs squirming in slimy, black ooze. I wipe my hand on my dress and say, "Gross."

"We can't stay here. We have to walk." He hurries to stand, to grab my arm, but I can't seem to move.

Warm wind flutters down from the tall snakelike trees, and a creature somewhere among them makes a grating, squeaking sound. I don't even have a guess as to what it is because we are in the Kingdom of Adas. The place my father vanished to for seven years. The place I have spent hours reading and rereading stories and myths about. Most importantly, we're in another realm without my mom or my sisters or a clue as to why we're even here.

The creatures who attacked us knew me. *I've not forgotten the scent of your magic, Florecita.* Then, they were dead. Where is their killer? I want to tell my dad what I saw, but I can't breathe. I hold on to a nearby tree trunk as I lower myself to the ground, fighting against my dad's hands and his pleading voice.

"Get up, nena." *Baby girl.* His palms, cold as the first snow, are against my cheeks. "Listen to me. I love you, Rosie. You need to know that I love you and I'm going to do everything I can to keep you safe. But I need your help, or they're going to find us. You *have* to get up."

I can't fall apart. Not here and not now. I have survived being turned into a ball of energy and being trapped in a tree. I have killed casimuertos and talked to the goddess of death. I have graduated from junior high school, so I know if I can get through that, I can conquer anything. I wipe my face and use the tree trunk to right myself. My legs are still trembling, from my swim. There will be time to freak out later on, when I'm in my room and Alex is making pizza and Ma is boiling estrella de anis and lemongrass tea.

Get it together, Rose, I think to myself.

My father's stormy gray eyes search my face, worry stitching deeper frown lines around his eyes, across his forehead.

"*Who* is going to find us, Dad?"

His voice is hard when he says, "Adas. The fairies of this realm. I will explain later."

"Not later," I say. "Now. Please. Why would an Ada remember me or want me?"

"It's just like the last time." He runs hands through his hair and glances around, like he's waiting for an attack. "The king of Adas sends bounty hunters to other realms. He's a collector."

"Great," I grumble. "I can offer up Alex's coin collection for our freedom."

He chokes out a dark, strangled laugh. "Not exactly. The king collects people—beings—with abilities. He brings them here. I don't understand why they would kill their own unless—"

I think of the rules of magic and snap my fingers, finishing his thought. "Blood portals to Adas require a balance of magic."

"Three people come out and three go back in."

"Then where is the third one?"

"That's why we have to go."

"Go *where*?" I hate having to ask these questions. I hate not knowing the certainty of things. "If we're in the Kingdom of Adas, then we're on an island. We're surrounded by water. If I know my portals correctly, and I'm pretty sure I do, they're one-way tickets."

"There's a village west of here. Olapura. We can find help. Here." Dad picks up a stick and uses it to draw a rough island-shaped map in the dirt. On the southeast coast, he makes an *X* where we are, then drags a line west. "We're not far."

I have questions about how far "not far" actually is, but I decide to keep them to myself.

He glances over his shoulder once, and there's a sharpness in his features that I haven't seen since he returned. Like he's aware. Like he's *awake*. The Kingdom of Adas makes him seem alive in a way he didn't at home. I have to ask a question that fills me with ice-cold dread.

"This village, Olapura—is that how you got back last time?"

"No," he says softly. He kicks the lines in the dirt to not leave behind a trail. I wonder if he always knew to do that or if he learned that here. "I'll tell you. Just—I know it's a lot to ask of you, but right now, you have to do what I say, okay?"

I want to say that he can't tell me what to do. He was a blank space in my life for almost eight years, and when he returned, he still wasn't there completely. I also want to say that at least neither of us have to be alone. I want to be mad. I want him to hug me. But I can't let myself feel any of those things, not yet.

"All right," I manage.

I keep my guard up as I take my dad's hand and follow him through the strange fairy forest. Every step lands on a jutting stone or branch hidden beneath soft earth. I lost my shoes in the water, and a petty part of me wishes Lula were here, so I could yell at her because I wanted to wear sneakers, and if I had, I wouldn't be barefoot right now. At least the packed dirt is soft, and I get better at avoiding sharp rocks and sticks.

At first everything looks the same. There are tall, serpentine trees as far as the eye can see. As we walk, I start to see the path between the trees that my father seems to know like the back of his hand. The rot of decaying leaves and mulch lingers in the air, like smothered, unturned earth. Like that creature's breath on my skin.

With every passing minute, I tell myself that if my sisters were here, Lula wouldn't despair and Alex wouldn't cower. They would be braver and they wouldn't have lost their shoes in the mucky pond. They would be stronger than I feel.

But when the snakelike trees grow sparse and give way to a wide river cutting off out route, I remember that my sisters did despair and cower. When she was in Los Lagos, Alex sank into her doubt and gave up her power. Lula was so afraid of letting go that people died. My sisters aren't perfect, but somehow, they pulled through. They chose to live and fight. I have to survive this place because that's the only way I can put my family back together.

"You know what's weird?" I say to break the heavy silence between us and get out of my own head. "I don't feel like I've left our realm. I know we *are* in another realm, but it feels familiar somehow."

Dad nods. Sweat runs down his temples as he kneels to splash water on his face and drink. I do the same.

"Not weird at all," he tells me. "The Kingdom of Adas was

created from the same earth we live in by El Terroz. Now it's shrouded by magic, with time and rules of its own. But once, long ago, during the time of the gods, it was just another island in the Caribbean Sea."

I think about the stories I've read about this place. In our family's Book of Cantos, there are only a few anecdotes about Adas, warning brujas not to walk between two ceiba trees under the full moon—but we don't have those in Brooklyn—and if you do get taken, not to eat the food or you'll forget your old life. None of which is helpful now, since our kidnappers used a portal. The only way in or out is with magic from the land. I hope we can find someone in Olapura who can help us.

First, we have to get to the other side of the river that blocks our path. It rushes so fast I know we'd get pulled under the minute we stepped in there. On the other side of the bank, the trees are thicker, taller. Their leaves create more shade, which means we'll have to find our way through the dark.

"Can we walk around it?" I ask.

"There's nothing on either side for miles but jungle, and this is the most direct route to the coast."

"What about when we parted the sea for Lula? Can we do that here?"

He stands with his hands on his hips, surveying the land in front of us. When he squints at the blue, cloudless sky, the wrinkles around his eyes deepen. "No, but I can get us a bridge."

A shadow passes overhead. It drifts quickly, unnaturally. My father's eyes are shut, his palms facing the heavens. Pinpricks of light lace around his fingers, and a memory of my mother unspooling her yarn to make us our winter scarves pops into mind right as a bolt of lightning strikes the jungle in front of us.

My father's eyes gleam as two sturdy trees fall across the river, their leaves at our feet, perfect bridges for us to cross. I recognize that look on his face. It's the same one I've seen on Lula when she heals a patient, when she graduated, when she does something so well she can't help but bask in it—pride.

I follow his lead, climbing past the head of leafy branches and onto the tree trunk. Instead of trying to walk across it like a tightrope, he crawls. My dress gets caught on a splintered spike of wood, and I rip the dangling strip of fabric, bringing my hem up to my calves.

"Don't throw that away," he says. "We might need bandages."

I shove the fabric in my pocket. There's already something there, and I realize I have one empanada and two chocolate bars from the party. They're soggy, but I tell myself it would be no different than eating cold pizza. I consider it a small boon, and we keep going. I grip the tree bark and try to focus on the gnarled roots on the other side.

"Rhett wants to take us camping," I say. "After this, I'm going to tell him to forget about it."

"Your mom hated when I took her camping."

I picture my mother's beautiful flowing dresses, perfectly lined lipstick, and her meticulous hair routine. I can't picture her having a good time. But then again, my parents had a different life once.

"The closest we got was summer at Coney Island," I say. "Or if Ma had time off from work, we'd cleanse our crystals in Prospect Park on a full moon."

We're about halfway across, and cold river water sprays on my skin. My arms hurt from holding myself up and my knees are chafing against the tulle of my dress. *Just a bit more*, I remind myself as a bird swoops down, almost too close. It snatches a silver fish from the river and keeps on flying.

"I should've been there," my dad says, the lament like salt on my wounds. "I'm sorry I wasn't."

"Not now, Dad. Please." Maybe I should be more compassionate, like Lula has been, but I can't find that in myself at the moment. "Were you in that village the whole time? Olapura? Is that where the salt mines are?"

"No. At first I was at the castle in the king's collection."

"The castle?" I repeat. That burning anger returns like a slap across my cheek, and I can't think straight. "Sounds fancy. Must've been nice. All this time—"

"You don't know what this realm does to you," he says, cutting me off. "I don't want you to know. We're going to get back home."

"What if we don't? What if we get to this village and no one can help us? No one even knows where we are! What if we're stuck here?"

He looks me dead in the eyes, Lula's eyes, and I press my lips together to stop from whimpering. He repeats, slowly, "We're going to get back home."

I nod, and we keep going in silence until we reach the other side, where the tree was splintered apart by lightning. The bark there is charred and smoke lingers. Dozens of shimmering emerald beetles crawl across the trunk, and I'm thankful that at least I'm not scared of bugs. Dad hops off first and helps me down.

I am eager to keep pushing. If I stop now, I don't think I'll be able to get back up. But Dad still stops to find a bowl-shaped leaf and uses it to scoop up some water, which I drink with relish. I taste minerals and grass. Probably still cleaner than tap water.

I drop the leaf on the ground and wipe my mouth with the back of my hand. "Where to now?"

"We follow this path to the top. From there, we'll be able to see Olapura." He hesitates, then says, "You don't have to pretend to be so brave, Rosie. It's okay to be afraid."

I level my eyes at him. He thinks I'm pretending? A mean, bitter thing slithers into my heart, and I welcome it. "You know, the day Nova appeared with you on our front stoop, the first thing I thought was that you were shorter than I remembered. Because my first memory of you was when I was three or four. I didn't know how tall you actually were or what your favorite food was or what would make you stop having nightmares the middle of the night. I didn't know how to care for someone I stopped missing years ago. And you know what? You don't know me either. Because if you did, you'd know that I'm not *pretending*. My sisters and I learned how to be brave from our mother."

His eyes cut to his feet. "You have a right to be angry. The things I did—it's my fault we're here."

"Tell me," I say, turning my gaze to the endless forests of undulating trees behind him. "If we're going to get to Olapura together, I need to know everything you know."

He clenches his jaw and nods. Try as I might, I can't find myself in his face or his voice or his actions, only fragments of my sisters. "All right. But we have to keep moving."

I push through the pain in my arms and the strange bone-deep ache in my fingers that has returned—along with the prickling on my skin that has nothing to do with the humid air and everything to do with my magic—because we can't stop moving until we're home. We walk, and even though I'm short of breath, I keep up.

"You've read about Adas," Dad says.

"I've read *Claribelle and the Kingdom of Adas.* But fairy-tale books aren't exactly history texts."

"True, but this one can be an exception," he says, stroking the last droplets of water from his mustache. *"Claribelle and the Kingdom of Adas* was written by Claribelle's youngest daughter. She grew up here and is part fairy."

"I didn't know that." I duck under the branch he pushes aside to let me through. "Alex met Agosto, the exiled king of Adas, when she was in Los Lagos. I know that there's truth to all myth. I just assumed most of it was made up."

"Every life is a story, and, in that sense, all made up." My dad keeps his pace but waits for me to catch up every so often, his stormy eyes always wary, always searching the shadows that surround us. "You'll see once we're in Olapura. Adas is a place of half-truths and whole deception."

I think of the stories in my book, the one still in the pantry. Tales of mermaids nibbling the meat off bones along a cove, artists kidnapped and brought to Adas to entertain the courts. Rival fairy royals in nearby islands. The infamous Bastard King who murdered his family to seize power. But there were also horned girls bathing in a moonlit waterfalls, queens who filled the world with gardens, magic so beautiful it could only be called miracles. Can it all be bad?

"How did you survive?"

"I had help," he says, but doesn't elaborate. "We might come from a magical lineage, but I grew up with a mix of mortal myths too. Sinmagos have their tales of *hadas*, but they're rooted in the European stories. Our Deos created Adas, the land and the creatures that populate it. I learned very quickly that some parts of the legends are the same."

"Like what?" We begin going uphill, and I grab hold of the thick vines that hang from the canopies for support.

"Lying, food, and names. Fairies of any kind can't lie, but their truth bends further than light. I tried not to eat anything when I first arrived, but the hunger won."

I focus on the ground beneath me, on moving as swiftly as I can over the mulch of leaves and soft earth. "Does the food make you forget right away?"

He shakes his head. "I've seen it in varying degrees on other creatures, but for humans? Humans don't stand a chance. Eventually, you forget your own name. Your home. Your loved ones. You might as well be another person. The land of Adas is paradise. It is made to make you want to stay forever, and the only way to do that is to leave your past behind."

I take a deep breath because I want to tell him that I wouldn't forget. I would be stronger than some sugar-covered flowers or magical mushrooms or whatever it is they eat here.

"Is the water safe to drink?" I wipe my lips.

He shakes his head. "It'll still have the effect, but it's better than dying from dehydration. If it's from a clear source and not contaminated."

"So, there's nothing we can do?"

"It helps to have a token. Magic from your realm slows down the forgetting."

Our realm, I think, but don't correct him. I hold out my hand to show him the bracelet Nova made for me. The pouch with the other two matching bracelets is in our kitchen. I wonder if my sisters have found it yet. "What about this? Nova would have blessed it."

My dad takes my left wrist, his thumb brushes across the silver sun charm. He looks satisfied. "Don't take it off."

"So I'm safe? What about you?"

He reaches into his stained button-down shirt and tugs at a gold chain with a circular pendant my mother gave him. She would have blessed it. "Nothing is safe here for mortals. Not truly. The creatures of Adas are eternal. The only way they see death is by inflicting it on things easier to kill."

My chest hurts from the uphill climb and sweat runs down my face. My tongue is so dry that just thinking about water makes me feel like a wet rag that's been wrung out. I stop to catch my breath. "Then why Olapura?"

He looks away abruptly. "There's a small human population there."

I wait for him to say more, but he doesn't. "If it's on a coast, does that mean there are ships?"

"Only fishing rafts," he says, mopping sweat from his brow with his sleeve. "Remember, there's a barrier of magic around the island that keeps it hidden, but we'd never get past the crabmaids and other creatures that feed on the reef anyway."

"Can't we fight them?" I ask. "I can borrow some of your magic and we can blast our way out."

Dad lets go of a defeated breath. "Even if we could, we're between Ponce and Caracas. That's about three hundred miles in either direction. I'm still Brooklyn raised, Rosie, and I can't sail a raft across the Caribbean Sea."

I try to wrap my head around the fact that we're somewhere in the Caribbean. I've never even been outside the metro area. I know that he's right. I know that every scenario he's listed has a higher probability of death than survival. I know that he wouldn't risk my life.

I take out the empanada from my pocket. I feel a terrible pinching in my stomach that has nothing to do with magic and everything to do with the fact that my last real meal was a bowl of Frosted Flakes and a banana early this morning because I was too nervous about my party. "It's a little gross with the pond water and all, but it's all we've got."

We break it in half, and it feels something like a truce. After devouring the meat-filled pastry (didn't even taste the algae), we keep walking at a brisk pace. There's a blister on my left heel, and I would kill for fresh water to replace the sweat soaking right through my dress.

Dad pulls out a tiny switchblade from his pocket, and I use it to cut the fabric I saved into strips. I wrap them around my heels, and it helps protect the blisters a bit. But it's a temporary solution, like that time we put duct tape on a pipe and ended up with a flooded bathroom.

I stop on the uphill climb, dig my toes in the soft dirt. Insects flutter all around in glistening jewel colors. Am I imagining the sea breeze? I can't even tell how far we've walked. A hundred New York

City blocks? A thousand? I try to picture the place we're headed to. Olapura. Ola. Pura. Even with my broken Spanish, I recognize the words meaning "pure wave." I think about the way my dad averted his eyes when I asked him what was there. He sidestepped the question by answering a different question—not a lie, but perhaps not the whole truth. What was it he said? *The things I did—it's my fault we're here.* I feel like there's a hornet's nest in my rib cage.

He realizes I'm not following behind him and stops. Turns. "Rose?"

"What are you holding back, Dad?"

His eyes scan the path ahead of us, where the trees begin to spread out. When the breeze picks up, I can smell the sea. Hear the waves. We're so close.

"You have your memories. How did you get back the last time?"

He stares at his shoes, muddy and scuffed. There's something resigned in the sag of his shoulders, the downward tug of his lips. His Adam's apple bobs when he swallows. "It's complicated. I'm not proud of what I did. I can't—"

"Try."

"The way I escaped—I don't know how to say this, so I'll start at the beginning. There was an uprising against the king. I took part in it. Most of the humans and adas responsible were executed, others caught in the middle. The truth is I don't know who opened the portal, but a group of us were sent through into the human realm, so we wouldn't be killed."

"Wait. You didn't mean to return?" I hate the weakness in my voice. I hate that my father won't look into my eyes. "So you ended up in Brooklyn by accident?"

His silence is made louder by the howl of unseen creatures, the calls of birds of paradise. Finally, visibly painfully, he says, "The portal led to the Everglades."

"Florida?" The sound of crashing waves in my ears intensifies.

I see the struggle in the way he shuts his eyes, the way his next words start and stop like a run-down car. I wonder what happened to him that is so difficult to say. I wonder if I'll be able to love him after I know.

"I was with other brujos. The first couple of weeks, we didn't remember anything, but flashes started coming back slowly. Some of the items we kept started making sense. Dean had written his address down when he first started to forget and kept it in an acorn. We went to Miami next, but Dean's house was abandoned."

"What about his family?" I ask.

"Time here moves twice as slowly as back home. Dean was taken when he was forty. He left behind a wife and adult son. He'd been in Adas some twenty-five, thirty years, and by then, everyone his family in our realm was dead. So we stayed in the abandoned house and found a high circle to help us get settled. They cast a memory canto to recover everything our time in Adas had buried."

"Your memories returned."

"Mine did. Dean's did too. Samuel, one of my friends, had been in Adas for nearly a hundred mortal years, and the canto didn't work on him. One night he walked into the sea, and we found his body washed up on the shore the next morning. He had been attempting to get back here."

I want to ask if my dad has tried to come back since. Didn't I ask La Mama for this? Didn't I want the truth?

"How did Nova find you?" Nova would never tell us. He said that was my dad's story to tell. Secret keeping is Nova's most infuriating quality.

"He came searching for a high circle who could help with his magic burns. Alto Brujo Benny did what he could, but nothing helped. Nova stayed with us for a few weeks, earning his keep. When he cleaned my altar, he noticed a picture I had of you girls, the one I kept in my wallet."

"That wasn't enough to make you remember while you were here," I say.

"I tried, Rosie. You don't know what being here does to you. It was like one morning I woke up and I stared at your faces, but I couldn't place your names or why I had the photo. I knew it was important, but I couldn't remember you anymore. I fell in line, and I fought and worked until I couldn't."

Maybe my mom and sisters had it right. I should have left it alone. I should have moved on and pretended nothing was wrong instead of digging and digging and digging.

"I don't understand." I wrap my arms around myself, as if I can create my own armor for what is coming next. "Your memory came back, but you didn't come home. How long were you back for?"

My dad rubs his lips together. He takes deep breaths, preparing to take this plunge. "Six months. Nova told me what happened with Alex and Los Lagos, and I knew I couldn't stay away anymore."

We are miles away from home, realms even. I don't have many test subjects, but I'm going to bet and say a heart can break the same way no matter where you are.

"Six months." In those six months, he might have been there

to stop Alex from trying to curse away her power. He might have stopped Lula from getting attacked, from raising the dead. In those six months, we could have tried to be a family for real.

"Would you even have bothered if Nova hadn't crossed your path?" I ask. I shut my eyes to clear my vision, but I can't stand the sight of him. "Did you even miss us anymore?"

"I missed you every day. Every day."

"Then why?"

He shakes his head, but that isn't a good enough answer. So I shout it again. I shout it until birds take flight around us and he grips my shoulders and reminds me that we are being hunted and we have to be careful and we are almost there and he will explain. Whywhywhywhy.

"*Why?*"

"Because I didn't know how to be the person you all needed me to be," he says. "I wasn't whole."

"Neither were we."

I turn to go, imbued with the knowledge that I can survive this realm because there is not a bruise or blister or cut that will hurt as much as the words my father has spoken. I have to get back to my mother, my sisters.

"Rosie," he says, and tries to touch my hand.

I slap it away, our magic clashing in sparks. "You don't get to call me that. My name is Rose."

"Not here it isn't. Names here can't be used to control you, but they're a part of you. The way your hair or nail clippings can be used in a canto to hurt you, they'll take your name and use it to find you or the people you love."

"Don't change the subject."

"You can hate me as much as you want, but that doesn't change the fact that I am your father—"

"Yeah you're my father now that the work is all done. You know what? I'm done listening to you. I have to get back to my family."

Olapura is waiting. The promise of a place where we can rest safely puts an intensity in my step, and I race past him to at least get away. At the very top of the hill, past the jungle trees and a snaking stream, I catch sight of a bright coastal town with colorful houses that line the sea cliff. The sun is so bright on the waves that I shield my eyes against the glare.

"Wait!" There is true panic in his scream that glues my feet to the ground.

When I try to whirl around, someone wraps an arm around my throat, followed by the sharp, cool sting of a blade. Three figures in emerald-green armor rush my dad. They bind his arms and cover his mouth with something I can't see. Dad tries to shout, but it's muffled. Without the use of his hands, he can't wield his power.

A fourth warrior weaves between the guards, towering over me the way she did in the park. Even without the hooded cape, I know it has to be her. She's the one who killed the other two adas and brought us here. Her voice is imprinted in my memory. She is different than I imagined, with bronze brown skin that glistens like dew. A body soft in a way that no one should look dressed in armor. The metal scales of her breastplate are the raw fuchsia of orchids, her pale pink hair is braided from the crown of her forehead and swept behind pointed ears and down her back. Eyes like pink amethyst and the wicked curl of a smile. There's a speck of dried blood on her apple-round cheek, smears of it on the bared skin of her forearms. She looks to be about Lula's age, but you never know with adas. They can live forever. She could be hundreds of years old for all I know.

"You," I say, struggling against the arms holding me back. The blade nicks my skin, and I feel a warm trickle of blood.

"Me," she says, retrieving an orange bell blossom from a leather pouch at her hip. She pulls out a clear, jellylike substance from the center and slathers it over my lips. My skin tingles, the sensation even numbing my tongue. "You are faster than I would have thought. For humans. Release the bruja, Alma, before she accidentally slits her own throat."

With a shove, I'm freed. But it's only for a moment. My hands are quickly tied behind my back, just like my dad's.

The pink warrior girl sheaths her sword, then motions to her guards. When she turns to walk in the direction we just came from, they follow obediently, pushing my dad and me along.

"There will be no more stopping. The Bastard King of Adas does not like to be kept waiting."

When the winds shift, I can no longer smell the sea.

When the world was drowned by sea,
El Terroz shook the mountains loose.
He cupped his favorite island in his hand
and called it Adas.

—BOOK OF DEOS

We pass Lagunitas Serpentinas, leaving behind the stench of rotting leaves and mucky water. The rocky soil evens out, but as the trees grow thicker and leafier, it becomes harder not to trip over the ropes of vines and roots. I've stubbed my middle toe three times and it throbs. My dad is somewhere up ahead, and when he tries to glance over his shoulder, he gets whacked in the head with the butt of a machete.

My breath is heavy, and I can barely get enough oxygen, let alone tell the pink guard where to shove her sword every time she pushes me to walk faster. Blisters swell on the sides of my feet, and a whine escapes my throat as we go uphill once again.

Two guards hack away at the overgrown emerald leaves and branches that block our path. Here, fat red birds watch from gnarled perches, some of them with human-looking eyes that crinkle with mischief. Tiny fairies with butterfly wings flutter close, until a hand swats them away. Snakes with scales so bright they look like neon signs wind around tree trunks.

My foot gets caught in a tangle of green, and I fall on my face and eat dirt. Two guards loom over me, grimacing.

"Alma, untie her before she strangles herself in the vines," the pink warrior says.

Alma steps forward. Her hair is a single green braid the shade of new flower buds. Her full lips curl around too-sharp teeth as she pulls a blade from her belt. Her brown eyes waver from me to her leader. "I beg your pardon, Commander. Are you certain this is the powerful being the siren spoke of?"

The commander says nothing but shoots Alma a death glare. In the next moment, the ropes around my wrists are cut. I sit up and massage my shoulders. The numbing goop over my lip slips off, leaving a rotten aftertaste. I fight the urge to puke.

"I think we have a misunderstanding," I say. My throat feels like I've gargled glass.

"Is that so?" The Commander speaks, her voice rough despite the humor in it. She squats to get eye level with me. Her cheeks are dotted with freckles, like someone blew dust in her face. I hate her for looking at me this way, like I'm as weak as I've always feared I am.

I hold up two fingers in front of my face, wave them from side to side, and say, "These aren't the brujas you're looking for."

The Commander smirks. "I went through a lot of trouble to find you, meat worm."

"Don't call me that!"

"Give me a better name, then."

Behind her the other green-clad guards stand at attention, waiting for their orders. Between them, my father's eyes spark with crackling lightning. Without the use of his hands, his power cycles within him. If he isn't careful he could give himself a heart attack and summon a bolt that could cleave him in half. I think about making a run for it, grabbing his arm and draining his power. Then what? I can hardly stand. The commander and her guards would catch up to us once again. With a flutter of his eyelids, his irises return to normal.

Perhaps he knows what I'm thinking, because he gives a tiny shake of his head. The slick substance over his lips prevents him from speaking. He only manages a muffled groan before a guard steps in front of him, blocking him from my line of sight.

"Eliza," I say. Rose Elizabeta Mortiz to be exact. Even before my dad's warning, Ma always told us to follow the same rules for magical creatures as we would for the average stranger danger. You can't just give your legit name to anyone who asks. "Your turn."

"Iris," she says. *Ee-reees*. The name is so delicate, so bright for someone with a smile that cuts like diamonds. I'm sure it's only part of her name. She stands, dusts off her hands, and says, "Make for the castle. We'll be right along."

"But—" Alma's next words die on her lips under Iris's pink-crystal stare. "Yes, Commander."

They forge a path through the brush, and two guards take hold of my father, shoving him along. Deep down, I'm relieved I don't have to continue fighting with him, but I didn't want *kidnapping* to be the reason for it.

Iris doesn't seem worried that I'm free of my bindings. I suppose, if I came across myself in this state—covered in dirt, sweat, blood and gasping for breath—I wouldn't be afraid of me either. She walks up to a tree beside us, climbing over a root as thick as my thighs, and pulls on a bell-shaped green leaf. She brings it over and offers it to me.

"Drink," she says.

"Pass," I say.

Her eyes widen, like she's not used to people rejecting her. "We have a quarter day to go. You need water."

Though moisture is thick in the air, rolling down soft flower petals and dripping from vines, the mention of water makes my dry tongue ache. I can hardly swallow.

"Fine," I mutter, and take the offering. I bring the leaf to my cracked lips and drink. The water is crisp, with the faint taste of flowers and something I can't quite put a name to. Not a flavor but a feeling, a brightness that surges through me. Standing doesn't hurt as much. The ache in my bones eases.

"Will you live through this, Eliza?" Iris asks, and the question, paired with her wicked smile, feels like a needle at my side.

"I know I will. I don't know about you though."

"You're not in the position to make threats, meat worm." She fishes back into her small leather pouch. It's that same orange flower. She scoops out the clear jelly from the center.

"Please don't," I say in the most pathetic voice possible. "I'll be quiet, I promise."

She hesitates, like she's trying to determine whether I'm lying.

I mean, I am. But she doesn't slather that stuff on my lips. Instead, she drops the glob of jelly in my palm.

"Cover your feet with this. It will protect your sores."

I do as she says. The jelly is firm and hardens when it contacts my blisters.

"Thank you," I say pathetically.

"Do not thank me. Walk." Iris motions forward.

We trudge over the cleared path left behind by the others. In the moments the rain forest creatures are quiet, I can make out the hacking sounds of a machete up ahead. I'm suddenly too aware of the stench I'm giving off. My flower crown is nothing but limp stalks and tangled in my hair. My skin itches as my mud-soaked dress dries. Meanwhile Iris glistens, not with sweat but with a natural radiance. Though most of her body is covered with the leatherlike armor, she seems impervious to the hundred-degree humidity. I regret not wearing shorts under my dress because my thighs are chafing painfully. The energy burst from the water is fading quickly, and I find myself falling, dragging like the round hummingbirds that flit near my face. No matter how long we walk, this jungle feels endless.

"You have to keep up," Iris snaps.

"That's easy for you to say."

Iris responds with the barest grumbling but slows a pace or two.

"Why are you taking us to the castle?" I ask. "What do you want with us?"

"You said you'd be quiet, Eliza. Do humans renege on their promises so quickly?"

"I'm not *reneging* on anything. Perhaps if you talk to me, it would distract from everything that hurts."

Iris's doubtful stare slinks to me, then back to the path ahead. If we're going to get out of here, I'm going to need all the information my dad can't give me.

"The king will better show you why you are here," she says. "But know you *will* be given a choice. As the kingdom's warrior, my quest was to bring you and your father to Adas."

I think of what my father said. He was at the castle as part of the king's collection. Is that what I'm meant to be? What did Alma call me? A powerful being. The surprise for them will be that a magical hacker isn't any good without power to *hack*.

"Why did you kill those creatures?" I ask softly.

Iris flicks an iridescent bug away from her face but doesn't appear bothered at the memory of her murders. "Don't they teach you humans anything?"

"I know stuff!" I shoot back more petulantly than I wanted. It's hard to be properly angry when I'm so thirsty and hunger gnaws at my insides.

"Blood portals to Adas are tricky. The same number of bodies that go in must come out. Besides, those bounty hunters were stealing from the king. I delivered their final payment for locating you."

"See, I was right about the portal thing. And wow, you'd do well in the cartel." I snort despite myself. Iris doesn't smile though. "How did they locate me?"

"Among the king's collection is a being who can sense power across the realms. For a time, your power was like a beacon." Iris ducks under tree branches and holds the leaves out of the way for me to pass as well.

I run my finger down one and lick the fresh water off my

fingertip. I've never heard of this kind of creature, but I don't want to meet it.

"Then, the beacon was extinguished. When you disrupted the protection on your home we could finally sense your power again."

"That's not right," I say. "I would never touch the protective wreaths on our doors." Last time that happened, these terrible creatures that were after Alex got into the house, and I got possessed by an ancient evil witch. After that, Lula and I braided the wreaths ourselves and secured them to every entrance.

"If not you, someone else," Iris affirms.

Wait a minute.

I suck in a sharp breath. The moment floods to the forefront of my mind. Me, running out the door. Slamming it so hard it shook. Hearing something fall behind me but not turning around to see it. When I study that moment, I realize I should have seen—I should have noticed. But I didn't because I was too busy shouting at my father. I did make the wreath fall.

I curse loudly as rage tears threaten to spill from my eyes, but I blink them away. "I have to go home. I shouldn't be here."

"And yet you are." Iris stops and faces me. Her brown skin shimmers bronze in the beam of light that breaks though the canopy. Her smile is as beautiful as it is deadly. "You cannot escape, Eliza. Your human mind is searching for ways to break free. I'd find you. You could swim, but there are monsters around this island that would devour you before you reached the barrier. Maybe you think you can get help from the other humans in the nearby villages. That's right—you were going to Olapura to find help. You need both blood and the power of Adas to break the seals of our realm. No one there would make you a portal because even if they don't fear the Bastard King, they fear me."

My pulse races. Right now, I hate her more than I've ever hated anything.

"You're angry," she says in that cold, hard voice of hers. Her crystalline eyes roam over my face. "Bottle your anger. Keep it close, because sometimes that is the only way you survive. I am counting on your survival, Eliza."

She doesn't wait for my response, only keeps walking. As we make the steep climb, I am grateful the path is dotted with withering leaves that are cool against my burning soles. My stomach is twisting with hunger pangs, and I am so desperate for water I lick the dewy leaves that hang from thick vines.

My only reprieve is when we start going downhill. A sea breeze shakes water from the dense canopy and delivers a cool spray to my skin.

As the sloping path levels out, the hard-packed earth turns abruptly to coarse sand. The guards and my father are like gems glinting in the distance. Out here, the sun is unforgiving without the coverage of trees, and the sound of birds and insects is replaced by the shuffle of our feet across hot white sand. The jelly has worn off, and Iris has run out of the orange flowers.

I was wrong when I said my father's revelation hurt more than any damage this world would do to me. The blisters on my feet give him a run for his money. The truth is, I don't want to stop walking. If we stop, then I have to confront my father again— and this king and the warrior girl's quest—and I don't think I can bear it.

I close my eyes and think of my sisters. I say their names over and over, like I can conjure myself into their thoughts by sheer will. We clamber uphill once again, the sand dunes burning my feet till I limp. I can taste the salt of the sea, hear the rushing waves, even if I can't see them yet.

There, in the distance, is a castle that shimmers as white as pearl against a sapphire sky. A golden flag waves in the stiff breeze.

"Welcome to Castillo de Sal," Iris says.

In *Claribelle and the Kingdom of Adas*, Claribelle was taken from the human world too, but when she was brought into Adas through a rippling portal (not a muddy pond), she saw fairies, stolen humans, and creatures in-between, running around the lush, green forests around the Castillo de Sal.

This feels wrong. The bone-white earth is deserted. Wind whistles across the wide expanse of sea. There's a stench beneath the salty spray, something that the acid on my dry tongue prevents me from identifying. My feet are covered in bloated blisters that pop like bubble wrap with every step I take. My throat is too dry to cry out as I fall to my knees.

"Nearly there, precious meat worm," Iris says, though I hear the worry in her voice. She slings my arm around her neck to help me along the rest of the way.

The archway of the castle is barred by two guards in green carapace armor, who form an *X* with their spears. They stand taller at the sight of Iris and let us pass.

I can barely see straight. My body decides to completely betray me. Perhaps it's the lack of food and water, or maybe it's the multidimensional travel, or both. Every time I blink, I've gone farther and farther into the castle halls. I lose time. And feeling in my legs. I'm aware of my father shouting my name from somewhere, but I don't—can't—respond. I'm floating, but after a while, I realize Iris is carrying me like a newborn in her arms.

"We'll get you all cleaned up before the fight, meat worm," Iris assures me.

I try to keep my eyes on her smooth brown forehead, the freckles on her cheeks that surely form a constellation. I try to speak to her. To tell her that I don't feel well. To ask her *What fight?* Then, the soggy, algae-covered empanada I ate earlier comes up all over the kingdom's warrior's chest, and I'm not even sorry.

7

The Bastard King of Adas wanted it all.

His reign just and true. His reign was her fall.

—CLARIBELLE AND THE KINGDOM OF ADAS:
TALES TALL AND TRUE, GLORIANA PALACIOS

I know I'm dreaming because I'm back in my house. It's just before the Deathday started, when my parents and sisters were preparing the living room. Alex traced lines on the floor with blue chalk, and Lula cut open a bag of sea salt to draw a perfect circle. Ma was mixing the clay that we draw on our faces, clay to make the dead feel at home and welcome because they've forgotten how to be around the living. I always thought it was a funny thing to do because I figured the dead knew exactly how to be around the living. It's the living who don't know how to be around the dead. No matter which side of the Veil you're on, it's hard to let go of a life.

Deathdays make everyone morose. Being a bruja means you're always waiting for something—your dead relatives, your powers, hunters to come run you out of town. And yet, preparing for my

Deathday was one of the most normal days we've had as a family in a long time, full of lighting candles, pouring salt, and pinning flowers in tightly braided hair.

I know that I'm dreaming because I keep seeing my family retrace those steps. Mom mixing and chanting. Lula with a secret smile on her painted lips, hands busy dusting a circle of salt. Alex concentrating on getting the symbols right. My dad cutting the stems of carnations for my crown.

I shouldn't have questioned our happiness. I shouldn't have poked and prodded. We were fragile things, and I broke us.

I know that I'm dreaming because when I wake up, I cry out as if I'm falling through a dark vacuum, and when I open my eyes, I'm not in my house, my city, my own realm even.

I'm in the Kingdom of Adas. The Castillo de Sal. And I'm alone.

Light floods my small windowless room through a rectangle narrow enough to fit just a hand.

I lick my lips and taste something sticky sweet, some sort of thick salve that cools my sun damage. My muscles ache as I push myself up to stand on the cool, gray stone floor. When I take a step, I find my blisters are nonexistent. There's only a faint redness where they decorated the sides and soles of my feet like old chicken pox scars. I rub the salve on my lips. It tastes like grass and fish oil. I have a flashback of the moment I got sick on Iris and cringe.

"Hello? I know you can hear me!"

An uproar answers, dozens, maybe hundreds of voices shouting at once as something heavy hits the ground. When I sit up, I take note of a short bench. The ache in my shoulder tells me I must have rolled off that. I pat the stone walls and find a metal bit protruding, linked to a chain. This is a holding cell.

I press myself against the door and curse every god in existence because I am a head too short to reach the window. I try to move the bench, but it weighs a ton. I try the handle, but there isn't one.

"Wait your turn," a familiar voice hisses from the other side.

I slam the wood of my fist. "What is this?"

She eclipses the light outside, a flash of green hair. She's clearly here to taunt me. "You're part of the king's collection now."

"Let me out!" I shout.

But there's a crackle of lightning and a thunderclap that booms louder than my voice. Is that my dad's magic? Half the voices out there cheer, and most of them scream everything from "cheat" to "rematch" to unintelligible cursing of entire family lines.

There's a brief moment when everything calms down enough that I can hear the slap of waves again, closer than ever before. I try to jump and see out the window but only catch snippets of a platform, a cliff, the sea.

My heart rebounds in my chest like a pinball machine gone haywire, and I take several steps back as the door swings open. I focus on Alma, her scarab-like armor catching the torchlight, her eyes filled with giddy malice.

"Where's Iris?" I ask.

"It's the king's attention you should be worried about," she says. "Come on."

"It would help if I knew what I was supposed to do."

Alma grabs my wrist and yanks me along to the center of the

platform I got a peek of. She flashes a cruel smile and says, "You fight or you die."

The arena juts out over the cliff's edge in a perfect circle. Ahead is the setting sun, the wild ocean, and the misty barrier of magic my father said cloaks this island. Waves crash so high sea spray kisses my face. For the first time I feel the slam of vertigo from standing near the edge of the ring. I scuttle back. Below me is a dark stain I recognize as blood. I turn slowly. Behind me is a sight I was not expecting.

The new roar of the crowd is deafening as I realize what is happening. A girl with ink-black wings flies above. Her face is stoic while her hands wield a ball of electric light. Her eyes flash. Long black hair whips across her face as her wings beat. Dust and sand get in my face, and I shield myself from an attack. But when I look again, the angel girl is gone. The only trace of her is the shower of sparks that fall over the crowd.

On the other side of the arena, a guard carries an unconscious body away through an archway. I take note of four identical cell doors to the one I was just taken from. Eyes watch me from the narrow windows. Is my dad in one of them?

You fight or you die. Alma's words echo as I take position at the center of this coliseum.

I let out a shaky breath as I scan the crowd gathered in the stands: Adas with wings. Adas with horns. Adas with the heads of beasts and the bodies of men. Humans with wine-stained mouths and glassy eyes. I can't help but be reminded of the time I had to act for my drama class. I was one of the witches in *Macbeth*, and when the curtain opened, I froze and just kept stirring the empty cauldron. Here, I have nothing to do with my hands except wipe sweat on my dirty, tattered dress.

Somehow, amid all of these bodies, I spot my father. I want to run toward him. But with a single shake of his head, I get the warning to stay put. He's in the center viewing box. From here, he appears unharmed and unbound, but there is a guard standing right beside him and the threat is clear. At the center of the crowd is a figure I immediately recognize as the king, if only by his glittering crown. Iris is to his left, and a horned boy dressed in gold to his right. When the king stands, the crowd's volume becomes a whisper.

"My beautiful beasts," he says, the sonorous boom of his voice is inviting. "Today we have a new addition to our collection of warriors. I present to you—Lady Siphon, daughter of El Fin!"

The what of what the? I'm pretty sure I'm the daughter of Carmen and Patricio Mortiz, but any sound I make would be utterly drowned out by this noise. The red and orange sunset floods the stands. Shadows lurch as bodies cheer for me. Suddenly dancing in my living room doesn't seem that bad.

What would my sisters do? Fight back. Something. Anything.

"Excuse me," I say. My voice doesn't even carry. My heart feels like a fist in my throat. "Y—you've got the wrong girl."

"Let's see the might of your power," says the king.

The louder they get, the smaller I feel, as though I'm shrinking in direct proportion to their cheers. The king of Adas sits and makes a flourish with his hand at Alma, who opens another cell door. Instinctively, I take three steps back.

A figure nearly six feet tall steps out. I bet *she* could see through the window on the door without having to jump. Panicked laughter scrapes up my throat as I watch her approach. The rope of silver hair atop her head makes her look even longer. She takes sure, confident steps toward me. The roar of the gathered crowd fuels the smirk splitting her round face. Tiny gems dot the toned white skin of her arms and even around the corners of her eyes.

Torches explode all around us as the sun finishes setting. Why couldn't this have been a fistfight or a sword match? I'm not great at either one of those, but Rhett insisted that I learn how to wield a weapon and Nova wanted to make sure I could throw a punch without breaking my wrist. For all of the newness and strangeness of my abilities, they don't do me much good without magic to steal from.

"Do we bow?"

It's the last thing I do before the silver-haired girl raises her hands to the darkening sky and summons her magic. Even I can feel the way the air is charged around us. I knew that feeling well when I drained some of my dad's power and conjured my own personal thunderstorm. But this girl's power is not lightning. It is light itself. She draws it from the very sky, and I watch in awe as she transforms it—shapes it—into a whip. She cracks it at my feet.

I throw myself back, but it isn't far enough. My skin burns where her whip wraps around my ankle. I scream and kick, but she drags me across the ground. There's a shrill wailing sound, and I don't realize it's me until she reels her weapon back. My vision is fuzzy at the edges, but I see her better now. Her nose is bruised between her eyes. Her bottom lip is split. I was wrong. Those aren't gems on her skin. They're freckles made of light, living constellations.

"You're the thing King Cirro has been searching for?" the star girl asks in a voice that reminds me of bell chimes. "I've done this a thousand times, little one. You're no different than the rest."

I push myself up and dust the bits of sand and gravel from my palms as she walks away. The audience is now standing and jeering. I can't even see my dad in the shadows. Did he have to fight too? Fight or die. Is that what he meant when he said he'd done things here? Did he kill? No matter. He can't help me from where he is. No one can.

"Finish her off, Alcyone!"

She readies her whip in the air.

I think of home. Somewhere in New York, my family is looking for me. If time is twice as fast in Brooklyn, then this is already the longest amount of time I have spent away from them. I remember my bruja lessons and how we had to memorize the names and cycles of constellations and stars. I remember Lula making up her own names when she forgot the real ones. Thinking of them doesn't have the effect I want on my power. There's a vacant well, a hunger instead. My entire body goes numb. I feel the ache in my bones. I smell the power amid the brine of the sea. I feel the pinpricks of magic, reaching and reaching. There is a distant voice calling out to me that wants to be heard.

When Alcyone attacks, I raise my hands to meet her.

I grab hold of the starlight whip. My power calls to it, devours it. Everything within me sings with magic and light so intense that, for a moment, I can't breathe.

"What are you—" Alcyone begins to ask, then falls to her knees. She shakes her head and lets go, forfeiting her whip. I hold it tight.

The crowd has turned in my favor. They shout my name: *Si-phon. Si-phon. Si-phon.* Their frenzy floods the arena as they break into fights of their own. Faces run with sweat and the nectar of fruit and drink. The power rushes through me, and I feel as if I'm ignited from within. I consider making her feel the way I did. My own anger and sadness throughout the day twists and pools into something dark, something I didn't think was there.

"Rose." My name is spoken calmly, and yet it cuts through the cacophony of the masses even though it's a whisper. There is only one person in this castle who would call me that.

Dad.

I drop the weapon, and it dissolves, leaving behind shimmering dust. My heart feels like it's sputtering, and I pant for breath. What was that?

Alcyone tries to swing at me with bare-knuckled fists, but I sidestep her and she face-plants at my feet. Her dark eyes are wide, her chest heaves with every gasp.

"What did you do to me?" she asks, unable to stand back up.

I did that.

I can't believe I did that.

"I don't—" I start to speak, but guards are coming to get her. They drag her away like the other.

"Tonight, we celebrate Lady Siphon," King Cirro says, the only voice clear enough to rise over the crowd. "Our last Guardian of Adas."

8

La Mama ripped fire from her heart

and strung it in the sky.

—TALES OF THE DEOS,
FELIPE THOMÁS SAN JUSTINIO

D ragged away from the seaside fighting ring, I'm unceremoniously deposited into a cavernous room. Thick candles flicker from indentations in the walls and drip wax from chandeliers above. The moon shines through the open double doors that let out to a balcony overlooking the waves.

"Don't touch anything," Alma warns, flashing her sharp canines as she slams the door behind me.

The room is empty. Every one of my footsteps is a sigh against the cold stone floor. I keep my hands around my waist as my muscles shake with the recoil of magic. What was it the king called me? Lady Siphon. And who is El Fin? That's not a Deo I've ever seen in our books. I shake my head to dispel the memory of using my power. But I can still feel the burn of starlight, how bright it was coursing through me.

I can't do that again. Not when I could hurt someone like I nearly hurt Alcyone. I don't know what came over me. When I used my magic at home, Nova or McKay or Dad didn't fall like she did. Somehow, I have to convince the king to let my dad and me go.

Iris said I'd have a choice, but the king's welcome doesn't fill me with confidence. *The Guardians of Adas* doesn't sound like a knitting club.

I circle the sparse room, tracing my fingertips along the cool white stone. It is no wonder they called it the Castillo de Sal. When I bring my pinky to my lips, salt spreads on my tongue. It's out in the sea that laps against the balcony, and it's here in these walls. One of the candles snuffs out, and I think of how I stood in front of La Mama's statue and asked for the truth, then tried to take it back.

In the corners of the room, cobwebs that look like they were spun out of platinum cling like tapestries from the ceiling. Birds fly in from the balcony and perch on crisscrossed beams where tangles of flower vines snake.

Despite the strange beauty of it all, I recognize this space for what it is—a war room. I've been in a war room before, when Brooklyn was under attack after my sisters and I trapped the goddess of Death and unleashed casimuertos on the city. That room had state-of-the-art holograms and tech that fused science and magic. *This* room has tables covered by scrolls of maps on parchment, and brass replicas of landmarks dot the landscape.

I peer closer at the map left out on display. It is wider than our dining room table, complete with colorful sketches of trees and rivers. I recognize Lagunitas Serpentinas and Olapura. I shut my eyes. We were so close. I shouldn't have insisted on my dad telling me the truth. I should have pushed my body harder to keep moving. But what was it that Iris said? She would find me. We never would have made it.

I place my finger on the map, to the white castle sitting on the most northeast side of the island. West of here is something called Girasol Grove dotted with sunflowers and two great rivers that cleave the kingdom in half. Then, there's a green valley on the western side of the island. At the center is a black mark that looks like someone spilled a tub of ink. I drag my index finger across it, but it comes away dry.

Then, there's a shuddering sound as the doors slam open.

"I didn't touch anything," I say, and keep my hands behind my back. But it isn't Alma the guard who enters. It's the king himself.

I have read about the Bastard King of Adas more times than I can count. I've stared at the blurry sketches in the pages of my book, a young man with a heavy crown of stars and gold crafted by the Deos themselves. Looking at him now, I know that those renderings were wrong. They didn't capture how his presence draws your eyes and forces you to look. Even the candles seem to burn brighter the moment he strides to the center of the room. He watches me back with eyes the rich brown of forests. His warm copper-brown skin is cast in shadow. His clothes are deep blue silk that ripples like the surface of water. High cheekbones and a full mouth give him the appearance of someone who is always just short of pleased.

When he takes another step closer, I realize it isn't the candles that are burning brighter. It's the pulsing light within his crown. Brilliant crystals cut like stars and twisted with gold sit perfectly on a head of straight black hair that spills over his shoulders. I find myself wanting to ask him if everything I've read is true—if he spent six days and six nights holding up a great ceiba tree to prove his strength to his future queen of Adas. Or if he regrets usurping his father's throne and banishing his brother Agosto to Los Lagos. Or if he really drank the sea in order to find the perfect pearls for his queen's crown.

I don't get to ask any of those things. The guard at his side sneers at me.

"Bow before the king!" Alma barks.

It's only the snap of her voice that pulls me out of my reverie. I hold on to the side of the map table to steady myself and realize there are two more adas gathered around the king.

"Peace, Alma," the king says in a deep voice that feels like the caress of a sea breeze. "Like all of my subjects, if the Siphon of Galaxies is to bow to me, it will be of her own accord."

Chastened, the guard stands back with the other two. Iris gives me a curt nod of recognition and keeps her hand on the hilt of her sword. Beside her is a male ada who writes furiously on a wooden tablet.

My heartbeat stutters when he stops and his eyes meet mine. His face is a contradiction, soft and square lines all at once. There's a streak of gold on each of his cheeks that matches the gold ram horns that sprout from his hairline and wrap around the sides of his head. Raven-black curls are pulled into a low knot at his nape.

I trip over my sweaty feet, and his wide, full mouth quirks into a smile as I stop just short of falling.

Iris makes a strangled noise, like when Alex thinks a movie

is overrated or when Lula realizes I ate all the chocolate-covered cherries. Looking at Iris now, without the threat of being captured or nearly dying from dehydration during our journey, she is startling, really, and I have to remind myself to close my open mouth.

There's a resemblance between Iris and the Golden Boy in the high cheekbones and the pout of her full pink lips. I bet they're related. But where he gives off a warm softness, she's the edges of a geode split open. Iris doesn't have horns, but her ears have sharper points than the boy's, and they're ringed with gold cuffs.

"Your power is divine," the Golden Boy tells me, still not taking the pen off his paper.

Nope, chastens a voice that sounds remarkably like Alex.

Hells yeah, please, follows Lula.

Oh no. My cheeks burn, and I breathe deep to snap out of this. Dad was right—everything here is designed to make you want to stay, even their lovely voices and lovelier faces. I should think of the painful trek from the ponds to here, the public fight I was subjected to, the sharp teeth of the guard. I'm not in my storybook. I'm in Adas, and I have to get home.

"Is anyone going to tell me why I was kidnapped and brought here or...?" I let my last word drag on and lift a brow. The more I blink, the more I get over the shock of their beauty, and the more clearly I can think.

"Can this truly be the siphon you spent so many moons searching for?" Alma asks, her words sweet, but I notice the way Iris's eyes narrow, a muscle jolts at her jaw.

"She bested the king's champion," she says. "The siren has not been wrong yet. And you forget your place, Alma."

Alma bows dramatically to Iris but does not lower her stare. "Apologies, Princess."

Princess? I gasp, then remember what that horrible creature in Alley Pond Park had called her. *Your Highness.*

Iris's features are schooled into cold indifference. I think of the girl who offered me water and carried me here. That kindness doesn't seem to belong to this girl.

"As long as her defeat of Alcyone was not sheer luck, she is the final guardian we've been searching for," Iris says.

"Wait a minute." I am too indignant to care that this is not how you address a girl with a sword. "You've dragged me through a muddy hole in the ground, across a jungle and a desert, shoved me into a magical boxing ring, not to mention you've ruined my birthday dress. The least you could all do is give me the courtesy of answering my questions. And while you're at it, stop talking about me like I'm not here. I'm literally in front of you."

The Golden Boy's beautiful mouth curls into a wide smile.

"Is it my age or do humans talk a lot more than you used to?" King Cirro asks, his brow furrowed.

"I can cut her tongue out, my king," Alma says, and metal sings as she unsheathes a small blade.

Let me at her, Lula says.

She can't hurt you. They need you, Alex says.

Even with my heart in my throat, I'm going to test that theory.

"While we're at it," I say, every ounce of fear and frustration since I've left home tangling up inside me, "I'm not going anywhere or guarding anything until I see my father. I'm not hurting anyone else or killing anyone for your twisted games."

"You're not here to fight in the arena," says the Golden Boy. "That was to see what you were capable of."

"You will be able to see your father again. But as my daughter said, the siren has not been wrong yet. She has found all of my creatures for me," King Cirro explains.

He moves closer to me. The lighting and magic of this island make it almost impossible to guess his age. In the stories he was centuries old, but here he looks in his thirties, and definitely not a man who could have two grown kids. I wonder why do eternal creatures want to grow to be so old if they cling to their youth? I'd hate to look fifteen forever.

The blue silk of his long robe floats around his feet. Under his gaze I feel both terrified and lucky to be given this attention. Each of his fingers is adorned with gems except for one bearing a simple wooden ring.

"The siren is wrong," I say, flinching when he cups my face.

His touch is surprisingly gentle, kind even. "You truly are the siphon," he continues, "imbued with the powers of El Fin, Deo and Master of Everything's End. You are to be one of the Guardians of Adas and save my island."

I don't think I heard him right. Not to mention I've never heard of a Deo named El Fin before today.

"I'm sorry, what?"

The king blinks away his confusion several times, and for a moment, the corners of his eyes wrinkle in the shape of spiderwebs. Then, they smooth out when his crown pulses brighter. He snarls. Kings must not like being told no.

"I am being patient with you. Human hearts are so very tender.

Believe me, it is best for you to agree to this and spare yourself true sorrow. You are here to save the Kingdom of Adas."

"Threatening me isn't going to get me to do anything," I say, sparks of anger rising within me. "Believe me, I can't guard anything. We're not even allowed to have pets anymore, so really, taking care of a whole kingdom is not in my cards. Trust me."

I rack my brain trying to remember my last tarot spread. When I got the Tower card, I just thought it meant that freshman year was going to suck. It has.

"The siren felt your magic." Iris's voice is the snap of a whip. "Years ago. Its pulse could be felt through the realms. A bruja unlike any other. Then, it disappeared before we could find it."

"I'm not your girl." I shake my head. They must be thinking about my sister, but I can't say that in case they kidnap her too. Alex is the one whose power unleashed one day, a wild, destructive thing she buried for years. She's the encantrix. My power is new and different, but it can't be stronger than hers.

How do you know that? Alex's voice asks in my head.

No one knows what you can do, baby girl, Lula says.

"You deny this honor I've bestowed upon you." King Cirro's face darkens. His benevolent façade slips. Who is he but the man who sent me to be kidnapped? A murderer. The King of Adas.

I point at Iris. "You said I'd be given a choice!"

"Allow me to present it," she says. "Lend your power to the Guardians of Adas or join your father in the prison tower, where he was relocated to after the match."

A red haze of fury clouds my vision. The buzzing feeling of my magic becomes a swarm beneath my skin, searching and searching for a power to draw. I ball my hands into fists and wish I had something to hit. Magic to taste…

"Father, Iris, if I may," the Golden Boy says. He holds his pen like he's waving a wand in the air. "Perhaps the siphon should understand her role in this. Her home is affected as well as ours."

"What do you mean?" I search the room for answers, but they wait for the king's word. Is that what he meant when he said he'd spare me sorrow?

The hundreds of candles in the salt-white room flicker all at once as a hard breeze cycles through. The king nods once at his son and gives a wordless command to Alma, who rushes out of the war room.

"I am Prince Arco, Scribe of Adas," the young ada says in a voice that reminds me of summer and the sweet tang of ripe fruit. "Lady Siphon—"

I don't want them to call me that, even if it sounds pretty when he says it. "Eliza."

"Eliza, then. A rot has taken root in our land." Prince Arco points his pen at the map. "With every turn of the moon, it spreads. My father, the king, has done everything in his power to protect us, but still it spreads. Vegetation, entire rain forests, even mountains have been reduced to dead earth. Nearly half of Adas has been rendered a desert. Do you remember what you saw around the castle when you were brought here?"

"'Brought' is a pretty generous way of saying 'kidnapped,' but sure," I say, and Iris makes like she's going to strangle me. Her brother stops her with a raised hand indicating patience. "I saw the castle."

"And around the castle?"

In my stupor, I remember thinking how empty the castle grounds were. It wasn't like I expected, like the stories with creatures reveling under the sun and around the trees. For the end of our journey, there were no trees in sight. "White sand?"

"Five moons ago, the land around the castle used to be rain forest. What was once trees and soil is now sand and stone. Here."

He draws our attention to the map in front of us and moves a polished white stone to the northern part of the island, where the castle faces the water. "This is the most recent rendering of Adas. Last moon, the land split right off during a tremor and sunk into the sea." Arco points to the jagged rocks around the cliff that look like a shark's open maw.

On the map, Olapura is marked by a silver fish while an emerald beetle, pink bird, and other bright animals denote villages in the center. Then the entire western half of Adas is desert. Right at the center is what I'd believed to be an ink stain. The rot.

Arco picks up a jagged black crystal—tourmaline from the looks of it—and holds it up for me to see. He sets it over the ink stain. "The heart of the rot is here. Since it began draining the earth of the western coast, it shows no signs of stopping."

"What is it made of?" I ask, taking the tourmaline from his hand. This is one of Lula's favorite crystals. She keeps it everywhere—on her altar, her car, her purses and jackets. She made a prex necklace out of it to pray to the Deos for happiness, to ground herself and find balance. I set it down, blinking tears before they can fall.

"Why does that matter what it is made of?" King Cirro asks harshly. "You are to get rid of it."

"It matters, *Your Majesty*, because in order to destroy something," I say, "it helps to know everything you can to fight it."

"We have never seen anything like it before," Arco says.

"You haven't seen it at all, Brother," Iris cuts in bitterly. "You have been in your study with your nose in your books and drowning yourself in rum and—"

"We mourn in different ways, Iris," Arco says, and there is so much sadness in his words that it twists in my gut.

Iris acts like her brother hasn't spoken and continues. "The rot, Eliza, is a black viscous substance. It spreads in poisonous veins that cling to the ground like leeches. We have brought weather witches, healers, fae from other lands and realms, all to reverse the damage. We even tried digging around it to rip it out by the root, and I lost my garrison to that pit. Nothing works."

"Then what makes you think that I can do something?" I say.

"You won't be alone." Iris's rose-crystal eyes flick to her father, then back to me. "The king has granted me permission to take the strongest of his collection to the outerlands."

"The Guardians of Adas," I say. I've refused to be part of magical circles and groups at home, and here I am. Lula will be so pissed.

"There are six of you. The siren and I will lead you to the rot. You will drink the blood of the gods and strengthen your power. We believe that together, you can fight back this plague devouring our island."

It's always blood, isn't it, Rosie?

When Nova's words come to me, I wrap my hand around my bracelet and let the anger I've reeled in all day surface. This isn't right. They *have* no right.

"Let me get this straight. You want me to go to ground zero of this rot to drink blood? I don't think so, Princess. What if we go the way of your garrison?"

She grits her teeth. "You won't fail. I won't allow it."

"See that you don't, Iris." King Cirro arches a thick black brow. "As for you, Lady Siphon, perhaps you'd rather join your father in the tower."

What do you do when a choice is not a choice? I am not a chess piece this king can move around. It feels like this king is trying to bluff, treating me like he's doing me a favor when all he wants is for me to do what he says without question.

"Then take me to the tower to be with him."

"How dare you?" When King Cirro speaks, something cruel tugs at his features, wrinkles webbing across his face. Gone is the young king who caressed me. Now, his face is splintering apart to reveal his true self, ancient and haggard. Then he takes a deep breath, the faint light of his star crown pulsing, drawing on its power until his skin smooths back into the face of youth. "It seems fitting that you should be the missing piece to the salvation of my kingdom when it was your father who set off its destruction. You owe this kingdom a blood debt, and it will be met."

Something cold goes through me. "What do you mean?"

"Why do you think your father was brought along with you?" the king asks, circling me, the ripple of his clothes like wings on a bird of prey. "I wanted the human who took up arms against me, after the rebels left my queen for dead, murdered. Your father set fire to my castle and then ran, like a coward. That is when the rot first appeared and took hold of my kingdom. I am benevolent. I am righteous. I am the true king of Adas, by root and blood, and no one—not you or anyone—will destroy what I have built."

I walk backward until I hit the wall. I press my hands, stinging with an ache for magic, against the cool stone. I tell myself that he's lying. Could my dad really have done these things? He told me about the uprising against the king, but he said nothing about having a hand in it. Then again, he also said nothing about his six months in Florida or his fake amnesia. What was it he said? *It's my fault we're here. I'm not proud of what I did.* Is my dad like this king? A killer?

"You, Eliza, are going to do whatever it takes to repay the damage done to me and mine," King Cirro says sharply, deep spiderweb-like wrinkles returning around his lips and eyes.

"Father," Arco's voice is a calming wave. He reaches out to the king's shoulder and gives him a gentle squeeze. But the prince's voice does something to me too.

I think of Alex and Lula and Ma back home. What must my mother be going through? It isn't fair that she has to relive my father's absence all over again. I think of Nova trying to get to a place he's never been before. I wonder if I can scream loudly enough, hurt badly enough that they can feel it no matter the distance. I wonder if I can get us out of this alive. If I can get us home. Because this mission doesn't sound like something I might come back from.

"If my father owes you a debt, then that is between you and him. I owe you nothing."

"In Adas, children carry the weight of their ancestors in their bones." King Cirro's lip quirks, a curious spark in the gold flecks of his brown eyes.

Iris, who has been silent during the yelling, glares at her father. Does she agree with his words? Does she feel the weight of everything he's done?

We're interrupted by the patter of footsteps outside the doors. They swing open, and Alma returns with someone by her side.

Every hair on my body stands on end. I can *feel* her magic even as she walks across the room—the siren who can sense power across the realms. The brown-skinned woman is bald, with gold tattoos around her temples. Her eyes are completely black, too large for her round face and gently pointed ears. There's a frailty to her body like a strong wind will carry her away any second. Her dress bodice is made of thin roots, and the skirt is hundreds of layers of ferns that drag when she walks. In her hands is a glass box lined with silver. Her unnaturally long fingers shield the contents.

Everyone takes a step back. Iris's eyes flame with fury while Arco tenses. Alma, for the first time since I met her, sweats.

"Xia," King Cirro says evenly, though the muscles around his left eye twitch. "Show our Siphon of Galaxies what the rot is capable of."

Xia places the glass box on the table. The sound of bees fill my head the closer she gets, and my hands tremble, like they want to grab hold of her and taste her power. I clasp one hand around the opposite wrist and squeeze for a moment until the sensation goes away.

"This is the rot?" I ask, dry mouthed.

"It is a piece of it," she says, her voice the tenor of a gong. "Like cupping water from a flood and hoping none spills."

She steps back. Inside the glass is a thin layer of black. It looks

109

like dried blood, cracking at the center. The king reaches for a vine that hangs from the ceiling. As his outstretched fingers near, a flower sprouts. He rips it off by the stem and hands it to the siren.

"This is all my daughter was able to gather from her failed mission," Cirro says. Only I seem to notice Iris wince at the words. "Xia's power can keep the abomination at rest, but it never lasts. Even removed from its source, it lives."

He brings the flower close to the glass, and slowly, the thing inside begins to move. He opens the lid and drops the flower. Within seconds, the black substance softens, moves like an ocean current around the stem and petals. It envelops the green and consumes it until there is nothing left. It begins slithering up the glass wall, and King Cirro grimaces at it with a look I can't quite name. Hatred is not enough. Fear, disgust. It's all there. But he doesn't move to close the box.

It is Iris who lunges forward and slams the lid closed. She keeps a hand pressed to it, her breath ragged as she glares at her father.

Xia taps her narrow fingers on the glass, head tilting to the side like she's listening to a voice the rest of us can't hear. "We have a full turn of the moon before it spreads again. If the rot moves past Adas, past our barrier, I fear the rest of the world is doomed."

"What say you now, Siphon?"

I should help my dad escape and make a break for it. Or take my chances swimming across the sea to get help. People can survive terrible feats just to get back to their families, to get back home. I've never seen magic like the rot. However it came to exist, it has to come from a great source of power. Bigger than me. What happens when this rot spreads? I owe nothing to this kingdom that took my father—twice. What will happen to my dad while I'm gone? I'm not finished being mad at him, but I'm also not done getting answers. Part of me wants to laugh because it isn't my family I picture now. It is McKay, the shape-shifter. His easy smile when he told me *There's always a new Chosen One around the corner.* I don't want it to be me. I want to read in my room and fight with my sisters and light candles at my altar and do my extra-credit homework. I wanted to fix my family, not the world.

My family is my world.

"I will join your guardians," I say. I think of every teacher who walked past me and asked me to speak louder, mocked the whisper of my voice. Lula would be louder. I clear my throat. I glance down at the map where the broken pieces of the island look like a shark's open maw. "I have conditions."

"Conditions?" He clicks his sharp nails together. "After what you've seen?"

"I am not of Adas. Where I come from, my father's debt means nothing." I stop and stack my words carefully. Doesn't it? Didn't I believe Nova was right and that we inherit our family's curses? "This is a new deal between you and me."

"Go on."

"I want assurance that you won't hurt my father while I'm gone."

"I make you this promise," King Cirro says, his voice airy but sure. "Before my children, my guard, and my siren, no harm will come to your father by my hand as long as you keep your word to use your power to heal my land."

One of the things my mother always told us was that magic, no matter how big or small, is a bargain with the universe. In a place like this, promises must have the same power. I want more time to think this through, but I know that no matter what realm I'm in, royals probably don't like to be kept waiting.

"No harm will come to my father by you or any of your kingdom," I add in a rush that surprises even me. "At the end of it all we get to go home."

His smile is like a beautiful blade. His hand is extended, waiting for me to grasp it.

"Eliza, Lady Siphon," the King of Adas says as he squeezes my hand. I squeeze right back. "We have an accord."

His words settle along my skin, and it feels like I'm being kissed by snow and the sun all at once. I have no question that there is magic in this promise, this bargain that I have made.

"Ready Lady Siphon to meet the others. The Salt Moon awaits." The Bastard King of Adas gives his back to us and stalks to the balcony. His voice is pitched low, but I can hear every word. "Everyone says they want to go home at first, but somehow, they never do."

9

Cirro stood over his father's body.
He picked up the bloody fallen stars and
crowned himself king.

—CLARIBELLE AND THE KINGDOM OF ADAS:
TALES TALL AND TRUE, GLORIANA PALACIOS

Alma shoves me down a long open hall. Iris follows close behind, and I'm not sure if it's for my protection or to make sure that I uphold my end of the bargain. Music spills from somewhere in the castle. The sounds are familiar in a way they shouldn't be. I focus on the flickering torches, the crawling sensation that lingers on my skin after meeting the siren and seeing the rot. Adrenaline catches up to me, and my mind reels. I am stuck on a dying island. I bargained with the King of Adas. Now I have to make good on my end of the deal. I curse myself because I should have asked for a weapon in addition to my father's safety.

I turn to ask for him. The king said I'd be able to see him again. But my fairy guards stop abruptly. Alma defers to the princess, and I wonder what happened between them that caused all the evil eyes being volleyed back and forth.

"I'll return for you, little siphon," Iris tells me before I'm uncer-emoniously shoved into a large bedroom. She shuts the door, leaving me with my mouth hanging open and a hundred questions dead on my lips.

"Jerk," I kick the door. It is, safe to say, pathetic.

Emotions crash over me. Losing control of my magic. Knowing my father's past. Being here. It takes a moment to realize that for the first time, I've gotten what I wanted all day. To be alone.

I leap onto the giant four-poster bed covered in sheer white silks that flutter in the night breeze, which blows in from tall arched windows like the steady breath of El Viento, Lord of Flight. Above is a skylight that frames the swell of the moon. My eyes begin to flutter closed when a pang of thirst overwhelms me. I get up and search the room.

There's a table with a ceramic jug that, on further inspection, is full of water. I unstick my parched tongue from the roof of my mouth and decide my thirst wins out. The water is warm and tastes like flowers. I spit a soggy stem from my lips.

"Ew," I groan.

The rattle of the door makes me jump. In comes a short ada with brown skin like worn, wrinkled leather. There's a silver tray full of fruits and flowers clutched in her long, bony fingers. Her ash hair is tied up in a knot and adorned with green berries. Narrow, beady eyes glance from me to the jug of water.

"Welcome, brujita," she says in a raspy alto. She picks up a bundle of wildflowers from her tray, empties the jug I just drank from, and refills it with fresh water and blossoms. "Offerings for the Siphon of Galaxies."

I definitely do not like all these things that people are calling me, but it's not worth correcting them. Besides, I wonder what she'd say if she knew her "Siphon of Galaxies" just drank old flower water. It's still a sweet gesture.

"Who are you?" I ask.

She shuffles to the bedside and rests the tray on the mattress. "None of your concern, girl child."

"I'm not a child," I mutter, but when I cross my arms over my chest, I definitely sound like one. If Lula were here, would she charm this old fairy into doing her bidding? Into helping? Alex would bargain, wouldn't she?

The ada stares up at me. When she frowns, her deep wrinkles gather like mango skin left out in the sun. I wonder how old she is. In my book of stories, there were some creatures born looking a hundred years old and others who remained children forever.

"Rude mortal children," she grumbles, ambling over to a narrow armoire. Despite the dim candlelight, her strange fingers seem to know exactly what she's searching for as she retrieves a flowing skirt and top.

If my mother were here, she'd slap the back of my head and remind me of my manners. It isn't this creature's fault that I was kidnapped from my realm and brought before the king.

"I'm sorry. I'm Eliza. What can I call you?"

"Palita," she says, her pink tongue sticking out a bit between the gap in her front teeth. "Come, come, bruja bruja brujita. We'll dress these wounds."

"We?"

She takes my finger and hobbles along, leading me through a set of doors that connect this bedroom to a large bathroom. Fat balls of light in every color dot the ceiling. There's a large tub made of stone in the pattern of fish scales, and glimmers like New York sidewalks. High-pitched voices laugh and splash water all over the floor. They're adas. About six of them. Three resemble Palita, with her wrinkled face, bodies adorned with dried fruits and baubles. The other three have reptilian features and slender bodies not a foot long, fluttering in the billowing foam of the bath. They all freeze when they see us.

"Is this what you do when my back is turned?" Palita snaps.

One of the lizard girls leaps into the tub, submersing herself up to her eyes. "We was only testing the temperature for the siphon, Palita our loveliest."

"See? They were only testing it," I say, and for the first time, I laugh without fear.

They get to go work taking off my dress. I try not to think too much about being naked in front of seven fairies. I try not to think at all as they take soft brushes and clean my skin with soaps and oils that smell like I rolled around in a field of flowers all day. Palita splashes me with salt water. It only stings on my cuts for a bit, then she applies a cool balm, and I think about how it wouldn't hurt at all if Lula were the one doing this. My wounds from the fight are throbbing, my skin raw where I was dragged on the ground. I think of the guards who carry the defeated away. If I hadn't had a lucky, desperate surge of power, I would have been carted away instead of brought before the king.

I clear my throat. "Could you tell me—where do the others go? The ones who fight and lose?"

"The salt mines, of course." A blue lizard fairy says, moving so swiftly she makes me dizzy.

How long did my father last before he was sent to the salt mines? I rub my temples, where a pinching pain spreads. When I close my eyes, I see the black ooze come alive and devour that flower. My nerves tangle in the pit of my stomach. "Oh gods, why is this happening?"

"Why does anything happen?" Palita asks, detangling my hair. The others wash the soap away.

It happened because I broke the protection wreath on my home and the bounty hunters tracked us down. It happened because I asked La Mama for the truth. Because my power changed and ruined everything. I have always loved being a bruja, but I'm not so sure if I love being this—magical hacker. Siphon. But I am not Alex. I will figure out my power so that no king or anyone can try to control me this way.

Palita's wafer-thin lips curl into an unkind smile. "While you despair, come and dress for the feast, even if you still stink of the iron and filth of your realm."

I frown at her but get out of the tub. I can't help but feel shame at the things I said to my father when he told me he came to the castle. *Sounds fancy. Must've been nice.* I wonder if the others are being treated the way I am. If they, too, have seen the king's true face beneath the beautiful one.

The crotchety fairy and her glam squad pat me dry, then slather me with oil I recognize as jojoba. It all feels like I'm getting prepped to be served up for dinner. One of the lizard adas with large yellow eyes picks up my index finger. She smells it.

"Strong, tasty magic," she says, her tiny sharp teeth flash with a smile. "Please, Palita, one nibble for our troubles."

I yank my finger back, but the ada is so small she holds on. Palita grabs a broom, the kind my mom uses to clean after rituals. It's made of a hundred skinny palm stems tied at the head with ribbons. I used to chase Alex around the house with one of those. Now, Palita slaps away the yellow lizard girl and kicks the others out.

"Go on, girl child," Palita says, smacking her loose lips together as she turns the broom to the floor and sweeps suds and water away. "Dress for your revel."

I grab a soft towel, wrap it around myself, and return to the main room. There are clothes laid out for me on the bed. Lula would love them. With knots in my stomach, I slip on the strange, gauzy underwear and long pink and orange silk skirt. Calling the material silk doesn't even feel right because it's somehow softer than that, like being wrapped in the wings of butterflies. The top is a yellow blouse that makes me feel like a sunset, and I thank the Deos that the Kingdom of Adas has a size eighteen.

The adas removed all of the flowers in my braid crown, leaving softer strands than before. I finger comb it over my shoulders. There is not a single mirror in this room, so I have to trust years of Lula's meticulous fussing that what I'm doing makes me look presentable. For who? The court? The king? For a flash, I think of Arco with his kind eyes and gold stripes on his cheeks.

"Get it together," I tell myself and lightly slap my face.

I drink the rest of the fresh water Palita brought on the tray, but my thirst isn't sated. I'm starving. I dig into the pocket of my old dress. Two chocolate bars. There's dried pond scum on the wrapper, but the inside is perfectly edible. I eat one in two ravenous bites that make my taste buds ache.

"Save your appetite for the feast," Palita says, reappearing as if from thin air. She sets a pair of snakeskin slippers at my feet. "Follow me, and keep up, girl child."

In the middle of the night, the Castillo de Sal is not the quiet, still place it was when I arrived. The Salt Moon has brought out the revelers and casts an incandescent light over everything. Wild palm trees as tall as buildings line a sprawling courtyard rich with twisting hedges. There are so many bodies that I'm afraid to keep walking out of fear that I'll get crushed by the throng.

"I will take you to the princess," Palita says, as she's folded into the crowd.

"Wait up!" I shout.

In the process, I step on the front of my skirt again. This time, I fall to my hands and knees on a white stone pathway. When I look up, Palita is gone and I have no idea which way she went.

Percussionists tap away a new beat that has everyone cheering and moving faster, shifting their feet across short, yellowing grass as I push myself back up and scan the crowd for Palita or Iris. I spot a head of pink, but it belongs to a lanky boy sitting at a fountain, batting his lashes at a guard.

To my right is a gathering of young fairies with silver, gold, and bronze horns, each set twisting in different shapes. They remind me of the kids at school dances who always look fashionable but bored. All of them steal my breath with their lovely faces made more radiant by the brightness of the moon. It's almost like it was lassoed and brought closer to this realm for this reason, so the court of this kingdom could party all night.

I think of a story my mom used to tell us when we were little—about El Papa, father of the Deos and partner to La Mama. He cut out his own eye to give light to the night sky. I always thought that sounded painful and gross, but my mom said that it was his sacrifice that allowed creatures of the night to live and find their way when they get lost. I'd scrunch up my face and say, "Ew. How could the moon be an eye?"

My mom would chuckle and say, "Maybe one day you'll stare at the moon and see El Papa's gift."

Here, at the court of Adas, under the biggest moon and more stars than I've ever seen in my life, I wish more than anything to see my family again. That would be my gift.

I pick a new direction, weaving through tangled couples. Long limbs snared around each other like the vines hugging the castle walls. Hips tick-tock to the beat, and I am an awkward, wound-up toy going the wrong way until someone stops me.

"Have you lost your way already, sweet girl?" the airy voice asks. A pair of brown eyes are so close to my face I have to take a step back to take in all of her. The ada is my height, with slicked-back blue and yellow feathers for hair and a small beak for a mouth. Her coloring reminds me of the parakeet Alex sacrificed on her Deathday—but I probably shouldn't tell her that.

"No," I say, capping off my words with a nervous laugh. "I'm just getting a proper tour of the place."

The horned adas I noticed before seem to have taken an interest in us. I don't know if this is a realm where I want to be noticed. They gather around, brandishing wooden goblets with gold leaf around the rims. The tallest of them has bright green eyes and black hair that shines like oil slicks.

"Keeping our guest to yourself, Caya?" he says, and I decide that everything sounds smug when an immortal creature says it.

"Of course not, Ixmel," the parakeet girl says.

A servant presents a drink tray, and everyone snatches fresh goblets from it. All eyes turn to me, waiting. Fairy peer pressure is even worse than high school peer pressure. I grab a drink and return their smiles.

"Let us toast to you, Lady Eliza," Ixmel says, bowing in my direction.

"Yes," says a girl with delicate gold horns and daisies in her hair. She's the only one of them with more rounded ears, more like mine. More human. Her face is unfairly beautiful, and her inscrutable gaze doesn't waver from me. "The savior of Adas and King Cirro."

"Blessings to his name," they all mutter in the way someone might say "bless you" when a stranger sneezes on the street and then never sees them again.

"Tell us," Ixmel says. "The king says that you will save us from the rot, that your magic is the most powerful in the realms, with the gifts of El Fin."

"Did he really? How generous of him." I raise the goblet to my lips. The sweet cane rum reminds me of parties at home. It occurs to me that these Adas would tell me so much more than the king and those close to him. I know if Lula were here with them, she'd get all the information she needed. I brush my hair back and flutter my lashes at Caya. "It might be the long journey here, but I'm having a hard time recalling who El Fin is."

Caya makes a small gasping sound, bringing her talon-like nails to her lips. "Why, the Deo who would end the worlds. When all life is lived and the sun and moon no longer rise, El Fin will be there to devour existence."

Ixmel gives a haughty laugh. "I suppose it is lucky for us he was banished by his siblings into the farthest reaches of the galaxies, never to be seen again."

The next sip of rum I take goes down my windpipe, and I'm a choking, stuttering mess. That can't be right. I've never heard of such a deity. And even if I had, there's no way that my power, my magical hacking, comes from *that*.

"Are you well, Lady Siphon?" Ixmel asks. "We can get help."

I shake my head quickly. This might be my only chance to get information from people not related to the king. "What about the rot? Do you remember when it first started? I'm sure it must have been terrible for you."

"As if it was yesterday," Caya says, ruffling her parakeet feathers.

"Three years, almost," says the delicate girl. She doesn't offer her name, so in my head I call her the Daisy.

"Not long after the uprising." Ixmel sloshes some drink on his chest but doesn't seem to care. "I remember because I was away with the princess on the Isla de Ayer, signing a peace treaty—"

The Daisy scoffs behind her goblet. "Is peace treaty what we call marriage prospects?"

Clearly, I have found the best gossip in all the land. When I drink again, the cane rum is sweet but doesn't burn like before.

Ixmel's smile is positively devilish. "Poor Princess Iris, having to fetch a new bride for her father while still mourning her mother's death."

The adas share a real, true moment of silence. None of the snide smiles reserved for the rest of the royal gossip. I think I understand Iris's anger a little bit more. Maybe the reason I was so surprised that she was the princess is because she never refers to the king as her father.

"I didn't notice a new queen," I say.

Ixmel's eyes sweep the crowd around us before he says, "The engagement never happened. We returned to bloodshed and ruin. On the night of the half moon, the outerlands split open and the rot spilled out."

Caya makes a strangled sound, like a bird being choked. "I was in my nest when the rot claimed its first forest. We fled here to the castle and have been here ever since."

"Everyone has made their way to the castle," the Daisy says. Her coral-pink lips glisten with drink. "It's easy to forget that the ground is crumbling beneath our feet when there's cane rum and food flowing liberally."

"Blessings to his name," they all say again with the same fake enthusiasm I reserve for when Alex cooks.

I want to ask why the rot started in the outerlands, and where the other Guardians of Adas are, and why do they keep blessing the king in that way, like someone is listening or watching them?

"Blessings to his name," a new voice says.

123

Caya squawks in response and the horned adas hurry to bow.

My movements are slow, fuzzy because of the sips of rum. I look up to find Arco. Under the light of the moon, he looks so impossibly not human. The gold horns sweep elegantly around the sides of his head. He changed into an open white tunic with silver thread that shimmers. When he stands still, it's like he's carved out of cold marble. But when he speaks, there's a warmth there that no other ada I've encountered seems to have.

"Lady Siphon, my sister has been looking for you," he says.

"I got lost and made some friends." I gesture to the adas, who are now tight-lipped in front of the prince.

"We won't keep her from you any longer, my prince," Ixmel says, backing away with his head still bent.

Then they're all gone, leaving me alone with Arco.

"Do you have the night off?" I ask.

Arco frowns, keeping his hands gripped behind his back. "What do you mean?"

"You're not writing anything down." I tap my nails on the sides of my wooden goblet.

"Not until my father presents you tonight. I'm prepared should anything out of the ordinary arise." The prince smiles and reaches behind his ear. His fountain pen. He hands it to me. The wood is smooth and elegantly carved with gold symbols. The metal nib still has ink dried on it. It's a strange thing to be holding in the middle of a fairy feast, but it's been a strange sort of day.

"So, you're like the court stenographer," I say.

"I don't know what that means, Lady Siphon. Come, I'll take you to the others."

He takes his pen back and leads me through the crowd. Walking with Arco is easier than following behind Palita, because he waits for me. That and people part for him. They bow and offer kisses and smiles.

The deeper we go into the castle gardens, the harder it is for me to focus. I remember reading about these feasts in my books, but seeing it in real life is different. This is the island created by El Terroz. He gave life to these creatures. Adas with skin like tree bark. Bright eyes that whorl like melted gold. Lashes that are soft feathers instead of hair. The sweatier and drunker everyone gets, the faster clothes seem to come off. I can't untangle my emotions, so I look away and focus on the things that are familiar. How strange it is that this ada celebration can remind me of home. Not the dirty dancing, but the other stuff.

The music has the same rhythm as my mom's favorite songs, and the trays of food are coated in salt and cumin and oregano. If I close my eyes, I'm in my living room again, celebrating an equinox instead. Maybe Arco is right. Maybe my power is the missing piece. Maybe I belong here and now. There is so much of my magic that I don't know about and haven't explored. A power that could come from a Deo I've never even heard of. Here, I don't have to pretend that I'm okay. I can just be.

We come to a stop at a throne carved from some sort of blue crystal. The ground beneath it is salt white, like the ground outside the castle walls. Behind the throne is a row of emerald hedges dotted with hibiscus flowers.

I want to tell Arco that this is the most beautiful place I've ever seen.

But that's when I see the metallic thing glinting inside the throne. I stagger back.

Petrified within the stone is an ada. His eyes are wide open, his final cry frozen forever.

I open my mouth and draw in a breath to scream, but cool fingers close over my mouth from behind and pull me into a hedge maze. The branches and leaves part, making room for us within the brush. Arco lets go but keeps his finger pressed to his lips.

"Don't scream," Arco says.

"You can't tell someone not to scream and then shove them inside a flower bush!" I hiss.

"I apologize. I should have warned you about the throne. I forget you've never been here. You mustn't bring attention to it when you're in front of my father."

"*Why?*"

"It upsets him. The last person who screamed was locked in the tower for an entire turn."

"Yeah, well, it upsets *me* when I see a body frozen inside of a crystal throne."

"It is not what you think."

"There's no way you know what I think," I say sharply. I realize too late that this is probably not how one should talk to a fairy prince whose father seems to have some serious issues. But Arco continues without pause.

"You think that my father is monstrous to do such a thing."

"Would I be wrong?"

"The ada within the throne is my grandfather, King Eterno. He and my uncle betrayed my father long ago."

I want to note that his father seems to get betrayed a lot, but that seems rude, so I keep my thoughts to myself.

"Why did he do that?" I whisper. It's not that I don't trust my voice. It's that an enclosed space shared with a fairy prince feels like it calls for whispers. "Put King Eterno in the throne, I mean."

Arco shakes his head, takes a step closer. Beneath the delicate floral spray of these purple flowers, there's the scent of salt and lemongrass on his skin.

"When Adas die," he explains, "when most creatures born of pure godly magic or the earth die, we return to that same earth. We become something more—a buttonwood or ceiba tree in the jungle, a cactus in the desert. Even the most ancient of mermaids become great coral reefs when they go beyond. Father won't give King Eterno the right to become something greater, so he—"

"Keeps him permanently iced while he sits on him every single day," I finish, grateful that the shadows of the hedge cover my grimace. "Kind of sucks being named Eterno and then being *eternally* frozen inside glass. I'm not sure if that's irony or just bad luck."

"You have a funny way of speaking." Arco's picks up a fallen hibiscus flower and tucks it behind my ear. A warm sensation spreads from that spot down to my neck. "We haven't had someone from your realm in my father's collection in some time."

Collection. I hate that he says that. I hate that his pretty smile and soft voice are enough to lull me into a false sense of safety. And yet, I wonder, is he talking about my dad?

"Can you take me to see my father?" I ask. "Please."

Arco steps away from me, standing directly under the silver

moonlight. I push down the swell of emotion that gathers in the pit of my stomach. I tell myself it's because I haven't eaten.

"This is as far as you can see him, Lady Siphon." Arco cocks his head to the side, a gesture I take to mean I should stand beside him. When I follow Arco's gaze up and crane my head back, I see a tower—the same one I first noticed when I was dehydrated and Iris had to drag me the rest of the way. There is a single small window at the very top, and a shadow paces back and forth in front of it. "He's up there."

"Your father said I'd be able to see my father again," I remind him.

"And you can. From here."

"But—That could be anyone!"

"I can't lie. Your father is in that cell tower."

I hate the way he carefully uses his words. I crack my knuckles. Ball my hands into fists. I remember how Nova corrected me, told me to never keep my thumb inside when I make a fist, otherwise I would break something. Would it hurt to punch a fairy prince?

I make a growling sound, anger rolling across my skin. "I hate all of you."

Arco sighs but does not defend his dad. "We must return to the feast. The presentation of the guardians will begin soon."

Our hands brush against each other, and I feel the buzz of my magic reaching. It's been reaching since we got here. Since I fought Alcyone and tasted her star magic. I scrape my nails against my palms to make the sensation go away. Arco doesn't seem to notice. The hedge branches answer to him, parting as we walk out and return to the garden throne.

"I apologize for upsetting you," Arco tells me. "Wait here. I'll tell my sister I've found you."

He takes my hand and presses a soft kiss to it, so quickly I wonder if I imagined it because then he's gone, blending into the revelry, which has tripled in capacity. Bodies press against each other, some with wings, some with horns, some with serpent bodies slithering all over the place.

I look back up to the tower where my father paces back and forth. Despite everything that's happened, I have to say goodbye. That this time he can't forget. That I will be back for him. But Arco told me to wait here.

It's a good thing I never said yes.

10

The girl was born in the cavity of her father's chest.

She began as small as an acorn and grew, always reaching

for El Fin's shadow.

—LOST STORIES OF ADAS, ARCO,
SON OF THE ORCHID QUEEN

The hedges open up for me like an embrace. I weave through the narrow path of the gardens and focus on the tower. I can't quite place why it feels familiar, or why the enclosed space makes my heart kick-start like a motor, but then I remember Alex recounting the labyrinth in Los Lagos. Her nightmares of teeth and monsters. This one is a bit different with wildflowers opening up to drink the moonlight, and couples searching for dark corners.

When I get to the other side of the hedge, I'm at the bottom of winding stone steps that lead to up to the tower. I peer down over the side of the wall at the roaring sea, the sharp rocks below. There are no guards posted and I know this will be my only chance.

From here I can see the entire gardens. The feast in full swing. It reminds me of the Mermaid Parade in Coney Island and how the crowds looked like one giant mass of arms and heads and legs. I see the blue glint of the throne and look away because I don't want to think of King Cirro trapping his father in there forever.

I reach the top of the steps panting and dry-mouthed. The open courtyard has four paths for me to take. Any of them can lead up, but which one? I look back down to the feast. No one seems to notice me up here. Sometimes you can be the most important or special person in a room or at a party and people still see past you because all they want is to be around you, not with you. That's fine by me if I'll go undetected.

The first archway leads to a guard post. The guard in question is passed out with his head on the ledge, black moss growing in the cracks of the salt bricks. I hold my breath and back away slowly. The second leads to a locked gate. The third leads to what might be the keys to the gate. Except the keys are with one of the four guards sitting around a wooden table covered in coins, jewels, and wooden goblets. I catch a glimpse of green armor, horns, and hooved feet.

I press myself against the wall.

"I should relieve Oyari," one of them says in a gruff baritone.

"Oyari has probably relieved *himself*," says a squeaky voice that reminds me of rodents. "Come, Niandro. Give me your wager before the sun rises."

There's the plink of coins. "My month's earnings that the Siphon of Rot doesn't make the crossing to the outerlands."

"I wouldn't be so sure," says a third voice. This one is low, contemplative. "You didn't see her when Princess Iris brought her in. I thought she'd die right them and there. But she lived and she defeated Alcyone."

They're *betting* on me? I am both indignant that they think I'm going to die and relieved that at least one person thinks I'm worthwhile.

"I'm with Niandro," says a fourth one. I recognize the voice as Alma and nerves twist in my gut. I should get out of here. But a masochistic part of me wants to hear what she is going to say. "That girl will be her own ruin. Let the princess have her way. She lost one garrison. What's another? Traitorous wretch. The princess cares for nothing and no one."

"Oye," the squeaky bookmaker says. "Don't let her hear you."

There another rattle, like dice or stone. Niandro's gruff voice clears. "Three stones that Prince Arco takes one of the river maids to bed."

Their laughter is booming, their voices getting tangled as they talk over each other.

"Prince Arco hasn't taken a mate since he became the Scribe."

"You're just jealous he has no eyes for you. Neither of the twins do."

"The king should have banished his daughter when he had the chance."

"I say the whole thing is lost. It has been."

"Oye, take his drink away before he makes us all as miserable as he."

"I mean it. I dreamt it. A dark wave that swallowed the island whole."

"In that case, I take my wager on the siphon back."

The shrill bookmaker cackles. "Too late! If these are our last days, I will return to El Terroz rich and with a belly full of rum."

"It's Niandro's turn to fetch the bottle!"

They descend into shouting, and then there's the clop of hooves on the ground. Approaching *me*. I flit as fast as I can to the fourth and final archway. The cacophony of the party covers my heavy breathing. I follow the steps that lead down narrow stone steps. I don't know what level I'm on or how to get back to the gardens. I'm so relieved to see a door covered in ivy that I don't think before I open it.

My path is interrupted by two small adas who remind of Palita. Their faces are less wrinkled. They carry trays with empty dishes piled taller than their eyes can see, which is probably why they walk past me like I'm not even there.

King Cirro's voice is like sandpaper against my ears. "If you lost her, I will have your head."

"She won't go anywhere. Not while we have her father."

There's a sound I don't recognize at first. It's a whimper, but part of me can't believe Iris would be capable of making that sound. "Your mother should have stopped pushing after Arco was born. All you have brought me is disappointment and ruin."

Anger plunges deep within me. How can he talk to her that way? I'm embarrassed for her, and then guilty because I did this. He thinks I'm gone. There's only one thing I can do. I step into the archway and announce myself.

"Finally!" I say.

King Cirro has Iris by her jaw. She looks like a rag doll, her long braids hanging down her back. He starts and lets her go.

"Lady Siphon," the king says, spreading his arms wide. It takes all of me not to flinch. "There you are."

"I got bad directions, and then I got lost in the crowds."

Faint light pulses from within the gems of his crown. From the depictions in my book, I always thought it would be brighter, more resplendent. The heavy thing tips forward and he rights it quickly. A sharp canine flashes when he smiles at me, taking my wrist to pull me into the somber sitting room.

"There you are. The court is eager to meet you," he says.

Iris opens another door on the opposite side of the room. She avoids my eyes, and her steely resolve returns. The three of us are quiet, but I'm accustomed to this kind of silence.

King Cirro doesn't let me go. I get ready for another long, winding path back, but we step out into the garden. At the throne. King Eterno frozen in an endless scream. When the door shuts behind Iris, branches and leaves grow over it. I look up at the tower. The light in the topmost room where my dad is being kept has gone out.

The music is replaced by an excited buzz of voices and crashing waves. The king's subjects all gather around the throne.

King Cirro is resplendent, dressed in all white, like a beam of moonlight come to life. He moves like a man who has always loved attention, and the creatures of the court shower him with kisses and flower petals from the palms of their hands and claws. I look over my shoulder and notice the Daisy and Ixmel. They don't smile but clap and go through the motions.

King Cirro sits, leaving me with Iris as my personal guard. A conch horn blows from somewhere, and the crowd parts to reveal Arco leading a procession of five I can only assume are the other guardians. I remember how the guard said Iris and Arco were twins. They could not be more different.

"Am I supposed to be up there?" I whisper to Iris. I have a terrible premonition it's going to be like getting picked on in gym class. "I mean, I'm perfectly fine waiting here until we have to leave for this crossing."

There a bruise blooming along her jaw in the shape of fingers, but she stands taller than ever. "The king loves spectacle, and you, Siphon, are now his greatest oddity."

"I'm not his," I whisper.

A smirk brightens her severe face before she returns her attention to the procession in front of us.

The guardians walk up around the throne, each one dressed in black scaled armor that hugs their bodies. The crowd cheers. I wonder if they've all been plucked from King Cirro's Sideshow of Death, or if they're new, like me.

There's a boy who reminds me of a tree with his brown skin and spring-green hair and eyes. The next girl has a head of silver hair like Alcyone, but with dark brown skin and younger features. Beside her is a dark-haired girl with pearlescent scars on both sides of her neck and patches of something glittering on the olive brown skin of her forearms. The fourth person is slim and tall with hair so black it's like an inkblot. The fifth is a girl with straight bangs that shield her eyes and raven wings at rest. I recognize her as the one who won her fight just before I did.

"Your turn, Siphon," Iris says, giving me a tiny shove.

135

ZORAIDA CÓRDOVA

I was right. This is exactly like getting picked last in gym. Possibly even worse because every ada and human gathered in the courtyard for the Salt Moon feast is staring at me. Why is this silence louder than music and the surrounding sea? I gather my dress, so I don't trip this time, and follow the stone path that leads to the throne area. Here there is no grass, only hard white rock. I stand beside the winged girl and allow myself to breathe for the first time since leaving Iris's side.

"My Lady Siphon!" King Cirro shouts my name as if he didn't just see me, as if I didn't just catch him saying cruel things to his daughter. He extends his bejeweled hand in my direction, and the crowd takes this as an invitation to keep shouting and throwing tokens of good luck at our feet—flowers, the caps of mushrooms, seeds, bits of rice.

King Cirro grips the armrests of his throne and, with some effort, pushes himself to his feet. It is a momentary crack in his appearance, the way his face changed in the war room when I wouldn't give him the answer he wanted.

"My kin," he says. "Today is the beginning of a new day for our kingdom. The Salt Moon has blessed us with the latest addition to my Guardians of Adas. Foretold by the siren herself, she has already bested Alcyone of the Starlark realm. I present Lady Siphon."

The king pauses for a unified holler from the crowd. I do my very best impression of a deer in the headlights, then wave while wishing I could vanish into thin air. Claws and hands slap my back in what I assume is *Congratulations* or *Welcome to our realm, please sacrifice your life for us or your father and your whole world dies too.*

136

As I'm given some space, I notice Iris is the only one, other than me, who isn't cheering. Her eyes are drawn to her father with the same anger she reserved for the rot.

"Tomorrow they make the crossing to the outerlands. But tonight"—King Cirro's voice is luminous and weighty—"we feast and pray the Deos light their path."

There's a ring of cheers and hooves stomping on the ground. The words, "Blessings to his name!" are shouted, but unlike Caya and Ixmel and the Daisy, these fairies mean it. It is a frenzy that unnerves me.

As soon as he sits, King Cirro is surrounded by dozens of adas who show their adoration by presenting him with small tithes—bowls of green berries and trays of figs dripping with honey, chalices brimming with spiced rum, and glass bottles filled with tiny bloody hearts.

My stomach cramps, and despite the gore amid the beauty, I realize I'm hungry.

"Do you want to dance with us, Siphon?" someone asks me.

I dab at the corners of my eyes and blink until the blurriness is gone. The five other members of the king's guardians lead me away from the throngs and back out into the gardens. I notice how they stay in the king's line of sight.

The one who spoke to me is the thin fairy with slender, sharp features and black hair that curls like wisps of smoke. Up close, I'm startled by how violet those eyes are.

"I don't know this song." But that's kind of a lie. The music isn't too different from what I was dancing to at my Deathday. There are just more pan flutes. I seem to have traded one party for another, and I'd laugh if half of me wasn't completely terrified of what I'm supposed to do now.

"I can introduce you to the song. Song, meet Eliza." Violet Eyes smiles, and I find myself laughing earnestly for the first time since we got here.

"Well, in that case," I say, and give a single shimmy of my shoulders.

"I'm Lin, and this is Calliope, Peridot, Márohu, and Nadira."

I can't keep track of all the names and faces. This is like the first day of school all over again, except here I can't get away with sitting in a corner and reading my book.

I swallow my nerves and ask, "Did you all just get here too?"

The tree boy, Peridot, shakes his head. "To varying degrees. This will be our first crossing."

"It was to be Alcyone's first as well," says Calliope. The only thing she shares with the girl I fought is the same silver hair and bright eyes. Where was it King Cirro said she was from? The Starlark realm. It sounds familiar, but I don't know from where. Her anger that I've taken her friend's place is clear.

"Yeah, well, saved her the trouble, I guess."

I remember the sensation of holding the whip made of starlight, the power of it. I rub my palms on my skirt until the feeling subsides.

The girl with wings holds a hand out in front of Calliope. "She lost in the arena fairly, Calliope. It's not this girl's fault. Besides, the siren chose her."

"She's not a girl. She's a leech." Calliope looks to the others, waiting for them to agree, but they don't. Peridot coughs behind his hand, but edges closer to Calliope to assure her of his alliances.

"I didn't mean to hurt her," I say, heart racing. I ball my hands against my belly. "I'm still getting used to my power."

"Then you shouldn't *be* here," Calliope counters. "You'll kill us all."

Lin frowns apologetically. But the Starlark girl is right. She's saying the things I don't want to say, don't want to even think. It's why those guards were taking wagers. They think I'm not ready. I'm not Alex. I said it myself. I don't know why it's worse thinking it in relation to this. Having your insecurities confirmed by strangers sucks. I breathe fast to stave off the tears that prickle in the corners of my eyes. That's when I notice Iris marching to our little group. I never thought I'd be so happy to see the angry princess marching toward me.

"Eliza, I am to escort you back to your room," Iris says, stopping at the center of us. "The rest of you make a short night of it. We leave before first light."

"But the night is young and we have a lot of *not dancing* to do with Eliza," Lin says, and is met by a round of stifled giggles— except from Calliope. I bet Iris loves her.

"Haven't you had enough feasts?" Iris asks, exasperated.

The girl with the neck scars, who I'm pretty sure is Nadira, raises her goblet. "We've had enough of many things, Princess, and somehow, feasts are not one of them."

Iris's eyes narrow, but I realize there's nothing she can do to the girl—nothing she can do to any of us without upsetting her dad or sabotaging the crossing. I know that there's one thing that scares her.

"Before first light," Iris repeats. Her eyes swivel to Nadira unkindly.

I wave at Lin and the others and follow Iris through the mass of bodies. I hold my breath as more trays of food are brought out bearing crackling fat over meats that smell an awful lot like roasted pork. Sharp hunger pangs stab at me, and I only walk faster because there's a small part of me that wants to stay to dance under the Salt Moon and shove food down my throat and laugh with all the beautiful, strange, wondrous creatures scattered across this lawn.

But then I think of King Eterno, frozen in that glass throne for all to see, of my dad waiting in that tower, of the wagers that I won't survive whatever this crossing is, and I force myself to keep marching behind the warrior princess. Her anger rolls off her in waves, and she periodically looks back to make sure I'm there. Where else would I go?

Iris says nothing when she deposits me back in my room, and that's fine because I've decided that I hate her and I hate this place.

I find my Deathday dress and dig in the pockets for the last candy bar I squirreled away and tear the wrapping open. I eat half. What if Nova's bracelet doesn't work and as soon as I eat the food of Adas, I'll lose my memories like my dad did? I know I won't be able to hold off for much longer. When I devour the chocolate, my taste buds explode with so much sensation that it almost hurts to keep chewing. I know that part of the hunger I feel runs deep for other reasons. The fear in Alcyone's face when I siphoned her starlight power flashes in my eyes. I can hear the buzzing sound of the siren's presence. The way my magic is reacting to this place scares me, and I have no one to talk to about it. What if being in Adas changes me in a way no one will recognize if I make it out?

When, I correct myself.

When I go home. *When* I see my family.

With my eyes closed, I breathe until I'm calm. As calm as I'll ever get under the circumstances. For a moment, my mind conjures a memory of Arco and hibiscus flowers, but I push the thought away because the following image is Iris being hurt by her father, and then I cycle back and think of mine.

I go to the basin to wash my face. Palita must have changed the water. She also left me a minty paste to brush my teeth with, alongside a leaf. A literal leaf.

I slip out of my clothes, then change into a gray sleeping shift that makes me feel too exposed.

I follow the cacophony of night creatures and raucous music to the open window. I wonder what my family is doing back home right now. Are they looking for us? Do they know Nova is gone too? What would my sisters do if they were here instead of me? I keep asking myself that question, but it doesn't matter, does it? Because they aren't here. I am.

I make a promise to myself, one only I can keep. I might be new to my power. I might be scared, hungry, tired, softer than the others. But no matter what it takes, I will find a way back home. I have to.

I am my mother's daughter, and she raised me to survive.

PART III

THE WARRIOR

11

El Papa unlocked the moon from his eye
and gave it to the night sky to watch over the darkness.

—TALES OF THE DEOS,
FELIPE THOMÁS SAN JUSTINIO

As much as I don't want to admit it, my first night in Adas is the best sleep I've ever had. I wake rested but ravenous, with my mouth tasting the way an old sneaker smells. When I rub my lips together, they crack. Palita is zooming around the room but stops when I sit up and kick off the covers.

"You best eat something. It's a long journey to the outerlands." She points to a small silver tray covered by a blue glass serving dome.

"Can you slow down for ten seconds? You're giving me whiplash."

Palita halts in front of me. Today she's got white flowers woven around the tiny bun atop her head. Her permanent forehead wrinkle of disapproval deepens. "A terrina is only as good as how quickly and silently they get their work done."

"Is that the kind of fairy you are?"

She clicks her tongue at me. "I'm no fae, girl child. I am a terrina."

Terrina? I want to ask her more, but my hunger wakes with the rest of my body, my stomach making embarrassing sounds.

"Eat," Palita grumbles.

I touch the leather bracelet Nova gifted me. I remember the worries I had from last night. After drinking sips of rum and water, I don't *feel* any different. How will I be able to tell? My dad said a magical token would help. I wonder if they're feeding him in his tower. I wonder what I'm going to have to tell my mom when we get back. If we get back.

I try to lick my teeth, but I don't have enough saliva, so I drink the fresh water. I hate that for the first time in my life, food makes me feel uncomfortable. "I don't know if I can eat that."

"You can if it's the only thing you've got." Palita shuffles over to a trunk and pulls out jewel-tone tunics and pants, leather sandals and belts. I wonder if the king hoards clothes just in case they have guests or a new batch of kidnapped humans.

"I wish I had a guarantee. Or at the very least a landline to our family psychic," I say, and chuckle to myself. The humor vanishes and worry returns. "I don't want to forget."

Palita does not stop working while she talks. "Does the tree forget the taste of rain? Does the mountain forget the sun at night?"

"I've never asked," I say.

The terrina chuckles, but I see the way her beady eyes linger on the treat on my bedside. "I forgot my name, so I took a new one. It was inevitable for me."

I reach for the nightstand and unwrap the half-eaten chocolate bar. I offer it to Palita. "Want a piece?"

"I lost the taste long ago," the Terrina mutters, but licks her lips, nonetheless. "I lost many things long ago. But the girl child is not Palita."

She takes the chocolate and eats it, wrapper and all.

Licking her fingers clean, the terrina gives me a curious smile and flicks my wrist, right where my sun bracelet is. "The girl child is well protected. For a time. There is so much of it in the eternal island of El Terroz."

I rub the spot above my wrist. When I close my eyes and press my fingertips to the silver pendant, I can almost see Nova hunched over his desk braiding the leather and blessing this gift. I see the light of his power.

I am protected.

"Wait, how long have you been here?" I ask.

"Never mind that. Eat." Palita shuts down the conversation by shoving my clothes into a bag.

Curious at the offerings of the morning, I lift the glass serving dome and find bundles of bright red berries that are covered in some sort of fuzzy hair, stinky cheese that looks to be made up of mold more than anything else, flatbread, and a glass full of juice.

"That doesn't look edible anyway," I say.

But once again, Palita is gone. I drink the orange-colored juice, and I'm surprised at the sweet taste of papaya. It's my mom's favorite fruit, but I always refused to eat it because of the way the seeds smell kind of like barf when you first cut it open.

When I'm finished, I wash my face and get dressed in the clothes laid out for me on a chair. There's a pair of soft riding pants the color of tree bark, a deep-blue sleeveless tunic, and a thin leather vest stitched with what must be the king's crest on the left side—a Pegasus taking flight from vines that drip rain from the thorns. I've never worn clothes that fit me this well, stretching over my wide curves and belly. I have to turn in the mirror over and over to make sure that it's me in the mirror. Lula always did tell me not to hide under baggy clothes.

"Are you done admiring yourself?" Iris's amused voice comes from the open door. Her two pink braids are tied together at her nape, and her fuchsia armor is fitted to every curve and lean muscle of her body. Her tawny brown skin is dewy, but I notice the bruise on her jaw, like a smudge of dirt.

My face turns red, and I stick my tongue at her back like the mature guardian I am. "Actually, I'm not, thanks for asking."

Iris doesn't smile exactly, but she doesn't grimace at me either. "Collect your things, Lady Siphon. We must leave now to make the crossing by nightfall."

I pick up the bag Palita made for me. I should have thanked her for doing that. As I fix the strap around my torso, I give my Deathday dress one last look. That gown has been through a sacrificial ceremony, a portal, and my first (and hopefully last) arena fight. But I won't have any use for it wherever we're going. *The crossing* doesn't exactly sound like we're sailing to a tropical paradise to drink virgin piña coladas. Still, I tug the ribbon from the waist and tie it around my ponytail. That way, I can keep a piece of it with me.

"I forget how sentimental human mortals are," Iris says, huffing as she adjusts her sword belt.

As she walks, I make a face at her back. "We can't all be heartless and immortal adas who don't know how to love."

For a moment, Iris stops. Maybe the heartless comment was way harsh. I'm about to apologize when she glances over her shoulder, her lashes fluttering slowly. A dark eyebrow quirks when she says, "On the contrary, Lady Siphon. Adas feel everything stronger than your kind, which is why we are able to understand our emotions instead of becoming ruled by them. It's also why adas make the best lovers."

Her mouth blooms into a smile as she turns, leaving me frozen speechless, my face hot enough to compete with the rising sun. I shake out of my silly embarrassment and hurry. Her legs are so long I have to leap three times to catch up to her.

The castle is, to put it gently, hungover as hell. There are sleeping adas everywhere—passed out in rooms with doors left wide open, in the arms of statues in the hallway, tucked away in little nooks inside walls, hanging from the chandeliers. There's a fairy with purple butterfly wings perching on the marbled horn of an ada sprawled out on the yard. I have never seen so many naked bodies before. My cheeks burn hot because I feel like I'm intruding on something that isn't meant for me to see, but this realm doesn't seem to have the same modesty rules as back home. I slap my cheeks and give myself an internal pep talk. *Okay, Rose. If you're going to survive this place, you need to stop blushing.*

"King Cirro wasn't kidding about the feast," I say. "It's like New Year's at my house. Though we never let anyone stay over unless they're too drunk to drive. And we have guest pajamas."

"They call him the King of Plenty for a reason." Iris's words are clipped. "They'll find a new reason to feast before the sun is at its peak."

"I thought they called him the Bastard King," I say, then slap my hand over my mouth.

This seems to elicit a chuckle from the warrior princess. "The king is called many things by many of our folk. However, the Bastard King of Adas is his preferred title."

Our soles slap against the cobblestones, and the first drops of humidity gather at my temples. "No offense, but why would he prefer that?"

"I suppose he believed it took the power from those who did not want him taking the throne."

"Did it?"

"You saw the state of my grandfather, King Eterno, at the Salt Moon feast," she says, and lets that hang between us as we enter the courtyard in front of the castle. She doesn't try to rationalize it the way Arco did. She's simply stating a fact.

Being out here, I vaguely remember her carrying me through the archways before I got sick on her. What good grace was returning for Iris is gone when she says, "Keep up, little Siphon."

"Yeah, well, I don't have legs as long as a giraffe."

She snaps around, flustered for the first time since we've met. "I do not have giraffe legs. And it is not my fault you are so small."

When we reach the sentries at the archways, I notice she slows down by a pace or two. The guards let us past, and at the sight of what's waiting at the bottom of the castle steps, I zoom past Iris. Waiting for us are the five other guardians, a dozen green soldiers, and black horses for each one of us.

"No way," I say, breathless.

One of the horses is a Pegasus eating from Arco's hand. Its

wings flap when I get close, and the warm breeze at the end of its feathers tickles my cheek.

"Oh my gods," I say, marveling as the creature chews and shakes its mane. In the light, the black sheen takes on the look of an oil slick, like a New York City street after the rain. "I can't believe it."

"This is Huracán. She was a gift from the king when I chose my future as Scribe," Prince Arco says, stroking the Pegasus on a golden spot between her eyes. It's only then that I notice the leather bag strapped across Arco's chest. I didn't realize he'd be coming too. He's dressed in a white open tunic, and a floor-length silk scarf is looped around his neck. I decide that Arco is the most beautiful ada I've ever seen in my life. He brushes back a stray raven curl, and the sensation of butterfly wings on my skin overwhelms me until I remember his tricky words last night. How stupid I was for thinking he would *really* take me to see my father. Not to mention what the guards said about him. Huracán whinnies, like she can sense my anxious stream of thought.

"I did not expect you would see us off, Brother." Iris leads her white horse between us. Its mane is braided with gold threads. I still can't believe they're twins. Together like this, it hits me. Arco and Iris. Together, their name means rainbow. I would point it out, except for the ire on Iris's face as her brother ignores her.

"Hello, Lirico," Arco says, to the horse with a gentle greeting. Then levels dark eyes to his sister's. "After you."

Iris tilts her head to the side. "Are you intending to join us? This is a perilous quest. Or has the king ordered you to?"

"It was my idea, not Father's. As the scribe of Adas, I must document everything, no matter how perilous."

"And how would you fight when there is danger? The pen tucked in your pretty curls?" There's a silent stare-down, and I wish I had something to snack on like popcorn or those Cool Ranch Doritos that Lula likes to hide in the pantry so Alex and I don't steal them.

"Even pens have sharp ends, Sister," he says, grinning despite the steel in his words.

"Very well." Iris gives him a curt bow, then turns to me with less ceremony. "Can you ride?"

"It's a bicycle with legs, sure."

Iris sighs and stalks off muttering about how she doesn't understand half the things I say. Her voice is commanding, doling out tasks, which are completed right away. Guards ready the saddles, and the other guardians and the siren climb aboard like pros with the exception of the winged girl, who must fly. Nervousness bubbles in my gut because, all of a sudden, the horse they bring over to me looks ten feet tall.

"Wait a minute," I say, realizing that six of the saddled horses given to the Guardians of Adas are not ordinary horses at all. They're Pegasi too, only their wings are strapped against their sides with thick leather straps. "Aren't we supposed to take these off?"

Arco shakes his head but keeps his eyes cast down. "My father won three dozen of these creatures from the king of La Isla de Anochecer. When they arrived here, six of them flew home, back across the sea. The others caught sickness and died. My father did not want them to fly away, and so he wanted to cut their wings. But I convinced him there was another way."

I want to say that there is not supposed to be sickness in Adas. All the stories call it paradise. But then again, we are going to destroy a rot that's killing the rain forests, so, maybe I'm wrong. I gently touch one of the feathers. The Pegasi can fly out of here. That thought is squashed when I consider that I would be leaving my father behind. I'd have to face my mother without him. I'd put my sisters in danger by coming back to rescue him. I wonder: Does he even want to be rescued? It took him six months of being in Florida before he returned home with Nova. I'd have these answers if I had only gotten to *talk* to him before we left.

Huracán huffs and shakes her mane. I choose to believe she feels my anguish.

"How come your Pegasus isn't bound?" I ask.

"A Pegasus is the hardest creature to break," Arco says, holding the beastie by the reins and giving her a gentle pat. "I was able to do that with Huracán, and so I am allowed to keep her free."

Iris gallops over on Lirico. "You cannot tame a Pegasus, Brother, only gain its trust. That is why Huracán has not fled, not because she is broken."

Arco takes a steadying breath but doesn't answer her. Instead, he helps me up into the saddle. When he lets go of my hand, a lock of his hair falls over his face. Lula always talked about how much she loved when her hunter's hair did that, and Alex is obsessed with playing with Rishi's new bangs. I never understood what the big deal was, but now, my fingers itch to reach for it. To tuck the curl behind his ear.

"Are you well, Lady Siphon?" Arco asks, and I realize he's been talking to me and I've been staring.

"Hmm? Oh, yes. Totally, thank you." I settle into the saddle and hold on for dear life. Ma, Alex, and Lula have all taken me aside separately and talked about boys and sex. Ma eventually stops speaking in English when she's flustered, and her Spanish syllables squish together in a beautiful but confusing way. Lula, on the other hand, had props—condoms and fruit. I kicked her out of my room. Alex was almost helpful. She said, "Don't be afraid to say what's in your heart, whoever they turn out to be." Nova was second worse in a protective-big-brother way. Everyone is so busy trying to protect me from something or other that I think they can't see past their own mistakes to realize that I'm not them. I let out a long sigh.

That downward mental spiral all because I want to touch Arco's perfect hair.

Okay, Rose, I reprimand myself. *You can't just forget yourself because a cute fairy prince smiles at you.*

Thankfully, Iris blows on a conch shell to alert us that we're leaving. Hooves pound on the ground, kicking up clouds of fine white sand. Two guards remain in the rear, waiting on me. One of them is Alma, who laughs under her breath. The other is a slender ada with pale green skin and a bald head decorated with intricate tattooed swirls around the back.

"Kick his flanks," Alma says, exasperated.

I remember that she thinks I'm a fraud. But she isn't the Siphon of Galaxies, or whatever I'm supposed to be. I am. I have to succeed if only so she loses a bet. And also, because the weight of this realm and mine is resting on my shoulders. Suddenly, I feel nauseous.

"I don't want to hurt him." I gently pat my Pegasus's mane, but my entire body is compressed into an anxious ball as he keeps his head down, eating the remnants of a pale purple fruit.

I give him a little kick, but he only glances back at me. What was the name they said? Damn Arco's perfect, distracting hair.

"Tortuga needs a bit of a firm hand," Arco says, cantering in a circle to get back to me. He gives the order for the guards behind us to go ahead.

"Apologies, my prince," Alma says. "King Cirro gave us orders to keep by your side."

Arco's dark brows draw together in a frown, and for the first time, I see the resemblance to Iris more than ever. "Very well, Alma, you may go. Vita, you may stay."

Vita's armor looks like hundreds of tiny scalloped green leaves stacked on top of one another. Instead of a sword or a bow and arrow, she has a spear with a bone arrowhead attached to her saddle.

I smirk at Alma as she kicks her steed and rides away. I'd snap my fingers at her, but I'm afraid I'd fall off.

When Huracán gets close, she nudges Tortuga's snout with hers, and we trot along at an easy pace. Huracán and Tortuga neigh and whinny at each other in a way that feels like they're having their own conversation. I've decided that I don't like horseback riding at all, and if I get any more tense, I'm going to petrify into a little boulder.

"What do you suppose they're saying to each other?" Arco asks.

I know he's trying to distract me with his straight posture and glistening golden skin and ridiculous smile. It's working.

"Maybe they're comparing their lunches or talking smack about us. Or Tortuga's complaining about how these straps are too tight."

"Uncanny, really." Arco laughs. I study his posture to copy it, which makes the ride less bumpy when I straighten. I have to keep remembering to look forward because, otherwise I'll ride Tortuga here right into the other Pegasus's wings.

We leave the castle behind for the cool shade of the rain forest. When the fork splits, we take a right and diverge into a path darker and denser than the one we took yesterday. Curious adas the length of my palm climb out from clefts in the tree barks and watch as our company rides across a gnarled path. Furry marsupial creatures scurry over thick roots scavenging for food before disappearing into holes in the ground.

Flowers unfurl their petals as Arco rides past them, and even low-hanging vines rise up so as not to get in his way. Beams of sunlight filter from gaps in the canopy and illuminate the golden prince. His horns become resting places for neon butterflies with long limbs and horned heads. After a moment, he is covered in them, a crown of wings.

My heart feels like it's sputtering. How can a place that sings with beauty also be home to seaside ring fights and a throne with an ancient king frozen alive inside of it?

Arco reaches for a flower growing from a vine, whispers something, and then plucks it. "A rose for your thoughts," he says.

I gasp so hard I almost choke. My real name on his lips is jarring and somehow feels wrong and right at the same time. How is that even possible for roses to grow on these trees?

Still, I accept the flower and bring it to my nose. It smells like the ocean, with a bitter fragrance laced beneath it. I tuck it behind my ear. That makes two flowers he's given me, but I'm not keeping count or anything.

"Were you talking to the flower?" I ask.

"I asked if I could have it for a gift."

He talks to flowers. Pass, Alex would say.

Where's my flower, though? Lula would ask.

"Actually, I was thinking about what you said when you shoved me in that flower bush."

"Flower hedge."

"Semantics."

His beautiful mouth curls at the corners, and when he tilts his head back, the insects hitching a ride on his horns flit away at the sudden movement. "Which part of what I said?"

"I don't understand why your dad won't let King Eterno return to the earth. That's an extreme level of petty when King Cirro was the one who betrayed his father first."

Curiosity brightens Arco's eyes. He touches the pen behind his ear. I wonder if he realizes he does that. His voice is deep but playful. "I saw you speaking to Gloriana at the feast. Did she tell you that?"

I think of the adas who surrounded me at the Salt Moon feast. Caya and Ixmel, and the Daisy girl with slender golden horns—so strange and delicate. Her copper-brown skin and lovely brown eyes. She seemed not completely human or ada. Despite speaking blessings to the king, her words felt vacant, like apologizing when you're just trying to bypass an argument. Like saying you're fine when you're not. Now I realize she never said her name.

"Gloriana?" Could it be? A thrilling sensation makes me forget I'm high up on a Pegasus and nearly lose my balance. "Gloriana Palacios, who wrote *Claribelle and the Kingdom of Adas*. She was there last night?"

"She was. I didn't know her stories were known in the mortal realm. Curious."

"It was a gift from my grandfather when I was born. I never met him, though. Most brujas my age act like they've outgrown fairy tales. They were comforting, like a verbal security blanket."

I don't know if I can feel that way anymore.

"My father outlawed them for a time, but I convinced him they would make him infamous. He rather liked the idea of that."

Gloriana's stories were all about the family feud between the court. King Cirro does not come out looking good in any of those. I think I liked them more when I could shut the book and not be threatened by the fairy king himself.

I remember King Cirro in the arena watching me hurt someone. How he looked at his son with adoration. How he reminds Iris of her failures and bruised her skin. When all you have about a person is stories, it is difficult to reconcile their myth with who they truly are. Maybe that's why Dad's lies hurt worse. For so long, all I had were stories. My eyes begin to burn so I clear my throat.

"The infamous Bastard King of Adas," I say but stop short of adding *with a tomb for a throne*. King Cirro has a long list of enemies. That makes me wonder—"What about the others who started the rebellion? Were they ever caught?"

"Does it matter?" It's the first time frustration edges his words.

"My mother taught me that magic is a bargain. A healer can take an illness away from someone and die from that very sickness. A bruja can conjure rain and then choke on water filling up their lungs. If the rot appeared after the portal was made by those who rebelled against your father, then perhaps it was created from the recoil of the portal magic. Blood portals are precise, after all. Anything could have gone wrong. If that's true, it could be tied to the magic the rebels used. So yeah, it matters."

Arco watches me for a long moment. I can't tell what he thinks of me or my theory, but at least I'm posing questions. King Cirro didn't even care as long as we get rid of it.

"There is no way to know the magic the rebels used."

"Why?" I ask, though I know the answer.

"They're all dead. Iris was tasked with hunting them down and uncovering their secrets."

"My dad didn't make the portal," I say defensively. But doubt seeds into my heart. But how do I know it's the truth? He's told so many lies...

"We know. Your father was the only one who couldn't be found until yesterday. The warding around you and your family is impressive."

"Did you speak to him?" I ask. "Is he well?"

"I assure you, Eliza, he is unharmed."

I think of my father in that tower. When I was little, the women of my mother's High Circle used to talk about how brave my father was—the handsome brujo who could conjure storms and fight back against hunters preying on magical beings. Why am I disappointed that the same man escaped this world by accident? Because someone else spared his life along with a handful of others. Why can't I focus on the fact that he made it home in the end?

"Wait," I say. "You said you knew my dad didn't make the portal. How?"

He rushes to answer. "It's not what you think. He was questioned under eleuthantila poison."

"You poisoned him?" I shout, and everyone ahead of me turns to stare. Tortuga is startled into a thicket of underbrush. "But my bargain—"

Arco trots to me and seizes my reins. "Your bargain was struck after. I've been told eleuthantila poison does not cause lasting damage to mortals when the antidote is administered. It was, Lady Siphon. Eliza…"

Guilt and anger sprout in my gut. They tortured my dad, and here I am laughing with the prince and gushing over a storybook author. I lift my face to the canopy. I wish I could scream so loud that the Deos would have no other choice but to hear me. *Take us home. Give us another chance.* Those thoughts flit past. I know La Mama has already answered my plea. *The truth. An adventure of my own.* Whoever said "be careful what you ask for" was probably the smuggest person on the planet.

I take my reins back and yank. Tortuga is devouring everything green within reach. Up ahead, the rest of the group is too far away.

"We should catch up," I say.

We ride in silence for a long time. Vita brings up the rear. She's one of those people who fill the silence by singing. Something about a princess who rose from the sea and delivered treasures to islands of the world. Those who know the words sing along.

Our caravan approaches a long curtain of vines that blanket slabs of white rock. They part. One by one, we go through a dark tunnel where iridescent carapaces flit back and forth, and glowing worms carve their own paths, though some are too slow to avoid the crush of hooves. I bite down my shrill yelps every time something brushes against my shoulder in the dark.

But as the cave brightens, the sight waiting for us at the other end makes my heart leap—miles and miles of sunflowers in a rainbow of colors lean toward the sun.

Arco returns to my side and says. "Welcome to Girasol Grove."

I look back. I hope my dad is safe. I hope my sisters are searching for us. I hope… Vines shut over the tunnel, and suddenly it hits me how very far I am from home.

12

La Flor wanted color among the green.

From her blood sprouted seeds.

From her seeds flowers bloomed.

—LOST STORIES OF ADAS, ARCO,
SONG OF THE ORCHID QUEEN

An overgrown path cuts through the sunflower field. Square cobblestones dot the ground, half-buried by moss and dried grass, like the earth is swallowing them little by little. Just when I start wondering if we're ever going to get off these horses, Iris's voice rings out clearly from the front of the caravan, telling us to stop.

Small clay houses are clustered on the swollen mounds. Some have roofs covered in thick heart-shaped leaves and others are completely open wooden frames with wild ivy and buds waiting to bloom. It seems like an inconvenient architecture for rainstorms, but maybe some adas don't mind getting wet. The sun is bright in the cerulean sky, and if we were at home, I'd say it was noon.

Vita helps me off my horse and I, graceful as ever, only stumble twice. She assures me that it gets easier, but I have my doubts. My inner thighs ache and my left butt cheek is numb. The ground feels like it's wobbling beneath me, and I'm already not looking forward to getting back up on the saddle.

"How did you find your first ride?" Arco asks.

I rest my hand on the leather wing girth, then pat Tortuga's side. "I can safely say that horseback riding isn't for me."

He chuckles, and I warm at the sound. I know, *I know*, that I should be mad at him. But an irrational part of my brain isn't listening.

"Perhaps you'd like flying better," he says.

His smile makes me feel flush. My heart squeezes with an unfamiliar sensation. I focus on the grove instead of his beautiful face. "Why are we stopping? I thought Iris said it was a long journey."

Vita's eyebrow quirks up just slightly, and I recognize that as the universal sign of someone who doesn't want to say the wrong thing.

"Brother." Iris cuts me off by trotting up to us. She doesn't look at me. "Would you put your pen to use and take inventory of the supplies Lady Kaíri is gifting us?"

"Wait, we're here for supplies?" I ask. I didn't consider that we are only carrying a few changes of clothes and water.

Iris dismounts in a graceful swing of her legs. She watches her brother as she says, "How could we ask the *great* king of Adas to part with his drink and food, when he has feasts to supply for?"

Arco gives a small shake of his head. Frustration draws a ruffled sigh. "Why take from the castle stores when there is plenty in our kingdom for all?"

"Is there?" Iris waits for his reply, but Arco says nothing as he adjusts the pen behind his ear and takes off on a road that snakes around the village.

"Why are you always so mad at him?" I ask the princess once he's out of earshot. I know it's the wrong thing to ask, but I don't understand their relationship. Even when my sisters and I fight, you can still tell we love each other. I don't get the same sense from the royal twins.

Iris glowers at me before saying, "Do not presume to know me and mine, Siphon. If I recall, your own words cut down your father's spirit. *Your words* are the things he will hold on to while he is alone in that tower. Now, stay with the others. I won't tarry here, and I don't need anyone wandering off, especially you."

My nostrils flare and I'm left with pent-up frustration as she walks away from me.

"Scout's honor!" I shout and cross my fingers behind my back as I salute her with a single finger.

I give Tortuga one last pat. He doesn't look up from chomping at the curly grass as I head to the bustling village market behind the other guardians.

Two plump adas with dark brown skin and white feathers for eyelashes sit on mats of woven leaves. They grind some sort of grain in large stone mortars and speak in a rapid-fire language I can't understand. A man with the thick, furred legs of a faun stomps around me, a clay jug of water nestled between his horns. Fairy children hurry behind him, carrying baskets of strange fruits. One girl with a tail like a lizard and fluffy black hair sticks her tongue out at me, the split fork wagging in the air.

I mimic the gesture, but she's already running away. A fat orange and brown fruit falls from her basket and rolls at my feet. I pick it up and smooth the dirt off. The waxy shell is so thin that when it breaks under my thumb, seeds ooze out of a juice-filled sac.

"Gross," I say, but then the smell is so familiar, I bring it to my nose. Passion fruit, I think. I've never seen it outside the frozen Goya packets my mom brings home to make smoothies, and I didn't expect to see it here, or to look like a thousand tadpoles gestating in an egg.

"If you're not going to eat that," Lin's friendly voice comes from my right, but in a flash, Lin appears at my left. I must be tired and seeing things. Not to mention starving. I present the passion fruit like I'm handing over a poison apple in a fairy tale. "My mother used to say parcha was the fruit of the gods, but really it was the best thing humans brought to our shores."

"Humans never bring anything good to any shore," Calliope says, arms crossed over her chest. Her silver-white hair is tied into two buns at the top of her head. "Especially your kind."

Does she mean brujas? She leaves me with that question and turns to a tiny vendor stall. Hundreds of flowers are stacked higher than the fairy who mans the table. He's like a living flower stem with thorns protruding from his joints and knuckles. Spindly fingers dip a rose into a bowl of sparkling sugar crystals. He blows on it and the petals part open, then hands the flower by the stem to Calliope.

It is the first time I see Calliope's smile, a real one. There's a brightness there, and the constellations that freckle her skin glisten as if reacting to this moment of joy. She plucks a strand of her hair—it glows, like the glow-in-the-dark necklaces my sisters and I once wore to the Dreamland Roller Rink midnight party. The thorned fairy ties the glowing strand around his slender neck like a necklace, and beams.

"Would you like one," the thorned fairy looks up with mud-brown eyes and a smile like a saw. "For a taste of your sweet power?"

What else do I have to trade with? My bracelet is not for sale. My earrings. My necklace. I was taught to never, ever, part with my hair, nails, or teeth unless I want someone putting a hex on me. I'm in a magical island, and I'm broke. Which is not so different than being in New York and broke.

"I'm fine."

"What's the matter, Leech?" Calliope asks.

She plucks the sugared roses one by one. Are these the same flowers my dad ate? My resentment and anger slam back into me, followed by that bone-deep pain in my joints, and hollowed hunger.

"I have a name," I say, lifting my chin.

Calliope licks her cupid's bow lips. "*Leech, siphon, devourer* they all mean the same thing in the end."

Leech. Siphon. Devourer. I remember disliking *magical hacker*. But now, after what I did to Alcyone in the arena, I hate to think that she might be right. Daughter of El Fin, Master of Everything's End. I think of what the ada Caya said last night. "El Fin will be there to devour existence." There's that word again. *Devourer*. It was a witch called the Devourer who tormented my sister and nearly killed my family. The Devourer killed countless people just so she could become a god. I'm *nothing* like that. I can't be.

I rub my hands on my sides as my tear ducts burn. Not wanting Calliope to see me cry, I turn and go.

Lin is beside me in a flash. "Don't go, Eliza. Iris wants us to stay together."

The softness in Lin's voice takes the heat out of my footsteps.

"I'm just thirsty," I say and muster a smile. "Look, there's a well."

Lin slows down, understanding in those violet eyes. "Don't wander beyond that. The sunflower fields all look the same, and you might get lost."

I nod like the good bruja I am and march over to the stone well. Wild patches of dandelions and clover blanket the grounds. Here, the buzz of the market is drowned out by the chorus of insects and birds swooping down on the grass to snatch their meals. In the distance, there's a thin stream snaking down a slope and, beyond that, more sunflower fields. Everything here is too bright, too vivid. It is like there is an entirely new rainbow of sharper colors. I never thought I'd miss the mundane brown, green, and slate gray of my city, but here I am.

I say a rezo to La Mama to guide me with her light, to La Ola to usher waves of calm, and to La Estrella to send me even the smallest bit of hope.

I pull a bucket full of water from the well and wash my face. But when I bring my cupped hands closer, something green and crystal moves across my palms. I let loose a shriek that shreds my vocal cords. Water sloshes over my front, and I shake my hands to get rid of the creature, losing my balance.

I wind up on my back and groan as I sit up. There, resting on the lip of the well, is a tiny frog the size of a quarter, with green translucent skin that lets you see its pink insides. Feeling utterly ridiculous at having reacted like that, I crawl closer. I can see its tiny heart beating. Bulbous black and red eyes blink at me. Its gullet extends, filmy like a perfect chewing gum bubble. It goes, *co-quí, co-quí.* These are not the coquí frogs I grew up learning about, but the song is unmistakable. Maybe it's a distant relative.

It's just a little frog. I reach out a finger to pet it, but a sticky pink tongue jerks out and lands in my eye. It jumps on my hand, then my forearm, leaving a slimy film behind. My eye burns, and I swat the critter away.

"What the—" With one eye shut, I grab for the bucket and splash water on my face.

Laughter erupts behind me, mocking and cruel. Calliope and a cluster of the village adas are watching me. One of the castle guards with lizard features has her sword in hand.

"We heard a scream," she says.

"It's nothing," I say, wishing I could jump away and disappear into sunflower fields.

"What is the matter, Leech?" Calliope asks. "Is the king's savior bested by a big scary bug?"

"It was a *frog*," I snap back. With my left eye still smarting and my skin burning where the creature made contact, I am a pathetic sight. Get it together, Rose.

Calliope holds her palms up, grinning. "Pardon me. A big scary frog. It is a wonder it took the siren so long to search for you."

"Why are you even here?" My voice is harder than I feel. "Do you have a daily quota for being a jerk?"

"I owe you a debt for what you did to Alcyone," she says. She carries no weapons, but I remember the star girl's light whip, and

I can only imagine Calliope has the same thing up her sleeve. Her leather sandals crush the path of dandelions as she gets closer.

"It's not my fault she was left behind," I say. "Take it up with the king."

"Are you afraid you wouldn't win if you fought me?"

"I'm not afraid of anything," I say, but when I say the last word, a numbness rings my lips. My tongue feels like it's swelling and my mouth is dry. Dozens of thoughts and memories crash down on me, unbidden and unwanted.

"I hear the quiver of a lie in your voice." She paces around me. "I can smell your fear."

"Fine." A broken laugh escapes me, and my words tumble out without permission. "I'm afraid of a lot of things, actually. I've got enough sense to fear the things that try to kill me like maloscuros and casimuertos." My hands tremble, and filmy green marks appears on my arm. My heart races and my mouth stings. "What did you do to me?"

Calliope's eyes widen, but she's no longer laughing. She shakes her head. "I didn't—"

Someone gasps, and I hear footsteps stomping somewhere as I fall to one knee. It's like my heart is being squeezed, tendrils of magic scratching up my skin that push out words I don't want to say.

"I'm afraid of failing a class for the first time in my life because no matter what I do, I can't seem to focus on school when there are bigger things to worry about. I was right about my dad, wasn't I? No one wanted to listen to me, but I was *right*." The inside of my throat burns, and I gasp. Emotions crash over me in waves. When I look up, the clearing is filling with bodies.

Lin and Peridot. More guards. They all trade glances and stare at me as if I've lost my mind, and I'm sure I have because I watch Lin vanish into thin air. Someone tries to grab me but I lash out. They're shouting to get help, but I don't feel like anyone can help me. I open my mouth to scream, but words froth out instead.

"I'm afraid my mother is not going to recover from losing my dad a second time and Nova's going to die. I'm afraid Lula is going to do something reckless and Alex is going to burn everything in her path trying to find me. I'm afraid of drinking a can of soda and rock candy at the same time in case it explodes in my stomach."

There are more translucent coquís hopping around the grass. They sound like tinkling glass with every bounce. I gasp for breath, my words crashing one on top of the other.

"I'm afraid that the siren is wrong and I'm not your savior and my magic is weak and I can't be the daughter of some god I've never heard of. I'm no one's daughter at all."

Blood spreads across my tongue as I bite down hard in an attempt to silence myself, but I can't stop. There is a fire burning within me that wants to be let out. I claw at my face and neck as Iris and Arco run toward me with Lin.

"I'm afraid of my power, and I can't control it."

The prince begins to reach for me. He's asking what's happening, but I put my hands up. I. Can't. Stop.

"Don't touch me! *You*. I'm afraid that I'm going to say something utterly stupid because you are so beautiful it hurts to look at you for too long." My heart races and my tongue swells more, a bitter taste like chewing on lemon rinds makes me grimace. It's hard to breathe deeply. Everything hurts as I sink into the clover and lie back, snot and tears running down my face. The back of my tongue hurts, like when you cry so hard and so long you're spent. I want this to be over.

"We have to take her to Kaíri," someone says. I can't recognize the voice.

Iris kneels next to me. She seems to be taking stock of my state, an angry frown on her forehead. "I told you to stay put, Eliza."

I hate that she sounds more worried than mad. It must be bad, then, because even her gaze softens.

Iris gathers me into her arms with little effort, like I'm a rag doll and I let her. I keep my palms firmly pressed against my face as if my skin and bones can shield me from this humiliation.

"I'm afraid of you too," I say, each word more painful than the next as her footsteps thud rapidly across the ground. "You're mean and beautiful and rude. I will never be as strong as you." I grunt and try to breathe. "Why am I saying these things?"

Surprise twists her pink mouth, bemused, angry. "Secretion from the crystal coquí will do that to you. Lucky for us, there is an antidote."

Iris carries me through a dense patch of sunflowers with jet-black seeds at the center. Lin was right. I would have gotten lost had I ventured in there, but perhaps it would have been preferable to being reduced to a blubbering pile of tears and snot.

"We're nearly there," Iris says, her voice like the croon of a dove.

We get to a house made entirely of entwined trees, with no walls except for the ivy and curtains of leaves providing cover from the sun. Iris carries me as far as the threshold. Inside there's a mattress covered in silks and pillows, and at the center of the hardwood floor, a perfect ring has been cut out to house a lily pond.

"Iris," a deep, melodic voice says behind us. "I'm overjoyed you came home."

I can hear Iris's sharp gasp, though the shock on her face rearranges itself quickly to her stoic steel. She whirls around, lowers me to stand but keeps an arm around my side to hold me upright.

Iris bows and says, "Lady Kaíri. I was going to look for you."

Standing there is an ada dressed in gossamer yellow. I blink several times, my eyes adjusting to her bright colors. She reminds me of Lula with her long perfect curls and dewy medium brown skin. But unlike Lula, large white, orange and black rings dot her muscular arms, like the pattern of a monarch butterfly, and her long lashes are tipped with yellow flower petals. She grabs my arm, running a thumb along the green mark that has begun to spread.

"Oh my." She clicks her tongue, but if she's worried that I'm going to drop dead on her doorstep, she doesn't show it. "Eleuthantila poison is a bitter thing."

I groan, unable to speak. The burning sensation is back, and my skin breaks out with sweat. Eleuthantila poison. That's what Arco said they gave to my dad. How long before anyone helped him?

"Bring her inside," the woman says.

Iris doesn't complain as she carries me into the open house. Kaíri unrolls a bamboo mat next to the lily pond and points to it.

"Set her down here."

Iris does as she's told, but I can feel her muscles tensing, see a twitch along her jaw as she does so. "I'll return for her."

"Iris, you do not have to go. It's been so long."

The princess only hesitates for a moment. She begins to turn around but stops cold. "We've already lost too much time because of this. We'll have to spend the night."

Guilt makes me shut my eyes. I rest my fists over my stomach and wish that the earth would swallow me whole, like those cobblestones we saw on the way in, like the overrun paths that stretch all over this island like veins to a wild heart.

"Of course," the woman says, her voice soft, but it doesn't hide the disappointment. I wonder who she is and why Iris hasn't seen her, why it would matter. I didn't think a princess had to bow to anyone except the king. "What is your name?"

"Eliza," I manage. My tongue is practically glued to the roof of my mouth. I might swallow it if she doesn't hurry.

She makes a *hmm* sound, like she doesn't believe me. I wallow in my own mixture of tears and homesickness as Kaíri gets to work. There's the slap of wood, the splash of water, a placid song hummed, the rustle of leaves around us. For a moment, it's like being in my mother's infirmary when she's cooking up a healing draught for a broken heart or creaky joints. I am filled with so much longing for home that when I open my eyes, a fraction of me expects to be back there.

But it's just Kaíri. She scoops up water from the lily pond with a wooden bowl. The water is pale green, but at least it doesn't smell like rot. She plucks two of her lashes and presses them between her fingers, rolling the petals back and forth until two fat drops of oil fall into her concoction, then offers it to me.

"Drink this. It will counteract the poison."

I bring it to my lips. I can practically hear my mother scolding me about taking healing potions from strangers, but if it's between this and biting off my traitorous tongue, then this eyelash juice wins. The instant the cold liquid touches my lips, the numbness fades. When I swallow, it only tastes like clean, fresh snow, the kind my sisters and I would collect in bowls that we left overnight on our roof and later loaded with fruit juice and condensed milk.

"Thank you," I say, trying my voice. I sound like I, well, swallowed a frog. When I hold up my forearm, I see the green stain on my skin is beginning to disappear. "What was that? The coquís in my world don't go around *poisoning* people."

In the few seconds it takes her to blink, the outer corner lashes are already growing back. She waves her hand over the pond water, and the lily pads move across the surface. Their shapes change to show the island of Adas, smack-dab in a turquoise sea. A smattering of pollen forms a mass to the south and smaller surrounding islands. It is the most delicate magic I've ever seen.

"Do you know the story of La Flor?" she asks.

I shake my head. "A flower goddess?"

The pollen takes the shape of her words, showing the silhouette of a god rising from the island. "When El Terroz first created Adas, he lived in solitude. But even gods get lonely, and he populated the island with the creatures of his dreams. Then, he gave birth to La Flor, who made flowers grow. She turned Adas into a paradise unlike any other. Against her father's wishes, she ventured across the seas and brought her gifts to the human kingdoms. But she also brought things back with her—humans who wanted a taste of magic and creatures that captured her heart. Over time, the power of Adas has transformed them. It is in the soil, the water, the air. The coquís have evolved to this."

The lily pond ripples and returns to its original shape, the pollen sinks to the bottom. I try to imagine this goddess. Creatures literally changing because of magic. "Why wouldn't they evolve to have three eyes or to actually talk?"

"That I don't have an answer to, but we become what we need to be for survival." She bats her petal lashes slowly, her smooth forehead creasing with a frown. "Perhaps because those born of Adas cannot lie, and so this creature took that magic deep into its skin and manifested it into revelation of truths, fears, desires. It became the magic it holds. The effect will be the worst for humans, more like poison because you are capable of true lies."

Kaíri holds out her slender hand palm up and a tiny crystal frog jumps onto it from one of the lily pads. I gasp and leap backward.

"Calm yourself," Kaíri says. Her laugh is so deep for how bright everything is about her. The crystal coquí blows its fat little neck out, bulbous black eyes staring at me as if it's a lapdog that wants a pat. It sings. As a kid, I heard this very sound in my mom's salsa records. I had to color in cartoon versions of their bodies for class projects on the rain forests of Puerto Rico and the frog whose song could only be heard there. Travel isn't exactly on the single-mom budget, but I always dreamed I'd be able to see them in real life. Kaíri lowers her hand to the pond to let the frog leap back in. We are surrounded by their music.

"No harm will come to you in my grove now. As for what else will become of you on your journey to the outerlands, I cannot make assurances, Siphon."

"How did you know I was the Siphon?" I ask.

Her black curls fall like ribbons around her shoulders. The lines on her skin seem to move. "News of King Cirro's latest addition to his Guardians of Adas traveled quickly. I assumed your troupe would arrive here for supplies, as my grove is the only village with enough to spare."

She doesn't sound upset, but I think harder about King Cirro. Shouldn't he have wanted to prepare us for our journey? Isn't our mission more important than some feast?

"My niece is the most determined I've seen her," Kaíri says, drawing my attention back.

"Niece?" I look back to where Iris stomped away, back through the fields. "You're the king's sister?"

"*No.*" I didn't think it was possible to imbue a single word with so much anger. She softens when she says, "My sister was their mother, Mayté, the Orchid Queen of Adas. Iris lived here before her death and for a brief period after the funeral at sea. I could not help her the way she needed it."

I lick my dry lips. I think of my family those first few months after my dad vanished. "I think that it's easy to push people away when you're grieving."

Kaíri offers a radiant smile. Rays of light shine down, filtered through branches and vines. "Iris does not want to realize that she is like her mother. Brave and so full of joy."

Joy? Are we talking about the same warrior princess? I must make a face because Kaíri laughs. I realize that even in a magical realm, the one place to get the gossip is the resident auntie.

"Rest now. You need your strength to train with the siren."

Train to fight a living, organic black hole. Pain spiderwebs across my temples. I don't want her to leave just yet. "Wait... Have you seen it? The rot."

Kaíri's tattoos stir again, and this time I know I'm not seeing things. It's like a nervous tic, reacting to her emotion. "No, but I have seen its effects and I feel them. I stood at the Pillars of the Sky and saw an entire mountain withered to cracked earth. The dwellers of Adas have migrated east for the last five turns. I have tried to accommodate as many as I can, but the others rush to the Castillo because of the king's promises."

I wonder what it's like for Iris to have to live with this every day since the rot appeared. She's tasked with protecting a whole island while her dad holds gladiator fights and drinks the night away. I think I understand her anger, more than ever.

Kaíri wrings a cloth to wipe sweat from my forehead, and when our skin makes contact, there's a static spark, and my magic lurches forward. The tattoos on her shoulders reveal themselves to be wings, sheer and filmy. They flutter frantically.

"I'm sorry. I didn't mean to," I say.

Kaíri shakes her surprise, her dark eyes looking at me with a new sort of awakening. Like she's seeing me again for the first time. "The magic of Adas is a wild thing, you'll learn. Sleep here tonight. I will have fresh water and food sent to you."

I watch her go. Her wings, too delicate to be functional, flutter as she walks. I lie back on the mat and press my hands on the ground, willing the sensation in my palms to go away. It's like something has burrowed beneath my skin. *Magic.*

I don't remember falling asleep, but the snap of a branch

wakes me. When I sit up, Iris is holding a broken twig in her hand. She's making a fire just outside the small, open frame house. Whatever she's cooking smells incredible. Even the memory of my humiliating display isn't enough to make my appetite go away.

"I know your fears," Iris says. "But if you're going to live through this, you have to be careful. You aren't good to anyone if you can't carry your own weight."

Begrudgingly, I walk over to her, stiff from sleeping on the ground and riding the Pegasus. That's going to be difficult to get used to. I take the unidentified meat-on-a-stick and tell myself it's just like eating corn dog at Coney Island. It's better than that, actually. It's salty and seasoned with familiar herbs. I devour it in two bites and lick my thumb.

"Where's Kaíri?" I ask.

"In her manor," she says.

"This isn't her manor?"

Iris stifles a laugh. "The Keeper of Paradise sleeps among the flowers. This was mine when we spent time with Lady Kaíri learning how to tend gardens. I never mastered the skill to make things grow, like my brother."

I think of what Kaíri said about Iris having lived here. She also said Iris was brave and full of joy. Did becoming the warrior of a kingdom crush her spirit? No. She's still fierce and seems to want this burden. I wonder what happened. What changed?

We eat in silence.

"You said you were afraid of me," Iris says after a while.

I shrug and stare at the crackle of fire. The sunset breeze is cool

against my skin and carries the earthy scent of the sunflower fields.
"Do you want me to be?"

"Most are."

"Do you want *them* to be? You said it yourself. If they don't fear
your father, they fear you."

"I have done many things in my father's name. I find having
people fear me means I'm never questioned. They do as I ask."

"I guess you and your dad have that in common," I say.

Iris doesn't say anything for a long time and when she does, it's
to tell me I can take the mattress and she'll sleep on the bamboo
mat. She lets the fire simmer to embers before she lies down.
Sleeping with open walls and ceiling is unnerving, but also nice. I
can see the swelling moon. It is the second night I've spent away
from home. I grip my bracelet and run through my memories of my
family. Nothing *feels* missing, but then how would I know?

I curl on my side. Iris lies so still I think she's asleep until she
lets go of a long sigh.

"I am nothing like my father," Iris says without anger or hurt. It
is assertive, a truth I know she believes.

I think of the king who parades his lot of kidnapped oddities in
front of his people and makes them fight, of the way he grabbed
Iris's face, of every single person who sings his praises without any
meaning, any love, behind those words. I wish I hadn't said that.

"I know."

Something that feels like a real truce settles between us.

"It's so peaceful here," I say.

Her voice is distant, heavy as she falls asleep. "It wasn't always."

13

Cirro held up a ceiba tree for six days and six nights.

To prove his strength as king.

To prove his love for Mayté.

—CLARIBELLE AND THE KINGDOM OF ADAS:
TALES TALL AND TRUE, GLORIANA PALACIOS

The early morning is cast in soft blue light. I take an inventory of my body. No numbness, lots of soreness, but I've felt worse after a ghost possession, to be honest. I sit up and find Iris is gone. Girasol Grove is serenaded by crickets and birds. Voices carry from somewhere nearby. I climb out of the little house but don't have to go too far.

I recognize Iris's cutting tone and catch a glimpse of Arco's golden horns. Yesterday slams back to me, and I'm glad he can't see me. I want to be so small that I can tuck myself into a tree hollow because I can't believe I said those things out loud. Thankfully, they're busy arguing.

"Then go back home, Brother," Iris hisses.

"Why do you insist on pushing me away?"

"You made your choice." She sighs. Stomps. "You don't have

to be here now. You've been perfectly content clinging to the king while I've scoured the realms for the siphon."

"Do not mistake my decision to stay by his side for apathy. You chose to go alone. This is my home too. Mother wouldn't want us to be like this. Can't you see that?"

"It doesn't matter what Mother wants, does it?" She doesn't wait for his response and marches away.

I start to run back to the little house, but "Stealthy" is not my middle name, and Iris is at my side.

"Good morning," I say. "Didn't see you there."

She's in the same scalloped armor, the same long pink braids, not a hair out of place. She turns sharp quartz eyes at me and arches her brow in a way that calls out my lie without a single word. "There's fresh water to wash up."

Sure enough, next to the lily pond is a bowl of water, mint leaves, and a natural sponge. I chew on the leaves and hope they're not there for any other purpose.

"You don't have to stand there," I say, wetting the sponge to wash up. "I can get back to the village center."

"We're not going to the village center." Iris has her back to me, fussing with the straps of her leather boots. "I'd prefer to keep an eye on you until we're at the Shuari rain forest."

"I thought we were going to the outerlands." I rinse out my mouth and dump the dirty water in the fire ring.

"We are. But the Shuari rain forest is the last stretch of green. That's where we'll make camp and find the blood of the gods."

"This isn't, like, real blood is it?"

"Why can't you be serious for once?"

"What am I supposed to do? Be miserable and guilty that the only thing my father gave me was a curse and also that things try to kill me all the time? I'm sorry, Princess, but this is the Siphon you get. Although, maybe you'd get along with my sister."

She watches me with something like amusement or respect. Whatever it is, she gets up and leads the way.

Iris doesn't bring up Arco or elaborate about the blood, and my survival skills tell me I shouldn't press. Instead, I follow the warrior princess through a different path in the sunflower fields. The sky is just starting to bleed orange and pink, and the flower heads perk up all at once.

In a clearing lined by tall grass, Xia, the siren, waits for us. Her dress is made entirely of wildflowers and bark. Sharp bones poke at the brown skin of her throat and shoulders. At her feet is the glass box with the sliver of rot, flat and cracked once again. My heart slams against my chest when I see it, the buzz of magic clear in the air and not just to me. Xia keeps tugging at the lobe of her sharp-pointed ears, and the girl with black angel wings watches the sky like she expects to see a horde of bees fly overhead.

The other guardians cluster, stiff and anxious as they wait for instructions. Kaíri is present too, sitting in a chair made entirely of yellow sunflowers, like they sprouted from the ground just for her. Iris remains with the guardians, while Arco, who's caught up to us, enters the clearing and goes straight for his aunt. He kisses her hands, and she brushes his curls away from his eyes. He sits on the grass with his leather-bound notebook and retrieves the pen tucked behind his ear. He gives me a sweet smile, and I can't hold his stare for long.

Xia commands our attention by standing at the center of the clearing. She bends down to gather a fistful of dirt. Shoots of grass and pebbles falls from the gaps between her fingers. She eats it. I glance around to see if this is strange to anyone but me. Only Lin gives me a look that says, *I hope we don't have to do that.* Xia crunches and swallows the earth. When she smiles, it is stuck between pointed yellowed teeth. "Yes, this will do. This, my guardians, is the birthplace of La Flor, daughter of El Terroz, and Keeper of all the World's Gardens."

This was definitely not in the Book of Deos back home.

"There are places on this island that pulse pulse pulse with magic of the ancients." She opens the glass box. This time she feeds the rot and lets it slither out of its container. Arco jumps to his feet. Everyone is at attention, Iris drawing her sword. My skin runs cold. What is Xia doing? "Harness it. When you dissolve this rot, you will be ready."

"Wait!" Arco cries. "You never said—"

The rot is suspended in the air. Xia keeps her hand up, the space around her undulating, creating a force field that pins the wretched thing in place.

"I may not be strong enough to face the source," Xia says, turning her face to Arco, "but this I can control."

"A little warning next time?" I mutter and keep my hand over my heart.

"Márohu, Daughter of the Winds," Xia says, beckoning her forth with the curl of a long finger.

The winged girl spreads her black wings. For the first time, I notice oil-slick feathers also grow in her hair, the same color as the ones in her wings. Her face is very much fairy-like with pointed ears and an outwardly curved nose. Her eyes are storm gray, like my dad's.

I can't hear what Xia whispers to Márohu, but the girl closes her eyes as Xia presses her palms against the air between them. The space ripples, as if Márohu is trapped within a clear wave. Her wings snap open more, as far as the wingspan will allow. She lowers herself to the ground, pressing her palms on the earth, then shoots upward, spinning in a powerful, graceful ballet with their wind. The air funnels around her, pulling particles of dust and pebbles from the ground in her own concentrated tornado.

Everyone shields their faces against the sting of the wind. Márohu climbs higher and higher, creating an electrical storm. She flies back down, toward the sliver of rot, when the air completely cuts out. Not because of her wings, but because Xia is doing something.

The siren pushes that ripple of her magic, counteracting Márohu's. And then the winged girl is falling hard and fast. Her arms grab at empty nothingness, and her legs flail uselessly. She is a comet shooting to earth. I turn from side to side as everyone watches, holding their breath.

"Hello?" I step forward. "Someone do something!"

Lin squeezes my wrist and presses a finger to their lips. I scream as I catch the terror twisting Márohu's face when she sees the approaching ground. She's going to crash into the earth and I'm going to watch her die. I brace myself for the fall that never comes.

Xia's magic suspends Márohu inches from the ground before letting her go. The winged girl hits the dirt with the slightest rustle of feathers and a defeated grunt.

"What the hell was that?" I shout.

Xia's gaunt face snaps in my direction. "She was not strong enough to resist my power and she fell. The rot will swallow you like it has the outerlands. You must learn to fight back."

I want to argue. I want to yell at her because this is a cruel, terrible way to make someone's magic flourish. I search for a memory of my old teacher. Despite our new differences, I can see her face. Her eyes lined with crow's-feet as she guided me through the Veil. I can see her, but when I can't conjure her name, my heart gives a hard thud and I remain silent.

Lin places a palm over mine. It is the strangest thing, that their touch brings with it a moment's pause, a calm that steadies my heart. Then, it hits me.

Valeria, I think. *My mentor's name was Valeria.*

"Peridot," Xia says, calling him forth. "Son of the Shuari rain forest."

Peridot steps into the center clearing next, his shorn hair the gradient shades of a dark forest. The fine twigs that sprout from the tops of his hands and around his ears move restlessly. The tree boy stands still for so long that I think his power might also be to freeze in place. But after a bit, veins throb at his neck and across his chest. The brown skin over his biceps takes on the texture of bark, and thick roots splinter the ground open and slither across the clearing like great serpents. They reach for the rot.

When Xia touches a single root, it withers and recoils back into the soft ground. I flex my fingers in anticipation of my turn. It seems that she not only senses magic but neutralizes it. That answers one thing the king didn't want to or couldn't answer. The rot is magic. A thrill runs up my spine at the thought of draining the source of the rot's power.

"Daughter of the Vicious Deep," Xia says, moving on.

Nadira takes Peridot's place. She scratches at scars on her neck. She shuts her eyes. Scales surface along her throat and forearms. They shimmer as magic vibrates within her. And I realize, they're not scars—they're gills. She's a mermaid. A stream of water rises beneath her feet, in the cracks of earth Peridot's roots left behind. She's drawing a current from beneath the island.

With the flourish of Xia's bony hand, the stream evaporates into a cloud of mist, and the mermaid crumples to her hands and knees, the blue scales on her forearms dissolving into glittering white sand. Nadira grunts as she gets up and joins the others who met the same defeat.

I glimpse at Kaíri, who grips the arms of her chair too tightly. Disappointment is plain in her eyes, but she keeps watching.

"Lin Octavio, Child of the Betwixt." She beckons them forward. Lin's winks a violet eye at me. Lin is the only one whose power I'm unfamiliar with. What does it mean to be a child of the betwixt? Also, I make note that Xia didn't call Lin *son* or *daughter.*

Lin draws a vertical line in the air. A fissure of violet light appears. *This* is Lin's power. I remember seeing them disappear earlier, but I thought I was hallucinating from the poison. Once again, Lin vanishes into the space between, thin as lightning, and then reappears a few yards behind Xia. I give a little *woo* of encouragement and clap, but a glare from Iris tells me it is not the right time.

Xia can't stop Lin from creating these rips in the air. One moment Lin's there, and the next they're stepping in front of Xia.

To the side of her. On the other side of the rot. Then back. I think Lin's trying to get inside of the siren's wall of magic. It is the only time frustration marks the siren's face, and I can feel the whistle of her magic in the air as she summons more of it. She shortens the range of the rift, so eventually, it's like Lin is only taking a couple of steps through the fissures of space they walk through, until the rift is barely a crackle and, finally, won't open.

Lin kicks at the air, then returns to stand beside me.

"What were you trying to do?" I whisper.

They muss their soft curls and wince. "I thought I could create a rift to shove the rot inside. But I couldn't even get close."

"Calliope, Last Daughter of the Starlark Realm," Xia says.

Last daughter?

Calliope lifts her head. In the daylight, the beauty marks on her skin look like dots of pure silver. Worried eyes dart at the royal twins and then the siren. "It isn't nightfall. My power comes from the stars."

"Is our sun not a star?" Xia asks, her voice distant. "Each and every one of you set your own limit. You might as well bury yourselves in a glass coffin and let your power wither away."

Lin and I look at each other at the same time.

"That seems extreme," I mutter, and they snort.

Someone, probably Iris, clears their throat.

When Calliope walks, each step is sure. Gone is the girl who doubted herself moments ago. She reaches a hand to the sky and reminds me of a star goddess. My favorite story of La Estrella was that she lassoed stars into constellations so she could find her way in the dark. She was never lost. Watching Calliope, her magic is just as beautiful, drawing down a ray of light between her hands. She begins to shape it into a sword. At the same moment, Xia waves a hand in the air, like someone erasing chalk from a board, and the light between Calliope's fingertips dissolves into stardust.

"Again," Calliope says, resentment and anger in her voice.

"Are you in a hurry to fail once more?" Xia asks, already moving to me. "Eliza, bruja of the Queens Realm."

"I'm actually from Brooklyn," I grumble to myself. I swallow the knot in my throat and take my place in front of Xia and the suspended rot. I exhale slowly, focus on the object in front of me. I know what I have to do: Touch the rot and drain it. Siphon its magic. That's what I am, isn't it? The only problem is, most of the time, I haven't used my power on purpose.

"You are the girl who knows herself the least," Xia tells me. She moves so quickly she's a blur, standing so close to me that my eyes cross. Her cracked lips pull back over pointy, crooked teeth. "You were the beginning and you will be the end."

King Cirro said something similar. That this started with my dad and the rebellion he was part of. If we are our parents' mistakes, shouldn't they be the beginning and us the end? That isn't right. I try to step back, but she gets closer still, her cold breath at my ear, her words only for me. "You have much to learn, Rose Mortiz."

I swallow the gasp that leaves my lips at the sound of my name. Of course, I couldn't hide that from someone like Xia, a being whose power is a lure for more power. Instead of a song that leads sailors to their deaths, she might just lead magical beings instead. I shake in place and I can still feel her magic, like a sunburn on my skin. The numbness returns.

188

"Go on, Siphon."

The hunger I've been feeling gets stronger. Xia's magic fills my senses. My head spins with the buzzing of insects, my heart murmurs. I draw a raspy breath as I grab for her, my magic driving through me, using me to get to the rot. For a moment, the hum of wasps fills my ears, and I think there's something else there. Someone calling my name. When I touch the black mass, it feels like my skin has been turned inside out. Needles of heat drive through my lungs and I can't breathe. I fly back and hit the ground so hard I see stars.

"Eliza!" Lin shouts. I hear their voice over all the others.

I moan and spit out the blood that fills my mouth. Footsteps form a mini-stampede, and when I look up, I am yards away from everyone else. Blades of grass poke at my tender skin and beetles crawl over me.

"What was that?" I groan.

My face is hot with embarrassment. Why did I think I would be different? Because I've been told that I am the one they were waiting for and Iris traveled across realms to find me? *Special. Chosen. Hacker. Siphon.*

"You are not ready," Xia's voice murmurs on the wind, but when I push myself up, she is standing exactly where I left her. "You must be ready."

I hate magical creatures and their cryptic talk.

Iris pushes past the others, wedging herself between Lin and Arco, already trying to help me stand.

"Are you hurt?" they all ask.

"I'm fine." I flex my hands, move my limbs to make sure nothing is broken.

Xia claps her hands. The sound pierces my eardrums. The others grimace and hiss, feeling the same effect. It is then that I notice petals dry and fall at the hem of her dress. Was that because of me? She won't meet my eyes. She stomps on the ground and says, "Márohu."

We go again and again, and though Xia gets slower, she still neutralizes each of our powers. None of us get close to the rot. It stays there, a stain, a blight, a pockmark. Worry settles over the group. Adas from around the grove gather around Kaíri. Faun children on wobbly, hooved legs and brown-skinned girls with rainbow petals for eyelashes. They watch us fail.

Xia walks off into the tall grass, the rot clutched in her arms. I wouldn't be surprised if she sleeps inside a giant flower or the hollow of a tree trunk. Kaíri announces that she's prepared a feast for the guardians. I want to ask what it is with faeries and feasts, but it's the same way in my community. Someone is always having a Deathday or getting married or having a name-day ceremony. Sometimes there's just the random Tuesday when all your aunts and uncles "stop by" and everyone spends hours in the kitchen telling stories about the days when brujas were at war with the hunters, or the miracles their grandmas performed. But I don't want Adas to feel like home. I already have one.

I follow the others and share in the defeated spirit. Calliope is beside me. She says nothing. Maybe she's too tired, because she doesn't even grimace when our eyes meet.

"What did Xia mean before?" I ask. "She called you the Last Daughter of the Starlark realm."

Calliope considers this. Her deep brown skin gleams with constellations. She is a living embodiment of La Estrella. "Do your bruja stories mention my home?"

I shake my head. I try to think of the texts I've read. Even though I haven't read them all, I know enough that there aren't stories of the Starlark realm, only a passing mention. "Not really."

She nods methodically and takes the end of her braid, unraveling her hair over her shoulders to tie it back in tighter plaits. "It was the dominion of La Estrella once, the way El Terroz created this land of Adas. Gods make homes for themselves all over the galaxies. We were the Starlarks, born of the star goddess herself. Do you see these markings?"

She extends her arm, drawing attention to her constellations. She has silver dots the way I have brown freckles and beauty marks. But hers connect with thin lines. It is the most beautiful magic I've ever seen.

"We bear them to guide our way home. But there is no home. Not anymore."

I speak the next words knowing I'm afraid to find out. But truth must be spoken, even when it hurts. "What happened?"

"A creature came to our land. A bruja." Calliope's light eyes flare with hatred. It is an anger I recognize in Iris. It is an anger I also recognize in me. Her bottom lip trembles, but she steels herself. Why don't people just let themselves cry? My mother is just like this. "That monster sucked the life out of everything. She left destruction in her wake. She had your power, but she called herself something else. Alcyone and I are the only ones left."

Now I realize why she was so upset that I took Alcyone's place. If I had let my power go completely, I could've killed one of two people left from an entire realm. The thought makes me sick to my stomach. Could it be that the witch who trapped my family and me in the realm of Los Lagos is the same one who forced Calliope to end up here? Coincidences are for mortals and sinmagos. I know, deep in my heart, that the universe, the gods of old and new, work toward something—a purpose, a goal, a series of events that can bring people together or break them apart. But then that leaves me with a new, terrible realization. *She had your power.*

My eyes sting. I breathe hard. "The Devourer?"

Calliope looks surprised. "How did you know?"

"My family *ended* her," I say because the rest is too much for me to handle. I can't be like her. Calliope is wrong. We are nothing alike. Nothing.

Calliope nods slowly. Her eyes roam my face like she is seeing something in my that she didn't before. "Then I owe you a kindness. Don't make me regret it."

Kaíri promised a feast and she meant it. The market of Girasol Grove is transformed. Rows of wooden tables are topped with sunflowers in every color. Bowls of paradise fruit overflow from ceramic bowls. Soft cheeses are drizzled with amber honey. Fried plantains laden with crispy meat make my mouth water. There are funny-looking mushrooms in a tray of dirt, and adas pick them right from the stem. Tiny bird feet with the talons still attached and fuzzy caterpillars are skewered and fried. Cold mango juice is served in small wooden bowls, and rose petals encrusted with sugar are served up on thick heart-shaped leaves.

It feels like every ada in Girasol Grove has come to our send-off. They kiss our knuckles and pile food on our plates. They call us saviors, protectors, and guardians. They want pieces of our hair and a bite of our fingernails, and I can practically hear Lula's voice saying, *Bruja 101: that's a no on gifting body parts.*

Vita and Iris move the villagers along. Arco sits across from me, deep in conversation with his aunt. I can see their resemblance in the shape of their smiles. Iris takes more after their dad, then, a beauty eternal and cold.

There's a crackle right in front of my eyes—magic, strange and familiar, traces a pencil-thin purple line in the air. It reminds me of the time a rock hit my mom's windshield and the tiny break spread up and down the whole glass. That is how the air rips open, and Lin steps out holding a wooden bowl filled with food.

"How *do* you do that?" I ask eagerly.

Shining violet eyes notice me as Lin steps out of the rift and sits to my right. "I don't know how, but ever since I was little, I could make myself appear somewhere else."

I thought my magic was unique, but what Lin can do is just as wonderful. "When I was little, my sister and I tried to write cantos to allow us to teleport. Turns out, that was not one of the gifts the Deos gave us."

"Teleport," Lin chuckles, and picks up a sugar-crusted flower petal to eat. "That's a funny word. Xia called me a living rift when I first met her. I can step through it, but I've never carried someone across."

"The first time I saw you do it, I thought I was imagining things. Are there others like you in Adas?"

For a moment, I wonder if I could siphon Lin's power. I could take myself anywhere. I could take myself home. I trace my Nova bracelet and feel ashamed at the thought. I can't leave my father, and I can't turn my back knowing what the rot can do.

Lin quirks an eyebrow. "I'm the only brujex I know with this power. My mother was an ada, but she didn't possess magic. My father was a brujo, like you."

"That word you used. Brujex? I've never heard that before."

Lin licks the sugar crystals from their fingers. "In Olapura, it's our word for brujos and brujas and people who are both or neither. That's why everyone calls me by 'they.' When I was little, my father boasted how he was blessed to have a firstborn son. Except I figured out that I wasn't a son. So he helped me come up with a new word. One that suited me. When there isn't a place for you in the world, you simply have to carve it out yourself. I'm a brujex."

"I like brujex."

I say the word a few times to get the recognition of it on my tongue, the feel of the vowels and exhalation of my breath. *Brew-hex.*

Lin laughs, a bright sound that reminds me of Lula so much that, if I closed my eyes, I'd swear she were here. I should be overcome with a sense of loss for my sister, but I perk up. I thought of her, I remembered her, which means that Nova's charm is working.

"How far is your reach when you rift?" I ask.

Lin shrugs. I don't know how, but I can feel their self-doubt. "Not far. My mother said the first time it happened was when I was a baby. I was in her arms, and then I wasn't. She panicked, obviously, and went searching for me around the house."

"Where did you go?"

"To my father in the next room." A smile, sad and full of memory, tugs at Lin's lips. "Sometimes I still want to do that—step through the rift and see my parents again."

"What happened?"

Lin digs a thumb under the rind of a round green fruit. The meat of it is pale pink and slimy looking, which they pop into their mouth. "They died during the uprising against King Cirro." Lin discards the shell of the fruit over a shoulder, then reaches for another. "Olapura was at the center of the uprising."

Olapura. That's where my dad wanted to take us before the guards trapped us. I lean closer to Lin's ear, so I'm not drowned out by the music. "What was the uprising over? The king said it was an attempt on his life. But why would anyone want to kill him? I thought he was the party king and gave everyone what they wanted."

"He does. Unless what he wants is in direct opposition to what others want. Isn't that why you're here?"

I nod and try one of the fruits Lin has been eating. I bite down into the meat, silky, like lychee but without a pit. "What did your village want?"

Lin's eyes dart to Iris, who is sword playing with ada girls using wooden swords. Arco and Kaíri must have left while Lin and I were talking. The revelers have spread out on the grass, bathing in the hot, glorious sun.

When Lin's sure no one is paying attention to us, they continue. "Even before the rot, the king took and took from Adas. He had to have the biggest revels, the most decadent feasts, the most curious creatures from all the realms. My family wanted to protect me and others. Xia sensed my power, and my parents didn't want to hand me over for the king's entertainment. Then there was unrest. King Cirro kept taking and taking. He stopped listening to the pleas of the folk. There was the revolt, and my parents died. I couldn't keep fighting against King Cirro. Now I fight for him."

"But you can go *anywhere*," I say.

"I was alone." Lin sighs lightly and says with regret, "Besides, I can protect the folk of Olapura now, as they did me."

That I can understand. I stare at Lin. Child of a brujo and an ada. A brujex. A living rift. An orphan. How can so many of us share the same kind of hurt? Is loss a thread that connects us, like the constellations on Calliope's skin? Is that why we are the ones chosen as guardians?

"What's upset you, Eliza?" Lin asks.

I shake my head and lie. "I'm just sorry. I know what it's like to lose a father."

Lin's thick black eyebrows furrow like caterpillars headbutting. "I thought yours was still alive—imprisoned but alive."

"He is, but he was gone for longer than I've known him. He was here, in Adas, for seven years of my life. When Iris kidnapped us, we were trying to reach Olapura before the guards caught up to us. Patricio Mortiz?"

Lin thinks on it for a bit, their face remarkably beautiful despite the frown. "My mother spoke of a brujo named Patricio once. I

196

may have been too small to remember him though. Our house was a safe haven of sorts for anyone in Adas who needed a home or was trying to escape the salt mines. My parents tried to help as many as they could."

"My mom has an infirmary like that," I say. I puff up with pride and beam. "She's a healer and a midwife to magical folk."

Lin's eyes widen with curiosity. "No wonder you seem comfortable in Adas. You must have had many adventures."

Now it's my turn to raise my eyebrows. "What do you mean?"

"I mean, the way you talk, the way you carry yourself—it's like you've already lived a dozen lives, and you're not afraid of anything. I could never speak to Iris the way you do."

My laugh echoes and heads turn to stare at me. "Me? No way. I mean…" I tell them about being locked up in a tree in Los Lagos, and as we finish the last fruits in the wooden bowl, lapping up the sticky juice that rolls down our wrists, I explain what the undead rising across the city looked like.

"Maybe, if time allows after this is over, I can take you to Olapura, where other brujexes live," Lin says.

Olapura. I picture a bright beach town with white sand and blue crashing waves. I picture brujexes walking around in the soft linens and chiffon that seems to be popular here because it's so hot. Tan hats woven from sun-bleached leaves to shield faces from the unrelenting sun. Lin goes on about the white brick houses with doors painted in pinks and blues and greens, so the goddess of the sea, La Ola, will be able to see them and stop the waves from crashing over them. That when they were little, Lin's father used to fry empanadas out of cornmeal stuffed with fish and crabmeat.

"My dad loved to cook once," I say softly. Now that I'm away from him, I wish I hadn't left things that way. I wish he'd been honest. I wish I didn't have to get the truth with magic. It unraveled too much. But now that I know what that feels like, I wonder if I was wrong to force his hand.

"Enough melancholy," Lin says, and tugs me to my feet. "Let's join the others."

We run through the tall grass, drawing faces on sunflowers as big as dinner plates. Lin tries to lead me through a rift but gets stuck halfway. Instead, they fall out sideways and I can't hold back my laugh. As the sun begins to set, I think about how we are going to have to train with Xia the whole way to the outerlands, and we *have* to make this work, because I can't imagine the sun not shining on this grove.

I wander off on my own and watch the band play. The trio is comprised of two men and one woman. The first is a man reclined on a green mound playing the accordion. He's barefoot, with a panama hat pulled low over his eyes. His curls are long, down over his shoulders, and there's a genuine smile on his face when he notices Lady Kaíri sidle up beside me.

Beside the accordion player, an older woman with dark hair and a white linen dress taps on a type of drum I'm not familiar with. The last of the trio is a man who reminds me of my dad, stroking a wooden instrument with metal prongs. Together their voices seem to fill the entire grove, telling the story of a goddess who carried flowers to human shores. I feel myself grinning, recalling the memory of a grandfather I barely knew who sang a similar tune.

"They're human," I say.

Kaíri nods. Her monarch wings flutter at her back. "Yes. I gave them a home here when they were ready to leave their world in the continent south of here. Not every being is taken. Some come seeking our magic, our secrets, or simply eternity."

"This feels different than the stories I read. The castle was different, too."

"Yes, Arco told me you grew up with tales of Adas. I wanted to show you the ceiba tree from one of them."

I gasp a little and eagerly take her delicate hand.

"Walk with me, Lady Siphon."

Bonfires are being stacked for later tonight, and as we stroll deeper into the rows of sunflowers, I'm overcome with a calm I never felt at the Castillo de Sal. Maybe it has something to do with the Grove being the birthplace of a goddess. Or the absence of King Cirro.

We can still hear the feast, but here the flittering sounds of insect wings and frogs is louder. I tense at the thought of the eleuthantila coquí, but another sight robs my breath. Down a green slope is a shady grove covered in flowers and fireflies. They blink in the coming dark. So many of them that it feels like stepping out into a field of stars. At the very center of it all is a great ceiba tree that looks like it is trying to climb toward the sky. The roots are elevated so high, you could fit an entire truck underneath.

I run down and stand at the mouth of the tree. Dirt hangs in clumps and I breathe in the fresh scent of earth. Even without touching the bark, I can feel how ancient is it, how the roots shoot back deep into the earth.

"This is the tree King Cirro held for six days and six nights to prove his strength and win Mayté's hand in marriage," I marvel.

I set my hand there and get an electric shock. I feel the ceiba tree groan and so I step back.

Kaíri smiles, but even in the fading light, I can see the doubt on her features. "That is a version of the story, yes."

"What do you mean?"

Kaíri rests her hand on the root. "When this ceiba would not move, King Cirro enlisted an ada to help uproot it for six days and six nights to prove to his beloved that his love was true and strong. He stood beneath it for those six days and six nights. On the seventh day, the tree would not return. Now it grows this way. I told you, the magic of adas adapts. Even its creatures. Even its trees."

I try to imagine adas like Peridot using their power of earth to remove something so beautiful. King Cirro wears the crown of Adas. He should have the same magic. Why lie? "How do you know that?"

"Because I was the ada who bargained with him."

I watch her lovely face. The sadness there. "Why?"

"Girasol Grove was the place where La Flor was born. Centuries ago, King Cirro wanted to clear this sacred land for his new palace. In exchange for raising the tree to impress his new love, he would leave this place untouched. He never told me the one he courted was my dearest sister. No matter what other reasons I found to dissuade her from the marriage, she would not listen. After all, I swore never to reveal my bargain with King Cirro to another ada." She looks at me. "However, you are not another ada."

"Thank you." It seems silly to thank her, but it feels like something that has weight to it. I'm just not sure what.

"We should return to the feast," she says, and I follow.

I wonder why she is telling me this. Arco told her I grew up on tales of Adas. Does she think I should know this truth, or does she not want me to believe anything good about King Cirro? I never thought to question which stories about him are true because I never thought I'd wind up here.

I can't be sure of her intentions, other than to take the story of king Cirro and the great ceiba tree as just that. A lie. A trick.

When we return to the feast, the grove is bathed in fiery light. Lady Kaíri is called over to a group of wrinkled adas who remind me of Palita. I turn to search for my friends.

Márohu is perched high up on a roof, her jet-black hair is so straight even the humidity won't curl it. Calliope and Peridot sit side by side. His jade-green eyes seem brighter when he looks at her. Arco is by himself, flipping through an old book. *He's a nerd just like me.*

Lin returns to my side in a violet flash, and shoves me gently toward the prince, offering me two ceramic cups full of sweet nectar. When I sniff it, I realize they also contain rum.

"Go help the princeling quench his thirst."

I take a deep breath and make my way across the village center. Arco looks up from his book, and his soft brown eyes notice me.

Márohu's shadow flies over me. Everyone notices the urgency with which she took off. Two adas with rabbit ears race past me, and one of the musicians strikes a wrong note.

Everything around us feels like it's in slow motion.

Then I realize, it isn't a wrong note someone struck, because it happens again and again. There's someone screaming.

Márohu returns, and this time there's someone in her arms. She flies to the ground. We gather around her. The child she holds has root-brown eyes with cedar bark skin. Thin branches grow from her temples, some of them singed at the ends.

"What happened?" I ask.

"There's more," Márohu says darkly.

Peridot breaks through the ring of adas around us, followed by Iris. The little girl recognizes him and leaps from Márohu's arms to his.

"Awáta!" he says. "What is it?"

She speaks so quickly I can't understand her. I don't have to. I see the strain in Peridot's eyes as we all turn. Dozens and dozens of the tree folk have entered the grove, some carrying small bundles, others carrying bodies. The setting sun casts a bloody glow across everything it touches.

I breathe hard and fast. There's a ringing in my ears as Peridot stands, clutching the girl in his arms. He turns to Iris and says, "The Shuari rain forest is gone."

14

The gods would not listen,

so she shook music from the sky.

—LA TORMENTA, LADY OF STORMS
AND WIFE OF EL CIELO,
TALES OF THE DEOS

I am accustomed to blood and death. Helping my mother in her infirmary and being able to see the dead helped me not harden my heart but make it bigger. Understand that violence happens. Understand that life is precious no matter if you're human or witch or werewolf. Understand that if we could help save someone, we should. I got all of that.

But I am not accustomed to this type of suffering. Healing a vampire with a wooden arrow lodged just above his heart is different than watching a mother carry two of her children in her arms after having walked for miles. I try to work on smoothing healing balms on cuts, but my mind returns on the rot. My theory that it could be connected to portal magic is flimsy. Because if that were true, then wouldn't the rot be over Lagunitas Serpentinas? Then, I remember the way my dad said the lagoon water had changed.

Wasn't there black moss growing over rocks? I tell myself that the two cannot be related, because the *thing* Xia has been carrying around doesn't feel the same. Unless, those were symptoms.

"Eliza, I need your help," Vita shouts.

I follow the guard. I focus on the folk of the rain forest. Shuari, kin of the trees. Kin of Adas.

We all work quickly, ripping cloth for bandages, putting out food, listening. The best thing I think I can do is listen when a little boy tries to tell me that he saw a great shadow blanket his home in the trees and swallow it whole. That is all anyone can seem to remember.

A young boy who reminds me of Peridot stares at a fire and pulls a blanket close. When I ask him if he is okay he says, "First, the earth shook. Then, there was nothing."

The Guardians of Adas retreat to the small house that used to belong to Iris.

It is late and the moon is a searchlight behind thick clouds. We gather around the lily pond and drink a bitter hot tea made from seeds and herbs meant to calm our nerves. It is safe to say, no one is calm.

"I thought the rot wasn't supposed to spread for another moon turn," I say.

"Where is Xia?" Iris asks.

Arco raises his head. There's a smear of dirt on his cheek. "She's in one of her trances. Perhaps we should consider returning to the Castillo de Sal."

"Retreat," Iris says the word like a curse.

"Regroup," Arco corrects. "We were going to the Shuari rain forest for the blood of the gods, but there is no—"

Peridot stands and interrupts Arco. "I beg your pardon, Your Highness, but I will not go back to the castle. I have to go home, even if there is no home left. I have heard the accounts. There may be parts that are untouched by the rot. I have to see."

"If we retreat," Nadira says, "there may be nowhere for us to go."

"That's easy for you to say. You can swim out of here," Calliope says bitterly. I wonder if she's recalling the destruction of her Starlark realm.

"But I'm not, am I?" says the mermaid. "I've seen kingdoms fall. I've seen as much destruction and death as you have. That's why I'm here. If this sickness spreads, not even the seas will be safe. I'm staying."

"You're all brave," Arco says, frowning. "But the Shuari said they were attacked by monsters. That is impossible. This could be something more none of us have ever faced."

"All the more reason we must keep going," Iris says. "We are the only ones standing between the rot and the rest of our kingdom. Our journey continues, for the sake of us all." Iris stands and faces us all. Stray pink curls wisp around her face. She's determined, strong. Like the warrior princess she is. Like a queen. "But I am not my father. I am giving you the choice of leaving and forging your own fate. Even my guards."

I know in my heart that there is no way out of this. I did not choose to be here. I think of what Alex and Lula would do. They fought because they had to right a wrong of their own making.

Perhaps King Cirro said that I was paying for my father's crimes, but still I have to stay. Nadira is right.

If this sickness spreads, not even the seas will be safe.

"I'm staying," I say. My voice feels so small, but they all turn to look at me. None of them look surprised, though, not even Calliope. I clear my throat and raise my cup of tea. "There's always a way. I know it."

Lin follows, then Calliope, Márohu, Vita and several guards, and finally, Arco. I am glad for it.

"To the true Guardians of Adas," says the fairy prince.

We toast and drink. The tea, to put it gently, is disgusting.

"I think I prefer my sister's champagne for toasts," I tell Lin after I've drained my cup.

It feels good to laugh with them. We all go to sleep on heaps across the floor. Nothing brings people together like the end of the world.

We're all packed and ready to go before first light. Kaíri and a cluster of adas are there to see us off. The grove is peaceful after last night's madness. I notice that there are two fewer guards than there were before, and Arco sends a third as a messenger to the castle.

Iris bows to her aunt but keeps a safe distance. "Thank you, Lady Kaíri. I won't fail you."

"I am not the one you owe a promise to," she says. The monarch butterfly markings on her shoulders move, raising up to reveal filmy wings.

Iris presses her lips together tightly but doesn't respond. I wonder what promise she means.

Peridot kisses Kaíri's hands and folds himself over in a bow. I do the same, which makes her laugh. Her palm, soft as a petal, caresses my cheek. This time, my magic doesn't react with the same static shock as when I first met her.

"You will learn the language of this earth too, Eliza."

I think I'm beginning to.

It turns out my second time on horseback is easier than the first. Vita and Alma take up the rear, driving a cart loaded with bags of fruits, corn, and grain. Lin is in front of me, whistling a tune that sounds familiar for no reason other than they must have learned it during our feast at the grove.

No one speaks. Calliope and Peridot ride side by side. Arco, despite having voiced his disapproval of the plan, returns to writing down everything he sees. Sometimes he mumbles things to himself, scratching his head with the butt of his pen. I wonder what he's trying to puzzle out. I've managed to avoid Arco's gaze since he wished me a good morning and I made the same sound as a gerbil caught in its hamster wheel. Vita lingers, always his shadow. Márohu, with raven wings, flies overhead as a scout.

As we plunge forward on to the outerlands, we have to ride slowly because the paths are too rocky. Sweat beads between my shoulder blades, and I feel my sore muscles acutely. Despite the hearty breakfast of bananas and hot cornmeal drizzled with honey and sunflower seeds, I'm hungry. Hungry for magic. I know it in the way the pads of my fingertips sting, searching for a power to latch on to. I think I'm ready to face the rot once again.

"We'll make up time once we reach the meadows," Iris assures us, then rides ahead. I notice the way she watches Arco. I wonder if she's glad that he's stayed. I wonder if she wanted him to go back. I'd give anything to have my sisters with me.

Nadira trots to my side. Her walnut-brown skin glistens with dew from the forest. The multicolored scales on her forearms look like metal plates. For a moment I think about the bets I overheard at the castle. Specifically, the one placed betting Arco would hook up with a river mermaid. I wonder if they meant Nadira. It is ridiculous that I should consider this now, but I'm only human.

"I grow tired of this silence," she says, squinting at the sun.

"Then you came to the right girl, because I have questions."

The mermaid smirks. "Go on."

"How does this work?" I point to her legs. "Is it an enchantment? A curse? A cyclical phase that has to do with the moon?"

She lifts her hair up, revealing a faded trident tattoo on the back of her neck. "River maids are different. They're not tied to the oceans and live equally on land. For us, an old sea king once took our ability to walk on land. Only ink from an ancient kraken gave us the magic to shift into legs."

"All mermaids have a magic squid tattoo?" I ask, only a fraction relieved. There are mermaids in Coney Island, but before this year, my family kept to ourselves, so we never met any. I think.

Nadira sneers, her upper lip curling on one side. "Those *chosen* by the king, of course."

"How does the king choose?"

Her lips remain twisted. "To his will. But the new king, he's young and idealistic. He's given us this new freedom."

"At least he doesn't sound like King Cirro," I say.

"All kings are the same." Nadira picks at one of her scales. It turns to fine grains of sand the moment it leaves her skin. "They are in the sense that they make their people believe they have no power."

"Then how did you come to be here? Did Xia find you too?"

"I came to be here because the seas were at war," Nadira says. "And I have not decided whether or not to pledge myself to the new sea king."

I can't help but watch Iris, a pink blur ahead of us. "So, you came to help a whole other king?"

"Royalty is interchangeable," Nadira says with a flash of pearly teeth. "But Iris and I met on one of her quests. She convinced me to come here to aid this land. I may not be from this world, but I am a mermaid. As long as there is water, I belong to it. That is where my fealty lies."

"Lucky for us there's ocean all around this island," I say.

"Lucky, indeed."

The path we take weaves through a beautiful landscape, the sunflower fields giving way to endless rolling hills interrupted here and there by wildflower meadows. Márohu circles overhead, her wings letting her coast on a breeze. The Pegasi all seem jittery, and I have to pull on Tortuga's reins to get him to settle down. It must be hard to watch another creature fly when your wings are bound.

Lin falls in step with us. They tuck a black wave behind a gently pointed ear. "We're nearly there, if you're wondering."

Nadira makes a face. "We certainly are not. We're not even at the rivers!"

"Or rather, sort of nearly there," Lin corrects. "That is, we're closer than yesterday. Sorry, I was hoping to put Eliza's mind at ease. She looked worried."

I laugh. "I'm not worried, though I probably should be. I'm having a hard time feeling like this is all real. I mean, I'm here and I feel *things*. I never imagined I'd be here alone. While I should be worried some creature is going to eat me, I keep thinking *wow* Lula would have wanted to run buck naked in that fairy garden."

"Is there nothing like Adas in your realm?" Lin asks, absent-mindedly running long fingers through the Pegasus's mane.

"There is," I say. "I had to do a project on national parks once, so maybe that counts, but I've never left my city. Until now."

"What's it like?" Lin asks, violet eyes brightening with excitement.

"New York?" I sigh. "Gray. Loud. Dirty. For a long time, we didn't leave the house. But sometimes my sisters and I would take the train from Brooklyn to Manhattan just for fun."

"I have been to this Brooklyn place," Nadira says. She turns up her nose and pinches it. "It was, how do you say, a dump. My gills were infected after swimming in that water."

"Hey now," I say. "That's *my* dump. Anyway, I swear, every time we go into New York, I think there is nothing more beautiful than the skyline of buildings and glittering traffic. I guess it's easy to see it as beautiful from afar when you're not knee deep in litter or crushed in a stampede during rush hour. But it's home."

Lin nods along to my words. For a moment, I think they might say something. I see the struggle there, but when they look over at the guards, they seem to change their mind.

As the meadows and hills open up, I let out a gasp of awe. I never knew that a place could be so beautiful it made you want to cry. We've emerged over a hill and between two great rivers that snake across the land. Birds flock across the cerulean sky, and even from this distance, I can see adas and animals roaming on the green. The air is so clean I feel like it is regenerating my city lungs.

"This is the Tanamá River to the left and to the right is the Solomía River," Lin says. "They stretch across the entire island, but the Tanamá ends in a lake in the south."

"And the Solomía?"

"The outerlands. We'll see when we get there, won't we?" Lin bites the inside of their lip. "And don't worry about being eaten. The only creatures bigger than us here are the Pegasi and the mountain tapirs, but they're vegetarians."

When Márohu circles back and signals that the coast is clear, Iris blows on her conch. We ride between the twin rivers that cut through the middle of the island. I grab hold of Tortuga's reins as tight as I can and sink down. I scream for most of the time we're riding, partially because we're going so fast, but mostly because I have never felt this kind of freedom. The wind is cold against my face, and the reverberation of hooves beating on the ground feels good in my chest.

It turns out that "we're nearly there" and "sort of nearly there" is exactly like the time Alex made me walk *two miles* around Central Park with the promise of "just one more block." Flanked by the two rivers, we follow an empty dirt path over the swell of hills and flat plains.

For so long, it feels like we're the only souls on this road, but winged adas fly overhead. I wonder if they're going to the castle the way the others had or if they'll stay in Girasol Grove. I try to imagine what it would be like if I had to leave my home for good. It did happen, back when the house in Brooklyn burned down, but at least there was *somewhere* to go. What if New York were being destroyed by something we had no control over? Where would we go then?

I'm pulled out of the melancholy thought spiral by the strangest creature I've ever seen. It has the shape, the long neck, four legs, and delicate face of a deer, but it is entirely pieced together from leaves, bits of grass, petals. Two branches twist where antlers should be. Bright river stones are set for eyes. I can see the hollow places of thin air where the leaves and bits don't quite cover.

"Ah, vientícos." I don't even realize I've stalled until Arco doubles back to get me. He adjusts the pen behind his ear, the smattering of freckles across his face look like dusted gold.

"Vee-ehn-what?"

Arco laughs playfully. "Vientícos. They're wind spirits. Iris and I used to spend days chasing them when we were little. They're supposed to be good omens."

Two others join, one in the likeness of a bird of prey and another that stares at me, piecing together *my face*. The one that has taken on my shape takes a step toward me. Her hair billows in the wind, each movement like looking at a flip book bringing a drawing to life. And then, a black shadow leaps behind her. My scream is lost in my throat as the furry creature takes a bite out of the vientíco. Petals and leaves flutter through the air and the others scatter. I clap my hand over my mouth and watch the mountain tapir, its strange, long nose wiggling as it chomps down on a creature I can't see.

"So much for a good omen," I say, and tug on Tortuga's reins to ride.

The wind carries the sharp smell of grass, bits of flower petals and leaves that made up the wind spirit. The sky starts to darken, promising violent weather.

Suddenly, everyone is in motion, trying to outrun the storm. My hands cramp from holding the reins too tight, but we're not fast enough. There is no cover out here to protect us from the rain that is now falling in torrential sheets, and Iris shouts for us to keep moving. Thunder rolls as fast as the dark gray clouds. If not for the stretch of blue in the horizon, I would think night had fallen. Despite my clothes clinging to my skin and rain running into my eyes and mouth, I am not afraid. My heart hammers with excitement. My blood rushes in my ears. I lick cold rainwater from my lips and turn my face to the sky. Beside me, Lin lets loose a howl, and Nadira's laugh cuts through the crackle of lightning up ahead.

When the storm becomes a drizzle, we slow. Vita runs a hand across her bald green scalp. "Commander, we should walk from here. The mud is too deep for the horses."

Iris surveys our sodden, dirty group. The only one who doesn't look like a wet alley cat is Nadira. At Iris's go-ahead, we dismount. Warm mud fills the empty spaces of my leather slipper sandals. I grimace, but no one else is complaining, so I swallow the *gross* that I was going to utter.

Trekking across mud is decidedly not as fun as riding in the rain in the middle of a thunderstorm, but we move slowly, steadily over flat terrain. I pant, my skin sticky with sweat. Stray vientícos follow us, and when they run across our path, the cool breeze that they carry is welcome.

Even the wagon packed with supplies moves faster than I do, my thighs burning the farther we go.

Iris lingers at the rear, her hair a deeper pink now that it's wet.

"I'm going as fast as I can," I say.

She glances over my shoulder, her hand at her sword hilt. "I know you are. It is also my duty to protect you. All of you."

"You're worried about monsters the Shuari spoke about," I intone.

"I worry because death—this kind of death—does not belong in Adas. These monsters shouldn't exist. They rot shouldn't exist. El Terroz created this land as paradise, and I intend to make sure it returns to that. Even still, I wouldn't want a creature gobbling you up."

I gulp. "Lin said there weren't any big predators. Wait, was that a compliment?"

Her brows go up, like she's weighing those words. "One can be small and deadly. There are fish in the river that, when swallowed by bigger fish, expand to rip its predator from the inside out."

"We don't have to swim any rivers, do we?" I ask, pressing my hand to my belly.

"We do not."

As the sun shines and the mud dries, my steps become easier. But when we reach our company clustered ahead of us, not moving forward, I want to point out that Iris is wrong about another thing.

We may just have to swim across a river after all.

15

The mermaid queen has a sweet song for me!

I must go find it at the bottom of the sea.

—WITCHSONG #23, BOOK OF CANTOS

The depression in the ground between the two rivers boxes us in so the only way out is across water or to double back.

"Is this normal?" I ask Iris, but she's already striding to the front of the group.

Nadira, who is closest to earshot, turns to me. She scratches at the pearly scars on her neck and shakes her head. "The rivers have flooded and filled in a break in the ground that shouldn't be there. There are no earthquakes in Adas."

I know we're both thinking of the rot and the accounts of the Shuari who recalled that the earth shook. The horses stomp around, and some of them rear back so far, they would have unsaddled their riders if we hadn't walked. Arco clicks his tongue and herds the beasts with Huracán at his side.

Iris turns to Peridot, who shrinks back at the intensity of her eyes. The delicate branches protruding from his hands twitch.

"Can you build a bridge from roots?" she asks.

"I can try," he says.

A buzzing sound approaches. Xia walks on bare feet caked in mud, her dress made of shimmering cobwebs clings to her, the glass box carefully resting on her hip. The sliver of rot inside is still.

"You will do it," the siren says. "You must speak to the earth."

Peridot gives a curt nod and raises his hands. We give him room. I remember the way my father conjured lightning and made trees fall. But out here, there is only grass and mud. Even though I keep my distance, I can feel Peridot's magic sift through the dirt. If I lower my ear to the ground, I think I might be able to hear it. Spindly white roots sprout upward, then coil back into themselves. They wither.

"Dig deeper, son of the forests, child of El Terroz," Xia says.

"I can't!" Peridot shouts, his eyes shut with strain.

"Siphon," she says. "Double his efforts."

I kneel beside Peridot and grab his hand. I have done this before. I borrowed Nova's power and conjured light. Dad's storm. McKay's shape-shifting. For nearly fifteen years before all that, I latched on to Valeria's magic and drained little by little, taking just enough that I was a different person completely. I know that I am different here, too. When I touch Peridot's skin, a shooting pain drives up the center of my arm. Worst of all is that it feels *good*. I can smell the raw green of grass, the roots, too far away. We reach deeper below. But beneath the ground trembling at our fingertips, there's a murmur. I can hear it whisper.

216

I wrench my hand free, and Peridot staggers back. Did he hear it too? I rub my hands on the muddy grass until the sensation goes away.

"It's not working," Peridot says, staggering into Calliope's arms.

I feel like I could leap across that river.

"What about the Pegasi?" Lin asks Arco.

He looks up at me, then at the others. "Even if I disobeyed my father for this cause, these creatures have not flown in centuries. Their wings were clipped. Lin, what about your rift?"

Lin shakes their head. "I've never carried another person before."

"I can carry you across," Márohu says, her waxy black wings at her sides. "We'd have to leave the steeds behind."

Vita steps in beside Iris, smoothing the sides of her cropped green hair. "It would be foolish to go on without the supplies. There is nothing in the outerlands anymore."

"We have to double back," Alma says. "You should have listened to the prince."

Before Iris can object, her brow already wrinkling with disapproval, Nadira runs up to the very edge of the newly formed river. The water is a muddy brown, and it is impossible to see how deep it goes.

"I have an idea. Wait here," Nadira says, before she pushes off and dives headfirst into the rushing current.

"Where are we supposed to go!" I shout, running to the edge of the bank. She's gone. "What just happened?"

"She's saving herself, isn't it obvious?" Alma mutters darkly.

"*Alma*," Arco says, his voice a deep growl for the first time since I've known him. "Tend to the Pegasi or return to Castillo de Sal."

She bows her head, her nose nearly touching the ground. The

green rope of her braid looks like a snake. "As you command, Your Highness."

"She'll be back," I say, anxiety knitting in my gut as I stare at the rushing waters. "She'll be back."

I repeat it while the guardians go another round with the rot in the glass box, and Xia until our magic is weak with failure. I repeat it while Iris, Arco, and guards scout in both directions along the river break.

But as the sky darkens and the first splash of orange hits the sky, I'm not so sure Nadira will come back. I feel like one of those women standing on a pier, waiting for a ship to return from sea, and then being sorely disappointed when it doesn't happen.

"Make camp!" Iris shouts. I can see the cracks in her exterior, in the way she fiddles with the straps of her horse, Lirico.

Tents go up just in time for it to start to rain again. Márohu prefers to stand outside and watch the lightning streak across the massive dark sky. I share my tent with Lin. We put our rolled-up cots side by side, the thin blankets surprisingly warm. Fireflies and a bit of spray from the rain come in, but it's better than being soaked.

"Do you think Nadira left?" Lin asks. Tiny lights pulse overhead.

I think of what she told me earlier. She would not follow a king, but she came to a place she doesn't know and risked her life. Why? Because she believed in Iris. "No, but I'm worried something might have gone wrong. We should scout in the morning."

Lin yawns and stretches. We both sleep with one leg sticking out of our covers. "Good night, Rose."

"Good night." But before I close my eyes, I realize what Lin just called me.

Lin's smirk is the definition of mischief, and it takes me a couple of blinks to realize that they called me by my real name. "When you were facing off with Xia I *may* have gone into the rift. I heard her call you that. I won't tell anyone. But why did you decide to use another name? Even if someone knows your true name, they won't be able to control you. You're human."

It feels so good to hear my name that I don't even care I've been made. "My dad told me not to give anyone my real name. If we had gotten away from the castle, if we'd gone into hiding, no one would be looking for Rose. They'd be looking for Eliza. Now, it feels easier to be someone else."

Lin nods along to my words, violet eyes crinkling at the corners. "You didn't strike me as an Eliza. Rose suits you—a flower so lovely no one is paying attention to the thorns."

"What about you?" I ask. "Is you name just Lin?"

"Lin Octavio. My father said I was named after his favorite month, October. Although I didn't really understand what *months* were. Then I realized he was referring to the turns of the moon. Why not just call them Pearl Moon, Blood Moon, Salt—"

"Moons are different in different realms. Or so my sister says. She's the only other person I know who's traveled to another dimension, and now me." We turn to face each other. I can see the sharp outline of their fairy features. "I like Octavio. My sister Alex's birthday is in October. She hates it because she *loathed* Halloween for a long time. She's a monster."

Lin gasps, almost swallowing a firefly that was near their face. "I thought you were brujas."

Laughing this way feels good, like bring cracked open to release bubbling pressure. "Not literally. Like, I call her a monster for things like buying whole-grain waffles and because she falls asleep at the movie theater and snores."

"I don't know any of the things you just said." Lin leans back on folded arms. "But it sounds nice."

"I wish I could bring you to my world," I say. "We have bacon and video games and chocolate-covered everything."

"Can I tell you a secret?"

"Of course."

"I went once. To your world." Their words have a sad edge. They speak so softly it's like confessing a fear. "It is the farthest my gift has ever let me travel."

"Where did you go? When?"

"I was searching for something that could explain my powers. My mother was an ada, but it was my father who had living magic. It was right after they both died, and all I wanted was to feel connected to them again. I wished so hard for an answer that I stepped through the rift and into the loudest, tallest place I have ever been to.

"For a few moments I was in a place called the Empire, surrounded by glittering castles and palaces. There were people all around me peering through lenses that could let them see as far as the horizon."

I stifle an excited squeal and clap my hand over Lin's. "You made it all the way to the *Empire State Building*? But if you could get there, why did you come back to Adas?"

Lin's violet eyes flick to mine, then there's a shadow there. A sorrow that I felt during my Deathday and when I learned the truth about my dad. It is the unshakable knowledge that things would never be the same, which is why I can't look away. "I didn't belong there. Perhaps, if my father had taken me, it would have been different. But there were so many people. A large iron beast nearly ate me. Humans stare too much, and at the time, I didn't know how to glamour myself to appear more like them. I felt scared, with nowhere to go, and the next thing I knew, I was back in the castle. Adas is the only home I've ever known. I have to play my part in saving what's left of it."

I squeeze Lin's hand. "You could travel that far even before the rot. Why didn't you say anything?"

"Because I tried, and it never happened again. It felt like a one-time thing."

I think of the way I used my power before I was aware of what I was capable of. What could I be capable of in a place made of magic? *Daughter of El Fin, Master of Everything's End.* I wonder, if I use my power to the height of its ability, could I end not just the rot but all of Adas? I picture Calliope sneering the word *devourer* and push the thought away.

"You'll get stronger," I say. *We have to.* Because there is not an option in which I don't get to go home.

When I drift off to sleep, I can hear the susurration of the earth. Is this the recoil of using Peridot's earth magic? It whispers to me. *Shhh. Shhh. Shhh.* I try to call out to it, but my fingers only dig into the dirt and feel nothing.

At daybreak, Nadira is not back yet. Iris and I seem to be the only ones who truly believe the mermaid didn't desert. It doesn't make sense that she'd leave us now, no matter what Alma thinks.

We wash up with fresh water from the Solomía. For a moment I wonder if this is what Alex went through in Los Lagos. Where did she use the bathroom with Nova and Rishi around? How did she handle always feeling like you smell like sweat? Did she have her period while she was there? Suddenly, I have renewed respect for my sister, and I regret never asking her.

When we're all done, Iris gives orders. We make contingency plans in case something has happened to Nadira. Lin dives into the river break and then reappears through a rift, soaking wet.

Calliope holds a blanket open for them to step into. "Well?"

"Too deep," Lin says between chattering teeth.

Iris nods once. Her calm is eerie, because I am more prone to worrying. I suppose that's why she's in charge. "I need two pairs of scouts to ride back the length of the Solomía and Tanamá. I don't care if we have to go the long way. There has to be a break somewhere."

As Iris rides off with one of the groups, the rest of us return to training. I change into a pair of brown leggings that remind me of armor and a tunic the color of a bloody sunset. My skin feels too tight, and my fingernails are filthy with dirt.

We're out of drinking water, so I take up a few of the water skins and hook them over my shoulder. Arco, sitting in front of the morning campfire, looks up from his reading. His hair is delightfully disheveled, and I can tell he slept out here under the cloudy sky.

"You shouldn't go off on your own," Arco says, shutting his book and throwing it inside his tent.

"Come with me, then," I say.

The grin he flashes is wry, and I try not to think too much about his canines being sharper than those of the average human. "Then you shall have me."

His wording is curious. I shall have him but in what way? Walking by my side? As my friend? As the boy that makes my stomach feel like it's a housing a hundred thousand butterflies?

"You came on this journey to write things down, right?" I ask.

Arco nods. "That is my duty, but I imagine there is so much more you'd like to ask me."

Honestly, there is so much that I want to ask him. About what he and Iris were like as children. What his favorite part of Adas is. What he would do if he weren't a prince. I kind of want to ask how old he is, but not really. I have Alex in my head going, *he's probably a hundred*. But it's just a crush. I'm allowed to have a crush.

"I mean, I could hear the scratch of your pen all night so it must have been important."

"I keep trying to make sense of it. Before the rot was advancing so quickly, I considered it was a plague from the gods." He glances at me, at my hands, and I shove them self-consciously into my pockets. "El Fin was the god who would end the worlds. All of them. But there was supposed to be a reason. If I can turn everything I have seen and know into words, I will understand something I have missed."

I shrug. "Sometimes people look to gods for answers when we have everything we need to fix those mistakes."

"You speak from experience."

I don't want to get into the mess with La Muerte last year. "One thing is for sure. The rot is magic. I can drain magic. But I'm not strong enough yet."

"The blood root will help with that," he says. Neither of us add, *if we can find it.*

We walk up a slope and my thighs burn, but less than they did during my first trek here. I feel stronger. From up here the wide white-capped river rushes.

"What else do you know about El Fin?"

"Nothing that we didn't know before. It was a god that rose from nothingness. The Deos slept too long or lingered past their time. He is stronger than Lady de la Muerte. I think he will take her, too."

I remember the old goddess. The cloak that dragged at her feet was made of souls, and her pale arms were covered in the names of the people she would reap. She said she never wanted to see our family again. Mainly Lula.

"The time of the gods is long gone," I say. "I think this problem is ours to bear."

He smiles at that, and we lower to the riverbank to fill the water skins. I watch his lean arms, the muscles that flex under the sheer fabric. He isn't weak. But I know that there are other kinds of strength besides waving a sword around.

"Why did you choose to be the scribe of the kingdom?"

Arco fills up three bags before he answers. "For a time, I hated every part of being my father's son. I ruined people the way he did. I drank entire cellars the way he did. I broke promises the way he did. There was something inside of me that was never satis-fied. After my mother died, I wanted purpose. By then, my father decided that he would never have an heir. Neither Iris nor I were worthy of his crown. I knew the way that I could keep my kingdom whole is by recording its history. But if we cannot defeat this rot, who will remember there was ever such a place as Adas in the first place?"

"Don't give up just yet." I manage a weak smile. He brushes my hair behind my ear. Then I go back to something he said. "What did Iris do that made her not worthy of the crown?"

"That is for her to tell you," Arco says. "But we both betrayed our father. I, by being a ruin to myself. I can say my sister changed when our mother was killed."

I think of the way my sisters and I were the first few years our dad was gone. Isn't this the same? Alex's anger bottled up so tight that she'd snap, Lula overcompensating to fill the holes in our hearts. What did I do? Talk to ghosts who no longer talk back. But my sisters were always there. I could count on that. "You lost your mother too. How are you changed?"

"We mourn in different ways."

I look into his eyes. I don't think I truly understood Arco until now. I thought he might just be blindly forgiving his father. But he's trying to see good in the king that I'm not entirely sure is there. It's King Cirro who should seek forgiveness from his children.

Suddenly I realize how close Arco is. Close enough that I can see flecks of gold in his brown eyes that match his sweeping horns. His breath is like sweet grass, and when his finger traces the length of my jaw, my entire body feels like it's floating. I'm going to kiss a fairy prince, I think.

But my thoughts are interrupted by shapes moving along the

riverbank. Goose bumps rise along my arms as two large creatures crawl out of the water like they're ready to take a bite out of us. Arco stands in front of me, and though he seems calm, his posture is menacing.

"What are they?" I ask.

They have mostly human torsos and the lower halves of crabs. They move from side to side on pointed legs, snapping coral-pink pincers in the air.

"Delicate treats," one of the creatures says, her voice like the rush of holding a seashell up to your ear.

"Little lost starfishes," a second one says. This one has a larger head, and when she speaks, her mouth is full of razor teeth. Beady eyes are set in a round head with sharp chins.

I glance around for something to fight with. We could run farther out, but they'd only give chase. And then what? Hope our friends at camp come and rescue us?

"I am the prince of Adas," Arco says, his voice is sonorous. "Return to the cove where you belong."

"There is no more cove." They move closer. One of them spits on the ground. "Rotten prince of rotten fruit."

I feel Arco's strangled shock. He struggles for words until he finally says, "I didn't know."

"That is why you have failed." One of them opens her mouth wide and lets out a screech. "Adas falls apart into the sea. No prince and no king no more."

"What have you seen?" Arco says, fear threading his voice.

"We have seen the belly bleed. There is nothing for us," the tallest one says.

"Our food spoiled."

"Our food *gone*."

"Your flesh will last us a for a turn at *least*, starfishes."

For a moment, I think a third one has joined because my blurry eyes only see a shock of pink. But when my sight clears, it is Iris. Her armor glistens like pink pearl as she lands between us and the crabmaids, her sword a deadly threat under one of the creature's throats.

"Do you want to live?"

"Yes, yes, my princess," the crabmaid shrieks, bowing at Iris's feet.

Iris turns to us, a deadly resolve in her eyes. Do I imagine the relief there, too? "Are you hurt?"

My mouth is so dry all I can do is shake my head.

"Away with you!" Iris shouts and stands at ease. The crab women leap back into the waters. When they don't resurface, Iris sheaths her sword and whirls on us with a scowl. Her long black lashes blink against the harsh sun. But when she looks at Arco, she rests her hands on his shoulders, her hand gently cupped on his face.

"Yurabas will make flutes out of your bones if you let them," she says.

"They said Adas was falling into the sea," he says desperately.

"Those creatures," I wonder out loud. "What did you call them?"

"Yurabas," Iris says. "They held the Court of La Bahia once, before the rot. Most of their kind has either left for kinder seas or perished."

"I thought you were going to kill her," Arco says softly.

227

Iris steps back, and I see the hurt flash in her eyes. She's returning to her steely mask, letting him go. "They scare easily enough. Besides, they have suffered enough loss. Do you think I'm a mindless killer, brother?"

"I'm surprised you'd care what I think of you."

I think of his words from earlier. What could Iris have done to make him think that? Then I also remember that he was going to kiss me, and I can't meet his eyes again. I busy myself picking up our water supply.

"Did you find anything?" I ask. "You're back sooner than I thought."

"Yes." Iris's stare goes from Arco to me, and frowns. "Nadira is back. And she didn't come alone."

16

King Cirro swallowed the sea
to find the perfect pearl for his beloved.

— CLARIBELLE AND THE KINGDOM OF ADAS:
TALES TALL AND TRUE, GLORIANA PALACIOS

T he sky is blue and cloudless now, the air smells the way Peridot's magic tasted. The camp is gathered along the lip of the rushing river break that blocks our way. Four bodies have climbed out of the water. Mermaids.

Only one of them is Nadira, her dark green hair nearly black now that it's wet. The other three have gem-colored eyes, deep brown skin, and ropes of hair braided with pearls and shells. Long, shimmering tails undulate and push them forward on round bellies.

Nadira transforms her tail, splitting it right where her fins meet. Her skin is dusted with the shining sand that once were her scales. Her gills flutter for air, and when she coughs up water, they shut once again.

"Apologies for being gone for so long," Nadira says. "But the court of the River Queen was harder to track than I thought."

"Mother Dayo," Arco says, wonder in his voice. "You have not been seen here in years. You honor the land."

The mermaid referred to as Mother Dayo sits taller than the other two, a crown of living coral and pearls atop her head. Scales the bright blue of a parrotfish cover her forearms, shoulders, her large breasts, and the sides of her wide belly. Her nostrils flare, but a curious, cruel smile plays on her lips. "We are here because one of our own called us. What do you wish, Children of Mayté, True Queen of Adas?"

Arco holds out a hand to Iris. To everyone's surprise, she takes it. But I have seen, even for a moment, how much Iris cares for her brother. If anything, they stand united at the sound of their mother's name.

Iris crouches down to be at eye level with the mermaid matron. The princess bows with reverence and says, "Mother Dayo, we ask for your help."

"Our grandfather, King Eterno, once gave you dominion over the rivers and waters surrounding Adas," Arco says. "Will you help us safely across this unnatural river?"

Mother Dayo's wide lips lift into a sneer. Her gums are ink black, her teeth sharp. "King Eterno gave me dominion over what cannot be claimed. And yet, my children and I have watched over the *forgotten* parts of the kingdom, may the Goddess of the Seas flood King Cirro with everything he deserves."

Behind her the two mermaids—one with golden dreads piled atop her head and one with a pink-scaled scalp—repeat Mother Dayo's blessing to King Cirro.

"You're a curious one," Mother Dayo tells me, as if noticing me for the first time.

"That's what I hear," I say.

"You know what is out there," Iris says, strength and calm in her voice, but I've been around her long enough to see her tells. She shifts her weight to the right side when she's overthinking, and she keeps her free hand on her sword belt like a security blanket. "Yurabas attacked my brother moments ago, so far from their southern cove. We are trapped here by this river created by the rot. There will be *no* rivers, no seas if we do not get across to the outerlands."

"I have never seen the land turn on its folk this way, and for that, I share your woe. The plague, for I believe it is a sickness, has disrupted both my rivers. My daughters and I can help you across, a single time." The mermaid turns her face to the side, stubbornness in her cobalt-blue eyes. When she stares into the midday sun, she doesn't even blink. Though her deep-brown skin is smooth of wrinkles, I can see how ancient she is in the sharpness of her eyes. When she turns to me, it is like I can *feel* her power, old as the seas. "In exchange for a favor and a promise."

"I will pay it, as long as they are favors and promises within my grasp."

"The favor is for all. I will tell you a story and you will listen."

Iris glances around, but there is not a single objection. I personally, would love to listen to an ancient river mermaid tell me stories.

"And the promise?" Iris asks.

Mother Dayo points a fingernail encrusted with miniscule barnacles. "Is not within your grasp. It is within his. Scribe. Come closer and I will whisper it to you."

I think of all the mermaid legends I've read. The ones where they sail off into the sunset and the ones where the creatures drag their prey underwater and watch them drown. I take a step forward, but Nadira puts out a hand to stop me.

Arco crouches down and gives the mermaid matron his ear. Shock widens his eyes. His full lips press into a thin line. Then resolve hardens his features. He nods a single time and whispers something to the River Queen that none of us can hear. Then, Arco returns to us.

Mother Dayo adjusts her weight, shifting her tail. Her gem-like stare bores into Iris, then scans the rest of us. Do our feet look strange to her? I have never seen someone so completely at home in their skin, scales and all, and I love this river queen.

"Listen to my song," Mother Dayo says, and her deep voice weaves a story like fine thread. "Listen to the short mortal life of La Flor. She bore fifteen daughters to inherit the island of Adas. The oldest, Dalia, to wear the god-forged crown. The youngest, to maintain paradise. The rest, to support their sisters.

"Dalia chose for herself a mate. King Suspiro was an ada half-born of the sea. He went to the ocean to pick the brightest jewel of the waves as a gift for his new bride. He swallowed the water, the current, the tide, to walk freely across the bottom of the sea floor. Indeed, he found his gem. King Suspiro swallowed the sea, but he forgot to return the sea where it belonged, and the first king of Adas drowned."

Mother Dayo sits back and watches our faces, lingering on me for longer than I am comfortable. I remember this story another way. In my book at home, King Cirro swallowed the ocean to find a pearl for Mayté. Is this another thing he took credit for, like the ceiba tree? I think of why the river queen would do this. Out of all the things she could ask for, including the crown of Adas for herself, she has done this.

"One of you knows the ending," the River Queen says.

Xia's finger drums on the glass box. The thing inside is flat and cracked. "I do know. In her grief, Dalia's reign weakened. The daughters of La Flor lost their throne."

"When I was a girl," Mother Dayo says, "I saw a queen wear the crown of Adas. My *hope* is that I will see that once again. Now, I will keep my part of our bargain."

The mermaids leap back into the rushing river, even Nadira. With Mother Dayo at the front, they create a rope across. Water rushes from both sides, creating tiny whirlpools at the center.

All at once, the four mermaids open their mouths and inhale. They drink the river, funnels of water rushing into their mouths, impossibly contained within their bodies.

Now, the riverbed is bare, a wide chasm that slashes across the Solomía and Tanamá. We can walk across. Iris and the guards set everything in motion. We travel across slick mud that suctions around our ankles, stepping on jagged stones. I remember falling through that portal, the choking sensation of dirt in my nose and mouth. I listen to Iris's voice as she leads us, guides us to the green bank of the other side.

When we are safe, Mother Dayo and the mermaids return the water to where it belongs.

"Brother," Iris says, "what did you do? What did you promise Mother Dayo?"

His smile is earnest, and if he has paid a steep price, we would never be able to tell. "That is between me and the River Queen."

17

When the time of the gods came to an end,

El Terroz gathered his siblings to help him forge a crown.

— LOST STORIES OF ADAS, ARCO,
SONG OF THE ORCHID QUEEN

We ride faster than before, trying to make up for the time we've lost. Even though Iris won't say it, I think that Mother Dayo's story upset her. No one seemed to know the original story that now King Cirro is famous for. I consider, why would she say that she's waiting for a queen to rule Adas when she knows there's a king at the Castillo de Sal? It almost sounds like encouraging Iris to usurp the throne, repeating her own father's mistakes.

We stop only once to distribute food but don't disembark. Nadira passes me something that looks very much like a tamale. I unwrap the green banana leaf and smell it.

Nadira laughs at me. "Are you checking for poison?"

I take a bite, and I'm surprised to find the mild sweet starchy texture of yucca. "Poisoned by olives, maybe." I pick them out and eat the rest in three bites. I throw the banana leaf in the grass, where a cluster of baby tapirs are grazing.

Tortuga shakes his mane, like he's affronted I didn't think of him. He returns to munching on the weeds and grass within reach. Vientícos in the shape of birds flutter around us, diving at my head.

"They seem to like you," Nadira says, gripping the reins again.

"The mosquitos seem to like me too," I say, scratching at my ankles, where I have dozens of bites.

As we ride, Nadira and I take up the rear. I wonder if it would be rude of me to ask her what it feels like to swallow gallons of water at once. I decide to do it anyway.

Nadira throws her head back and laughs. "I am a mermaid, Eliza. I simply made room for it."

"But where does it go? Did you swallow any fish in the process?"

"If I did, I spit them back out."

"My sister used to tell me that I tried too hard to rationalize magic, but I just like to know."

"I'd like to know what promise the prince made to Mother Dayo. You don't break a promise with the sea easily."

We return to silence and ride on, catching up with the others. The Tanamá River on the left splits south and the Solomía snakes into the Shuari rain forest. Iris is at the lead, trying to calm down Lirico. His white mane is shaking from side to side, and we are not even in the shadows of the trees yet.

"Stay together." Iris and the guards draw their weapons, but all I can think about is the group of Shuari tree adas walking into Girasol Grove talking about shadows and monsters. We approach a rain forest that feels quiet and empty in a way the plains we've just crossed are not.

Whatever tore through here was full of rage. Iris shows no signs of slowing down. Márohu's wings are a black beacon where she's scouting ahead. I notice the way Calliope reaches out to Peridot, squeezing his hand once. Something howls in the distance, but Vita assures me it's some sort of monkey.

For the first time, I notice abandoned wooden houses built up in the trees. Ladder bridges connect one to the other, some of them broken off and hanging, split open on vines. Adas lived here. Adas ran from this place. They died. A body is propped up against a tree. His eyes are closed, and he's begun to fuse with the dying bark of the trunk. I remember what Arco told me about the creatures of Adas returning to the earth. Becoming something more.

Márohu's shadow flies directly over me and into the trees.

Except when I look up, I see her crouched up ahead with Iris. Whatever just passed me wasn't the winged girl.

I open my mouth to call out to the others. Every part of me is frozen with alarm as a hiss emanates from the shadow of the canopy. Tortuga rears and bucks. I scream and try to hold on, perpendicular to the ground. My feet are stuck in the stirrups, but I feel myself falling, my limbs twisting at a painful angle that I know will break me in half. Before I hit the ground, someone grips my shoulder. There is darkness—a black so complete it feels like vanishing from existence.

The world comes back into focus in a rush of color and noise.

The rain forest. The road. Lin. They stand next to me, violet eyes wide. I know there is no time to ask what they just did, and why we are six feet away from my Pegasus. For now, we run with the others as fast as we can.

"Eliza!" someone shouts my name.

"I've got her!" Lin cries out. We hold hands and try to catch Tortuga, but my Pegasus lets loose a terrified whinny and takes off.

"What was that?" I ask, panting as I run at Lin's side.

"I don't know. There's something in the trees."

"What happened to 'no predators in Adas'?" I demand, panting.

"I can be wrong from time to time."

Hooves on the ground pound like thunder across a sky. I glance behind us, where the cart of supplies is catching up. The guard at the helm whips the reins. She extends a hand to help us up, but terror blanches her face.

A creature erupts onto the road. It's hunched over in a crouch, its body a gleaming carapace of deep green with sheer, filmy wings. Sinewy arms end in sharp pincers that slash at the air.

"Run!" the guard shouts as a long blue spike rips her chest open, bright scarlet blood running down her armor. An unfamiliar warmth sprays across my face. She looks down at the hole in her body, legs flailing as she's lifted from the cart and dragged into the cover of leaves in the jungle. A putrid stench fills the air.

I shove Lin out of the way as the horse runs wildly past us, dragging the cart behind it. My body shakes with fear. I know I should run. I want to run. But I replay the guard's death over and over. I see the fear frozen on her face.

"Eliza!" This time it's Iris who shouts after me. "Lin!"

She gallops back on her white-and-gold horse, Vita and two other guards riding at her side. Lin slings themselves onto the saddle behind Iris.

I reach for Vita's hand, but a second creature returns and cuts us off, crawling out onto the road on clawed feet. This one comes close enough that we can see its face. Pointed teeth line a rounded reptilian mouth that snaps, a bright red tongue moving in the air as if it's sensing, smelling. A long, barbed tail that ends in a sharp scorpion's hook.

Iris lets loose a bloodcurdling scream, waving her sword in the air as she charges the creature. She slices the tail's hook clean off, but the beast doesn't go down. It pounces on her. Iris leaps off the horse with her hands around the hilt of her sword. She drives it through the creature's back. Blue blood bubbles through the wound and splatters across her cheek.

Vita dismounts and runs over to her commander. Using the tip of her spear, she leans down and examines the creature.

"What in the name of El Terroz is this beast?" one of the other guards asks.

When I'm sure the first thing out of my mouth won't be a scream, I say, "These are the monsters the Shuari spoke of."

Iris pulls out her sword and wipes the sticky blood across her thigh. Her dark brows are knit together, but her voice is soft. "There should be no creatures like this born of Adas."

"They came from somewhere," Lin says, holding the reins of Iris's horse.

"Lin, ride ahead with Zuri. Tell the others to keep going and don't come back," Iris says. "Vita, Emmen, with me."

Lin shuts their eyes tightly. Zuri, a bulky guard with raven hair in disarray, leaps on the horse. A rift erupts, brighter than any they've conjured before, and they ride through. The crackle of magic sparks in the air and then vanishes with a pop of static.

"The other monster could return," I say.

Iris sucks in a breath, her eyes like daggers behind me. "They *have* returned."

Iris is right. There are half a dozen of them, smaller than the first two but with the same sharp teeth and hooked tails that move in the air like they're searching for a target. She cuts down two of the monsters, drenching herself in putrid blue blood.

"Get Eliza to safety," Iris commands.

I pick up a thick branch from the ground, ready to fight or hit a home run, I'm not sure. But I'm not leaving her alone. "We're not going anywhere without you."

She sees the weapon I've chosen and gives a strangled laugh. With a single look to her guards, they grab me by my shoulders and heave me onto the saddle. I scream and shout for them to put me down.

"We can't leave Iris there! Vita! We can't!" A cold wind encircles me, carrying a thousand leaves in the shape of a bat. A vientíco! I instinctively thrust my palms in the air and grab hold of its power. The magic of the wind spirit floods my senses. I'm encircled by leaves and bits of branches, anything light enough to carry in a breeze. I wrestle free from the guards' hold and I lash out, slamming a hard gale at the reptilian beasts. They fly away from a cornered Iris and roll across the ground.

One of the creatures gets back up and advances on Iris, its pincers inches from her face.

I grab hold of the power coursing through me and release it again, controlling the wind. It picks up rocks, pelting the creatures in their eyes. The beasts screech and scatter. Iris catches up to one and drives her sword through its shell. Vita tries to steady her Pegasus, so we can climb up. I jog to her and Iris.

Iris holds her side, panting, a real smile on her face. Wild and true. And gone just as quickly.

One of the monsters returns. Its tail drives through the air, then slams into Vita's horse. The guard tries to throw herself off, but another pincer appears, latching on to her shoulder. We scream as they are both dragged into the dark of the trees, lost behind leaves. Iris chases after them, and Emmen runs after the princess.

The air is thick with the stench of decay. There is so much blood running down my cheeks. Blood has never really bothered me. We sacrifice it. We clean it up when my mom treats serious wounds in her infirmary. But for some reason, Vita's blood on my face mingling with the rotten blue blood of the beast makes my insides feel like dice set to roll.

I can feel Lin's magic before they reappear. Violet eyes take in the mess they left behind. Sorrow, regret are both there.

"We should go," Lin says, and presses a sure hand on my shoulder.

"We can't leave her."

"And we can't stay here."

I fold myself in half, holding my stomach as I retch from recoil and nausea. I have to keep it together.

After what feels like ages, there's movement in the brush. I grab my stick but sigh with relief when I see the green armor of the king's guard and Iris.

They have Vita slung over their shoulders. Her eyes are rolled back, and blood streams out of the wound on her shoulder.

"Help me get her onto the saddle," Iris says.

Emmen gives me a desolate stare. She knows what I do. With a wound like that, Vita's going to bleed out before we get where we need to go.

"Leave me," Vita chokes.

Iris cries as she falls to her knees, Vita in her arms. "Help. Please. Eliza— Lin—"

I wish I could do something. I wish I had my mother's power to heal. I wish I could do more than stand about uselessly as the life drains from this girl's body.

Vita looks up at Iris. "It was an honor to serve you, my—"

Iris keeps a hand pressed over the open wound. She's forehead to forehead with the girl. I'm struck by her vulnerability in this moment, and she must feel it because in the next, Iris sets her eyes on me.

"I told you to go."

I inhale. I am familiar with the resentment that comes with surviving when others don't. "If I had, then you'd be dead and we would be mourning *you*."

Iris looks past me to the other guard. "We will bury her, but not here. Help me, Emmen."

Emmen nods, her raven hair unraveling further from her long braid as she struggles to drape the dead body over the saddle. Lin attempts to make another rift, but their power fizzles from overuse.

We all walk, clutching our weapons. The forest has a dead quality. Not even the timbre of insects disturbs the silence. There is only our heavy tread and heavier breaths. We find another Pegasus farther down the path, stomping in circles, unsure of where to go. Emmen mounts it and rides ahead to find the others.

When we get to them, standing at the edge of a steep, rocky cliff, no one speaks. No one asks questions. There will be time for those later.

For now, I take in the sight of the desecrated rain forest. It's like El Terroz took his axes and cleaved a chunk of it away.

At the roots of the last tree marking the end of the Shuari, we put Vita to rest. Iris rips apart her tunic and I hand her a salvaged waterskin. She does her best to clean the girl up. She is a blur of movement, gathering stalks of leaves and any flower she can find to cover the wound. Last, Iris lays Vita's broken spear on her chest. I don't know why I'm so surprised by this gesture.

Iris turns to Peridot, who waits nearby. He controls the roots of the tree like he's tugging on marionette strings. They wrap around Vita in an everlasting embrace.

I can hear the Solomía river, though I can't see it. The tree line ends abruptly. We stand on a cliff shelf overlooking a desert that extends far and wide. I think back of the map on King Cirro's desk. It didn't know the ruin justice.

We make our own route of hard-packed earth and climb down. Our horses skate and tangle on slick stones, but Arco and Emmen herd them down the steep drop. Dust fills my nose and mouth. Roots jut out from the ground, and there's a trickle of water that must be runoff from the river. We scramble down for so long, night catches up to us. Calliope lights the way.

When we get to the bottom, I realize why we couldn't see the Solomía. The river has found a way through the cloven boulders, waterfalling down the face of the cliff. Around it grows lush palm trees and flowers. It is the last stretch of green for miles.

An oasis.

PART IV

THE ROT

18

The crown was wrought from gold
and seven stars and vines of thorn.
A goodbye from the gods of old
A gift for the queen unborn.

—LOST STORIES OF ADAS, ARCO,
SONG OF THE ORCHID QUEEN

Stepping onto the grass of the oasis feels like being in a realm within this realm. But at the same time, it is a boundary line, the place where life ends and the rot begins. Beneath flower-scented breeze is the decay. Too tired to speak, we all trudge along a path cut through dewy grass. As night falls, the guards hold red lanterns up high and lead the way.

The remnants of tiny wooden houses is all that's left of the adas who live here. Relief that we're going to be allowed to sleep slips away as we keep going. But eventually, the guards gather large stones and create a circle on the sand. Within it, Zuri builds a fire, and the other guards stand around us like sentries, trading lanterns for torches, while a group scouts the oasis for dangers.

I settle myself on the ground and hug my knees. I can't let myself fall apart yet. Not now. But I can't stop seeing chests cracked open in front of me. I can't stop wanting that sensation of drawing the power from the wind spirit and using it as my own. For the first time since being in Adas, I'm cold down to my bones.

I edge closer to the flames and watch the siren. She clutches the glass box on her lap. The creature within glides slowly from side to side like it's searching. Has she fed it? Or can it sense that it is near its whole being?

The food that remains is passed around, but I don't have an appetite. I overhear one of the guards say that we only have rations for two days, max. One responds with, "Have my share. We're not surviving that long."

"Xia," Iris says, blue and red blood dried on her hands and face. "What were those creatures?"

The siren's face is lit by firelight. Her black eyes are pools of onyx. Her movement is twitchy, and there's something familiar in the way she stares at the sky. Like my dad used to when he was remembering. Like I used to when I was being hounded by spirits.

"The rot is changing. Moving. Leaving things behind," she says.

I frown. "But what *are* they? If the rot is like a cancer eating away at this land, then how can it *make* things?"

"I didn't get a good look at them," Nadira says softly.

"They swarmed like blackflies over a mud pit," Zuri says.

"How many more can there be?" Márohu asks.

"What if—" I hate what I'm going to suggest. I hate even thinking it. "What if those creatures are adas?"

"Abomination," Emmen whispers.

There's the pop of the fire, the steady rush of the waterfall. I feel my heart thud louder and louder when I remember Vita's scream.

"How can that be?" Nadira asks.

"The rot has been spreading for some time," Arco says. "But these creatures are recent—"

"They're my retinue," Iris says, her face still as marble as she watches the fire. "When we tried to excavate the rot, they fell into the pit. Xia is right."

Uncertain glances are traded across the firepit. Fear sits alongside every one of us. Then come the suggestions of leaving. Abandoning the island to the rot. That is the one thing that is impossible. If I abandon Adas to the rot, then I abandon the world outside the magical barrier.

"There's nowhere to go," Calliope reminds us. "We keep fighting."

"We will die," one of the guards says softly.

No one responds for a long time until Xia says, "Do not despair, Guardians. Hope is like the stars above."

Yeah, out of reach? I think to myself. But even I can't bring myself to say it.

"Rest." Iris stands, her hand fisted around the hit of her sword. "In the morning Peridot will lead a search for the blood root."

He nods, but his confidence wavers as his eyes drag up to the towering cliff that used to be his home.

"You will drink the blood of the Deos," Xia says in her detached, buzzing voice. "Your power will bloom, and the rot will become uprooted."

We make camp in the small wooden houses we saw when we first arrived. I climb up the ladder that wheezes with every step I take and mutter good night to the others.

I grab the lantern hung above the door, though I'm still only able to see two feet ahead of me. The flap of wings beats loudly above, and I catch sight of Márohu taking her lantern higher into the trees. I don't blame her for wanting to have her own space.

I know I'm the only person in my room, but I have the sense that I'm not alone. I used to feel this way when I could see spirits, feel the pull of the Veil. Being here, in a room with a tidy bed under a sheer canopy to keep away mosquitoes and shutters that flap open and closed in the breeze, I can't shake the sensation that I'm walking in someone else's skin. Who lived here? What were their last thoughts? If I were still a seer, I would be able to have impressions of that. No other seer I knew *liked* being able to talk to ghosts. But I did. What kind of person misses *ghosts*? I miss that power. I miss the thing that I thought I was.

I sit on the bed and find a soft pair of pants and a linen top. I change quickly and am about to go to wash my face and body as best as I can when I hear a soft *tap tap tap*. There is no glass in this tiny wooden house, but I'm almost sure I heard it.

Then I realize it's coming from the lamp.

I lean in close to the red light, and there, a tiny fist pounds at the glass. The ada has a smooth red skull and glowing skin, like lava running beneath black stone. Her body flickers like a firefly.

I remember when I was eight, there was a boy who lived next door to us for a summer. I wanted to make friends who *weren't* related to me, but we weren't really allowed because sinmagos don't understand our power. They never could. I decided to try anyway and invited him into our yard, where he gathered fireflies into glass jars and shut the lid because he liked to watch as they glowed and glowed and then fell to the bottom. I punched him, and he chased me into the house. When he saw our altar covered in offerings and dripping candle wax, he called me a freak and pushed the votive candles on the floor, smashing a statue of La Viuda, Goddess of Widows and Keeper of Small Sorrows. Then he ran back out and I never saw him again.

I don't remember his name. I don't remember what I told my mother when she asked me why I broke the candles. I haven't thought about that boy in such a long time. But I wonder if the food is having the opposite effect on me. Instead of forgetting, I'm remembering things I thought I'd buried, each one a candle sputtering out and then reigniting.

I pull the latch on the lamp and the glass door swings open. The fairy zooms at my face and presses a kiss on my nose. It's like letting a match touch your skin immediately after blowing it out, but it doesn't hurt for long. I press my finger on her smooth, bald head. But instead of letting go, I close my fist around her body. Heat blooms on the pad of my hand, fine red lines singe up my fingers, and I hiss at the heat of this magic, like the time I burned my hand on a hot pan. I can't let go. I smell embers and shut my eyes because this feels good. Better than good. I feel lit up from the inside, my heart echoing loud in my ears. Raw, bright magic.

Then a voice wriggles through my thoughts. Nova's voice. *Remember yourself.*

I stumble back, wrenching my hand open.

The fairy falls with a hard thump.

"No, no, no," I hiss, my vision hazy and ringed with red. I drop to the floor to gather her into my hands, but she makes a sharp little cry. "I'm so sorry. I didn't mean to—"

Her sharp teeth close around the side of my finger, and then she's off, a pulsing red star fading into the night.

I crawl into bed and ball my fist, cradling it against my chest. The bite throbs, the magic still burns fine red lines across my skin, filling the lines of my palm. Worst of all is this feeling, deep down in my bones, like my power is just stretching, as if I've only scratched the surface of what I am capable of.

That night my sleep is restless. I can hear someone cry out in their sleep, others snoring to the rhythm of night birds and crickets. I dream of my sisters calling out my name, my father praying into a wall of sea.

I don't know if it's the urgent need to relieve myself or if it's because I'm not used to sleeping under a mosquito net in an abandoned shack, but I wake up before even the sun. I examine my hand and find little blisters where I siphoned the lava fairy's power last night. Relief washes over me because I can't feel her magic—or the ravenous need for it that followed. Now, I'm just hungry, and I have to pee.

The others seem to still be asleep as I climb out of bed. My eyes feel swollen, and I'm aware of every muscle in my body in ways I never have been before, mostly because they *hurt* in ways they never have before. In the blue dawn, I can better see the small room. There's a wooden trunk covered in fine dust. I rummage until I find a clean cloth and decide to use it as a towel.

I retrace my steps back down the wooden ladder as quietly as I can. Last night's path is marked by our dried footprints in the mud, leading me through ankle-tall grass peppered with fallen fruit from tall palm trees. Water rushes from the nearby waterfall, and that only kicks my pace into overdrive.

I have never had to think so much of my bodily functions before Adas. I tuck myself behind a tree, but nightmare scenarios of poison sumac and ivy flash before my eyes. The mental spiral doesn't stop there. I notice the army of ants crawling across the dirt and leaves. *What if there are snakes in there? Snakes would be better than those things—*

I shake my head and keep going. As I trudge out of the patch of oasis and onto the desert in search for a place to return to humanity's most primitive function, I'm a little disturbed that my mind put a question like *Will I get out of here alive?* right up there with *Do fairies even poop?*

Then I think of Iris asking me *Are you ever serious?* Maybe I should be. Maybe that's what's been wrong with me this whole time.

I breathe in the cool morning air, wrinkling my nose at the stink of rotten eggs that comes with it. There is nothing but dry earth marbled with deep cracks. *Don't step on a crack. You'll break your mama's back.* That's what we say on my block when you walk to the bus on long stretches of broken sidewalk.

I was wrong to call this place a desert. Some *deserts* at least have life—cacti, snakes, scorpions. I close my eyes against the breeze and I don't feel anything. Not the way my power has felt with the rest of Adas, like magic clings to the air itself. This land is dead.

The first signs of sunrise break along the horizon, and I notice a patch of dry bushes and warped leafless trees that grow low to the ground. A fallen tree has been under the sun so long, the trunk appears smooth and white.

My bladder might burst from holding it in too long, so I find a spot between two of the warped trees and squat. As I try to not pee on my feet, I pray to the Deos that in addition to no poisonous leaves, a snake or something worse doesn't crawl up the mud cracks and try to bite me.

The sound of a throat being cleared behind me makes me jump and nearly fall on my face.

"Did you sleep well?" Iris's voice comes from behind one of the bushes.

I use the towel I brought along, and a ridiculous sense of shame washes over me as I pull up my pants. If I keep walking straight, I'll go back to the oasis, but why stop there? If I keep going in any direction, I'll get to the sea. There's no avoiding Iris, so I kick dust and sand over the wet earth and face her.

"Did you sleep *here*?"

Iris is sitting alone on a second fallen, bleached tree, this one so white it reminds me of bone. She peels a brown-skinned fruit with the small knife she keeps at her hip, the rind dangling in one long strip.

Her hair is loose and tumbles down her back and over her shoulders in cotton-candy-pink waves. She'll never look human.

Her ears are too pointy and her eyes too much like pink diamonds. She's strong and delicate all at the same time. But somehow, she almost looks vulnerable. Her armor rests at her side, and I'm glad I'm not the only one in pajamas.

"No, Eliza, I did not sleep here. I wanted to get my bearings before we begin our search," she says. When she smiles, I know she's amused but not making fun of me. At least that's what I want to believe.

"Oh, yeah, me too," I say, parting the brush to get closer. I feel the urgent need to talk, to say anything even if it's a lie. "I usually get my bearings with morning yoga and a yerba mate latte."

"Why are humans so embarrassed by their bodies? To be human and mortal means to be in a constant state of decay. You needn't be ashamed."

"When you say it like that, it seems so poetic," I mutter. "That's also rich coming from an immortal being whose job it is to be beautiful."

"You think I'm beautiful, Eliza?" She narrows her eyes and her attempt at a smile is full of sadness. "Beauty means nothing if it means being still, stagnant. If your time in Adas has taught you anything it should be that."

Iris straps on her breastplate over her thin top and pulls on leather boots. I follow sheepishly at her heels, the sticky scent of flowers in bloom clinging to her hair. I imagine Kaíri and her sunflower fields.

"I owe you a debt," Iris says, and I imagine how much that must cost her to admit. "You saved my life."

"I should have done more," I say.

"Vita and Lukano knew what the crossing meant." Lukano. The other guard we lost. I never even knew his name.

"Because you lost others the last time you came here," I say.

She nods and fiddles with a strap on her belt. A butterfly with fuzzy blue wings has made its all the way out here. It tries to get close to Iris, but she bats it away. I think of how the creatures were drawn to Arco too, the first time we left the castle.

"This will work," Iris says, and I'm not sure if she's trying to convince me, herself, or both. "Come. I need everyone searching for the blood root."

We split into groups to climb back up to the top of the cliff. Peridot and Calliope. Lin and me. Arco and Nadira. Iris and Zuri. Márohu flies overhead. A cluster of guards in their beetle-green armor are spread out for our protection. I glance over my shoulder once. Arco's soft brown eyes settle on me. His smile devastates me in a way that shouldn't be allowed. Not when we're racing to find the one thing that can strengthen our powers to defeat this rot and it's like looking for a needle in a stack of more needles.

"Hey, Lin," I say. "What used to be here in the outerlands? Further out past the Shuari."

"It's hard to imagine, but this was once a cloud forest," Lin says. Lush black curls twist around gently pointed ears like tiny tentacles. There's something in those violet eyes that strikes a memory, though I can't tell why, because I've never met anyone with violet eyes like Lin's.

We both glance back to the waterfall that disappears into a basin of the oasis, then back up the steep scramble to the jagged cliff.

"Do you remember it?" I ask them.

"It was the most beautiful part of Adas," Lin says. "King Eterno and his family held court here, before King Cirro. The Ceibos Mountain. I came here once as a child with my parents. It's all gone now."

"I never thanked you for saving me," I tell them. I breathe harder and harder, my heart racing as we climb. The sun isn't even at its zenith, but the oppressive heat already has me sweating. "Someone once told me that our power can stretch to amazing lengths when we need it to."

When we get to the top of the cliff, I'm overcome with vertigo I did not have yesterday. Perhaps it was all the adrenaline or the loss of our guards. The rain forest all looks the same from here. But in the morning light, we can see the rot.

Behind me there's the sound of guards gagging. Even Calliope shudders at the sight of it. I make the symbol of the Deos over my face, trace the circle of La Mama and the crescent of El Papa.

Inside the chasm is a swollen black mass, like a severed organ. It doesn't seem right, doesn't belong in this place of shimmering seas and sunflower fields and rivers. At school, they showed us what a smoker's lung looks like when it was beyond healing, and I can't help but think of that when I stare at this. It fills the cracks in the splintered earth, filmy tentacles reaching and reaching for something to hold.

"That is the heart of the rot," Iris says, staring with her crystalline eyes, her body facing it, like she's thinking of running to jump in and attack it with her sword. "When I brought my garrison here, they drowned in it. The rot was less than half this size."

"Every living thing can be killed," Márohu says, her wings twitching.

Gods can't. What if it isn't alive? What if it's something else? I want to ask. But when the tentacles of black ooze spread, I'm sure it has to be.

"Iris," I say, and her attention snaps to me. "How—? What are we supposed to do?"

The princess keeps her gaze on the rot. "You do everything Xia asks of you."

"Get to searching," I say, then grab Peridot by the sleeve. "What does the blood of the gods look like? I assume it's a metaphor, but no one answered me."

Peridot shakes his head, but he can't keep himself from smiling and that feels like a win. "Like a blue hand made of roots with bright white ends."

We spread out but stay within earshot of each other. Peridot uses his magic to lift the roots of trees and uncover sheets of ivy and underbrush. Desperation thickens as the day passes by, the rot within eyesight as a reminder that every moment we can't find the blood root, we are failing.

I crouch down to the ground and lift a huge fan leaf. Beneath are dozens of black beetles. The memory of those creatures—the blackfly-like monsters—slams into me and I let out a scream.

"Eliza!" Márohu shouts.

They all freeze, raising their hands to draw on each and every unique power they possess.

"I'm fine, it's fine, I'm fine," I say quickly. "It's just beetles."

"Perhaps we can take you to the underwater caves, where you can poke sea dragons for your amusement," Calliope says, and despite her anger, there is also fear and, worst of all, helplessness.

We keep searching until we lose the light, and hope begins to fade even from the daughter of stars.

As the sun begins to sink in the turquoise sky and cloying heat has burned the top layer off my skin despite the shade, we retreat empty-handed into the shadows of the oasis, under massive palm trees leaves budding with pale green coconuts. Sweat pours down my face and neck, between my shoulders. Wild grass tickles my ankles along an untrodden path. Here, a weak breeze pushes flowers in so many colors, they might make up a new rainbow, new colors, new patterns.

We round a cluster of boulders covered in grasshopper-green moss, a city of skinny blue mushrooms grows tall and spindly, and spiderwebs glisten with dew, stretching over every surface.

If I didn't know about the pit of ooze a few miles west of us, I'd think I was still in paradise. I stop to take in the sight of a waterfall. It has layers, a natural, narrow shelf about halfway up, surrounded by vibrant emerald vines that fall like Rapunzel just let down her hair. A pool of pristine water stretches before us in bursts of blues that shift under fading rays of light.

"Thank the Deos" is all I manage to say as we trudge across grass and stones and fall at the mouth of the small pool. I cup my hands and drink until I feel replenished, then splash the cold water on my face.

We devour fruits, more cassava and plantain, and the last of the cheese wrapped in green leaves. I haven't seen any cows or goats, so I don't want to ask where the milk comes from. Even as I eat, all of my insides are one collection of knots, sort of like the cables behind the television.

As the others have stripped down to their birthday suits and float in water that shines like azure glass, I dig my fingers in the earth. The weariness in my bones goes away and the tightness of my sunburned skin feels less itchy. I feel like I'm drinking in the purest, cleanest source in the realms. When I brush my hands clean, there's a spot of dry grass where there wasn't before. I reel back and look at my hands, but I no longer feel the pull of the magic.

Lin disappears through a rift in the air and reappears at the middle rock shelf, where a narrow cliff juts out of the waterfall. Even Calliope cheers Lin on to jump, and they do, diving headfirst.

When they resurface, splashing everyone around them, Lin says, "Careful down there. Nasty rocks."

Like when I touched the grass, this pool calls to me. If I close my eyes, I see a busy sunny beach, and three smiling faces. Then I blink and the memory is gone, my mind foggy. But now that my belly is full, the rest of me wants other things. A cold, delicious dip in this water. A tiny taste of the magic that is thick in the air. The electric buzz on my skin returns. The soft bubble where my blister was this morning thrums.

Iris strides over, her worry mark deepened. She's taken off her breastplate armor but kept her sleeveless tunic on, her light brown skin shimmering where her shoulders are bare. She keeps her sword at her hip.

"You're not in the water, Eliza."

"Tell me something I don't know," I say, but her smirk is knowing. "I'm just wrestling with my very human, very mortal shame."

Part of me wants to prove that I am all of the things that Lin suggested I was. Daring. Brave. A little shameless. The kind of girl who had fought monsters and pushed back the dark. It has nothing to do with loving my body. I do. I love my thighs and arms and cute waist and my soft belly. So, what if I have to strip down in front of fairy, immortal beings from across the realms? I'm fine with that.

"Iris, what happens if we don't find the root?"

"I can't accept that possibility yet, Eliza."

"I don't know. I feel like a part of me is expecting someone to appear, to find their way to me. To save me."

"That doesn't sound like you." Iris undoes the sword belt around her curvy, muscular hips. "What is it, Siphon? I recognize that inscrutable look on your face by now."

"What's the deal with this oasis?"

Iris sits on a boulder close to me. Even though Nadira is the actual mermaid, Iris could very well pass for one, with her bright pastel hair and piercing eyes, the sharp points of her canines when she smiles that way.

"A legend," she says.

"I like legends. Come on. Tell me a story."

"What has gotten into you?" She's trying not to smirk, so she sniffs and tugs off her boots, unraveling the laces in the same speedy way she does everything else. "Very well. They say that when El Terroz shaped the eternal island of Adas, and La Flor gave her favorite creatures the ability to sow flowers into the earth, and El Papa made adas themselves using the favorite parts of his beasts, the stars went to war."

"What do stars have to fight about? Who gets to skate on the rings of Jupiter first?"

Iris squints at me in the way she does when she doesn't understand what I'm saying. "What do siblings ever fight over? A parent's love. Toys that break easily. No matter the reason, one of these stars fell to Adas, right in the Shuari forest, wept, and created this pool. Perhaps this is why the rot couldn't claim this bit of green. My mother called this waterfall Milagritos when I was a girl." *Little miracles.*

Perhaps the miracle is that Iris is telling me about her mother. I spent so much time reading stories about lands that were supposed to be myth and have come to find that they have their own tales too. Does that mean I'm living in a myth within a myth?

"Come on, Eliza," Iris says, voice husky and irritated once again. "You smell like a human."

"I am a human," I say. Then I hear a croak in the sunset shadows. "Wait. Are there any of those poison frogs?"

Her laugh is surprising, like a burst of sun after rain. "No. The eleuthantila coquís prefer to gather at the grove."

Then she peels off her underclothes and jumps in. She swims across and surfaces at the mouth of the waterfall. Nadira is in her full mermaid tail, combing tangles out of her hair. Arco floats by, his torso bathed in so much light he looks like he's made of solid gold.

I dig my fingers into the soil like earthworms burrowing deep.

There is something so refreshing, so soothing, that this earth makes all my aches go away.

I strip off my clothes. There's a tan line around my wrist where a bracelet must have been. I scratch at the spot and feel a hollow in my heart. It goes away when I breathe in the green, cool scent of the oasis. I recognize this calm. Haven't I felt it before? It is a peace that cannot last, so fragile, it cannot be peace at all.

19

Las Memorias, sisters two,
One who forgets and
One who things of you.

—TWIN SISTERS OF THE WORLD'S
MEMORIES, BOOK OF DEOS

I wake to a tremor. Rocks tumbling against my roof and trees swaying. We don't have earthquakes where I come from. Wait. Where do I come from? It doesn't matter, because I roll off my bed and onto the floor. I go to the doorway and stand within the frame. The sound is terrible, like a giant biting into the side of a mountain.

When it's over, my insides are still shaking. I run out and into the firepit area we made the first night we arrived. The others come here instinctively, in various state of undress.

"By El Terroz, it's spreading again?" Alma screams.

"I'll fly overhead," Márohu says.

"Not alone," Arco tells her. "I'll take Huracán."

"And then what?" I ask.

Iris presses her fingertips to her temples. "The rest of you, spread out. Find that gods-forsaken root!"

My ear feels like it's clogged with water after swimming. There's a rushing sound, the howling of wind. I need to see it. I need to see the rot.

"I want to go with you," I tell Arco. He looks like he's already about to say no. "You said you thought I'd like flying better than riding a horse. Or were they just pretty words?"

He stands so close to me I realize for the first time he and Iris have the same freckles across their jaw and nose bridge. "Yes, Lady Siphon. I'd like to see whether or not I'm right."

Arco leads me to the stables. Lirico, and the other Pegasi stomp restlessly, but Arco doesn't seem worried. He goes right for Huracán and feeds her a diamond from his pocket.

"That's a really expensive horse," I say.

Huracán neighs as if she understands me and agrees.

Arco leads Huracán out of the stables, fishes a key from his pocket, and unlocks the leather wing girth. Before it hits the floor, Huracán trots a few paces ahead. Her wings spread wide, her head rearing with a joy even I feel in my bones. She kicks up on her hind legs and just when I think she's going to take flight, she settles back on the ground and returns for another treat.

The other Pegasi are restless though, so I ask, "Do you think we should let the others out?"

"Now is not the time." He gives a small shake of his head.

When *is* the time?

Arco keeps Huracán steady so I can mount. He helps me up, and I suddenly feel very tall and very precarious. Arco swings himself up gracefully. I'm not sure where to put my hands so I hold on to the saddle horn as Arco steers us away toward the desert.

Huracán flaps her wings, taking long stretches, like she's getting used to the feeling of being free again. We trot straight ahead, kicking up dust. Márohu flies low beside us. She whistles between her fingertips and Huracán neighs back. I feel Arco's laughter reverberate against my back, and I can't help but scream as we take off.

"Hold on, Eliza," he says at my ear.

I glance down, and I have the strangest sensation of spinning in place. I put a hand over my eyes and brace for the tickling sensation in my stomach. I press myself against Arco's chest to have something solid to lean against.

"Open your eyes!"

"No, I think I'm fine like this!"

His laugh vibrates right through me. "I won't let you fall."

I believe him. I take a series of deep breaths. If I look down, I know I'm going to want to scream. But there's also something thrilling about flying with my eyes closed. The feel of wind through my hair. The fine mist of clouds against my face.

"Take your time," Arco tells me, and it feels like we're coasting on a stream of air.

The sun feels brighter, palpable. I drop my palms from my eyes and look down. Huracán coasts on the breeze, and Márohu looks like a superhero in flight a few yards away, leading us toward the rot.

Below, there is nothing but the desert, with cracks so wide and deep, that this high up they look like blood vessels bursting across an eye.

When I glance over my shoulder at Arco, our eyes meet. The wind is too loud for me to be able to tell him what I want to say—that this is the most incredible thing I've ever seen. That up here is the closest thing to magic that I could hope to feel without using my power. I don't even feel like I'm going to fall anymore, not with his arms on either side of me.

We fly past the desert cliffs and over roaring waves that crash against a cove that's white as bone, either bleached by the sun or covered in layers of salt from the sea.

"The last time I was in your realm, there were wild horses all over the islands," Arco asks.

"When was the last time you were there?"

A strange voice trills through my head, *He's probably a hundred.*

He looks deep in thought. "I'm not quite sure. My mother had a favorite island: Borikén."

A feeling strangles my heart. A memory of someone confiding in me. She says, "One day, we'll save up some money and get to go there to see where your father's people came from."

Not someone.

My mother.

I breathe in and hold, squeezing the empty spot where my bracelet was. I pinch my skin so hard I draw blood, so hard I will remember. A fog lifts from my mind where the memories of my family, my whole life, lie. *Alex. Lula. Mom. Dad. Nova. Alex. Lula. Mom. Dad. Nova.* I exhale.

"It's called Puerto Rico now," I tell Arco.

"It's straight ahead," he says. "Past the mist that keeps Adas hidden from your world."

My longing for home pulls like threads on a tapestry coming undone. We can leave now. I thought I had somewhere to get back to, but I can't remember what it is exactly. It is slipping behind a foggy glass wall again. "Can we go there?"

"I would grant you this wish, Eliza, but—"

The rot. The new. The guardians. I shake my head. "No, I know."

We coast in a circle, Arco navigates west, and that's when that helpless feeling of falling returns, because we are flying directly over the black gash in the ground. Arco keeps one hand on the reins and one around me.

Beneath us is a pit as wide as a lake, with hundreds of rivers of thick black sludge spreading from the center, wretched and all-consuming. Its vile stench radiates. I try to make a shape out of it. A heart perhaps, black and rotten to the core. I can feel its power even from up here, coating my skin like mud on the day I was brought here.

"Lord Arco!" Márohu shouts over the breeze. She flies to us, moving to the same rhythm as Huracán's. "There's runoff in the north. It wasn't there yesterday."

Between the beating wings and whistling wind is a hissing sound I've heard before. I thought the rot sounded like a swarm of bees. But what if it is something else. Someone else. *Shh. Shh. Shh. I. Am. I am.*

I am what? Is this what Iris's garrison heard before they drowned? This cloud of sound wrapping around their heads. My skin crawls, and I need to get away from here. Away from Arco and down below.

I need to be inside the rot, swimming within the darkness.

"Eliza!" Arco shouts. He squeezes the air from my lungs. "What are you doing?"

Márohu tries to reach for me.

Huracán swoops to the side as Arco shouts, "Eliza!"

My arms are stronger than they once were, and I elbow him.
There is *magic* down there, and I have to have it. I need to have it.
"You don't understand. I have to see!"

"Make me understand," he shouts. "Think of your father. He's
waiting for you!"

That's when the haze clears, and I realize what I'm trying to do.
I feel myself floating in open air, Arco grabbing for me. His hands
close on my forearm and he yanks me back onto the saddle.

We fly fast and hard, Huracán careening against the wind. We
land with a clapping trot. Arco leaps off the saddle and pulls me
down. He holds me by my shoulders, and for the first time since
I've known him, he is angry.

His fingertips brush my hair back as if trying to see if I am okay,
if I am still me, and I am honestly not sure I am. "Make me understand, Eliza. What possessed you to try to jump?"

I swallow the anxious knot in my throat. His hands fall to his
sides, and everything, from the tips of my toes to the inside of my
head, buzzes. Is this magic or something else? It doesn't let me
focus, and maybe that's what he wants. Maybe that's why he stands
so close to me.

His full lips part, and I count seventeen freckles so far. I kiss
him. I kiss him and my heart feels like it's vibrating in my chest. I
kiss him, and I know it is my first one.

But when I break away, I can still see the cancerous rot that
fills the desert. It overpowers even Arco because it actually spoke.

I am.

I think of how ancient that power felt. How Xia said that there are parts of this island that have a pulse. They are markings of the Deos. Divine. An idea blooms through the fog of my mind.

"We need Iris and Peridot," I say and leave the confused prince of Adas in my dust.

I find the tree boy working with Xia in the green of the waterfall. His palms are on top of hers, and the waves of their magic slam into me. I shake the sensation off and sit.

"Speak, Siphon," Xia tells me.

"The rot is a Deo," I say.

They both blink at me like I've gone mad. My hands shake and I slap them against the ground. "Listen to me. We were flying over the rot, and I could hear it. It had a voice. This entire time we've been trying to figure out why our powers don't work. It's because the rot is divine."

They still seem unconvinced, so I continue. "Think about it. This is the source of the rot. The legend says that the stars wept on this earth. The oasis remains intact. It has to be because the god can't destroy it."

"Why wait until now?" Peridot asks, biting a new leaf jutting out of his nail like a cuticle.

I think of everything that I've learned. We are myths inside a myth. The biggest myth of all is the king. "King Cirro's deceptions. King Cirro depleting the land. Everyone keeps saying Adas is paradise. But it has also evolved, like Kaíri told me. His corruption has evolved into the rot. An abomination of the gods who created this land."

"Uprooted," Xia says, shaking her head, "you are uprooted, Siphon."

"If that is a god," Peridot says, "nothing we do will help."

I shake my head. "You're wrong. Bruja 101: Our powers are their powers. Brujas were gifted with the magic of the Deos, but so were all the creatures of their realms. You were created by El Terroz. Even Arco and Iris are descendants of La Flor, and Calliope from La Estrella."

Peridot grips my shoulder to still me. "That doesn't change anything if we don't have the blood root."

"You have raised trees. I've seen you. Uprooted, like Xia says. We have just been looking in the wrong place."

I point to the top of the waterfall, where there's a jutting cliff with an overgrowth of vines. The Oasis was spared by the rot because something is protecting it. The blood root.

"Trust me," I say. "And if I'm wrong—"

"Don't be."

"Run, Guardians," Xia says. "You have not yet begun to become uprooted."

We can't wait for Lin and the others, and so we grab hold of the vines spilling down the waterfall. I have chosen the worst time to become outdoorsy, but I focus on the top of the cliff, on the blood root, on knowing that when I consume it, I will be more powerful.

Peridot gets to the top first, but I follow suit, heaving myself over the rock shelf. Dark curling vines blanket the floor along with flower bushes in species I've never seen before. I remember Kaíri saying that La Flor created the flowers of this world and tended to the gardens. They come in sharp pinks, delicate blues, and even black orchids with neon hearts.

Peridot takes a deep breath, and when he extends his palms over the blanket of vines, I feel the ground murmur. My stomach tightens waiting for another quake, but it doesn't come. I remember the way the Shuari girl spoke to Peridot. She was speaking another language. The language of trees and green things. What was it Kaíri told me?

You will learn the language of this earth.

"You know the language of this earth," I tell Peridot now. "Stop doubting. Listen to it."

His magic unfurls like a coiled vine, tiny green leaves sprout at the tops of his pointed ears. I can taste dew in the air, the bright green of chlorophyll, and then the blanket of green parts. White tendrils sprout from the dirt, followed by gnarled blue roots that look like fingers clawing out of a grave.

"There," I say, and surge forward. I dig up the little roots.

Peridot lets out an excited holler that echoes. I open my arms to hug him. When I inhale his scent, I can feel the buzz of the power he conjured. It fills my senses so that all I want to do is breathe in and in and in.

Peridot's green eyes go wide, mouth agape, gasping as I draw out his magic. My power feels like wires frayed at the edges, sparking and sparking as if searching for something to ignite. There's a brightness in my line of vision that blinds me. My muscles are paralyzed with the need to consume. I am too elated to breathe. I feel weightless. Every cell that makes me unique has come apart and is floating away like dandelion fluff.

I have never felt this way and I want it to stay.

I siphon more power.

Fingers dig into my skin, trying to pull me apart.

But I control the roots around us, buried under a dark magic that stifles them, beneath the layers of decay and rot. They relinquish the hold around me and push the others away.

The rhythmic beat of Peridot's heart is trapped in my mind along with a voice. It's as fast as a bass drum going *bombombombombombombom.*

Remember yourself, a voice whispers.

I blink.

Someone is crying.

Shaking until they can't shake anymore.

I could float like this forever, adrift in a sea made of stars.

"Eliza," Peridot whimpers, and then I hear it. The beat has slowed down. *Bom. Bom.* And then it stops.

Glee and misery vying for space in my heart, I let go. I scramble to where Peridot lies unconscious, the blood root between us.

All at once, I realize what I'm doing. I gasp as I release my hold on him. When I look at my hands, thin, fragile shoots sprout from my nails. *More,* my power screams.

"No, no, no!" I cry. *What have I done? What did I do?*

"Get away from him!" Hands shove me away. Calliope punches me hard when I try to reach for Peridot again. She doesn't understand. I want to help. "Don't touch him!"

Lin appears in front of me. They rest a hand on my shoulder and whisper, "Stay back, Eliza."

"But I can help—"

"You've done enough," Márohu says, her voice like an anvil as she flies above us.

"He's breathing," I hear Calliope say. "Lin, help me get him down."

Peridot is in Calliope's arms, unconscious, but at least he is breathing. The Starlark's eyes lock with mine. "You're going to regret this."

Márohu holds me around my waist. I grab her arms to siphon her, but her power is not like the others. It is a part of her in a way that I cannot replicate or drain or taste. She drops me on the ground. The waterfall rushes silver beneath the swelling moon.

Lin, Márohu, and Nadira stand back. We are alone, and I know, when I look into Calliope's eyes, that the night isn't over.

"This is far enough," Márohu says. "We have the blood root. We don't need to do this."

"You made a mistake, Eliza," Lin says. "We can fix this."

My power hums along my skin with anticipation as Calliope draws on the stars. Her fingers, splayed to the sky, create a beacon for the staff-shaped prism that appears in her hand. A silver aura surrounds her. It is so bright I have to look away.

But then, she charges at me.

I make an X with my forearms to shield my face. My limbs tremble against the impact and I absorb the starlight, then kick her stomach.

Neither of us fall. She breaks her starlight spear in half. I summon her starlight and mold matching batons. I skid on to the ground, kicking up dirt and going for her leg. Calliope rolls to the side but lands on her feet, her weapons displayed at her sides. They flash like lightning and shadow, and for a moment, I'm frozen. Someone shouts my name, tells me to move, but I can't.

A stinging pain hits my shoulder as Calliope strikes. I breathe through the burning sensation that spreads from where she cut me and grab her baton. It bursts in my first as I siphon its power. She kicks my legs from under me and I fall on my face.

"Eliza!"

"There is no shame in surrender," Calliope says, stomping over. All I can see are her feet.

The ache is overpowered by the strange hunger of my magic. I trace my fingers on the shimmering dust of her disintegrated weapon. I grab a fistful of it. If I close my eyes, I can see the star this belonged to, see the burst of its power. It whispers my true name.

"Should I accept this fetal position as defeat?"

Remember yourself.

There is no *me* in Adas. Rose Mortiz, the brujita, the quiet little sister, the good girl, can't be here. There is only room for Eliza, the Siphon of Galaxies, Daughter of El Fin, Master of Everything's End. Rose is gone.

I throw the stardust in her eyes. Calliope cries out, lashing out with her last baton. There's the *thwack* of our weapons. For a moment, I'm pushing her back.

For a moment, I'm winning.

My sore arms are strengthened by a rush of adrenaline. Sharp, ragged breaths fill my lungs.

Then, Calliope recovers. She conjures starlight around her fists like knuckledusters and slams that rage into my chest. Its force knocks my fighting sticks somewhere in the dark. It doesn't matter. The bright, beautiful scent of her starlight overpowers everything around us. The rot. The dead earth. The blood flowing from my nose and split lip.

My mind is murky, my body hungers for magic.

Before Calliope can pull more starlight, I barrel into her. We slam to the ground. The beat of thunder rings from somewhere. I close my fingers around Calliope's wrist and gasp as I siphon her power. The sky feels closer to the ground, like if I reach up, I'd be able to pluck a star and bite into it like low-hanging fruit.

It is different than the other times I've used my power. Now I know why it took me so long to know myself. I pushed my abilities down because I didn't want to accept that I could be different, different enough to be less than good. Someone who doesn't *borrow* a power but takes it. Harnesses it until there is nothing left. I didn't want to face that I could devour the magic from a being like marrow. I didn't want to break out of my safe, run-down home. But I was never really safe, was I? There was always something that would come for me.

Tsst tsst tsst, shhh shhh shhh, the rot calls out to me, *I am waiting*.

It is only then that a scream breaks through the torrent inside my mind. The breath is kicked out of me as I reel backward into the waterfall and down into the cold current below.

20

I sang for you and you did not sing back.

I waited for you and you did not come back.

—SONG OF LA TRISTESA, GODDESS OF ALL
THE WORLD'S TEARS, BOOK OF CANTOS

Remember yourself. Remember yourself. Remember yourself.

It isn't the sinister murmur of the rot that fills my head but an even, familiar voice. Someone that makes my heart ache with love and worry and enough panic that I gasp.

Water forces its way down my throat.

There's a pressure in my chest that feels like it's pushing me deep into the earth until I crack open.

Lips press against mine.

I choke and cough and spit water. The rawness of my throat hurts first. I float out of my thoughts and back into my body as people shout my name.

"Eliza! Eliza, wake up!"

"Rose," Lin whispers from somewhere.

Awareness jolts back into me, oxygen fills my lungs, and I see a face inches from mine.

Rose quartz eyes. Fairy eyes. Warrior eyes. Iris sits back, something like relief on her stern, lovely face.

I turn over and cough my brains out, water stopping my words from coming.

Nadira sits on the grass. The sheer ends of her mermaid tail are shifting, moving as her fins become slender feet, and her tails tears into her legs. Pain flashes across her face, but it's only there for a moment, like it's an uncompromised part of her.

If my throat didn't burn so much, I'd scream my admiration for her, but all I can croak out is a small, "Thank you."

"Thank Lin," Nadira says. "They saved us both. Carried us through the rift. How did you manage to get sucked into a tunnel beneath the waterfall?"

My throat burns. My chest aches where someone hit me. "Lucky, I guess."

Then I remember. Peridot and Calliope. I hurt them with my power. I search for them, but they're not in the waterfall clearing. "Where—"

"Peridot and Calliope are recuperating," Lin answers before I can finish.

"I'm sorry," I say. "I don't know what came over me."

Iris watches me carefully, like she's assessing a bomb. Her soft pink curls have come undone and her eyes soften, almost pleading. "We're so close, Eliza. Hold on."

I swallow the guilt and tears that flood the hollow places in my chest where my spent-up magic is. I breathe deeply.

"Where did you go?"

"Hunting," Iris says. When she stands, I see the thing behind her. A boar with a broken-off arrowhead still embedded into its skull. "We have the blood root. Tonight we feast. Tomorrow we attack."

The boar has golden tusks jutting from an open mouth. Even with carrying the weight of such a creature, Iris is infuriatingly fast. She peers at me from under her arm. Her upper lip has a speck of blood on it, which she licks away. I'm not sure if that thrills or terrifies me exactly. Both, maybe.

We follow her to the other side of the oasis, where Alma and Zuri are clearing a pit. Peridot and another guard are carrying fallen branches. Calliope is sharpening a stick. When she sees me, she wields it like she intends to drive it through my chest.

"I'm sorry," I tell them. "I couldn't control my power. I never wanted to hurt you. Either of you."

"Consider my kindness to you repaid," Calliope says, then sits back down and gives her attention to Iris.

"It's tradition before going off to battle—we have a feast." Iris looks at every single one of us. "You've all earned it, don't you agree, Brother?"

Arco is in the middle of writing something down. His fingers are stained with ink. I have the strangest sense of déjà vu. Brown eyes flecked with gold wink. "By the Deos, are we in agreement?"

I rub the tan line on my wrist, then jump into action to help prepare dinner. Nadira helps bring fresh water to clean out the boar. I never realized how hairy they were.

Márohu and I gather fruits from nearby trees. She plucks passion fruit from their stalks. They're covered in a fuzzy skin that blows away with the graze of her thumb.

"Why haven't you flown away?" I ask her, reaching into the leaves for a plum. I bite into it. The tender meat is the sweetest thing I've ever tasted, warming my skin, my insides. Even if it stings my cut. When I lick my fingers, I think of Arco's lips against my own. Should I talk to him about it? Does he hate me now that he's seen my true abilities?

Márohu's wings twitch. I wonder what it feels like to have the weight of them at all times. Though I suppose it isn't any different than arms or legs, just like Peridot's finger twigs and Arco's horns.

"Sometimes," she says, "when you're alone, one place is better than no place. I've been searching for somewhere to belong that gives me the same feeling as when I had my sisters, or when I fly. You have sisters, you know what it's like."

I do? First comes confusion. Then numbness behind my eyelids. I have sisters. I know I do. The same panic I felt underwater when I couldn't breathe returns because I try to hold on to their faces, but it's like falling without the safety of someone catching you.

"Eliza, are you coming?" she asks.

I assess the fruits fallen on the ground. Some of them have split open, quarter-sized beetles feasting on the dripping juices and meat. "I'll be right there."

I can't remember what I was supposed to be doing.

I take my basket of fruit and go to the waterfall. When I press my hand over my heart, the beat is erratic. I pace back and forth in the same spot so much that I've flattened the grass beneath my feet. I go through everything I've done during my time here. How many days has it been here? I mark them in the dirt, but some days felt longer than others and then I start again, retracing my steps. My head feels *heavy* in a way that makes me want to lie down and bury myself under the dirt.

That's called being dead, Rose.

Rose.

That is not my voice speaking to me. That voice is so clear, so very familiar, and not. It is my sister's voice. But which one? I have sisters. I have a mother. I have a father. But when I try to picture them, there is a warped glass and shadows behind it. My mind is like swiss cheese, like gaps in a forest canopy open to let in the light.

"Eliza?" Iris calls my name. "There will be time for sorrow when we're finished."

"I can't remember them," I say, squeezing the tan line around my wrist. There is a bruise already beneath the skin. "I mean, I know they exist. I know they're there. But I can't see them. Is this how it starts?"

Iris walks to me and picks up a fat orange in her hands. She brushes dirt away from the skin. "You're forgetting. You lost your bracelet around the time we got to the Oasis, but I can't be sure."

"What do I do now?" I shout.

"You finish this," she says softly, with a weariness that hasn't been there before. "You help me finish this, and I will do everything in my power to get you back home. I will take you to the human realm myself and make you remember."

I shake my head and point my finger like a gun at her shoulder. I push her, but she doesn't even budge. "I should never have made that deal with your father."

"Do you know why humans forget when they come to Adas?" she asks, but I think she changes the subject because the mention of her dad lights up the rage in her eyes.

"The food."

"Yes and no. Everything about this island is magic. Dregs of a lonely god seeking a place to hide from the rest of the world. That's the story at least. Mortals come here, and they sing and dance and eat. They take, the way the king takes. Maybe that's their exchange for their enjoyment. The price of living in paradise."

I blink blurry, burning eyes. "I didn't want to understand him, but I think I do."

"Who?" she asks.

"My father. He forgot me, and now I'm forgetting him. By my account, We're even."

"You'll never be even," she says. There is the slightest whimper in her voice. "You'll never be even as long there is no real forgiveness."

"What did he do to you?" I ask her.

"He betrayed my mother, and so I tried to kill him. I failed," she says, choking on a laugh. "My mother convinced him to spare me and allow me to spend years in exile at Girasol Grove. There, I would learn to serve the crown. I did that. I served the king and my mother was murdered. That, Eliza, is why King Cirro and I will never be even. Don't let your heart fester like mine."

We sit together for a little while longer. I realize that Iris and I not only share the same anger, but also the same hurts. Only, if I stay here long enough, I could forget mine. I could just be. Being with Iris reminds me of a warm, safe place. I strain to see the location, but there's a light hanging above me and a book in my hands.

"Your anger is yours to feel," I tell her.

She hands me the fruit, smirking. "Come, brujita. We have a feast to get to."

I bring the rind to my nose and inhale. The brightness of the citrus tickles my nose, and all at once, I see them, clear as if they were sitting with me in the pantry. And I remember—

"Just say the magic word."

"What's the magic word?" I ask.

What is the magic word?

When we make it back, the boar is crackling in a great firepit. Xia stares at the sky beside a clay pot brimming with stewed greens and mushrooms. The guards have removed their breastplates and one of them taps a beat on the hollow husk of a tree in a rhythm that is as familiar as the magic buzzing on my skin. Laughter and chatter mix with singing. Even Calliope wears a small smile as she sits back and watches the sunset, her hand threaded with Peridot's. Lin plays a game of catch-me-if-you-can with Iris, and she never does. Lin is so fast, sometimes I miss the moments they vanish. But I feel the crackle of the rift. I know that I'm not forgiven, but the blood root gives us a little bit of hope.

Arco sits quietly beside me, shoulder to shoulder, jotting down things. I look over at his paper. Part of me wishes that he'd been drawing stick figures this whole time, but I catch a sentence. *When the time comes, crown the queen.*

After the boar is eaten down to the bone and the juice is squeezed from every fruit and the music becomes part of the vibrant buzzing of night, Xia is ready with our blood of the gods.

Here, straddling the line where the oasis meets the desert, the six of us lie back, our bodies positioned like points of a star. We are scrubbed clean, dried, and fed, and we stay silent.

That is, until I decide to ask, "What does the blood of the gods *taste* like?"

Iris blows out an exasperated breath from outside the ring, and I catch Arco stifling his laugh with a fist while holding his wooden tablet with the other. Is it me, or are they both relieved at the ill-timed humor?

"It isn't a joke, Eliza," the warrior princess says.

I motion to the pot of slimy blue water. The root has turned white, now that all the color bled into the potion. "I'm not joking. I want to be prepared."

"This draught is a means to a gateway," Xia says sharply. "You will step into a dreamscape, and it will taste like your deepest fear. When you drink it, you must see past that fear to understand the source of the power within you. Once you have faced this, you will be able to access your abilities as they were meant to be."

I give her a small nod to tell her that I understand. "Great. But it still smells like dirty egg water."

"What if you pretend it tastes like chocolate?" Lin says beside me, wriggling on the ground like they can't get comfortable.

"My mother used to cook figs in butterfly honey," Márohu volunteers in the small voice of remembrance. "I'll pretend that's what it is."

"Nothing is better than ripe apricots in the warm months," Peridot says, blinking at the stars.

Calliope makes a dreamy noise too, but, whatever she's recalling, she doesn't share her story.

"Last night, I dreamt of how sweet a shark's heart can be," Nadira says, and we all sit up and turn bewildered eyes on her.

"It's a delicacy in the sea kingdom," Nadira says.

I grimace. "You drank a whole river for us, so I'm not going to comment on your food preferences."

Xia clears her throat and stomps her bare foot, kicking up fine dust. "Silence, star children. Silence is required to walk on dreams."

I glance up at the sky, dotted with unfamiliar constellations. What must my family be doing while I hallucinate for the sake of my power?

I turn my face to Lin and whisper, "I'm afraid."

Lin's finger hooks around mine, and a comforting peace settles across my chest. I have felt this calm before. "I am too."

Xia is pouring the liquid into everyone's mouth. When she reaches Lin and me, she lingers. There's something sharp in her strange black eyes, the look of someone who knows more than they're willing to tell.

"Stay close to each other," she says, and her voice is surprisingly gentle. "The root has a way of showing us things we'd rather not see. It is a long journey to walk alone."

I can hear the scratch of Arco's quill moving furiously. I drink the smelly tea, trying my hardest not to gag. I have a strong suspicion that this is what the water under the third rail tastes like.

I think of what Xia said about the dreamscape, and I take Lin's hand. I close my eyes.

Then, laughter echoes around me.

The memories I've felt evaporating like mist return all at once. My sisters' faces. My mother. Nova. My dad. Lula's laugh. The one that tells me she finds something truly, deeply funny, a laugh like wind chimes and bubbles in a summer breeze.

"Lula?" I shout. But I can't sit up.

An invisible weight presses down on my chest, and my skin tingles with the numbness that comes when your foot falls asleep, only it's everywhere—my eyelashes, my fingernails, the roots of my hair, my teeth.

I realize I'm still holding Lin's hand because suddenly there are two heartbeats thudding in my ears, and I'm not sure which one is mine.

I am sure that the sky is falling down, stars and the light of moons coming closer, and I'm sure that when I turn my head and look into Lin's eyes, that same sky cracks open.

"Rose?" Alex says.

The smell of fried bacon and burning sugar assaults my nose. I could scream at the way my body shakes because I'm back in my kitchen.

I'm home.

"Come back!" I shout, panting as if I've run a hundred miles. "Where did they go?"

My voice echoes in the expanse of galaxy. We're standing in an empty, glassy black. At our feet and all around us are stars, the ripple of deep greens and celestial purples.

"The dreamscape must have pulled us back," Lin says, violet eyes roaming the emptiness. "I don't know what else it could be."

I reach for a star floating by, but my fingers close around air. Lin's hand is the only solid thing I can grasp. There's weight there, an anchor that keeps me from floating into the wide-open space.

"How do we get back there?" I ask them.

Lin's hair blows in the breeze as uncertainty tugs down at their lips. "Xia said we have to face our fears. What are you afraid of, Rose?"

I go through the catalog of things that I admitted at the grove—growing up a bruja meant I played with tarantulas and snakes, cleaned dead bodies for funeral rites, have been possessed more times than I can count. Those are not the things I'm afraid of. Memories of the last year and a half hit me.

I can see the maloscuros attacking our house and scarring Lula. My breath catches when I remember being possessed by the Devourer, the warning she had for us. I remember the deep, restless dark of being trapped in the Tree of Souls in Los Lagos and waiting. Just waiting with no reassurance of when or *if* Alex was going to come for us. I remember the fear I hid those first few days my father was back—fear that he wasn't real, that he was some sort of revenant or demon sent to trick us, to lull us into a false sense of safety. There's knowing Lula was straddling the world of the living and dead, and the sight of the things she brought back with her. I think of the moment I knew that my magic was never going to be the same, that I would never be the same, but everyone around me had seemed to move on, so why couldn't I?

True fear that has sunk teeth into my flesh and rattled me—but the worst fear is this moment of clarity because that means understanding the hunger in my heart. Of all the monsters, the gods, this is it. I saw the truth in Calliope's eyes and in the aftermath of what I did to Peridot. I share the same power as the woman who almost ruined our lives and none of us knew. What if, despite everything I've been through, I don't know who I am at all?

Remember yourself.

"I'm afraid my power is destruction," I say with a deep breath. "You?"

"Being alone," Lin says, and I feel myself twinge at how easily that answer comes to them. "So alone that there is no one there to think of me or care for me. So alone that all I'll ever be is a rarity for a mad king to use as a weapon because there is no one else."

Stardust and spiraling lights move while we stand still.

"Look." I point in the distance.

Here, the dreamscape clears and reveals the cerulean sky and white waves of Adas. A brown-skinned fairy woman in an orange dress stands at a cliff's edge. She's in the light, her hair a tumble of black curls, her webbed fingers reaching for a man with his back turned. He is cast in the shadow of a passing cloud. He leans in to kiss the woman's cheek, then casts a fishing line into the water. She rubs her pregnant belly.

There's a loud swell of thunder and lightning in the horizon, clouds churning and twisting like a stampede rushing the sea, a large wave climbing higher and higher, threatening to swallow us all.

288

Lin staggers back as the image fades and the dreamscape returns, leaving them breathless. "Those were my parents."

"Quick, try to use your power," I say, pulling on their hand. "You can get us back to Adas."

Lin shakes their head because, once again, we are not alone.

There's a woman just a few yards out of reach. I *know* her. I've never seen her like this, young and standing straight as a pole, but I would know her anywhere. My great-grandmother Mama Juanita. Her dark skin has a shine to it, and in her hands is a sphere of conjured light so bright Lin and I have to look away.

I call out to her, and she whirls around. The bottom of her dress is frayed and splattered with blood. She's surrounded by brick in a dark alley. Her black eyes look right through me and focus instead on a maloscuro with claws and sharp teeth. It lets out a pained howl as my grandmother's magic burns through it.

"Mama!" I cry, because I want her to stay. I want to step into this memory and have her look back at me and know that I'm here.

She vanishes as the stars shift to reveal a man sitting on a river-bank. His pants are rolled up to his calves. His white skin is freckled along his arms, and his dark hair is covered by a wide-brimmed hat. His fingers move swiftly, weaving a net that seems to glint in the sun.

"Who is he?" Lin asks me.

"I think it's my ancestor. Philomeno. My mom used to tell us of her great-grandfather. A poor fisherman from Spain who tried his luck in the Americas and ended up in a river town along the coast of Ecuador. He could weave nets that caught fish by the hundreds. No one knew how he did it." But in this light, in this memory, I can see the magic he wove into the threads with tired, calloused fingers.

"Magic," Lin says at the same time I think the word.

When he casts the net in our direction, I hold my arm to shield my face reflexively, but when I look again, he's gone, just like Mama Juanita.

"Is it working?" I ask. I hold up my hands. Am I supposed to feel different? I have admitted my fear and I can taste it, the sorrows of loss a bitter, palpable thing. I have seen my ancestors. What more is there?

When the dreamscape sky returns, we're floating in it. Lin grips my hand tighter.

"Rose, I know I heard you," my sister whispers.

Alex. I want to pick a direction and move toward her, but her voice seems to come from everywhere all at once.

"Alex! Can you hear me?"

She doesn't answer back, and I can't tell if I imagined her calling out to me through space, or not.

"Who was that?" Lin asks.

Relief helps me breathe. "My sister. Can you take me to her? Please, Lin."

"I can't, Rose. I've tried before. I'm not strong enough."

"Don't you see? You already did it." I press my hands on both sides of their face. "You did it when I was falling off Tortuga in the Shuari rain forest."

"That was a short distance." Doubt creeps into Lin's voice.

I'm sure of it now. I know. "Just before we got to the dreamscape, we were there in the kitchen. You *are* strong enough. You did that."

Lin nods and holds out a hand sideways. I hold my breath as a splinter of light opens. It's different from the other moments we've seen. Lin's parents and my ancestors were in the past. When Lin steps into the rift and I follow a step behind, I know we're going to the present.

But Lin isn't on the other side. My instinct is to go find them, but I am glued to the floor of my kitchen. My house. My realm.

Roosters line the windowsills and cover the fridge as magnets. Wind chimes made of seashells and clear quartz twinkle in the breeze that pushes through the open back door. This is not the kitchen I grew up in. The floors are stone tiles, and the counter doesn't have any scratches. The stove is twice as big as our old one, but on top is a pan burned so black we should have thrown it away years ago. Bacon sizzles inside it, and a pancake in a separate pan has just started to bubble. My mouth salivates with the thought of its taste.

"Alex, something's burning!" my mom shouts from somewhere in the house. The living room maybe. I knew this house was too big for us.

She slides across the floor in her socks and flips the pancake to the other side. Too burned.

"Alex," I say, and reach for my sister, but my hand goes right through her.

There's a chill, like wading through a cold, dense fog. My lungs feel too tight, my chest swollen with all the things I want to say but can't—*I miss you. I can't do this by myself. I made so many bad decisions. Please, help me.* I say her name the way I would call on one of our Deos. "Alex."

She gasps and spins around. Her big brown eyes dart to the soft orange walls. The color came with the house, and none of us liked it except for Dad because he said it reminded him of his favorite ice cream from when he was little, and Ma said that he remembered wrong because it wasn't an ice cream but a candy, and then there was this sadness, so we let the soft orange walls grow on us, like this pain that we just can't seem to shake. Was he lying about that? I wonder if pain is woven so deeply into our roots and that's the reason no one in my family can find the strength to be happy, truly happy.

"Ma!" Alex shouts and runs out of the kitchen. She still can't see me, but I know she felt me. I know that's why she's running to get help.

"You left the bacon in the pan!" I yell. I try to turn the burner off but I'm a ghost, a shadow. How can I even be sure this is happening? That I'm not creating this scenario out of the deep sadness of missing my family?

I follow the sharp chatter of my mom's and sister's voices down the hall, into the infirmary on the first floor. The three twin beds are neatly made and empty. There's a floor-to-ceiling wooden rack full of herbs and supplies. Ma's work desk has been shoved to a corner, hundreds of papers stacked on top. The entire wall where it used to sit is now covered with a map of New York. There are pins pushed into different parts of the city. Angry circles and frustrated lines crisscross the landscape. The most startling part are the pictures of me and Dad. Mine is my graduation photo from junior high and Dad's is at least ten years old.

They're searching for me. For us.

When Mom turns around, I notice her hair is covered in a scarf like she doesn't have time to get it done. Her face is heavy with unshakable worry, and the lines at the corners of her eyes are deeper than before.

How long has it been? I look for a newspaper or something with the date, but they're all buried beneath books and junk.

"Ma, I'm right here," I shout. I try to pull on her blue blouse. I try to smack my hand on the wall. To rip up the signs that show how gone I am.

"Tell me you feel that," Alex says, standing in front of our mom with her hands extended to the air.

Ma touches her chest. "What was that?"

"I think the canto we did yesterday woke up some sort of spirit," Alex says, stroking her chin with her index and thumb.

"No, stupid, it's me!"

Ma looks around the room. I wonder if she knows that Alex is wrong but won't bring herself to hope. I wonder if she's had it with losing so much that she doesn't have any faith left.

"Please don't give up on me," I whisper.

Ma sniffs, her face twists into something terrifying. "Alejandra, you're going to burn a second house down. Do you think houses grow on trees?"

"I mean, technically…" Alex shrinks into herself and follows our mother back out of the infirmary and to the kitchen. Burned bacon overpowers every other smell, including the incense smoke wafting on the windowsill and the jars of dried flowers and herbs that line the shelves.

I stand in front of the wall with the map. They've circled Alley Pond Park and our house.

"Do they always yell like this?" Lin asks, stepping inside the room.

I clap my hand over my heart. "There you are!"

"I take that as a yes." Lin's amethyst eyes crinkle. They go to the window, where a plume of incense smoke dances beside a geode the color of their eyes. They reach their hand toward the geode, but slender fingers go right through. "Curious. I was able to bring us to your realm but because our bodies are still in Adas, only our dreamscape selves made it. I always wondered what it would be like to be a ghost."

"We aren't *dead*," I correct. Then add, "I hope."

But something feels dead in this house. Despite my mom's and sister's usual yelling, there is a different kind of quiet. Where is Lula? Have they heard from Nova?

Alex charges back into the room, Ma right behind her.

"Leave it, Alex."

Alex carries a bundle in her arms and throws it on one of the infirmary beds. "There's something here. I thought—I thought I heard her."

"You did!" I yell.

Lin takes a deep breath. "They can't hear us, Eliza."

"No, but it's the only thing I can do. I have to at least try."

Alex digs her fingers through her hair. Is it longer than it was when I left? That's when I notice she's wearing the bracelet Nova made us. I clutch my wrist where I lost mine.

"Remember when I was in Los Lagos and I went through Campo de Alma? That's what this feeling is like. There's something in this house."

Panic shoots up from my toes to my temples. I turn to the things my sister threw on the bed—a slab of palo santo as large as my forearm and a glass bottle full of cloudy water. I know if I unstoppered it, I'd get a fishy whiff of water from the Coney Island Sound. It's a Banishing Canto for spirits.

But I'm not a spirit. I'm right here.

"No, no, no!" I yell at them.

"I know you're upset," my mom says, her voice tinged with something I've never heard before. "But we've been through this. There's always an explanation."

"You taught me that some things can't always be explained." Alex yanks a glass jar from the top shelf. She squeezes the bottle against her chest to twist the top.

"I can be wrong, Alejandra," my mom says. There it is again. This is a woman who raised three daughters on her own when she thought her husband and the love of her life had walked out. A healer, a believer in light and hope. She taught me how to fold empanadas, to make the clean, even lines with the prongs of a fork. That cooking was a magic of its own sometimes. For the first time in my life, she sounds irreparably defeated.

"Maybe you're right," she tells Alex. "Maybe the spirits are here to tell us that they're—"

"You can't say that!" Alex shouts, her body a living tremor. The jar of sand shatters and spills all over the floor, and for a moment, the walls and floor shake, moving like an Etch A Sketch clearing itself. "You can't even think that!"

Dead.

My mother thinks I'm dead, because every time she finds happiness, it gets pulled right out from beneath her.

But I'm not dead.

"Mamá," I say, weak and desperate.

"I shouldn't be here," Lin says. I want to tell them to stay, but I don't want to see this either.

"We've searched for nearly a month," my mother says.

"Gods, Mom, it's barely been three weeks!"

"There's no trace of them. None. Not from the police. Not from any magical being we have talked to and I am tired. I wish—"

"I can't listen to you right now," Alex says, and turns her back on our mom. She conjures a flicker of flame and lights the end of the palo santo. "You were like this the first time Dad went away, and for years, *for years* we put up with it. I can't do it anymore."

"Neither can I," she answers. "Lula is off somewhere putting her life in danger with hunters. Nova is Deos knows where. You've lost days of your studies, and you're making yourself sick with all of this. Every time the wind blows, you think it's Rose sending you a message. Every time you dream, you think Rose is waiting for you in the desert of Los Lagos. Spirits lie. Spirits trick you because they can. I feel beyond broken, baby girl. My heart can't take this anymore. It simply can't."

They stand face-to-face. My mother looks so small, her blouse too big for her around her shoulders. I've brought this pain to my mother. I've taken away her faith.

"You have to try to hold on a little bit longer," Alex says, and the tremble in her voice has nothing to do with her magic. She takes a deep breath and doesn't let go until our mother walks out without saying another word. "It's okay. I'll hold on for the both of us."

Smoke fills the room as the flame consumes the palo santo. Alex raises the jar of salt water high above her head. But she doesn't smash it. She hesitates. Gives up. And runs to her room.

I follow her. The door is shut, but that's never stopped me before. It's just easier now that I can walk through walls. Alex grips the ends of her altar as if it's the only thing holding her up. Most of the flowers are dead except for a bouquet of fresh pink roses with a card bearing Rishi's name on it.

"I'm going to find you, Rosie," Alex says as her exhale blows out a couple of the candles.

"I'm right here," I say, and when I do, I let that fear of forgetting fill me from the tips of my toes to my hair follicles. I think of the anger I felt toward my dad. How that led to us being found. I wanted to use my power to bring my family together, but I am watching it drift further apart. I reach out to her, but instead, my fingertips hit one of the roses, and that familiar hunger returns.

The petal withers and turns the brown of dried blood as it falls on Alex's hand.

"Rose," she says, and this time she sounds sure.

"Yes!" I shout. Lin sticks their head back in. I focus on the roses. Nothing soothes the senses quite like roses. Another petal withers at my touch.

Alex sees right through me with glossy eyes. "Withered petal means yes and no withered petal means no."

I tap the next one.

Alex touches the air around me. "Are you right around here?"

"She's very much like you," Lin says.

"She wishes," I say, and touch the roses.

Alex sits on the floor in front of me. Her bottom lip tugs at the sight of the decayed flowers. "Damn, Rishi's going to kill me. But she'll understand. Are you with Dad?"

I tell myself I shouldn't lie to her. I'm so close to touching that rose when Lin shakes their head.

"Are you safe?"

"That's debatable," I mutter, and touch a petal.

"Where are you?" she whispers.

I shake my fists. "Yes and no questions, Alex."

She presses her hand over her forehead. "Are you in Los Lagos? I mean, of course you're not. I already checked. But just in case."

I reach for the petal and see a different kind of magic imbued within it. The love Rishi and my sister share. I use that to wilt the top half of a petal.

"What the hell is that supposed to mean?" Alex yells, then breathes through her frustration. I want to hug her and tell her everything that's happened, everything I've seen. "You're in another realm, just not Los Lagos. But which one?"

I grab the rest of the flower and the entire head crumbles. "I need you to focus."

The ground beneath us begins to move.

"Rose?" Lin shouts, and lunges for my hand.

"Not yet," I say.

I look back at Alex, sitting on the floor, sifting through the wilted rose petals. She yells my name. I grab another flower head just as Lin rifts us back into the dreamscape.

The stars are all falling, and so are we.

21

Mayté traveled from island to island,

gifting the mortal world with gardens,

just like her mother, La Flor.

—LOST STORIES OF THE DEOS, ARCO,
SON OF THE ORCHID QUEEN

I sit up and can't catch my breath. The sensation of falling never quite stops. My eyes sting, everything just a bit blurry. The dreamscape has been replaced with dawn. The others are slowly getting up, stretching and rubbing their eyes. Somehow, we've ended up in different places—Peridot on a nest of vines, Nadira facedown in a bed of grass. Calliope a few yards away groaning as she tries to stand. Lin is beside me, and when they sit up, they gasp so deeply they vanish.

"Lin?" I say, my voice as groggy as I feel.

"Something's wrong," Calliope says. She's haloed in flickering silver light. The constellations on her dark brown skin are brighter than they have ever been. She presses her ears closed. "Does anyone else hear that?"

It must be Márohu. Wings beat above us, and she glides down, landing in a soft crouch. Her pin-straight hair falls neatly around her face. Gray eyes are threaded with electricity. "That was—"

"Different?" Nadira suggests, picking grass off her face. "I want to do it again! I was back home in the western seas."

Calliope is fascinated with the way her magic springs to her fingertips without having to yank it from the sky. It's within her. "Peridot, look."

He runs over to her. The Shuari boy has stretched nearly half a foot, his muscles more sinewy. The branches around his head have sprouted into a full crown of leaves and acorns.

"Lin?" I repeat. Everyone has gotten a boost in their magic, but what about Lin? What about me? I'm not taller or glowing or anything like that.

The fire has gone out, but there's still one stubborn ember. Then, a vertical line of violet light cracks the air open. Lin. This time, I can see the dark space past the rift. That dark, endless space that connects the places Lin teleports to. The brujex stumbles out and very gracefully falls on their back beside me.

"Are you okay?" I ask.

"I'm still trying to figure that out," Lin says. There's something strange in their violet eyes—wonder, fear, all of it—but they don't let go of my hand. None of the other guardians were with us, and we say nothing about having traveled back to my world.

I assess my body again and do notice something different. The hunger I'm used to feeling isn't there and neither is the bone-deep pain. Instead, there's something else. It is like I'm lit from within, my heart strong, steady.

Realizing we're awake, Arco and Iris run over. When I try to get up, my hands come away wet. I examine my palm, expecting to see blood. But the stench hits my nose. Rotting, putrid black.

The ground quakes, and we tumble. I hear the murmur beneath the land stronger than ever.

I am.

I am.

Xia makes a shrill sound that terrifies us all. Behind us the oasis is dying, wilting, and shuddering apart. Rocks fall and fill the pool beneath the waterfall, and trees lie in gnarly waste.

"Get up. We have to go," Lin says.

Rivers of black spread across the desert, rolling in like a high tide, and from the cracks at our feet.

The rot came to us.

And so has a swarm of blackflies.

22

*Olvidame draped herself in shadows
and roamed the roads of the world,
forgotten.*

—LAS MEMORIAS, TWIN SISTERS OF ALL
THE WORLD'S MEMORIES, BOOK OF DEOS

The rot travels in thick, glossy black veins, swelling out of the marbled cracks in the earth. I remember how I almost fell inside of that pit because I was drawn to whatever was inside. It's trapping us in. A dust storm is coming from the distance, dotted with those monsters—the blackflies. They bring a clicking sound, like metal tapping on glass, as they crawl out of the heart of the rot.

Their bodies are smaller than the ones from the Shuari. But they have the same reptilian eyes and same barbed tails, attached to black, armored humanoid bodies. Their mouths, full of sharp-ridged teeth, snap like bear traps as they advance. The guards are at our side at once, raising spears and swords. The Guardians takes their stance.

"Zuri, take my brother and the siren to the stables," Iris shouts, her voice ascending over the buzz of insects. Some of the black sludge has gotten on her face, bringing out a ferocity I knew was there but haven't seen truly unleashed. Her braids whip as she turns. "Spread out! We will never have another chance to fight back."

"We should retreat," Alma says. I do not relish in her fear the way I thought I would.

"There is no retreat. We are the only line of defense for Adas," Iris says, glancing back. I see what she sees. If we climb up the side of the cliff, we'd be easy to pick off by having our backs turned. We have as much of a high ground as we're going to get in the remains of the oasis. Iris thrusts her spare short sword into my hands. "This is the end that kills."

There are so many blackflies. My gut tightens with cold dread. I see split guts and blood. Ruin and dead earth. Creatures that might have been adas once. But then, I remember the dreamscape. My sisters. My mother, giving up. I have to be strong enough for all of us.

I squeeze Lin's hand. A familiar pulse of magic reverberates between our palms: strength. Our magic undulates in a protective aura. The spark of stars, the swell of oceans. The life of trees, the power of flight. A kinetic hum rises from within me. We run. The swollen veins of it pop under our feet. The breeze dies. For a moment, the outerlands are deafeningly silent.

Then, Iris strikes first, emitting a howling scream.

Her gleaming sword cuts across a barbed tail that would have impaled her. She whirls around to finish the creature off by decapitation. Black rot spews from its skull and splatters on Iris's skin.

I feel myself moving in slow motion. All I see are monstrous limbs and sharp teeth. All I feel is the heat of the dead outerlands. My feet drag. My muscles are heavy. I swing my sword at a blackfly to my right. Stabbing something in motion is harder than it looks, but I catch it by its open mouth. The creature writhes as I pull my sword back and mirror Iris's move to hack off their stingers. I wipe my face of the hot oozy blood and the salty spray from Nadira's summoned water magic. Two more appear to replace the fallen blackfly.

Nadira and I remain side by side with Iris, a triangle of steel and waves. The mermaid offers her hand to me. Green scales rise to her forearms like glimmering shields. "Use my power."

There is no time for hesitation. I don't want to be a power that steals, and drains, and takes. I want to leave something good behind. I want to join her power to make something stronger. I grip Nadira's arms and the cold rush of her magic cycles through me. I remember standing on the beach with my sisters and parting the sea. This time, I take just enough that it won't weaken her.

"Concentrate on the sea beneath us. Pull the current to you," she says.

I thread my fingers with hers and my power is at ease, not drawing her out anymore, but alongside her. I see the shape of the sea, the millions of molecules that form the ocean, the life within it. I can hear the sound of the waves approaching, roaring into a crush like the voices of the Yuraba crabmaids. Streams of salt water blast into the air, clearing the rot that clogs the arteries of the outerlands. They slam down like the fists of an ancient sea queen.

Nadira and I share a victorious smile as six of the blackflies are decimated, their carapaces cracked like eggs. Only two of them get back up. But they're faster, adapting.

"Lin!" I shout. "Can we send these things through a rift?"

They wipe rot off their face. "I have to find a dead world. We can't let this happen to another world."

Calliope flings bolts of starlight, saving us from being devoured. Her eyes brim with tears but her voice is even. "My realm. The Starlark. There's nothing left."

"I need time," Lin says, rubbing their palms together. Purple light splitting the seams of empty space. "I've never made such a portal."

I squeeze their shoulders. "No pressure. Love you, bye."

I ready myself to keep fighting when Arco rides into my line of sight on Huracán. His face and torso are splattered with sludge. Huracán rears and pummels the blackfly in front of me. I did not realize Pegasi teeth were so sharp because it bites through the monster's shell.

"What are you doing here?" I shout.

"Get up!" He steadies the jumpy Pegasus. "There are too many. We have to retreat!"

I search for Iris, but she's moved farther away. She fights like she was born to it with fury in her blood. Nadira follows at her side, and I can sense her pulling at the waters again, drowning the desert of the rot.

"I can't leave them," I tell Arco.

"I thought you might say that." His smile is amused. He dismounts Huracán and whispers into the creature's ear. Then he slaps her on her side and she rides into the fray, crushing and ripping blackflies with her teeth. Her hooves splash in the pools of salt water and sludge.

Wild, giddy excitement floods my veins as Arco takes my hand

and we regroup with the others. He doesn't have a weapon, but climbs up and behind the blackflies, snapping their necks. Even though they are vile, and even though they have sprung out of this rot, he whispers something every time he brings one down. A prayer? A curse?

I whirl around for a moment. Just a moment when I see a dark spot at the corner of my eye. As I turn back toward him, a blackfly knocks Arco down with a thrust of its snout. Even as I push my body to move, raise my sword, pull at the dregs of Nadira's power within me, it is no use.

I shut my eyes and scream.

Arco grunts. The creature makes a terrible screeching noise.

When I reach them, Arco is laying beneath it, his fountain pen sticking out of the beast's eye, piercing right through its brain. When he retrieves it, the pen drips with ooze. I shake with relief and wrap my arms around him. Arco tilts my chin up.

"My fight is not yet over, brujita."

A few yards away, Lin has cut a rift as wide as a door. There is nothing inside but black space. "Now!"

"Hold that thought," I tell Arco.

"Guardians," I shout. "Together!"

Márohu leaps up high and spins and spins, conjuring fast cycling winds. She is a tornado, capturing dozens of blackflies and shattering them against the jagged rocks of the cliff. Calliope fights with two spears made of sunlight, leaping in wide arcs that send the creatures into a dizzy spin, making them perfect targets. Peridot's thick roots push through the ground, ensnaring the blackflies and dragging them back to the rift.

But as we move the wave of blackflies and rot toward the divide, the ground splinters with an earthquake. Lin is thrown several yards away. Their rift vanishes with a booming slap, like thunder.

It didn't work. Iris is on her knees, staring at the mass of monsters re-forming. Under it all, I hear the sob that wrenches from her.

There are too many of them. More erupt out of the rot, dozens and dozens of them.

"Lin, can you get us out of here?" I yell.

"To me!" Lin hollers, running back to us. We stagger and stumble to regroup in a tight circle. We stand back to back. Lin cleaves the air in two. But as they try to open a rift, the cracks beneath our feet split wider and wider, widening like jaws.

"Peridot!" Calliope shouts as she reaches for him. His feet straddle both sides of the ground. He teeters sideways, and for a breath, he is grasping at air.

Márohu is a flash of black feathers swooping down to catch him.

I grab Calliope by the back of her tunic as she hangs precariously on a ledge. She clings to me. With another seismic shake, our slab of rock breaks off, like a chunk of ice separating from a glacier.

"I got you. I got you."

But truly, it's Lin who is saving the pair of us. They slide across the ground and rip through the air. We roll out of the second rift onto more solid earth.

We all stand at the mouth of the precipice and watch a chunk of stone, the very slab Calliope and I were on moments ago, float atop the mouth to the ocean of rot rising too quickly. Even blackflies drown in the muck, returning to the soupy sludge they crawled out from.

ZORAIDA CÓRDOVA

From here, it looks like El Terroz tried to hollow out the ground, and filled it with decay.

"Why is this happening?" Lin asks behind me.

I try to parse out the different types of magic in the air. The buzzing sound break apart Each one has a distinct voice, racing through my thoughts. Even the rot.

I am waiting.

"It's waiting for something," I say. "Or someone."

I lock eyes with Iris. She's bleeding where tooth marks puncture her shoulder. There's something terrifying about the fear filling her quartz eyes as she watches the rot beating like a bloody heart. "Retreat. *Run.*"

"Lin!" I shout. There is nowhere to go but climb up the cliff because ahead of us is a great, black sea. "You can do this!"

Lin concentrates on the space in front of them. Just like in the dreamscape, their power splinters the air. This time, they pull on the seams to keep the door open. It holds! But as we start to file in, clouds of gray dust cling low to the ground, filling our noses and irritating our eyes. I can't see my own hand in front of me, only gray clouds.

"I'll clear this," Márohu says. She pushes up, spreading her wings, and clearing enough of the dust storm that we can see each other, when a blackfly plunges out of the ooze and stabs her. Her howl of pain rings through the air as black feathers flutter to the ground. Iris and Peridot run to her aid.

"Here!" Calliope conjures orbs of light to mark the entrance.

"Hurry!" Lin grunts through the strain of wielding their magic.

The blackflies are unsticking themselves out of the primordial ooze in the pit. Calliope conjures a sword of starlight and slashes down creature after creature. She kicks the dead blackfly over the ledge and helps Iris carry an unconscious Márohu through the open rift.

"Eliza," Nadira says. I whirl around to find her staggering, a hand clutched at her side. I grab her. Drape her arm over my shoulder. Feel her magic buzz along my skin. Beads of sweat bubble across her forehead. "I didn't see it."

Peridot and Arco are each helping injured guards through the rift, and they can't help me. Alma is rushing in after them.

"We're almost there," I encourage Nadira. Suddenly, she feels so very weightless.

"I still wouldn't choose the seas, Eliza," Nadira's says between pants. "I was brought to these shores for a reason. I know that. We all were."

Nadira and I stumble and fall. I hold her in my arms. Her eyes turn the white of sea caps. Her brown skin becomes translucent. I remember Arco's words at the start of our journey. *We become something more.* Even mermaids.

"Rose. My name is Rose."

"Rose," Nadira whispers, pressing a cold, wet hand to my cheek. "It suits you."

The mermaid's grip around me vanishes. Her eyes widen with surprise. She looks down. White surf froths from her mouth, and from the cavity in her chest, where a stinger protrudes.

"No!" I wail.

I try to hold on to her, to grab her, to make her stay. But at that moment, she becomes sea foam in my hands, seeping into the desert.

"Behind you!" Lin cries, arms shaking as they pull one side of the rift open. It shrinks, threads of lightning caught within it.

Then a blackfly crawls on top of me. I want to scream, but I choke on salt water dripping into my mouth. I grip the monster by its throat and feel the rapid pulse of magic that comes from it. My power draws on the creature's life force. I hear the whisper of the rot. It is the thing that spawned these creatures. There's more beneath. The first rising dawn, like I'm back in the dreamscape. Something ancient and cursed. Something that needs to be heard. Divine, but not a god. The rot shows me its heart.

I am.

I am waiting for you.

It fills my mind with her memories.

She is a girl running wild across rain forests and fields. She has violet hair that fades to white at the ends like the flower she is named after, skin kissed golden by the sun. Long lashes made of petals flutter at the corners of her eyes. Contrasted sharply against her beauty are rings of thorns that grow around her throat, her wrists, her ankles. Where her feet touch, flowers sprout. She kisses the rough bark of trees and reminds the island that it is loved. She rolls down hills with her sister—they are twin girls, the last of their line, with fierce hearts and kind souls. Kaíri tends the gardens, and Mayté the forests and beyond. She walks across the sea and helps life bloom even in the ocean's depths.

She is a girl, older, watching blood spill over the land she loves so much. She touches the blood of the fallen, and it becomes moss.

The new king, Cirro, chooses her and loves her for a time.

She sits beside her new husband after his conquest. His dark hair falls in sheets down his back, and she is in love with the onyx pools of his eyes, his brown skin, the flush of his lips when she kisses him beneath La Mama's sun. Wherever she goes, Cirro follows. Flowers twist from the forest floor where she steps. He plucks them and dresses his hair with them, to smell her, to keep her with him.

But over time, King Cirro changed. He became fickle and, greedy, ravaged other islands. He was not the king she had believed.

Mayté loved him still, loved him more when their children were born. Twins born under the blissful omen of a rainbow. "Arco and Iris," the king said, and then did not see them again until they could walk.

He returned to her like the tide. There was no room for her in his bed. Cirro spent his night and days feasting, from the Howling Moon to the Salt Moon.

Mayté watched her children grow. Arco grew slowly, quietly, like a bloom that thrives in the dark and survives the cold. Iris preferred to run wild. Her scream could be heard across the rain forests. They grew that way, twisting, becoming the only versions of themselves they knew how.

Arco became lost.

Iris became her fury.

Fury toward her father for letting the kingdom rot. Fury toward her mother for withstanding it.

Mayté watched Iris plan her deed. Train her arrow at the king's heart. Iris never missed. She let the arrow loose, but at the last second, Mayté was at her daughter's side.

Mayté held her daughter and gave her all of her strength, all of her magic. "If you murder your father, there will be no hope for Adas. Our blood seeds this land. You are goddess born."

Mayté watched her daughter's anger change, transform. She watched her daughter choose a life of steel and blood. She watched her leave.

Mayté opened the portal when the rebels came. Enough. She had had enough cruelty. Enough bloodshed. Enough of Cirro corrupting her mother's island. The paradise of the gods.

On the night of the Manatí Moon, King Cirro found her. Held her like he hadn't in so long. She did not see the dagger but felt it pierce her heart. She could not breathe as she fell, as he rang for the guards, as the castle fell into chaos. She could still hear his voice, a whisper: "You should have let Iris kill me when she had the chance."

Mayté the Orchid Queen was dead.

She was sent out to sea, but she returned. Beneath the waves. Beneath the island that was her by root and blood.

She returned for him.

I am waiting for you, my love and my end.

PART V

THE RIFT

23

She forgot her name for a spell.

Forgot her mother tongue, her mother too.

But she learned the language of the rainforest.

—CLARIBELLE AND THE KINGDOM OF ADAS:
TALES TALL AND TRUE, GLORIANA PALACIOS

Even as I watch Mayté's memories, I cannot breathe. Not until I push her magic out of my system. I am still in the rift, my hands covered in rot and Nadira's death. Lin is shouting my name. We are stuck because of me, because of something I've done.

"You can't stay in here, Rose," Lin says, pleads.

I know that I can't, but I wish to stay in between nothingness. Maybe if I stay here long enough, everything will hurt less.

"I know it's tempting, but you have to come back. The castle is falling—"

The castle. We're back at the castle, which means we have to see the king. My bargain is broken because I failed. *Get up*, Rose. *Get up.*

I take their hand, and familiar magic pulses through us. Lin pries the rift open once more, and the pitch-black of the in-between becomes a sea. Dark waves beat against the side of the castle. My eyelids are heavy, but I can't fall asleep. When I rub them, a sticky black crust comes away on my fingers. I try to turn on my side to hack up the viscous black that spews out of my lungs. But no matter how much I cough up, I feel like I will never rid myself of the putrid power of the rot.

Lin helps me sit and bring a water skin to my lips. I let the crisp, clean water quench this horrible thirst. Nothing helps with the bitter taste of it though.

We're far away enough from the rot that I can't smell anything but sea brine. I take note of a large bedroom with a bed frame built into the wall. Fireflies cling to the gnarled vines. Every leaf has fallen and withered on the mattress, on which lie Zuri and Emmen. Two terrinas tend to their wounds.

"Welcome back, girl child," Palita greets me in her hoarse little voice. A strange part of me is relieved to see her again. The terrinas carry bandages and dirty water away on their trays.

I sit up on my knees. Iris leans against the frame to the balcony watching the waves reach as far as the banister. Xia and Calliope treat Márohu's injured wing. Peridot is resting his head against a wall, and Arco is washing up in a clear water basin. The water is a dark gray.

They all look at me expectantly. I can see the question on the tip of their lips. Where is Nadira?

"Dead," I say.

There's a collective exhale. I should be used to dead by now. Haven't I said that over and over again? I push my feelings down, because I know this is not over yet.

"Where are we?" I ask.

"My chambers," Iris says.

"When I made the rift, I thought of home, but Iris went first," Lin explains.

I notice the weapons hanging from the walls. Swords and arrows. Several animal trophies, and a tapestry of a regal fairy with delicate thorns around her throat, and orchid sprouting from her ankles. Mayté.

I am waiting for you, my love and my end. I have to tell them. I have to say something. But when I try to speak, my voice is nothing but scratches. I think of Nadira dissolving in my arms.

"There is nothing left of her," I say.

Lin lowers their head.

"She vanished into nothing." I look at Arco, who holds my stare. "I thought she was supposed to become something greater. Something *more* than this. Isn't that what you said of Adas and magical beings?"

"Maybe if she'd been in the sea," Lin says. "Maybe if she were older. I was there once when a young one died. He'd returned from the human realm with iron poisoning. He simply withered into nothing. Not even grass. But an elder in my village—she became a ceiba tree."

"So what?" I say, my voice escalating. I wish I could reach down and scrape out the burning sensation. "You have to be old before you're special? That's not fair. That's *not* fair!"

Lin wraps their arms around me, and for a moment, I want to push away the embrace. I want to kick and scream. I want to rub sand on my skin until it's raw because I can still feel the rot, burrowed within me like larvae. Maggots. Arco and Iris's mother.

But I only hold Lin tighter. They anchor me.

"Carry Nadira to your everlasting shores," Xia says.

A heavy silence stretches between us all, and for a long time we only listen to the sound of waves.

"What do we do now?" I ask.

I push through the stiffness in my legs and join Iris. From here I can see the waves, and the waxing moon, red like the bottom half of a Iris's swollen mouth. Her eye is swollen, too. Her hands are wrapped, but blood still seeps through—the injuries that show how hard she fought. My heart beats wildly thinking of what I have to tell her. She told me she tried to kill her father, and that she was punished for it. But what will she do if she knew the truth?

If you murder your father, there will no hope for Adas.

She grips my shoulder, and I wince.

"You lost your bet," I say.

Iris makes a strangled laugh. "I won. You made it to the outerlands. What is it, Eliza? I know you well enough by now to that you don't hold back."

It is Xia whose voice surprised me. She nods her bald head slowly. "Ahhh, the Siphon has heard the rot. Tell us what even I could not hear?"

Zuri and Emmen. Calliope and Peridot. Lin and Arco. Xia and Márohu. They all turn to watch me, but it is Iris's stare I dread. How can I keep this from Arco and Iris when I know firsthand how lies destroy? The sweeter the lie, the harder it is to lose a taste for it.

"I siphoned the rot from one of the blackflies. It showed me what's in there."

"The Deo?" Peridot asks skeptically.

Could she not know? What if she runs me through with that sword after I tell her because she thinks I'm lying? I *can* lie, after all. My heart squeezes painfully.

"The rot is Mayté," I say, looking from Arco to Iris. Then to the tapestry of her on the wall. "The rot is your mother."

Arco staggers back, pressing a hand on the bare skin of his chest over his heart. "That can't be. She wasn't buried. She'd told Aunt Kaíri that she didn't want to be buried because she didn't belong to one place. We built her a barge and filled it with everything she'd need in the next life."

Iris pounds her fist against her chest. I can see how she is held together by silk threads. "I shot the arrow that set her pyre aflame in the open seas."

I want to take it all back. Maybe the rot was lying. But why would it? Why would she?

Iris turns to me now, her eyes shrewd, as if she can see through my lies—as if she wants me to be lying. "Tell me, Eliza, Siphon of Galaxies, how that *thing* could be my mother."

I shut my eyes and warm tears fall. "She's waiting for the one who killed her. She's waiting for King Cirro."

Her bottom lip trembles. Then Arco is there, holding his sister while she curses every god in existence. Glistening tears fall down their cheeks. It turns out, like everything adas do, they look ethereal. It is a strange thing watching an immortal being mourn.

"I will utterly end him," Iris vows.

Thankfully, it is the siren who waves her finger. "The princess cannot end anything. You are the beginning."

"Enough, Xia," Iris says. "How could you not know?"

"The Siphon was the one who could hear her. The Siphon is the one who is the daughter of Everything's End."

"Is there a way to stop this?" Márohu asks, wincing as her wing twitches.

Peridot clears his throat. "If the rot—the queen—wants King Cirro, then why shouldn't we give him to her? After all he has done."

Zuri sits up, bowing to Iris. "Your Highness, may I speak?"

"Of course, Zuri."

The guard has duende features, with a twisted nose and sharp bottom teeth. "The folk, those who are loyal to the king, will not betray him."

"If you or Arco kill your father, you would be corrupting your own blood. That's what started this," I explain everything I say. I spare no detail. Iris knows I'm telling the truth when I describe the moment she had with her mother. "We have to separate him from the crown."

"My father will not give up his crown easily," Arco says. "It was forged by the Deos and binds the ruler to Adas."

It is magic. I can siphon its power enough to get it off King Cirro."

"And then who will wear it?" Calliope asks. "You?"

I scoff. "Have you seen the infrastructure in the outerlands? No thanks."

"Princess Iris," Emmen says. "Is it not obvious? The River Queen foretold it. She would see a queen on the throne of Adas again. She is nearly two millennia old."

Stiffly, Emmen rises from the bed. Her auburn hair is matted with rot and her shoulder is bandaged, but steps forward. "You are my Queen of Adas, and the only one I will recognize."

"The folk love my brother, not me," Iris says.

"I take great pleasure in saying this, Sister." Arco bears a crooked smile. "But you are wrong."

Emmen shows no sign of getting up from her bended knee. Zuri makes the same vow.

"You're the only hope for Adas." I get down on one knee and look up at her. She looks both flattered and terrified. "You searched the realms for magical guardians, you led us to the outerland. You're the rightful queen of Adas. And if I'm going to pledge myself to you, I should tell you, all of you, that my real name is Rose."

Iris returns my bow.

Márohu rises and does the same. "You gave me a place to belong when I had nowhere, not even the skies to turn to. I pledge myself to you."

Calliope follows suit, drawing a new constellation over her heart—an iris flower. Then Peridot and Lin. Arco steps forward. He looks at his mother's likeness, then at Iris. I remember the words he wrote in his book.

He pulls out his fountain pen from his pants pocket and offers it to her, joining the rest of us on his knees. "You have my pen, sister. When the time comes, I will crown the queen."

Iris stands tall. Bruised and scarred, covered in blood and rot, she is every bit the depiction of a warrior princess. No. She's a warrior queen.

"I accept your pledges and will honor them," she says.

323

I get up. "Now comes the tricky part."

Calliope shakes her head, silver strands shimmering around her shoulders. "How do you unseat the current king without restarting the corruption and bloodshed that led to the rot across the land?"

"As we speak, the entire castle is full of revelers," Lin says. "They're everywhere. In every part of the courtyard, the gardens, the arena."

"All of Adas has come to escape the effects of the rot, not caring that there is nowhere else to go," Arco says gravely. "Father loves an audience."

"Okay, I have a plan," I say. "But it might be dangerous."

"Might be or is?" Calliope asks dubiously.

"I've never tried it so I can't tell, can I?" I think of the kind of king that Cirro is. He has created stories of himself that magnify who he truly is. But even a king can't escape the truth. "I'm going to need my father's help on this one."

It's my first political coup, so Zuri and Emmen go over my plan again and again. Márohu, because she can't fly, will be our lookout. Arco and Iris will do the only thing they can. They'll face their father. It's up to me to get the crown.

"Wait," I say, and look around the room. In the excitement, the horror of it all, I forgot something. "Where's Alma?"

"She didn't come with us," Iris says.

"I saw her." Alma the guard who was sent along with us for King Cirro. Heavy footsteps come from outside. A stampede of them. Everyone is on their feet, drawing weapons as the door slams open.

King Cirro stands at the threshold with Alma and a dozen guards. His crown is tipped forward, the light within the stars faded.

"Treason," he bellows. "I should have expected no less from you, Daughter."

Iris looks at me and Lin. "Go!"

"But—"

I hear the crackle of Lin's violet lightning, feel the void of the betwixt, before we step out inside a cell. We're in the prison tower.

At first, it's so dark I can't tell if anyone's in there. Then there's the spark of light, and a torch light ignites. A perfect circle is cut out of the brick behind him, just large enough to fit his fist through to touch the open air, to see the full moon when it aligns.

"Dad?" I shout. I think about how the first time I saw my dad standing on my front porch, I didn't recognize him. He was a skinny, strange man that Alex let in. I realize, I forgot him once too.

My dad lifts his head but does not move. As I step inside the cell, he blinks over and over. He grips the gold pendant under his filthy tunic. I can feel him trying to convince his mind that I'm here and I'm real. But his eyes—Lula's eyes, bright and gray and full of recognition, have tears racing down his face when he sees me. Then, past me.

One word echoes through the stone room. "Papá?"

But it's not me who's spoken.

It is Lin who approaches slowly, like they're walking across a tightrope trying to get to each other.

Lin holds a trembling hand to my father and asks, "Papá, is that you?"

24

The Siphon of Galaxies will learn

her greatest power is her heart.

—LOST STORIES OF ADAS, ARCO,
SONG OF THE ORCHID QUEEN

Watching my dad hug Lin Octavio, my friend, my sibling, I suddenly, finally understand.

I understand why my father would go from being completely content one minute to overcome by sadness the next. I understand his faraway stares, not from lost memories but from losing something else. Someone. A child. It's the same way I felt when Alex was trapped in Los Lagos. Knowing she was somewhere we couldn't reach was like living with a piece of my heart missing. Now that I'm here, my mom and sisters are going through it again. I understand all this.

But in this moment, I don't think I will ever understand why he didn't tell us.

I take a deep breath.

I clear my throat.

"Dad," I say, and even though it's only one word, my voice breaks.

"I don't understand," Lin says, and despite my best efforts, I can't meet their eyes.

"Oh, Rosie," my dad says, trying to come to me. To grab my face, streaming with tears.

I shake my head. Part of me doesn't believe it. How long was Dad here? Almost seven years for us. Double the time in Adas. Lin is younger than me. I want Lin to know that I am not crying because of them. I have to focus on the main reason we came here. My nose is stuffed and runny and I sound like a child instead of someone trying to save an island from destruction. I wipe my eyes with the backs of my hands. "We need your help."

"You have to let me explain," he says. "Both of you."

"The rot is spreading, and King Cirro just arrested my friends." All of it, everything about our retreat and my entire plan to make Iris queen of Adas, comes out in a whoosh. "Now we have to improvise. I need your help."

My magic stirs. It whispers along my skin as if to tell me that I'm not alone, even when I feel it in my core.

"Rose," Dad says.

"Are you going to help us or not?" I ask.

"I am." Dad stares at Lin and me. "But in case something happens to me, I owe you my story."

What I need is time. I need time in a place that practically fabricates it, and all the while, I haven't been able to use any of it. Not to adjust to my powers or race across the island or to understand how fast your world can change with a single truth.

I have no choice but to face him and Lin. My sibling. My kid sibling. My best friend in this wretched place. How many times did I feel they were familiar? That laugh like Lula's, that smile like Alex's. They have the same nose as Dad. Now I can see it. How didn't I see it before? What do they have that is like me? A strange, wonderful thought occurs to me—I am not the baby Mortiz anymore. I turn to Lin. They must be confused and scared, and I'm only thinking about myself.

"You said your parents were dead," I say.

Lin bites on their bottom lip to stop from crying. "I thought that too. We thought you died in the rebellion. She stood there every night waiting for your body to wash up and it never did."

We. I realize I saw them in the dreamscape.

Dad turns away from us. His shoulders shake. He is nearly bent over crying for another woman who isn't my mother.

"What happened to her?" he asks Lin.

"She tried her best to protect me, but they found us. She was sent to the mines and didn't make it out."

I think of my mom sitting at home. What if she didn't come back from work one day? At least she was able to get back to us every night. Lin didn't have that. Lin lost more than I did because they didn't have Alex or Lula or me. I grab their hand and squeeze. Reassure them that I am here. I won't leave them.

"That's why you stayed in Miami," I say. The anger has left my voice. All I ever wanted was the truth. But I know I would not have forgiven him if he'd told me this back in Lagunitas Serpentinas.

"I wanted to tell you all," Dad says, facing the circular cutout in the tower. We all watch the red half-moon line up. "When I came here—I gave myself to the king in exchange for Alex. I'd made a bad deal with an ada. I followed him here in exchange for something that could help control her power. It was so unpredictable back then. But it turns out that the ada was a bounty hunter. He did give me the draught, but by then, I was already in King Cirro's gladiator ring."

I find myself smiling. Alex always did blame herself for Dad leaving. How different would things have been if we'd known that he'd been tricked?

"That's when I met Graciela. Lin's mother. We fought together in the arena. I used a different name: Octavio."

"Then you forgot," I say. It is a fact. One I know, too well now. He nods.

I have more questions now that there is no time to ask right now. I know that no matter what, I have to get us all home.

The ground trembles, and I reach for my dad. I can feel his chest shake with sobs.

"What will you tell Ma?" I whisper.

He takes a deep breath, and for the first time since my father has returned to my life, his eyes are clear, his voice strong. He says, "Everything."

I open my arm to let Lin into our embrace. The world might be falling apart at the seams, but at least, for the moment we are together.

We do not have to search long to find our friends. Everyone, from the terrinas to the guards loyal to Cirro, is talking about the public trial the king was going to have for the traitors. We do not even have to hide, but we do try to blend in. Dad and Lin wear flower crowns, and I pull on a purple cape to cover my rot-ruined clothes.

The Castillo de Sal is brimming with bodies. It is nearly impossible to move through the throngs. Worse than any traffic jam, any concert in Coney Island, anything I've ever been to before. Plus, the adas here have horns and thorns protruding from a lot of extremities, which makes it dangerous to navigate through the gardens.

We follow the flow of the crowds into the seaside gladiator ring. From this side of the stands, it looks just as intimidating as the night I fought Alcyone. The waves are dark, the horizon tinged red from the moon.

I recognize some faces around in the stands—adas who were at the Salt Moon feast, Gloriana with her delicate golden horns. Shuari folk who I last saw at Girasol Grove. When I scan the stands, I notice Kaíri. What must have happened to her home to have her come here? I wonder if she suspected that the rot could have been her sister.

"Be careful," I tell my father, squeezing his arm. "My bargain with King Cirro is broken. Anyone here can—"

He flashes a rare smile. "I can take care of myself, Rosie."

When the ground trembles, the arena goes silent. I think about how if this doesn't work, we go down this with island.

Just then, King Cirro enters the arena. He's trailed by a retinue of guards. I catch Alma's green braid swing at her back. She pokes and prods the crowd to cheer, to scream, to hoot and holler so loudly I bet you could hear us past the barrier.

I catch a bit of conversation from the adas behind me, decked in sheer linen and dripping with jewels. "It's the last I'll get to wear them."

"I hear King Cirro is calling tonight the feast to end all feasts."

They have no idea how right they are.

Alma blows on a conch shell, then gives the floor to the king. He is swathed in gold silk. The stars of his crown emit a weak pulse of light. That doesn't belong to him.

"My kinfolk of Adas," King Cirro bellows. His sharp stare cuts to the cells housing his prisoners. "I have been betrayed."

He pauses for the gossip and whispers. He pauses to let adoring subjects throw flowers at his feet. How can they watch their island drown and still adore him?

I squeeze Dad's shoulder, our signal, and he climbs up higher and higher in the stands. I force myself not to look back. Not to worry. Focus on Cirro.

Then he continues. "I entrusted six Guardians of Adas to save us from this rot. Instead, they have turned my children against me. They have deepened the wound in this land. But tonight, I will save our kingdom." He waves a hand, and the cell doors are opened. The prisoners are bound and gagged. With a show, they are marched to the very edge of the arena that juts out over the crashing waves.

Iris, Calliope, Peridot, Márpohu, Zuri, Emmen, and Arco.

A sharp cry goes up from the stands. I recognize Kaíri and her kin. I recognize Alcyone, the Starlark, by her silver hair. Clearly this is not the reaction King Cirro wanted. So, he presses. "My guard has told me that the rot demands satisfaction. And I, your faithful king, your true king, will give it to you."

"Ready?" I ask Lin.

Their violet eyes spark with purpose. They take my hand, and we step into the rift. We stay in the strange, dark calm for a moment. When the door opens up again, only I step out onto the arena.

Dad is my own personal special-effects master, calling down fat bolts of lightning that illuminate even the sea. People duck, and I do my very best not to flinch.

"Siphon," King Cirro says. "What an unexpected pleasure. I was told you didn't make it out of the outerlands."

"You were told wrong." I turn to the spectators, which buzzes with energy. "I am here to challenge King Cirro to a fight."

The King sneers at me. His eternal features drain for beauty. The king I had dreamt of once is long gone. "And what is the occasion of this challenge, if I might ask?"

I bare my teeth. "For the honor of a queen."

"Arrest her," He waves his hand.

"Arrest me?" My voice is sharp and clear despite my trembling legs. "Are you not the king who held up the great ceiba tree for six days and six nights with your sheer strength?"

The audience hollers. I take a few steps closer to him. He says nothing.

"Are you not the king with the daring and power to swallow an entire sea?"

This time, they notice that he doesn't answer.

"Are you not the king who held Queen Mayté in his arms and then stabbed her through her heart?"

King Cirro lunges for me. It was stupid of me to count on his rage, his brute sense of power. He chokes me. But I grab for his crown. My magic unwinds like a spool of thread. I sink into the brilliant light of La Estrella's seven stars, the eternal magic of La Flor's thorn vines, and El Terroz's treasured gold. Together they created this for a queen. But it was stolen, taken, uprooted with hatred and violence. It is the same violent act that wrenched open the curse on this land.

"You did this," I tell Cirro as he loosens his grip on me. "You ruined her, and you tried to ruin your children. You are no king."

He falls at my feet without his crown. Everyone is screaming. I am shaking so much I am afraid I will shatter.

"Rose!"

I whirl around. At the center of the arena are the guardians. No one, not even Cirro's guard, threatens me as I hand the crown of Adas to Arco. He raises it high. His dark eyes take in the crowd, his sister kneeling at his feet, and then me.

"I, Arco, Scribe of Adas, Son of the Orchid Queen, crown you, Iris, Warrior of Adas, the True and Fair Queen of Adas."

The seven crystals give off a pulse of magnificent light.

And then, the world is torn in two.

25

The girl still hungered for the world.
She ate the sea and swallowed the moon.
She is the girl with all the power.

—WITCHSONG #5, BOOK OF CANTOS

The arena splinters down the center. Bodies run and fly away. The first signs of morning brighten the horizon. And Iris is the queen.

A queen who picks up her sword and joins her soldiers as they fend off those still loyal to King Cirro. Arco said to anticipate it. But I would expect that on the tiny occurrence of the island still breaking apart into the sea, Cirro's guards would see reason.

The first part of my plan is complete. The second one is harder. It does not seem to matter that he killed his queen, or that his words bend like a trick of light. There are those who throw their bodies in the way. Not many, but enough that it takes time to bring him to me.

I can hear Mayté's voice now, buzzing with expectation, like she can feel the change in the power of the land. Rot bubbles up from the new cracks in the ground.

Calliope and Peridot drag the king, draped in gold silk, across the arena. I remember scraping my skin here. I remember getting the first taste of my power. There's a smear of rot on his high cheekbone. A terrible cry ripples through the crowd as the earth shakes.

The Guardians of Adas gather around me. We started this together, and we will end it this way. I say a silent prayer for Nadira. Vita. For everyone who died because of him. I hate that I have this anger in my heart. But now I think of the mermaid girl who was there to laugh at my jokes, who pulled me out of the water. Nadira said, "I was brought to these shores for a reason. I know that. We all were." She was right.

The only way to heal Adas is to start anew. Arco and Iris, descended from La Flor, can't kill their father. But I am not descended from La Flor. I am a bruja, a witch, the Siphon, Daughter of El Fin, Master of Everything's End.

There are many different kinds of ends, and they don't all have to mean death.

"Cirro, Bastard son of King Eterno, Ruin of Adas," Iris says, meeting her father's eyes. "I sentence you to an end eternal."

I shut my eyes. I breathe in the salty sea air, the shimmer of sunrise, the layers of magic that fill this island. From seed to root to hair follicle. From the barrier that surrounds it to the rivers that run deep.

The rot has been evolving, turning into a living thing. Iris's garrison went in and out came the blackflies. Like all things in Adas, it has become something more. And I have to get rid of it, uproot it like a tree with rot at the core.

I summon the rot. The way my father conjures lightning and

Nadira did the oceans, I latch on to the thing that makes the rot destroy. I know I am capable of that. It is not my curse to bear. But it is a curse I choose to save this realm, and my own.

My lungs begin to burn as I hold my breath with the strain of magic. The darkness threatens to overwhelm me, close over me. I focus on the limits of my power—power so great I have seen it raise the dead and vanquish evil. Power so small I have seen it woven into fishing nets to feed hungry bellies, to soothe fevers and toothaches, and to provide light during a very long night. My power is my family, even if they are scattered across realms. Alex and Lula and Mom in Queens. Nova just a few islands away. Dad and Lin feet away. They are always with me, and as long as I know that, my power is endless.

Mayté's voice slithers across my skin, and I realize I am not the only one who can hear her say, "*I am waiting for you, my love and my end.*"

Cirro opens his mouth to scream and the rot plunges in. Watching it feels like hearing a scream played backward. Guttural, terrible, cruel, endless, like he was. When it is over, I can feel the entire island sigh.

Lin's rift crackles like one of Dad's lightning bolts. A wide doorway opens.

I shove Cirro into the great, dark, empty.

26

Socorro, socorro, mi Estrellita,

que me ahogo en lamento.

—REZO TO LA ESTRELLA, BOOK OF DEOS

Alta Bruja Lady Lunes taught me that the price of magic is not always fair. I know that, but as the Castillo de Sal erupts into celebration, I don't care. The recoil of using my power feels like I've been pressed to death like the accused witches of old.

For a moment, I watch every single smiling face. Calliope with her star-bright hair. My father, saying hello to old friends. Kaíri paying tribute to the queen.

For a moment, I sit down to rest with my feet dangling over the ledge of the fractured arena. Arco comes to sit beside me. We are all filthy from sweating and fighting, but somehow, like most of the adas, he manages to look breathtaking.

"I have something for you, Rose," he says.

It's kind of strange having him say my name after calling me one thing for days, but I like it. "I do like presents."

The prince of Adas hands me a beautifully carved fountain pen. I can feel some sort of magic, but I can't be sure if it's in the wood or the steel nib.

"I thought you gave yours to Iris," I say.

He grins slyly. "I do have more than one."

For a moment, I start to laugh.

But then a scream erupts. We rush to the center of the arena, where Lin is slumped in Dad's arms.

"What's wrong with them?" I shout.

"I don't know, one minute we were talking and then Lin just fell."

Lin's purple light shatters open. The sound is all wrong, like metal being warped.

Cirro steps out. His hair has turned to ash, and his skin sags off the bone. How did he get out?

Iris pushes her way through the throng. Calliope is there beside me wielding a spear of light.

For a moment, I think I'm safe.

"You took everything from me," King Cirro says. I see the glint of steel.

Calliope thrusts the spear through the old king's head and kicks him back into the infinite dark. I let go of my pent up breath. Arco is standing in front of me. He falls, a slender dagger driven through his heart.

27

La Flor rested her head between two rivers and slept.

It was the best place to spend eternity.

—LOST STORIES OF THE DEOS, ARCO,
SON OF THE ORCHID QUEEN

Some things can't be fixed by magic. Growing up in a house with its own infirmary, I know it better than most brujas. My mother might have been able to heal wounds and deliver babies safely into the world, but if she'd always used magic, it would have resulted in her death. Magic has a price. She pulled back a werewolf, who'd been shot seven times by a rogue hunter, from the brink of death. She slowed his heart rate, so he wouldn't struggle and bleed, then dug out each bullet, and I remember holding one of our cereal bowls to catch them. I shut my eyes and counted as each plink of metal hit the ceramic. She didn't wave her hands and close his wounds. She taught me how to make a poultice to fill the bullet holes to keep out infection. Then, we waited. We hoped. We prayed. Healing takes time.

It is only because I am my mother's daughter that I act fast. Lin and Iris are on either side of me. Iris cradles Arco's head, her tears fall on his forehead, mix in with his. My dad helps me remove Arco's tunic. It takes all of me to not shake apart. If I do, Arco will slip away.

At the corners of his eyes, his tears turn into golden petals. *No no no no no no. We broke their curse. If he dies, Arco will become the rot.*

"Take me to the Tanamá to rest," Arco says.

"Don't leave," I say. I look up at my dad. My hands are covered in Arco's blood, trying to keep the blade from moving. "*Help* me, please. Please."

He knows what I know. The knife could be the thing that's stopping him from bleeding out, or it'll do more damage on the way out. Without healing magic to keep his heart rate low and heal blood vessels, there is nothing I can do.

"Take me home," I tell Lin. "My mom—"

But Lin is still recovering from their rift. Something broke. Something broke and let it out.

Arco lets go of a shuddering breath. His chest moves slowly, laboriously. Veins darken beneath his torso. His lashes become petals, like his mother's, only they're scarlet. Iris smooths his forehead and presses a kiss there.

That's when I notice she's changing too. Her skin glows from within, her hands touching the ground are surrounded by new grass. Stems shoot out around us all. She looks at her hands, and where there was blood is dandelion fluff.

"What's happening?" I ask. "Iris, what if he—"

"He won't. I won't let him." Iris brushes away tears. "Take out the blade. I can do this."

I do as she asks and let go. Iris presses her hands on Arco's bloody chest. I stand back as he gasps at the pain. A green vine, thick as thread, rips into his wound and stitches the gash closed.

"Rose," he whispers. He catches my tear with his fingertip. "Think of me, from time to time."

Around us, every creature and folk in the castle emerges and gathers. Arco's eyelashes flutter closed. His mouth is parted for his final breath. The hand that clutches his sister falls to the side. The Castillo de Sal weeps for the dead prince.

28

To sea, to sea.

My love has gone

to sea, to sea.

—WITCHSONG #18

We do not go home right away.

Iris changes right in front of us day by day. Blush pink roses bloom in the empty spaces of her crown. She has gifts that King Cirro did not. When she holds out her hands, the whole earth answers. Like El Terroz, she makes new land where there was nothing before. She is the queen that Adas waited for.

The Guardians of Adas travel with our queen as her personal guard for a few days. First we carry out Arco's final wish. We go to the Tanamá river. Along the way Iris replants trees where they withered. At the place where a new river cut across the other two, she raises hills with new breeds of flowers. She names them after Nadira, their petals a green of the sea.

I am not sure how I'm supposed to mourn for a boy I cared about. This is one of those things that no one ever taught me. For the first few nights after, I would cry for no reason. Simply because Palita set a bowl of fruit in front of me or because the sun was shining.

I have only ever mourned for family and friends. I have spent my entire life so used to death that I thought it would get easy.

In reality, sometimes, I feel like I will never get better. Sometimes I feel he should have let Cirro stab me.

When I say that, Iris reminds me that she lost her twin.

"Sometimes, I think that missing my brother is like missing a part of my being. But then I remember he is returning to the Adas, and in that way closer to me than ever before."

We lay Arco to rest in the perfect hill, which Iris spends all day tending to. I write him a letter using the pen he gave me. But then I feel ridiculous. Still, I tuck it into the soles of his slippers, so that my words will always be entwined with his roots.

We keep going west. Iris doesn't say it, but she hopes to find her mother's body. We pass the spot where Vita was buried, and Iris adds new flowers around the trunk of the tree where there is a mound of moss in the shape of a girl.

Past the oasis, the ground is still the same marbled desert, but instead of a crater that looks like an oil spill, there is dry ground.

We walk instead of taking horses because when Iris takes a step, grass grows.

Finally, at the center of where the rot used to be is the queen of Adas. Mayté is breathtaking even in her preserved former state, with her golden-brown skin, pink petals resting over her cheeks, and her orchid tumble of hair that reaches down to her calves. Her hands rest over her stomach, like she was positioned that way by someone who loved her.

It is strange not being able to hear her.

A hill rises before us, Mayté at the very top. All around her, a garden blooms—and keeps on blooming.

Iris walks from one end of the island to the other once more without us, breathing life where it had been taken before. She steps out of her armor and is dressed by the island. Bark cinches around her waist, leaves and petals hug her hips and thighs, draping elegantly and kissing the ground at her feet. She's different, but when butterflies and birds try to rest on her shoulders, she flicks them away, and I light up with warmth because she's the same girl I knew. Fierce, defiant, with thorns guarding her edges.

"I wish we could go with her," Lin says. "But it must take time to rebuild so much that has broken."

We ride back to the castle, stopping at Girasol Grove to spread the news. But when we get there, Kaíri already seems to know there has been a shift. She weeps for Arco with us. She heals our bodies. We sleep for days before we travel back to Olapura. Lin and I are never far apart. At first, Dad is quiet around us, but by the time we get to the coast, we trade stories of Alex and Lula. Even of me.

"Your first word was 'juicy,'" he tells me, the lines around his eyes crinkling.

"No way," I say. "Mom says my first word was *Mom*."

Dad throws his head back and laughs. His curls, the same soft curls as Lin's, are long. But despite Dad's beard, he looks like he's rejuvenated. "That's what she wanted you to think. You'd stick your entire fist in my orange juice and lick your fingers. It was a mess. I wish I had pictures. I wish—"

It's times like this when the sadness creeps back in. Sometimes I find him crying when he stares at the sea. Sometimes he wonders out loud if my mom will forgive him. The truth is I don't know. All I can hope for is that when we get home, my mom hasn't given up.

We busy ourselves with rebuilding the castle. Peridot and the folk of the rain forest use their power to fill in the gaps of the towers. Terrinas hurry from one end of the castle to the other. Xia prepares the new throne room for the queen's return.

When Iris arrives at the castle, she's greeted by all of Adas. Terrinas and Starlarks and all sorts of folk and humans gather along the towers, the walkways, the gardens. Everyone wants a look at the new queen. I catch a fraction of her profile as she enters the throne room with Xia.

Calliope, Peridot, Márohu, Lin, and I slump around a tree growing at the center of where the arena used to be. The only way to save the structure from collapsing was for Peridot to grow a tree at the center. Márohu's wing is still healing, and she hates being locked on the ground for so long, but she seems to be enjoying the food and gifts that people bring us.

Calliope picks up a slice of mango and sprinkles fat sea salt crystals over it. "You'd think we'd get an audience with Her Royal Highness. Especially you, Leechling."

"I told you to stop calling me that!" I shout, but they all fall about laughing.

"Are you sure you won't stay longer?" Peridot asks.

I shake my head. "We've been away too long. Plus, there is no way I'm repeating freshman year of high school."

On the evening of the feast, I get dressed with Palita's help. The castle is in full swing, bodies crammed into every possible corridor and hall.

I walk down to the gardens and pass a fountain with a golden statue of a boy with the head of a jaguar. Water trickles from, well, *everywhere*. When he winks at me, I realize that he is not a statue at all. A moment after the creature scurries away, two fairies come over, and before I can warn them, they cup water from the same fountain and drink.

I go farther into the castle, past bird-faced fairies, with their cackling laughs and bright feathers, past a blue-skinned girl pressed against a girl with goat horns swept back over her shaved head. I can't help blushing and pick up my pace, nearly bumping into a group of Terrinas carrying trays of chicken hearts wrapped in bacon and chunks of crispy pineapple burnt to a crisp, topped with sugar-crusted grasshoppers.

"Care for a treat, girl child?" Palita asks me. It's my last day seeing her and I find myself reaching to hug her. But she jumps away and smacks my leg with her wrinkled hand. "No tears for the brave girl."

"I'm not that brave," I say. "Hey, Palita. Are you sure you don't want to go back to the other world?"

"There is nothing there left for me, girl child. Just because I came from a place does not mean I can return to it. The new queen. She will be a good one."

I smile at the thought of Iris. When I look down again, Palita is gone.

I head back to the feast. Guitars seem to strum from every direction, and I tap the beat of the drum on the top of my thighs. In a small garden with overgrown dandelions and fat fireflies, I see a boy with golden horns just like Arco and I feel the air kicked out of my lungs. It isn't him, of course. He is part of the land. He is life in a way I will never be.

Iris does choose the moment I'm ready to cry to appear. She's in an elaborate dress made of tiny river pearls and silk that moves like the sun over water. It is a gift from Mother Dayo.

"You look like the sea, Rose," Iris says.

"Wide and terrifying?" I ask. My hands go to the front of my dress. The seamstress who made it was an ada about a foot tall with long, pointed ears and brown pom-poms for hair. She draped the fine blue silks until it started to take on the shape of a dress. After wearing dirty armor and bathing in nature for a week, the baths here are practically five stars.

"Breathtaking." Iris takes my hand and guides me down one of the many paths that lead to the garden.

When the ceremony begins, the bodies crowd around everywhere except the throne. Rum flows into goblets and the folk clap and stomp and howl for Iris, the True and Fair Queen of Adas.

Before Iris sits, she releases her grandfather from his petrified prison. The enchantment melts away, unraveling the blood curse. Eterno, the former king, does not truly wake. A long sigh leaves his body, trailed by black butterflies. His eyes flutter, but they never open. Then he transforms. His body dissolves into a small mound of grass and his bones and antlers spiral and braid into a new throne.

Iris takes a seat. Gloriana, in a sweeping silver-threaded dress, is the first to pledge her allegiance to her cousin, and the leaders of smaller courts follow. Kaíri offers the queen a gift—a dagger with a curious hilt designed to look like a twisted vine.

As queen, Iris decides to give out knighthoods.

"See?" I mutter to Calliope, who truly believed Iris had forgotten about us.

I knew she wouldn't.

Iris calls me forward first. A small part of me wants to stay and truly see what life is like in this castle, what it would be to live in a kingdom I helped save. I take shallow breaths as I kneel in front of her. She takes her sword. I stare at the grass and focus on a tiny blue flower that grows between her bare feet. The sword taps my shoulders.

Iris says, "Rise, Rose Elizabeta Mortiz, Knight and Savior of the Kingdom of Adas."

The feast goes on into the morning. I spent the night dancing with the other guardians under the full moon and then under the rising sun, knowing that some things end for no good reason.

"Look!" someone shouts and points at the sky. Up above are seven winged horses circling the castle. It feels like a sign for some reason. None of the Pegasi have left, except for Huracán.

When it's time to say goodbye, suddenly it feels too real and too soon. Xia lingers in the garden shadows, talking to a bird perched on her finger. But then her eyes find me. We share a silent good-bye. I hold my breath as Lin creates a rift. The folk of Adas throw flower petals, well wishes, and salt as we go.

Iris takes my hands in hers.

"I don't like goodbyes," I say.

"I hope you like gifts," she says, impossibly beautiful in her living crown.

"You already gave me a knighthood. I would have settled for a medal. I could have put it next to my science fair trophies. But gifts work."

Gloriana comes over with two leather-bound books. One is filled with Gloriana's stories. One is Arco's. I think of him scratching the side of his head with the butt of his pen and I let that fill my heart.

Peridot gives me a glass box with trinkets inside. A raven feather, a vial of stardust, a spindly branch that looks like a wand, and a seashell. That feeling swells again, like hearing a song after a long time and remembering what it meant. A capsule of a time and a place. I don't want to forget. Iris is next.

"If you get bored of being queen, you should be my pen pal," I tell her.

"Perhaps," Iris says. She hands me a small bundle in a silk sachet. "I wouldn't want to lose a wager."

"You made a new bet on me?" I feign indignation.

I hug her, and I don't care that I'm crumpling my dress or that I'm crying away the delicate fairy makeup they put on me earlier or that she's the queen and I'm a human bruja.

"Plant it under the new moon and put a drop of sugar water in it," Iris says.

I commit her to memory. The soft curl of her pink hair that falls over her shoulders. The serious set of her eyes. "You'll make a fine queen, I'm sure of it."

As I step through the rift, I promise myself I won't look back. I whisper it: "Don't look back don't look back don't look—" But even as my eyes sting, I turn. My breath catches. Arco is there, all gold and stars and perfection. A ghost. A memory. Then, gone.

But I, Rose Mortiz, am not gone or lost.

I am home.

EPILOGUE

El Fin waits in the wings.

His greatest gift to the world is time.

—LOST STORIES OF THE DEOS, ARCO,
SON OF THE ORCHID QUEEN

W e appear in the kitchen. Is there a word for the feeling that comes with returning to your life after being gone for so long? The plants along the window are leafier, and there are two new rooster magnets on the fridge. Soft smoke billows from a seashell bowl on the kitchen island, the sage burnt to the end.

"Welcome home, Lin," I say.

Dad leaves Lin's pack on the table, and I set down my gifts from Adas. The last thing I want is Lula asking me why I didn't bring her any souvenirs.

"No one seems to be home," Dad says.

Knots twist in my stomach. If not for the signs of life in the living room, I'd be afraid they picked up and left. Quiet is something our house has never been. I remember walking through this kitchen door and down this corridor on my Deathday. I remember the animals that found their way inside the house. Now, I wonder if that was because of Iris searching for me.

When we get to the living room, relief and worry collide. The furniture has all been pushed to the walls and the rugs rolled up and left limp in the corner. There's a circle of symbols drawn in chalk.

Mom and my sisters are lying at the center, forming a triangle. Within the triangle is a map skewered with pins. A postcard from the Dominican Republic, my book of Adas, Dad's photo from when he and my mom eloped without telling their parents.

When I take another step, Alex's eyes snap open. She looks from me to Dad to Lin. There's confusion, relief, definitely tears.

"I knew I heard you," she says.

They scream so loud the neighbor's dog barks. I run to my mom. Everything is too blurry, but we hug and cry and thank the Deos. There are too many questions.

What happened? Where were we? How did we get back? Who is Lin?

But Lula is very concerned with what I'm wearing.

All of it can wait. Dad and I hold Lin's hands. I feel them trembling with fear and excitement, with the newness of all of this. I get to be the big sister now.

"This is Lin Octavio Mortiz," Dad says, looking directly at my mom. "My child."

Some parts are easy. Ma welcomes Lin with her whole heart. *Blood of my blood*, she tells them. We don't get lost in the house as much anymore, especially now that Lin has their own room. They're going to go to school with Alex and me soon, and when we bring Lin to meet our cousins and circles, everyone makes Lin feel at home. One of the kids, Jesse, who was having a hard time at home, falls in love with the way Lin calls themselves a brujex and adopts it for themselves. We work our way toward a new community, making room for others. Lin and I tell everyone stories of our adventure. Until Lin snitches on me about Arco, and then Alex and Lula won't leave me alone for *weeks*.

Some parts are difficult. Lin doesn't like human school, but Lula thinks the Thorne Hill Alliance can help them. A few nights after we got back, I heard Ma crying by herself in her infirmary. When I asked her about it, she said it was because she was overjoyed that we'd returned, but I didn't totally believe her.

"It's okay to be upset," I told her. "I was upset. Not about Lin. But because Dad had this whole other life without us. But I was there, Ma. In one day, I could feel how strong that magic was. If it wasn't for Nova's bracelet, I don't know what would have happened to me."

"You're different," she tells me, tears in her eyes. "I'm proud of you."

Magic transforms you.

Sleeping comes with its own adventures. I read the book Gloriana gave me and sometimes, at three in the morning, I use Arco's pen to compose letters I don't know how to send. I wake up screaming, Lin appearing in front of me to tell me that I'm

353

dreaming. Then we fall asleep side by side, adrift but not alone in our nightmares.

Dad is different too. He wakes up early and the house fills with the smell of freshly ground coffee and bacon. He packs sandwiches and blends smoothies for Lin and me to take to school on Tuesdays because we *hate* the fried fish stuffed with cheese that they serve. Dad plays music on Sundays and invites long-lost friends. He fills in the gaps of our memories, and we fill in the gaps in his.

There are truly terrible days with fights and words full of resentment, or wishing things had never changed, or wishing we could hold on to the bitter ache in our hearts because it's so much easier than forgiveness.

But there is forgiveness. I see it in the way Ma brushes Dad's hair behind his ear and the way she fusses over the wrinkles in Lin's clothes. In the way Lula and Alex bring Rhett and Rishi over for dinner because there is nothing more important than family.

There are moments when we hold our collective breath, when we know that we aren't whole as long we still don't know where Nova is. Alex and I replace her corkboard with a new map, the single postcard he sent with the message "How's the snow?" and nothing since.

"We'll find him," Alex says, but I notice the way she scratches at the markings laced into her skin, a promise she made long ago that ties her to Nova in life and death.

One day, Ma walks into my room. I'm writing in my notebook, Lin is trying to understand mortal history and finds it illogical, Alex is cursing her English teacher's name, and Lula is trying on my fairy-made dress. We stop what we're doing and stare at our mother. She's wearing her cleaning-day hair scarf and T-shirt that says *My Child is an Honor Roll Student*. Clearly from my school.

"I already did my laundry," Lula says defensively.

"And I'll replace your jar of baby teeth, I just had to do this thing for a friend," Alex says, not looking up from her book.

"What friend?" Lula asks.

"I have friends," Alex snaps.

Lin snorts before pillows start getting thrown.

"I need everyone to cancel what they're doing in two weeks," Mom says.

"Why?" I ask.

"Because we're having Lin's Deathday."

It's spring, and the flower Iris gave me has bloomed. It is a rose-orchid hybrid with a riot of pinks and oranges, managing to capture the perfect colors of a sunrise in the outerlands.

"I'm ready for a vacation," Lula says the minute I step back in the kitchen for Deathday preparation. "Hey, you know a girl with a castle in the Caribbean."

"She's a *fairy queen*." I roll my eyes at her. We're supposed to be putting the final touches on preparations for Lin's Deathday party, but mostly she's been texting and eating the cupcakes I bought for Lin. It feels good to be irritated with Lula over little things like this. I have missed her voice, her good heart.

Ma is mixing clay in a bowl. "Oh, good, Rosie," she says, not looking up. "Make sure Lin's sacrifice is ready for tonight. And your father needs help upstairs with the flower crown. Don't let me forget I had to use the neighbor's oven for the pernil because I've got two lasagnas and a turkey in ours."

I answer every command with "Yes, Mother," while Lin does their best to not laugh out loud. They're dressed in a violet knee-length tunic and matching pants brocaded with silver thread. "I'll go with you."

"Are you okay?" I ask. "I'm afraid I've been asking that a lot lately."

"I will be fine, Rose. I do hope Lady Carmen starts letting me help."

"Don't worry. The first new few months at our house are guest mode. I just don't see how I saved an entire fairy realm and still come back here and have to do everyone's chores."

Lin smirks, scratching at their pointed ear. "It is dreadfully unfair."

We find Alex and Dad in the study. The maps and missing-person web my sisters had up has become a collage of dead ends searching for Nova. Dad's on the phone, while Alex is furiously typing on the laptop.

"You rang?" I ask. Alex places her finger to her lip and darts her eyes toward Dad.

He sighs hard. "No, I appreciate it. Let me know if anything comes up."

"No news on Nova?"

Dad tries to put on a good face for us, but I can tell it's another dead end. "No news. But I finished the crown. Let's have a look."

"Pa," Lin mutters, embarrassed. The crown is made of heart-shaped ivy and white flowers with purple hearts. It fits perfectly over Lin's dark curls. Dad fusses so much I snicker.

"I'm sorry, kiddo," Dad says. "I want this to be special for you."

"It will be."

There's a loud screeching coming from upstairs. We rush in Lin's room to check on the squirrel Lin chose for their offering. I took them to the park, and they went wild over them. Apparently, I failed to notice there were not any squirrels in Adas. The creature is happily chewing on carrots without any signs of distress.

I check my room and find the source of the screeching is a bright turquoise bird with black tail feathers and a strange curved beak. Its talons are too long, perched on the railing of my bed. When I reach for it, it turns beady black eyes that look aware. There is magic in this bird. I can feel it. I reach to touch its resting wing and notice a small scroll tied to the leg.

It reads "Tell me a story."

I grin. Since coming back. there are plenty of stories I could tell. But they all belong to Lin and their first time around the city—first time meeting other magical beings, first time trying ice cream, first time going to high school with humans that stare far too long at their slightly pointed ears and violet eyes.

"I'll have something for you soon," I tell the bird, and it bows its tiny head at me before taking flight.

I return to my family, to our Deathday.

Yeah, some days are good and some bad, some neither. But we are making it work. Magic transforms us.

We light candles and walk Lin through the rites of calling forth our ancestors. Everyone comes forward, Papá Philomeno and Mamá Juanita and even Tía Rosaria, because family is more than blood.

There is singing and food, and this time no one has to convince me to dance and dance and dance. My magic hums against my skin, wild and free and mine.

When everyone has left and the leftovers have been wrapped in aluminum foil and cake sent away in plastic containers, my mind won't let me sleep. I read my letter.

I bring out my quill pen and press the tip to a blank page.

Tell me a story.

AUTHOR'S NOTE

BRUJA, BRUJO, AND BRUJEX

During a book event for *Labyrinth Lost* I had some wonderful readers ask me if they could be a bruja in my world and still be nonbinary. I realized that in all of my world-building, I had defaulted to the gender rules of my first language. I left out a whole bunch of people from my books! I've thought about it since, and so, in the Kingdom of Adas we are introduced to a "brujex." Brujex is a word I've created for the character Lin, and nonbinary or gender-fluid brujas. I hope you can share in a bit of this magical world, too.

HADAS VS. ADAS

To all my Spanish speakers, yes, I know Adas is spelled differently. The proper way in Spanish is "hadas." It simply translates to "fairy." There fae are rooted in European traditions and came over with the Spaniards. I grew up on "cuentos de hadas" and I do recognize that I'm doing my own thing by changing this spelling to suit my needs. When I set out to create this magical kingdom, I wanted to separate the fairies from Europe from my original island located smack dab in the middle of the Caribbean. Welcome to the Kingdom of Adas.

KINGDOM OF ADAS

The inspiration for this magical little island, completely overrun with rot, came to me when I first wrote *Labyrinth Lost*. I had a vague notion that the third book would take place here, and that it would be connected to Daddy Mortiz's evolving story. The first thing I wrote for it was the book of stories, *Claribelle and the Kingdom of Adas: Tales Tall and True* by Gloriana Palacios. Gloriana is Agosto, the Faun King's half human daughter. She wrote these stories because it was her only way to process growing up in this island where she straddled the magical worlds. As I wrote *Bruja Born*, I started tweaking the mythos. Who are the Deos that are at play? Each book introduces you to a new one. La Flor and El Fin are some of my favorites because they just want to be left alone and do their thing. This is serious deity #goals. Once I figured all of that out, I needed to give Rose a journey. This island is inspired by Puerto Rico, Ecuador, Colombia, and I hope that readers can recognize nods to these cultures. I never want to take an existing god and plop them into my world, which is why I challenged myself to give Adas its own origin story using the Deos from the Brooklyn Brujas series and mixing it up with what I imagine a Latinx fairy would be like. I would spend my whole life making up new myths if I could.

ACKNOWLEDGMENTS

I'm going to get this question a lot, so, yes, *Wayward Witch* was the hardest of all three Brooklyn Brujas books to write. Rose is such a special character, and I wanted to get her bright, sassy, fraught voice *right*. I have a ton of people to thank for being alongside me in development. To my #TeamBrujas at Sourcebooks: Nicole Hower and the art department for this cover. It is magic. The brilliant editors who had a part in each of the Brooklyn Brujas: Aubrey Poole, Kate Prosswimmer, and Molly Cusick. To the whole team: Dominique Raccah, Steve Geck, Cassie Gutman, Beth Oleniczak, and Jackie Douglass.

Thank you, Cat Scully, for bringing the Kingdom of Adas to life in map form, and to my copyeditor, Gretchen Stelter.

When I started writing this series, I was paralyzed with the thought that no one would understand it. Perhaps it was too strange, too Latin, or too unfamiliar. But I wrote despite my fear because the Mortiz sisters have occupied a part of my mind for about a decade now. I owe so much to every reader, librarian, teacher, friends, family member who helped me share this dream.

To my agent, Victoria Marini and the team at Irene Goodman Literary Agency, as well as Heather Baror at Baror International.

To these wonderful minds who beta read Rose's journey and poked holes at my story until it was finished: Tessa Gratton, Diya Mishra, Brendon Zatirka, Brandon Will, and Lindsay Warren.

To Dhonielle Clayton for being an incredible friend, podcast cohost, and for solving this ending. You are one of the best people in my life. To Victoria Schwab for giving me a place to work on this book in Scotland. To my girls I couldn't be without, Natalie Horbachevsky, Sarah Elizabeth Younger, Christine Higgins, and Natalie C. Parker.

For my family. I love you so much, I'd definitely travel into a fairy realm to save all of you.

ABOUT THE AUTHOR

Zoraida Córdova is the author of many fantasy novels for kids and teens, including the award-winning Brooklyn Brujas series, *Incendiary*, and *Star Wars: A Crash of Fate*. Her short fiction has appeared in the *New York Times* bestselling anthology *Star Wars: From a Certain Point of View*, *Star Wars The Clone Wars: Stories of Light and Dark*, *Come on In: 15 Stories about Immigration and Finding Home*, and *Toil & Trouble: 15 Tales of Women and Witchcraft*. She is the coeditor of *Vampires Never Get Old: Eleven Tales with Fresh Bite*. Her debut middle grade novel is *The Way to Rio Luna*. She is the cohost of the podcast *Deadline City*. Zoraida was born in Ecuador and raised in Queens, New York. When she isn't working on her next novel, she's planning a new adventure.

#getbooklit

Your hub for the hottest in young adult books!

Visit us online and sign up for our
newsletter at FIREreads.com

 @sourcebooksfire

 sourcebooksfire

 firereads.tumblr.com